The Final Entry

The Haighdlen Chronicles
Book 3

Mary S. Catlin

~To my family, friends, and teachers. ~

———————————

Explore maps and more at

www.maryscatlinauthor.com

———————————

LEAFBROOKE
LOCKESBARROW
THE TRAWLEY ISLES
PLADIAN OCEAN
IADAEN OCEAN
HAIGHDLEN
SAPIENCE SEA
ROZATHIAN OCEAN
VYNCHIA
VACILLIAN SEA
MERCHANT GULF
N
THE FOUR KINGDOMS

CHAPTER 1

Elise Laurille knew better than to gamble with fairy magic. If her limited experience had taught her anything, it was that the outcome would *always* be the opposite of what she anticipated.

Why should I expect anything different this time?

Because there was no other choice.

She had already spent the better part of a week time traveling with friends through a diary to uncover secrets about her family's past. However, the clock in her grandmother's present-day living room showed she was only gone mere hours.

How can that be?

Elise nearly died seeking the identity of the spy responsible for the future downfall of her family's kingdom, Haighdlen. Not long after, Elise's boyfriend Gavin was kidnapped by the same elusive spy and forced to join Queen Rona's army. The journey to rescue him alone came with its own risks and revelations, resulting in the loss of more precious fairy magic that could've helped them along with the diary.

The same one Rona now possessed.

To make matters worse, Elise's grandfather Derek Laurille was struck by Rona's curse right as they were sent home. Now Elise and her three friends were left fearing Derek's fate as well as Rona's looming plans.

Still, something else plagued Elise's mind about returning to Joranna's house. . .apart from Gavin, Mitch, Darcie, and herself, no one was home. Her family should've been there, and Elise had a growing suspicion it had something to do with the fact that Gavin saw only blank pages in the diary before it brought them back.

Without it, Elise needed another source of magic to help the Laurille family. Since the extent of her newly discovered powers was uncertain, Elise prayed Joranna's antique scarf was the answer.

She gripped the silken fabric tightly. Sewn by fairies and gifted to Joranna by their king, its magic was the only chance Elise and her friends had to make it back to Haighdlen.

The irony of their situation didn't escape Elise's notice. After days of wishing and praying to return home, here they stood seeking a way back through another magical item.

Hoping to summon the scarf's magical energy, Elise clenched her eyes shut and focused on what she wanted most. She hadn't received proper training like her extended family, yet with every unsuccessful passing moment, her desperation grew.

We need to get to Derek. Take us to Derek. Show us what we need to do. Please. Please. The image of her grandfather falling after being struck with Rona's magic was all she could think about. *What if we're too late? What if we're stuck here? No, I can't think like that. I need to think about the magic. Focus, Elise.*

"Elise, it's working!" her best friend Darcie cried.

Elise, Gavin, Darcie, and Mitch all stared in awe as the scarf began to glow before them.

Yes! I can't believe it's actually working!

"So, we'll head back and check on Derek," said Mitch with a shrug. "Then what? What about Rona?"

After a tense silence, Elise straightened her shoulders and replied what she had already accepted in her heart. "It's going to have to be me. I'm going to have to defeat Rona."

Gavin, Mitch, and Darcie began to argue against her declaration, causing Elise to lose focus on the magic. As the illuminated garment flickered, she waved away their overlapping interruptions.

"Guys, stop. Just grab on, and let's handle it when we get there."

I don't expect them to understand. Not yet anyway.

A swell of energy coursed through Elise's fingertips once all the noise ceased, and she concentrated again.

Take us where we need to go. Please work. We need to get back.

"I don't like this," Mitch said, glancing around the empty room as if he expected a ghost to materialize from the walls. "It's just a scarf. You can't expect something to do what you want just because it might have a *little* magic."

Darcie shushed him.

Block him out. If you don't believe this will work, you'll never get back.

Again, the light flickered before dying out.

Darcie stomped her foot. "Ugh, see what you did, Mitch? You made Elise lose her concentration! Do you want this to work or not?"

"He's right though." Gavin stared at the scarf in Elise's hands. "Sure, fairies made it, but how do we know it can be a portal? Maybe it's just something they expected Joranna to wear."

Elise wilted. Was it so ridiculous to hope for a way back without her family's help? They had come this far, and risked too much, to try forgetting it all now. She met Gavin's gaze.

The two had yet to talk about what transpired while Gavin was captured, but Elise felt an awkward, ugly amount of tension festering between them. As much as she wanted to hear every detail, Elise knew her family's safety needed to come first.

Elise focused on the carpet rather than at any one of her friends. "Fine. We can forget it. Y'all can go home after all."

"Oh no, you don't." Darcie's pestering, bossy tone that she was known for pulled Elise out of her thoughts. "You can have your pity party later. No one's leaving except through *that* scarf. Now everybody shut up and let her concentrate. Go on, Elise."

Knowing better than to argue, Gavin and Mitch watched Elise expectantly.

She cleared her throat before trying again. . .and again.

"What if you tried wearing it?" Darcie offered.

Elise felt ridiculous but took her friend's suggestion anyway. *We've tried everything else.*

For a moment, she felt nothing but embarrassment with everyone's eyes on her. Before she could remove the garment, however, it began to shine so brightly that all four teenagers had to shield their eyes from the flash. Only when it dimmed could Elise process that someone was whispering in her ear. She looked over her shoulder towards the voice but didn't see anyone.

"Do y'all hear that?"

"Hear what?" Darcie asked.

"That voice." Elise turned in a full circle without finding the speaker. The whispers were so faint she couldn't make out actual words.

"Nobody's talking," said Gavin.

I'm hearing things. I've gone crazy.

Elise's heart raced as she yanked the scarf from around her neck and threw it on the ground. The voices stopped. She backed away from the pile of fabric and began pacing to steady her breathing. Despite her best efforts, she was unable to calm down before becoming enveloped in a full-blown panic attack.

She saw her friends' mouths moving, but her brain couldn't process what they were saying. They couldn't possibly understand the paralyzing fear jolting through her veins like electric shocks. From a young age, Elise feared her anxiety would cause a nervous breakdown, and hearing voices no one else could triggered the nightmare within her. It felt real in a way she couldn't put into words.

Elise's shallow breaths came faster and faster until she thought she would pass out or throw up. Either outcome would be welcome. She hated this part. It didn't matter if it was the hundredth time or more, they all felt like the first one.

She started to leave the room, a common coping mechanism that usually helped, but froze when Gavin grabbed her hand. Elise's thoughts raced like a tornado as sweat coated both of her palms.

I'm crazy. I've finally gone crazy. I knew this would happen. I'm hearing things that aren't there. Nobody else heard it. That's not good. That's not good. Why did we ever come here? What are they thinking about me now? Gavin's going to leave me for sure. He knows I'm insane.

"Elise, calm down," Mitch said.

Tears welled up in Elise's eyes. She couldn't look at anyone. Through her mental fog, she caught pieces of her friends' conversation.

"Don't say that," Darcie snapped. "She hates that. Plus, it doesn't work. She has to come out of it on her own."

Elise stared down at her hand as Gavin squeezed it. Closing her eyes, she forced herself to exhale slowly. As her breathing relaxed, she thought back to when Gavin saw her panic for the first time while rowing on a lake. He had been so patient and helpful, much like he was at that moment.

All signs of irritation were gone now as he rubbed small circles on the back of Elise's hand while assuring her that she was safe. If Gavin noticed how clammy her skin was, he didn't show it.

At long last, the turbulent storm clouds of doubt and fear parted, and she could process everything again. Pulling away from Gavin, she wiped both palms dry on her skirt. Right on schedule, shameful tears stung the back of her eyes. "I'm sorry," she whispered.

This is so embarrassing. I don't want to be this way. I wish I could make it stop.

"Don't be," Gavin said. He hesitated before wrapping his arms around her.

As both stood in a silent embrace, the fabric of Gavin's collared shirt tickled her nose. Elise inhaled his familiar scent and felt her remaining tension vanish as she melted against him.

I missed you.

He kissed the top of her head. "I'm right here. You're safe."

She tightened her hold on him as if he were the source of her oxygen.

"What did you hear?" Mitch asked when Elise and Gavin pulled apart.

"I-I couldn't make it out, but I also didn't feel in control of myself, and that's always been a fear of mine." When no one responded, she felt the need to elaborate. "That one day I'm going to go crazy, and no one will want to be around me." She let out a dry, hollow chuckle, trying anything to lighten the mood and distract herself from more irrational thoughts. "I guess it. . .freaked me out. That's all. I'm sorry."

"Don't be and quit apologizing. That'd freak me out too," Darcie said. Giving her friend a hug, she looked down at the scarf. "But you know you have to put it back on, right?"

I was afraid she'd say that.

"You don't have to," Gavin said. "We can find another way."

"Like what?" Mitch argued. "It's the only other thing we know that has magic."

"A minute ago, you doubted this whole plan," Darcie pointed out. "What changed?"

"The scarf is talking to her." Mitch pointed at the garment. "*Something* was working. Put it on again."

When Elise hesitated, Gavin picked the scarf up and held it out towards Mitch, who flinched. "See? You're scared of it too. So, leave her alone, okay?"

"Hey, I almost died out there, man! Forgive me if I don't trust any of this crap."

Gavin glared at his best friend. "You're not the only one."

Elise felt a shiver course down her spine. She had so much to learn about Gavin's terrible endeavor in Lockesbarrow. The truth was, they had *all* struggled in one way or another, and if she didn't do everything she could to end this forever, what was the point of entering the diary in the first place?

Mustering what little courage she could, Elise took the scarf from Gavin and wrapped it around herself once more.

"Try to focus on what the voice is saying," Darcie insisted.

Elise nodded before closing her eyes.

At first, she could only hear her own uneven breathing. Then, following a familiar flash of light, the whispering resumed.

Goosebumps prickled her arms as her anxious thoughts screamed out to flee the situation. Elise's toes curled as she rocked back and forth, determined to stay put and hear the words. Ignoring

Darcie, who shushed Mitch again, Elise was surprised to realize that the voice was growing louder. . .

A beating heart in every stitch,
Doomed follies on the rise,
One need only summon truth,
To conquer grounded lies.

Elise's brows furrowed as the riddle repeated three more times.

What are 'grounded lies'? They're going to flip out when I tell them. It doesn't make any sense. I'll never get us back to Haighdlen at this rate.

Elise sighed as she removed the scarf from around her neck. Did she want to defeat Rona? Yes. Did she want to save Derek? Of course, but if she were being honest with herself, all of that seemed out of reach.

I can't tell them how I really feel. I put them all up to this. They're here because of me. How would they react if I admitted that I want to go home after all?

At that moment, the scarf flashed like a bolt of lightning, causing all four to jump back with cries of terror.

The light flickered before burning so brightly, Elise couldn't look directly at it.

Is this working? Is it finally going to take us to Derek?

Elise chuckled in disbelief before urging her friends to grab onto the silken garment.

Hearing the echoing riddle ringing in her ears—this time as an urgent chant—Elise watched as Darcie grabbed Mitch's wrist before stuffing a piece of scarf into his hand at the last second before all went dark.

CHAPTER 2

Elise moaned as her muscles spasmed. Struggling to stand, she felt as if her limbs were made of concrete. She took in the surrounding forest area. If the bright crisp gold and reddish orange foliage was anything to go by, it was autumn. Unable to discern if the scarf sent them all backwards or forward in time—or even to Haighdlen, for that matter—Elise felt her barely quenched anxiety resurface.

This isn't where we left before. Are we in Haighdlen? Where is everybody? Derek isn't here.

Dusting the dirt off her dress, Elise felt a sharp pain against both palms where splinters had pierced into her skin upon landing. She was able to pull three out on her own, but the remaining ones proved to be too deep. She then attempted to remove twigs that were tangled within her hair.

The sound of crunching leaves made her jump, but she visibly relaxed when she saw Gavin.

"A little scraped, but not too bad. You?" He chuckled as Elise's fingers got caught. "Here, let me help." Gavin removed the offending twig she had been after and tossed it onto the ground. After she thanked him, he shrugged with a small smile before the same awkward silence from before filled the air between them.

Elise broke eye contact first and glanced around. "Have you seen Darcie and Mitch?"

Gavin pointed over his shoulder. "Mitch is snoring away somewhere over there."

Elise's brief smile fell when he didn't continue. Her brows creased. "And Darcie?"

"I haven't seen her."

The color drained from Elise's face.

Did she not make it back with us? Is she still at Nana's?

Whirling around, Elise cried out Darcie's name before Gavin shushed her.

"Cut it out!" he hissed. "We don't know where we are or what's here!"

"How else are we going to find Darcie?" she argued.

"By staying alive long enough to look for her!"

Elise hated to admit he had a point, and perhaps screaming at the top of her lungs in a strange place probably *wasn't* the brightest idea.

"What're y'all fighting about?" Mitch stumbled through the piles of leaves and fallen branches. With an audible yawn and wearing a bemused expression, he rubbed the back of his neck. "Where's Darcie?"

When Elise informed him that she was missing, all traces of drowsiness vanished from his face. Instantly alert, Mitch's movements took on a frenzied, hectic state as he sidestepped the other two.

Elise and Gavin followed his lead. For the next half hour, the three scoured the surrounding woods looking for their friend.

"She's not here, guys," Gavin called out, waving the others over to him.

"We can't stop. We have to keep looking." Panting, Mitch continued to scan the area. A layer of sweat glistened along his furrowed brows. "She could be unconscious somewhere."

"Do we know if she made it here at all?" Gavin asked, echoing Elise's previous fear. "Maybe she's still at Joranna's house."

"This is great. Just great." Mitch raked a hand through his hair as he paced around the other two. "Let's head back and check. Where's the scarf?"

Crap. He's going to kill me.

"I-I don't have it," Elise confessed. She held out both palms. "It was missing when I woke up."

Mitch looked from Elise's empty hands to her face with a scowl.

Anticipating an outburst, Elise stepped closer to Gavin. "We'll find her. I promise." She could tell by the way his nostrils flared, coupled with the twitching muscle in his cheek, that Mitch wasn't convinced.

He hung his head. When he finally spoke, Mitch' voice sounded flat, defeated, and lifeless.

"How many times am I going to regret not getting in my car?" He clenched both fists by his sides before sucking in a breath through gritted teeth. "It's either prison, magic, or a near-death experience. Are we just supposed to keep blindly following you?"

His stare pierced through Elise's eyes, sending a cold chill down her spine.

"Mitch, I understand—"

"No, you don't understand," he snapped. "That's the problem. You don't understand anything that's going on. We keep getting by with dumb luck, but you're going to get us killed. If anything happens to her—"

"Hey! Ease up, man." Stepping between them, Gavin rested a hand on Mitch's chest.

"No, *you* ease up!" Mitch shoved Gavin away from him. "Aren't you tired of it? Gav, you got ripped away from home, kidnapped, and somehow made it back alive. We had the chance to go home. We could've avoided all of this! Derek was always going to die, so why do we care?"

Did he really just say that?

Mitch jerked his chin towards her. "How do we know she's not using her magic on us right now?"

Elise's chest fluttered as a fresh bout of anxiety did a somersault in her stomach.

"Mitch, go cool off," Gavin warned. "*Now.*"

"Or what?" Mitch argued.

Although Gavin was often the calmer of the two, Elise knew her boyfriend also possessed an untamed temper when provoked. Gavin's stiffened shoulders made Elise wonder if their altercation would turn physical.

I have to do something. This isn't going to help us find Darcie.

Someone was going to get hurt. She just got Gavin back, and Mitch had also recently suffered a near-fatal encounter in Lake Mirage. Tensions were high as it was. They didn't need to start turning on each other.

Elise touched Gavin's elbow before stepping in front of him. "Both of you need to stop. This isn't going to get Darcie back."

"We wouldn't have to if we had gone home in the first place," Mitch countered.

Heat rushed to Elise's cheeks as she glared at him. Deep down, she knew his anger spurned from worrying about Darcie, but that didn't give him any excuse to attack her. "Will you get over that already?" Elise snapped. "You're here now."

"Because of *you*!" He sneered at her. "All of this is because of you."

"Shut up, Mitch," Gavin said. "I swear, if you don't back off and—"

"It's *always* going to be something with her, Gav!" Mitch blurted out before Gavin pushed him to the ground.

Elise couldn't admit it out loud, but having Gavin stand up for her meant more than he would ever know. However, it was hard watching the two friends fight.

This is *all my fault.*

Ignoring Mitch's grumbling, Gavin turned back to look at Elise. "Can your magic help us? Or that voice you heard? What did it say?"

In all the excitement, Elise had forgotten about the voice. She closed her eyes and tried to remember the riddle. "Something about a beating heart, rising follies, finding truth, and grounded lies."

Gavin tilted his head as a line appeared between his brows. "What does that mean?"

"Nothing." Mitch dusted himself off as he got back up on his feet. "It doesn't mean anything. It's another distraction to throw us off."

I wish I had the scarf with me right now. How did that stupid riddle go? "'*A beating heart in every stitch,*" she began, struggling to piece the puzzle together. "Doomed rising, no, '*doomed follies on the rise.*'"

Am I even making sense? Seeing Mitch roll his eyes, Elise supposed not. She wiped both hands along her skirt, immediately regretting it due to the splinters, and paced while collecting her thoughts. "One should find the truth. . .Um, '*one need only s-summon truth,* and. . .'"

Mitch growled as he turned and punched the nearest tree.

Elise flinched when she heard his painful grunts. "'*To conquer grounded lies.* That's it!" She repeated the entire riddle.

"I still don't—" Gavin paused, watching Mitch shake his injured hand. "I still don't know how that can help us."

"Me neither." Elise took a deep breath. Maybe it was time to tell him they landed there because she wished to go home, not knowing the scarf would follow its own path. "But I think I know why—"

She froze. Only when Mitch stopped grumbling could she hear it again. It was a familiar noise that sounded like. . .snickering. Her heart threatened to leap out of her chest. There was only one sort of creature she knew that snickered like that. . .

Fairies!

"Do y'all hear that?" she hissed, silencing the boys who had begun to argue again. For a moment there was only the surrounding sounds of nature—birds chirping, the wind whistling through the overlapping trees. . .and there it was again! Elise jerked her head upwards, convinced she had seen a small ball of light disappear into the thick coverage of leaves above them.

"Ugh, not again. Please, no." Mitch tilted his head back with a groan as he cradled his injured hand. "Not them."

"Hello?" Elise shouted up into the trees. She shielded her eyes against the harsh rays of sun that managed to penetrate the foliage. "Can you hear me?"

"Elise, what are you doing?" Mitch asked. "Don't get them involved!"

"Right now, they're our only chance to find Darcie," she snapped. When he didn't reply, she called out again.

"Maybe he's right, Elise," Gavin said, cutting off one of Elise's attempts. "Let's try something else."

This time, no less than six balls of light emerged and hovered over their heads.

Mitch backed away before shielding his eyes. "Cover your eyes guys. Their dust *really* stings."

Elise thought back to the night they followed her mom through the forest. Mitch was hit directly in the eyes with fairy dust. She couldn't blame his hesitation to get the mischievous creatures involved, but she had to try. Elise couldn't make out any of their faces from where she stood, but she made the attempt to look at each fairy as she spoke. "We used the scarf you gave Queen Joranna, but I think something went wrong."

"Of course, something went wrong!" a squeaky voice called down from one of the lights. "It wasn't yours to use, now, was it?"

"Typical human," said another, clicking its tongue. "Stealing whatever they want."

Don't fairies take whatever they want too?

"I say we kill them now and be done with it," suggested a third voice with a drawl of boredom.

A sickening sense of dread pooled into the pit of Elise's stomach as the other lights bounced in agreement.

"We're not afraid of you," said Gavin.

Elise shook her head as Mitch uncovered his eyes.

What is Gavin doing?

"Gav, shut up! What're you trying to do?" Mitch hissed. He ignored Gavin's attempt to shush him, and instead closed the distance between them. "We won't find Darcie if they put some stupid curse on us."

"Wise words coming from the foolish one," one of the lights called out before a ring of laughter spread again.

Mitch glared up at the taunting fairies. "Go ahead, Elise. Set them on fire or something."

Elise suppressed a smile at the idea she could control any type of magic with that kind of precision. Mitch hadn't been far off when he labeled their progress 'dumb luck'.

"Look. Can you help us or not?" Gavin asked the fairies.

"Now, that depends," said a deep, alluring voice to their right, "on whether or not you *want* to be helped."

All three teenagers jumped as a tall, mysterious man emerged from behind a tree.

Who is that? Has he been there the whole time? At first captivated by his regal robe dragging through the multicolored leaves, Elise's mouth dropped open when she noticed an impressive pair of wings.

"Bow to King Horanis!" shrieked one of the fairies before all of them landed on the nearest branch with a bow of their own.

Horanis? But he's so. . .can he really be a fairy? He's bigger than we are!

Elise felt Gavin tug on her sleeve. He and Mitch were already kneeled on either side of her, most likely feeling the same stunned, speechless terror she was. Following their lead, she hiked up her skirt while bending down.

"Hello, Elise," said the winged man.

Elise felt as if she swallowed a jagged icicle. She was frozen to the spot, unable to form a response. King Horanis was nothing like she expected, *if* she ever thought about him before. Both of her arms felt numb, and she made the mistake of looking directly at his face. Heat rushed to her cheeks. "H-how do you—"

"Oh, you're very well-known in *our* kingdom." Horanis circled around them, much like a predator would its prey, but kept his eyes on her.

Elise's heartbeat throbbed in her ears as she stared into his piercing gray eyes. Words poured from Horanis's mouth like warm honey, and his chiseled features were that of a man in his mid-to-late thirties, but she knew better than to judge a magical being by appearances only. Intimidated by the king's unwavering stare, Elise looked down at the ground where fallen twigs snapped beneath his feet as he walked. A pile of leaves dragged behind his garment.

"*Your* kingdom?" Gavin asked. "Aren't we in Haighdlen?"

Horanis paused in front of them. "You were. Now you're not. There are kingdoms *within* kingdoms."

Elise and the boys exchanged dubious glances.

"I don't get it," Mitch said. "We never left the forest."

Horanis smirked as he regarded him with menacing amusement. "And unless you return my scarf to me, your beautiful friend won't either."

CHAPTER 3

"Simply produce my scarf, and you may have her back." Horanis's already regal stance was amplified by his impressive wingspan as he studied them. Had he not just confessed to holding Darcie captive, Elise would've found him irresistible. He resembled the majestic, domineering creatures she had only read about in storybooks. There was a silky, seductive—no, *ethereal*—quality to the way Horanis moved and spoke that kept Elise on edge, anticipating what he would do next. In the back of her mind, she wondered if his appeal was purposefully controlled through his magic to lure people in.

Did he lure Darcie in? Is she hurt? Will he kill her?

"W-we don't have it," Elise said. "It disappeared when we landed here."

"Pity." Horanis shrugged as if he had only misplaced a common trinket before stroking his chin. "She will make a perfect wife for one of my lords."

Mitch leapt to his feet with startling speed. He tightened both fists until his knuckles turned white. However aggressive he may have wanted to come across, Mitch was meek compared to the fairy king.

Horanis chuckled. "She is already spoken for, I see." He sized Mitch up and down before his face split into an impish grin. "What is she worth to you?"

"Look around." Gavin spread his arms out on either side. "We don't have anything to give. Just free her already."

"I'm afraid that's not how this works." Though replying to Gavin, Horanis kept his eyes on Mitch while he spoke. "Make an offer."

Mitch relaxed both hands, but his skin remained splotched and heated.

Elise wondered if the king enjoyed getting her friend worked up. Given Horanis's perverse merriment, she assumed he must do this sort of thing all the time. She watched a multitude of emotions play across Mitch's face, ranging from calculating, fearful, to rage. His raw, unchecked vulnerability unnerved her.

Mitch is going to lose it any second now. He looks insane.

Elise jumped when Gavin squeezed her hand, luckily avoiding the sore skin. *He's scared too.*

Horanis, however, wasn't at all fazed by Mitch's temperament.

Mitch's shoulders fell as he hung his head. "Then what?" His voice was lifeless, resigned, and Elise hardly recognized him.

"We negotiate a trade." Horanis swiped a long lock of hair out of his eyes before he gestured towards the forest path. "Then you all go skipping about on your journey."

Don't do anything stupid, Mitch. We don't have anything to give them. There has to be another way. Elise waited with bated breath for one of the two men to speak. *And if we don't?* "What if we don't?" Elise asked, surprising herself by blurting the thought out loud.

The fairy king shrugged once more. "Then we have reached an impasse and I must kill you."

How can he be so calm about all this? You'd think he was discussing the weather!

"Mitch, let's go," Gavin said. "We'll try to find the castle. Maybe they can give us something to trade so we can—"

"No." Mitch shook his head but kept his eyes on Horanis as if expecting the king to spring a sneak attack.

"Gavin's right," said Elise. *That's a great idea. We can get what we need and come back for Darcie without anyone getting hurt.* "We can come right back—"

"I said *no!*" Mitch snapped.

Elise looked up at Gavin, who shook his head not to say anything. Both watched as Mitch and Horanis squared off, ready to make a deal. Horanis's anticipation was palpable, and his eyes glinted with mischief, reminding Elise of a crooked salesman. There was no way they could trust anything he said. *Mitch has to know this guy won't play fair. What's he doing? Why won't he listen?*

Another agonizing moment of silence passed. Taking one last look around the forest, Mitch took a deep breath and cleared his throat. "Let her go. Take me instead."

What!

The forest came alive as both the visible and hidden fairies chimed out their excitement. There were snickers, laughs, and jeers coming from all directions, all encouraging Horanis to take the offer while Gavin and Elise pleaded for Mitch to stop.

Elise watched as the trees shook violently, sending a flock of startled birds flying into the sky with wild chirps and squawks as well as autumn leaves fluttering to the ground.

"Ooh, take the deal!" said a twinkling voice louder than the rest. It belonged to a ball of light that bounced back and forth between Mitch and Horanis. After a couple of somersaults, it lowered onto Horanis's shoulder before dimming out to reveal a small fairy girl.

Hey, wait a minute. I know that fairy.

"Thicket?" Elise asked.

Thicket smiled, crinkling her freckled nose, before speaking into Horanis's ear. "Can I have him? Please?"

"No! You got the last two. It's *my* turn to torture!" said a gruff little voice.

Elise recognized the second voice as Hemlock, an irritable yet equally mischievous fairy. *There were always three of them together. Where's Sage?* She looked up into the trees, but didn't see the younger, wiser fairy who had always helped her.

Thicket and Hemlock argued until their mousy voices overlapped one another.

Elise winced against the ringing in her ears. *Ugh, I wish they'd stop. I'm getting a headache. What do they even want Mitch or Darcie for?*

Horanis massaged the bridge of his nose before commanding they be quiet. "You must forgive my children. They can be quite a nuisance."

Children! Horanis is their dad?

The startling confession rendered the three teenagers speechless. Elise stared between the fairies, while Gavin and Mitch gaped at each other. The latter looked as if he were attempting to solve an advanced calculus problem in his head.

"So. . .are they," Mitch asked Horanis, struggling to find the words as he pointed above his head, "are all of these your kids?"

The branches of the surrounding trees shook with howling laughter. Elise supposed there must have been at least a hundred more hidden fairies in the area.

Horanis struggled to hide his humor as he regarded the three travelers. The corners of his mouth curved upward into a wry smile. "These three are plenty, I assure you." He cleared his throat before continuing. "But enough of this nonsense. Where's Sage?"

"I'm here, Father."

Elise's heart fluttered when she saw the smallest blond fairy responsible for their past triumphs land on Horanis's other shoulder. Even in the presence of his father, the little fairy wore a solemn, stoic expression.

I'm so glad to see him! He'll help us for sure.

"Sage, there you are." Horanis held his hand out towards Mitch. "You remember our gallant young friend here. He's just offered himself to take the girl's place. What say you to this?"

"Why do you seek his advice?" Hemlock asked. "I'm older than him."

"Or me," Thicket pouted. "I'm the oldest!"

"Silence, you two!" Horanis hissed. "I've decided that since Sage has yet to receive a human, I'm giving him the choice of which one he'd like."

Thicket crossed her arms with a petulant scowl.

Hemlock, on the other hand, flew to hover in front of Horanis's face. "Father, no! Sage has done nothing but disgrace us in front of these humans. He's helped them multiple times despite our objections and doesn't deserve such a choice!"

"Hemlock's right, Father." Thicket pointed to Gavin. "We nearly died in a fire the last time we helped *that* one."

The blood drained from Elise's face. *What are they talking about? What fire?* She still had so much to learn about what really happened when Gavin was captured by Rona. Elise looked up at her boyfriend, but he shook his head to drop it.

"Is this true, Sage?" the fairy king asked. "Are you helping humans without charge?"

"I've always required payment," Sage replied, "but I have accepted less than most would with regards to *her*."

Elise gulped when Horanis and Sage looked at her. *What're they going to do?*

"You detected it as well?" Horanis asked.

Detected what?

Sage nodded. "I did."

What're they talking about?

"As I expressed to them before, she has a caged power within her," Sage added. "A purity that Rona both craves and fears."

Horanis hummed. "Let us hope you are right. However, there's still the choice between our hero here and the maiden. Which would you prefer to take?"

As pale as Sage was, Elise believed Mitch surpassed him. Her friend's face was as white as a ghost. Though he tried to harden his stance, Elise could see his hands shaking.

Thicket and Hemlock whispered their choices into Sage's ear, but he paid them no heed.

Elise bit her lip as he scanned the area. As much as she appreciated his help, Sage always took forever to speak or make decisions. Elise swallowed a groan and suppressed the urge to stomp her foot. Offending the *one* fairy who would most likely help them wasn't the smartest plan.

At long last, the smallest fairy answered. "I desire neither."

"What a waste, as usual." Thicket clicked her tongue. "Can we not banish him already, Father?"

"I'd never turn away such a prize," said Hemlock. "The girl is lovely, yet Sage turns his nose up at her. Nothing is ever good enough for him."

Horanis turned to face Sage with furrowed brows. "Why will you not choose?"

If Sage was intimidated by the discerning looks aimed at him, he didn't show it. "I don't possess the same visceral need for torture. I have no need of a human." He glanced over at Mitch. "His sacrifice for her release should be payment enough to let them both go."

Elise thought Thicket would explode. The fairy's face was an ugly shade of purple as her face contorted with rage. Hemlock wasn't any better, ripping at his hair as he paced on a nearby branch.

Horanis isn't going to like Sage's answer. Maybe I can make a deal with them instead.

Elise licked her lips as she mustered the courage to interrupt the fairies. "What if I made a deal of my own?"

Thicket, Hemlock, and Sage hovered in balls of light near Horanis's face as the fairy king studied her. The balls of light whispered into his ear, but she couldn't hear what they were saying. "Did you not say there is no scarf nor money? Please enlighten us as to why we should hear any offers."

"What are you doing?" Gavin whispered.

Elise felt her stomach do a somersault as her knees began to buckle. She took a deep steadying breath, willing the panic attack that was creeping up to go away. With a hopeless sense of dread, she looked down at her shoes as she addressed the family of fairies. *Here goes nothing.* "I would like for you to give us our friends back and send us to Haighdlen Castle."

Crossing his arms, Horanis scoffed. "Anything else?"

Elise made herself look up. She knew by the glint in his eyes that he was only humoring her, like an adult speaking to a child about Santa Claus. Beside her, Gavin rocked back and forth as if itching to add something. When he met her eyes, she nodded for him to add something.

"I also want my friend's medallion."

What friend is he talking about? I have way too many questions for him if we ever get out of here.

Hemlock spluttered. "What makes you think we have it?" Puffing out his small chest, he glared at Gavin, Mitch, and Elise.

"It's been months!" Thicket added.

"I know you're all greedy hoarders who will keep something as long as it hurts someone else," Gavin said.

He's going to get us killed! To Elise's surprise, Thicket beamed with pride as she landed on her father's shoulder.

"Indeed." Thicket gestured for the other two to land as well. "It's always worked out for you before. You could sound a *bit* more grateful."

"That's right," said Hemlock. "We've done nothing but save your foolish necks. It's never enough, is it? Look at you, making demands again. Let's take all four of them, Father. They've had more than enough chances."

"My disobedient children make a fine point," Horanis said. "But let me see if I've got this right. You wish for me to release your friends, send you all to the castle, *and* return a traded medallion. . .for nothing?"

It does sound stupid. No one in their right mind would make a deal like that. We're dead for sure. "I'm going to take care of Rona. If you help me, I can save everyone."

After a brief pause, the trees shook again as waves of laughter erupted from the colony of fairies. Horanis joined them.

Elise felt two inches tall, but she didn't want to let them know they had gotten to her. She couldn't blame them. There was nothing about her appearance or past that would suggest she could destroy an evil sorceress. "I know it sounds crazy, but—" as she pointed a finger at her chest, something crinkled against her skin. Elise pulled out the picture her mother had drawn during Ruby's fifth birthday party. As wrinkled and stained as the paper was, Elise could still make out herself and Ruby on a unicorn together. She ran her fingers across the page, remembering that fateful night. Not only had a fire been set in her bedroom, but it was also when she and Gavin kissed for the first time in the royal gazebo. Elise looked up at Gavin, who shook his head.

"Elise, don't. That means so much to you."

Elise sniffed and blinked back oncoming tears. *I don't see how they would use it, but it's all I have to give. We need Darcie and Mitch safe before we can go to the castle. I don't know what that medallion means, but it's obviously important to Gavin, so it's worth it.* Holding the drawing high in the air, she cleared her throat. "Would you accept this?"

Shaking his head, Horanis chuckled again. "Absolutely not. I cannot—"

"*I* accept it." All eyes turned to Sage on Horanis's right shoulder. "I will help you get to Haighdlen Castle and try retrieving the medallion."

"Sage, what has possessed this sort of behavior?" Horanis asked his son.

Before Sage could answer, Thicket tugged on a strand of Horanis's hair. "We've tried telling you this for years, Father. Ever since that girl showed up, he's done nothing but defy your rules."

"He's damaging our reputation, no, *your* reputation," Hemlock argued. "He's giving away everything for a filthy piece of paper. And what for?"

"*It* is valuable," Sage replied. "If you ceased your bickering a moment, you would sense its value to her. A sacrifice of this magnitude is worth a great deal. It is difficult for her to part with it." Sage's wings hung low behind him as he looked at Elise. "I take no pleasure in causing you pain, but I must take payment for such demanding favors."

I understand. Elise nodded while trying to keep tears from falling. She suspected that Sage sensed this too.

"No, you must take *more* payment!" Thicket hissed. "She asked for three favors—that's three transactions!"

"I don't wish to play this game any longer," Sage replied. "Father, please use the scarf and help them. Find other humans to play with, for these have important fates."

How does he know that? Wait, did he say scarf?

"Hold up," Mitch said. "What scarf?"

Sage ignored him. "She's given all she has, is the only one able to vanquish Rona, and stands the only chance of setting the timeline right."

Okay, Mitch heard him too. He said scarf. What timeline is he talking about? What's wrong with it?

Horanis looked between Mitch, Gavin, and Elise. Several moments passed as he assessed them individually.

Elise blushed under the king's stare, especially when he stopped to give her his undivided attention. She tried avoiding his eyes, but something pulled her gaze to him.

Please. Please let us go. I need my friends with me, and we need to get to my family. I can't wait much longer.

"Fascinating." Horanis hummed again before addressing the three travelers. "Very well. My son makes a compelling argument. I shall send you to Haighdlen Castle. On my terms, of course." He pulled the silk scarf from his sleeve and shook it out.

"Are you kidding me?" Mitch roared. "*You've* had it this whole time? And you were going to punish us?"

"But why?" Gavin asked.

"Because I could," Horanis said with a shrug. "It was a great game while it lasted, but Sage is right. If you're going to mend the timeline, you'd best be off."

Elise couldn't hold her curiosity in any longer. "What timeline are you talking about?"

"The one Rona created," Thicket said. "She's gone and altered time itself."

"Nothing is as it should be," Hemlock said. "You'll see."

"She has the diary," Elise said to Gavin. "Do you think she's changed anything about my family?"

"You need to go. Now," said Sage. He nodded towards Thicket and Hemlock, who flew over to collect the drawing in Elise's hand before giving it to Horanis. They both disappeared into the tallest tree behind them before everything grew still. Less than five minutes passed before they returned with a medallion dangling between them.

Gavin reached up and caught it in midair. He ran his thumb across it with an unreadable expression that pulled at Elise's heart.

Who does it belong to?

"Now, where's Darcie?" Mitch spun around as if Darcie would appear out of thin air. "I want to get out of here."

"All in good time," Horanis said, examining the drawing. "Such sentimental value." He turned to face his youngest son. "Does this satisfy you?" When Sage nodded, the fairy king continued. "Very well. Despite our interference, it appears my son is pleased with your deal."

"Great," Elise said. "Now, what can you tell me about this timeline problem?"

"Oh, I could tell you plenty," Horanis moaned. "But I won't."

"Figures," Mitch whispered under his breath.

"I will leave you with this," the fairy king added as the scarf began glowing in his hands. "It won't do any good to ask anyone else. They won't know anything other than their current reality."

"Then how can we fix it?" Gavin called out as the wind picked up.

Autumn leaves began swirling as the scarf burned brighter. Horanis smiled with a wink. When he spoke, his voice echoed around them as he shrunk down to the size of the other fairies inside a glowing orb of light. "Forget what you know."

What does that mean? Elise screamed when the scarf flashed like a firework. She shielded her eyes and clung onto Gavin. *What's happening?* The forest grew dark as the sound of Horanis's sinister laughter faded into the distance.

CHAPTER 4

Elise gasped as she was shaken awake. Gavin's hand rested on her shoulder, and it took a moment to realize where she was. Although covered in the same autumn blanket of leaves, there was no mistaking the manicured beauty of the royal garden. She smiled up at Gavin before memories of fairies came flooding back to her. Bolting upright, Elise scrambled to her feet. *Where's Darcie? Did she make it?*

Her breath hitched when she saw Mitch sitting next to Darcie's unconscious body. Mitch looked up at her with bloodshot eyes. He wiped his hand across them as Elise knelt across from him.

"She should be awake by now. I've tried everything." Mitch's shallow breath rattled in his chest as he shook Darcie's shoulder like Gavin had done to Elise. "Her breathing's not right either. Something's wrong."

Panic flooded Elise's body. "Are you sure?" She placed her ear against Darcie's chest. Elise could hear a faint heartbeat, but it certainly wasn't following a steady pattern. *Darcie, no. No, you can't do this. You can't.* She clasped her hands on top of one another like Vaughn taught her when they saved Mitch from deadly mermaids. Each attempt pushed the splinters deeper into her skin, but she ignored the pain. After twenty or thirty compressions, Elise paused again to listen for a stronger heartbeat. "Gavin, maybe you should try."

"I've tried all of it." Mitch's voice was lifeless as he looked down at Darcie. His features darkened as he clenched his jaw. "It would be like the fairies to kill her, anyway, wouldn't it?" he choked out. When Elise didn't answer, he spun around and doubled over as his body shook with broken sobs.

Gavin placed a hand on his best friend's shoulder, but Mitch pulled away. Shaking his head, Mitch could do nothing but cry her name into his hands.

Elise's chest tightened as she ran both hands through her hair. It was only then she realized how many leaves and twigs were trapped within her tangles. She would have to worry about that later. *This is a nightmare. It can't be real. I can't lose Darcie. I have to do something. Maybe my magic can help. If I could reach my Aunt Sarah, she could heal her quickly.*

Knowing she didn't have the time or ability to reach her aunt, Elise placed her hands on Darcie's cheeks and concentrated on what she wanted.

Wake up, Darcie. Don't die. Wake up. Stay alive. We need you. Please wake up now.

Elise opened her eyes but saw no change. Mitch's guttural cry tore through what resolve she had left, and Elise lost control of her own emotions. Hugging Darcie against her, Elise rocked back and forth, letting her tears fall into Darcie's hair. *Please, wake up. We can't do this without you.*

"Maybe there's another way," Gavin said. When Mitch and Elise looked up at him, he took a deep breath. "We're in a magical kingdom. If Elise's magic won't work, maybe another kind will."

"Like what?" Elise asked. She would try anything to help her best friend.

"Like a kiss."

Is he serious?

"Now's not the time for jokes, Gav." Mitch sniffed and used his shirt to wipe his face.

"Yeah, we really need to think this through. She's still breathing. It's not far to the castle. Maybe we *can* reach Sarah in time to—"

"Guys, I'm serious," said Gavin. "It works in the fairy tales. What about this place makes you think this isn't a fairy tale? We were *literally* just sent here by fairies."

He's got a point. Anything could work. "Yeah, but it has to be a true love's kiss or something like that," Elise pointed out. She and Gavin paused before looking at Mitch, who shook his head.

"No, forget it. It won't do any good anyway."

Elise rolled her eyes with a groan. *This is taking forever. We don't have time for this.* "But what if it does? We need to hurry before a guard hears us or something." She looked around for any eavesdroppers. "Come on, Mitch. Wouldn't you rather be wrong than not try?"

Mitch scowled before roaming his eyes across Darcie's sleeping figure. He mulled over his options before shaking his head as if to wake himself from a bad dream. "Guys, this is stupid. There's no way—"

"Just shut up and kiss her already!" Gavin snapped, attempting to keep his voice low.

Please. Elise pleaded with him to try whatever it took to wake Darcie up. Seeing Mitch hesitate again, she propped Darcie up into a sitting position against her.

He shook his head once more. "She'd punch me if she knew," he whispered with a grimace.

Poor Mitch. Elise reached out as best she could under Darcie's weight and placed her hand on his shoulder. "Not if it saves her." When he looked into her eyes, she watched his expression soften.

Mitch took a deep breath and braced himself for what he had to do. With a nod, he beckoned Elise to push Darcie closer.

Expecting him only to lean in, Elise was surprised when Mitch pulled Darcie into his arms completely. Sensing the awkward intimacy on Mitch's part, Elise backed away and stood by Gavin a few feet away. She intertwined her fingers with his.

Both watched as Mitch cradled Darcie's head against his arm. He caressed her cheek before whispering something into her ear.

What's he saying? This is driving me crazy! Come on, Darcie. Wake up. Please wake up. This just has to work.

Mitch sat back to gaze down at Darcie's slumbering face. With one last glance at Gavin and Elise, he closed his eyes and pressed his lips softly against Darcie's.

There were no immediate signs that the kiss worked. Fireworks didn't shoot off, fairy dust didn't burst into the sky, and the only sounds came from various birds above them.

Elise felt as if her heart jumped into her throat. *Why isn't anything happening?* She stomped one foot as fresh tears fell down her cheeks.

Mitch's own tear-stained face fell as he carefully lowered Darcie to the ground where she continued to lay motionless. He met Elise and Gavin's eyes before shaking his head.

Elise buried her face into Gavin's sleeve and sobbed until her chest ached. He wrapped one arm around her and the other around Mitch. All three shook, overcome with grief, and held one another while Elise's thoughts screamed in her head that none of this was real. *It can't be real. This isn't the way any of this was supposed to be.*

The sound of a groan brought Elise out of her despair. Peeking over Mitch's shoulder, she perked up when Darcie sat up and stretched out her arms. *Darcie! She's alive!* Without a word, Elise pushed past the boys and ran to her best friend, attacking her in a tight hug. She clutched her best friend so tightly there was a very good chance Darcie could be in pain, but that would only be more proof that she was alive.

Darcie squeezed her back as the boys approached.

"Elise, what's wrong?" Darcie asked when Elise pulled away. She looked warily between all her friends. "Why're y'all crying?"

"We. . .we thought we lost you," Elise said.

"Why would you think that?" she chuckled. "We just left your grandma's house. It looks like the scarf took us where we needed to go. Isn't that the gazebo over there?"

Gavin, Mitch, and Elise exchanged anxious glances.

"What? What aren't you telling me?" Darcie's eyes widened as she looked at all three. "Okay, seriously, someone say something. You're freaking me out."

Gavin spoke before Elise could find the right words. "You were taken by fairies. The king fairy, actually."

Darcie laughed as she stood. "Yeah, right. Come on, guys. We can play pranks later. We have to get to the castle and check on Derek."

"He's telling the truth," Elise called out as her best friend walked away. "If Mitch hadn't kissed you, then—"

"*What*?" Darcie spun on her heel. All traces of humor were gone as she glared at them before fixating on Mitch. "Excuse me?"

Elise gulped. "Darcie, it was the only way to save you!" She motioned for Gavin to chime in when Darcie began stomping back towards them.

The tips of Darcie's ears were red hot as she stopped in front of Mitch. Before Gavin could say anything, Darcie grabbed two fistfuls of Mitch's shirt and shook him. "*Why* would you do that? If I was asleep, why would you do that without me knowing? Ugh, I could just punch you!"

"Told you," Mitch said to Elise.

"Don't look at them. Look at *me*!" Darcie demanded, forcing his attention back on her as she jabbed a finger against his chest. "You had no right to do that. Do you hear me? *No* right!"

"Yeah, well, you don't have to worry about it happening again, all right?" Mitch yelled back at her. "Next time, it'll be because you asked me to."

"*Next* time?" she shrieked, ignoring her friends' attempts to shush her. "No, there won't be a next time, Mitch, because there shouldn't have been a *this* time. Ugh, what were you thinking?"

"I was thinking I'd lost you, okay?" he shouted. Closing his eyes, he took a deep breath and tried again. "We thought you were dead."

Darcie shook her head, still unconvinced. "We traveled like we always do. So, why would this time be—"

"You don't remember anything that happened?" Elise asked.

Darcie groaned in frustration. "The scarf just brought us here, and I took a little longer to wake up. Big deal. Don't try to excuse what Mitch did with a stupid story about—"

"No, Darcie," Gavin said, interrupting her. "No, we didn't just travel back. We've been here a while, but *you* weren't there when we woke up."

Darcie released Mitch's shirt but remained silent.

"We looked everywhere, but we couldn't find you," said Elise. "When the king said he wanted to keep you, the only way to save you was to pay them, but we didn't have the scarf he wanted back, so—" She gestured towards Mitch.

Darcie's brows furrowed in confusion.

"Mitch offered to take your place and stay with them," Gavin said.

A tense, awkward silence filled the space between them as Darcie processed everything. "Then, how did we *all* get away?"

"Turns out those three fairies we met before are the fairy king's kids and he had the scarf the whole time," Gavin said. "One of them took Elise's drawing as payment. He said there's some timeline for us to fix, and then they let us go."

"But when we got here, you were under some curse or whatever," Elise said. "We didn't know what else to try."

Mitch, Elise, and Gavin waited until the full realization dawned on Darcie's face.

Elise knew Darcie felt betrayed, but she hoped learning the truth would allow her friend to forgive them. Especially Mitch.

"And you," Darcie said to Mitch, "you offered to take my place?"

Mitch nodded.

Biting her lip, Darcie drew tiny circles in the dirt with the toe of her shoe while she pondered everything.

She has to know we're telling the truth. Elise held her breath.

When Darcie lifted her blushed face, she no longer appeared frustrated. Instead, she wore an expression of shame, embarrassment, and something else Elise couldn't decipher. Rather than speak right away, Darcie closed the distance between herself and Mitch. Upon reaching him, she searched his eyes in silence.

Elise didn't know what her friend was attempting to find, but she desperately hoped for Mitch's sake it wouldn't start another argument. *What is this going to do to him? Is she still mad?*

Mitch was at least a foot taller than Darcie. Yet even while towering over her, his tense shoulders and wide eyes gave him away.

He looks like he'd rather face Horanis again than make her upset.

Darcie waited until Mitch met her eyes. "Do it again," she whispered.

Elise and Gavin exchanged another anxious glance.

Failing to hide his confusion, Mitch tilted his head with a shrug. "Do what?"

"Kiss me."

Mitch looked as if someone was about to dump a bucket of ice water over his head. He glanced over at Gavin and Elise with a dumbfounded expression.

"You said the next time would be when I asked you to," Darcie reminded him. Taking his hand, she interlocked their fingers together. "I can't believe you sacrificed yourself like that for me."

Mitch grew serious as his eyes darkened. "Yeah, I couldn't just—"

Darcie pressed a finger against his mouth.

The two stared at one another, sharing more with silence than was possible with words. Standing on her toes, Darcie snaked a hand around Mitch's neck and pulled him lower until their lips crushed together.

Mitch's tense demeanor melted away as his arms wrapped around Darcie's waist.

Elise felt her heart swell. Seeing Mitch and Darcie finally give into their desires clouded all their problems for the time being. *About time!*

"Let's give them a minute," Gavin whispered, causing Elise to jump. When she nodded, he led her to another section of the garden.

Once they were alone, Elise was unable to contain her excitement. "Can you believe it? I'm so happy for them!"

They finally gave in to each other's stubbornness.

"Me too," he said, sitting down on a nearby bench. He patted the empty space next to him and waited for Elise to sit. "He's liked her for a really long time."

She rested her head against Gavin's shoulder. *I've missed this.* "That was a good idea you had about the kiss. I thought we'd lost her." Elise closed her eyes, relishing the feel of both the sun and cool autumn breeze against her face. In that moment, she and Gavin were the only two people in the world. *I just hope nobody finds us here.* The perfect moment was short-lived, however, as Elise winced when he pulled her hand towards him.

"What's wrong?" Gavin was suddenly upright—completely alert. After studying her open palms, and seeing the handful of splinters on either hand, he sighed with relief. "Why didn't you tell me earlier?"

"There was kind of a lot going on," she replied with a sheepish smile. Elise nodded when he offered to remove them and braced herself. Clenching both eyes shut, she bit her tongue so as not to cry out while he took each piercing splinter out. If the process hadn't been accompanied with pain, Elise would almost label it an intimate, romantic gesture. She exhaled slowly once he finally tossed the last one on the ground. "Thanks."

"You're welcome." He gave Elise a lopsided smile before removing a leaf from her hair. "Now, *this*, I can't help you with."

"What are you talking about?" Elise ran a hand through her hair and felt countless tiny broken twigs and crispy leaves tangled within her frizzy red locks. Unable to contain an embarrassed chuckle, Elise feigned a pout as she yanked a few unwanted pieces out. "Why didn't you say anything earlier?"

Gavin shrugged with a smirk. "There was kind of a lot going on." He laughed at her answering glare. "I wouldn't bother anyway. You'll never get it all out without a bath."

She leaned back into his embrace with a defeated sigh. "Let's hope we get one soon. At this point, I don't care how many maids try to help." It was a known obligation that the castle staff helped them bathe and dress, despite their own reluctancy.

Gavin kissed the top of Elise's head and caressed the side of her arm. Locating the gazebo nearby, he cocked his head towards it. "Feels like forever ago, doesn't it?"

She nodded with a contented yawn. *Our first kiss. It does feel like a long time ago. How has it only been a few days?* Elise tilted her head back to share a sweet kiss with him. It was still surreal to have Gavin back. There were countless moments on their journey to save him where Elise feared it would never happen. Her train of thought continued wandering, again speculating what all Gavin had experienced while they were separated. She felt the weight of Gavin's head increase as his breathing slipped into a steady pattern. *Is he asleep?* Chancing a peek, she noticed his eyes were closed. *He's exhausted.* It broke her heart to see how worn out he was.

"What did she do to you?" she whispered, caressing the back of his other hand. While Elise was merely thinking out loud to herself, it shocked her when he replied.

"Not here." Gavin sat up with an audible yawn as he stretched, causing Elise to scoot over. "Maybe later."

She frowned. *Why won't he tell me? Is he hiding something?* Elise opened her mouth to ask him but was distracted when Mitch and Darcie came into view holding hands.

"Are y'all good?" Gavin asked with a smile.

"We're good." Darcie beamed before giving Mitch's hand a squeeze.

I don't think I've ever seen her look so happy. Elise couldn't have been more thrilled for her friend. Nodding towards the castle, Elise suggested they find Joranna.

"Wait!" Gavin hissed, pulling her behind him. "Someone's coming."

Elise heard footsteps approaching. They would be found any minute now. *This isn't where I want them to find us.*

"Over here!" Mitch whispered, pointing to a section of hedges that would conceal them. He waved his arm until the others were crouched in safety before also hiding.

It took a moment to get adjusted where all four could properly see who was coming. *Who would be coming this deep into the garden in the middle of the afternoon?* No sooner had the thought left her mind than Ruby and Charles walked into the gazebo.

CHAPTER 5

While the autumn weather was one indication to time passing, Ruby's rounded stomach confirmed just how far Elise and her friends had traveled into the future.

"I thought they weren't allowed to see each other," Darcie whispered.

"Knowing my mom, they still aren't," Elise muttered.

Princess Ruby was known to break the rules for the fun of it, often causing problems for others, particularly Elise. Fortunately, for now, Ruby hadn't seen the four teenagers. She was more preoccupied with the gentleman accompanying her.

"I don't get it," Mitch said. "I thought you said she was getting married off because of the baby."

Elise shushed him when Ruby and Charles started talking. *He's right. She was supposed to get married. I wonder what happened. . .*

"We should be safe out here," Ruby whispered, scanning her eyes around the gazebo.

"Ruby, this isn't a good idea. We should head back," Charles replied.

"Not until you tell me everything you know. Richard has sworn the doctor to secrecy and Mother doesn't leave Father's side." When he didn't reply, she continued. "We're all going mad with worry. Sarah is in hysterics, Ian keeps to his room, and you're the *only* one I can depend on at present. Why all the secrecy?"

"It's for the best, Princess."

"Don't use that excuse," she spat. "You sound like one of them. You're better than that." A hush fell between the two. "Richard might believe what he's doing is for the best, but if Father's health is declining as rapidly as I fear, we have a right to know."

Charles frowned with a sigh.

Why is it being kept a secret?

Stepping closer to take his hand, Ruby pleaded with her eyes. "Charlie, it's *me*. Whatever it is, please share it. You're Richard's closest friend. Surely, you know *something*."

Avoiding her gaze, Charles pulled his hand away. "I can't. I'm sorry." He cleared his throat and stepped back. "Sunset is approaching. Allow me to escort you back to the courtyard and—"

"Don't bother." Ruby jerked the front of her skirt up with a huff. As she shoved passed him, Charles reached out and grabbed her arm.

"Quit pouting," he growled. His face was mere inches from hers, but there was no denying the unspoken restraint behind his tone. Charles' glare softened into a pleading stare of his own. "Just do what you're told, *please*."

"Are you sure your mom *never* mentioned this guy?" Darcie whispered.

Elise shook her head. "She never said anything about him, but he was clearly the love of her life." *I'm dying to know why she cut him out of her life.*

Pulling her arm out of his reach, Ruby turned away from Charles before stomping out of the gazebo.

Elise panicked, afraid the two would walk out of earshot. *Why can't he give her a straight answer? Is Derek okay or not?* She pressed herself against the hedge, desperate to catch any more of what her mother and Charles were saying. It looked as if the latter convinced Ruby to return since Elise saw her mother come back into view. Rather than here what was said, she heard a scuffle behind her followed by the sounds of crunching leaves and someone whimpering. She turned to see Mitch's hand across Darcie's mouth.

"What happened?" Elise asked.

"Mitch stepped on my foot!" Darcie hissed once she pulled Mitch's hand away from her mouth. "Ugh, seriously, why did you do that?"

"There was a bee! I'm sorry," he argued back when Darcie rolled her eyes.

"Good going, Mitch," Gavin whispered with a chuckle.

"The thing was massive! It kept flying around my head. How was I supposed to know her foot was there?"

Seeing Darcie open her mouth to respond, Elise shushed them before their argument could escalate anymore. Gritting her teeth, she took a deep breath. *Ugh, these two get on my nerves sometimes. What all am I missing? I can't hear a thing.*

"What do you mean you are not able to see me again? Since when has it mattered before? We have been secretly meeting for months!" Ruby snapped.

Elise didn't hear Charles' reply, but judging by the sneer on Ruby's face, it wasn't what the princess wanted to hear.

"You dare to blame me for that?" Elise heard her mother ask. She wasn't sure what Ruby was talking about, which only managed to irritate Elise more.

"I never said anything about blaming you," Charles replied. "The least you could do is listen without jumping to conclusions about matters you know little about!"

"I would know more if you would simply tell me! About us, about my father, or anything!" Ruby grabbed her skirt once more as she stepped up to him. "I am not a child anymore. Neither are Sarah and Ian. We deserve to know the truth without being left to Richard's will. You know as well as I do the power has corrupted his good sense."

"*Careful,*" Charles warned, glancing around to insure no one was listening. "He may be your brother, but it could be thought treasonous to defame the man being crowned king in the coming days."

Ruby's face paled. All signs of anger wilted from her features as she froze. When she spoke, her voice was on the verge of breaking. "Days?"

Elise held her breath. *Oh no.*

"Possibly hours," Charles admitted. "Prince Richard has already ordered for the coronation preparations."

What!

Hesitating on the spot as Ruby broke into tears, Charles gave in and pulled her into his embrace. For a moment, the only sounds were the princess's muffled sobs against his shoulder until she pressed against his chest to gain distance.

"*Who* told you this? I demand you tell me this instant!" she sobbed, wiping her cheeks. When he didn't answer, she glared daggers at him and lunged forward, slapping her hands desperately against his chest. "Why will you not answer me?" Ruby shrieked in hysterics.

Charles remained stoic, allowing her to take her outrage out on him, even when Ruby screamed inches from his face before she finally tired herself out and leaned back against the gazebo railing.

Ruby's makeup smeared further across her face as she continued wiping oncoming tears away. Placing a hand under her rounded belly for support. Wincing, she held her other hand up to prevent Charles from approaching as she steadied her breathing. "How my mother did this four times is beyond me. Do *not* come any closer," Ruby commanded when Charles tried taking another step to assist. "I require *nothing* from you." With one last deep breath, she was able to correct her posture and continue. "That is how you want it. Is it not?"

"Ruby, this is for the best as we—"

"It is Your Highness or Princess to you," she corrected. "If our friendship cannot continue, then I suggest you address me properly before corrective action is taken. We both know you wish to remain Richard's little lapdog."

"I never wished for this to—"

"Yes, you did," Ruby argued. She paused to hold back more tears as she cleared her throat. "The night you kissed me. From the moment you declared your affections, you have been trying to recant them."

"Do you think it was easy for me?" Charles tensed his shoulders as his words spilled from his mouth like fire. "Do you think I rejoiced all those nights I helped you over the wall so you could carouse with strangers?" When she opened her mouth, he closed the distance between them. "No, *Princess,* you will stay and hear every word of this."

"How dare you—"

"Put up with your childish antics for so long?" he offered, ignoring her answering glare. "It was not without its challenges I can assure you." When she sidestepped him again, he backed up five or six steps to remain in front of her. "You will not treat me as you have done everyone else, because I have done what no one else would even against my better judgment. You do not like to be held accountable for your actions, but in a few months' time or less," he said, nodding towards her stomach, "it will be out of your hands. Now, I do love you. Every part of me longs to reach out and touch you, but I. . ." He closed his eyes, restraining himself. "I simply cannot."

"No, you *will not*, because you are choosing to run away from what we could become. You push me away, yet every time I leave, you follow. There are stolen touches, kisses, glances. . .just enough hints to betray your true desires before you retreat like the *coward* you are!" Ruby shook her head in disgust. "Maybe, if circumstances were different. . .if I were not a princess—"

"If the child were mine," Charles blurted at the same time.

Ruby froze once more, staring in shocked silence at the man across from her. Regaining her composure, she held her head high as she looked into his eyes with a solemn yet defiant expression. "You have said enough. This is the last time I shall bother you. Good day, Lord Fenton."

Charles hesitated.

Elise's heart broke watching the exchange. *Mom, I'm so sorry.* "We need to wait here before we follow them."

"I think we need to let her know we're here before we try sneaking in," Mitch said.

"Why? So, she can know we were listening?" Elise asked.

"I can't believe he said that to her," Darcie whispered. "Poor Ruby."

"Yeah, that was low," Gavin said. "She's going through enough, but Mitch is right. We should talk to her before we try going into the castle. I really don't want to end up back in a cell."

Elise sighed. "Okay, hang on. I'll get her attention. It doesn't sound like we can rely on anyone else right now."

There was a part of Elise that was scared to go back to the castle. It wasn't because she and her friends had just arrived. It was because Elise didn't know what to expect. If the fairies were right, and they usually were, then everything would be different. It sounded like Richard had grown even more conceited and corrupted than in their original timeline. Elise's mind traveled back to a conversation she had with her uncle at Joranna's kitchen table.

"Elise, I may be one of your biggest challenges later on. All of my life I have wanted to be my father. I have wanted to be what he stood for. I don't know how far into my mother's diary you are going to travel, but as I grow older, I will become arrogant. I will not fear anything, and that is dangerous. Do all that you can to convince me of my weaknesses. It is the only way I can get stronger. Convince me that I am not him."

Elise fidgeted with her hands. *How am I going to do that?* No matter how she approached the situation, it sounded like a death wish. Standing up to Rona was one thing, but standing up to her own uncle was another. A wave of panic coursed through Elise's veins as she pondered how far Rona's meddling went. *We also have to somehow get the diary back. Things are just getting worse and worse.*

Biting her lip, Elise kneeled to pick up a pebble. Saying a quick prayer, she tossed it towards Ruby. The pebble bounced a couple of times but fell short of its target. Elise tried again, but the second and third pebbles didn't travel far enough either.

"Move, let me do it," Mitch said, nudging his way past her.

"Mitch, I've got it," Elise argued.

"Clearly not. We're going to run out of rocks waiting for you."

Elise glared at him but allowed Mitch to take the lead. She watched him close one eye as the tip of his tongue stuck out while he aimed.

Rocking his hand back and forth near his ear as if about to throw a dart, he finally released. Mitch's pebble went further than all of Elise's attempts before hitting the ground with a couple of extra bounces. It landed near Ruby's foot, but the solemn princess didn't notice.

"Want me to try?" Gavin offered.

Mitch groaned, patting the ground until he found another pebble.

It's not as easy as it looks, is it? Elise got a sick satisfaction watching Mitch also struggle to reach their target. After two more failed attempts, he was able to toss a pebble far enough until it bounced off the gazebo railing next to where Ruby was standing.

The princess jerked her head towards the hedge. "Who's there? Show yourself!" Ruby tensed, shielding her stomach with both hands until Elise and the others stepped into view. Upon recognizing them, the princess relaxed her shoulders with a deep breath. "It's you! I thought I'd never see you again. When my friend returned claiming he had been robbed, and saw no sign of you, I feared the worst."

Elise realized she hadn't considered Ruby's reaction to Vaughn's interference. The princess had arranged a meeting with a friend with letters of safe passage to Vynchia. When Vaughn showed up in possession of the letters instead, they followed him believing he was Ruby's aid who would lead them to Gavin.

"We were tricked by the same guy," Darcie said.

"And your Elven bottle necklace is gone." Elise's mind traveled back to the soul-crushing moment when Rona dumped out the remaining fairy magic. Gavin saved them by activating the diary before she could even think about finding it. "I'm sorry."

"Never mind that. I am glad you are safe."

"We're sorry about Charles too." Gavin nodded in the direction Charles walked away.

Realization dawned on Ruby's flushed features as she shifted her gaze anywhere but theirs. "I-I don't suppose you heard us just now."

"We did," Darcie said.

"We're so sorry," Elise added.

"Yeah, he's a jerk," said Gavin. "Don't listen to him."

Ruby smiled with a heavy sigh. "I wish it were that easy." She drew small circles with her fingertip along her belly. "But he is right. No respectable man wants anything to do with me these days."

Elise's chest tightened as she felt her temper flare on Ruby's behalf. "Why? I thought you were supposed to marry someone before you started to show?"

Ruby chuckled. "I am not sure where you have all been these last months, but much has changed. Those plans were forgotten long ago."

I don't understand.

"So, you're stuck here?" Gavin asked.

Ruby nodded. "I am restricted to the grounds with an early evening curfew to be indoors."

"That sucks." Mitch shook his head. "They're treating you like a prisoner."

"It's just a baby!" Darcie gestured towards Ruby's stomach. "Why is your mom treating you like this?"

"It is not her," Ruby said. "I doubt she is fully aware of the measures in place to shield me." The princess stared off into space as her thoughts traveled far away from the garden.

A cold chill coursed through Elise. *She's completely isolated from everything. Why isn't Joranna helping her?* Elise ached to bring up the latest conversation between Ruby and Charles, but she thought it best to stay quiet on the subject. After all, they needed to focus on getting into the castle.

"Since we just got here, could we talk to the queen?" Elise asked. "We want to check on the king too."

Ruby returned her attention to the four travelers before shaking her head. "I can get you as far as the main hall. I am afraid Richard's study is the furthest you will get to Father."

Richard's study? He's already taken it over? Why is no one allowed to see Derek? Feeling her adrenaline build, Elise exhaled slowly. *Calm down. It's a step in the right direction. Maybe I can use my magic to get further.*

"That would be great." Elise plastered on a grateful smile.

"Could we get cleaned up before we see your brother?" Darcie nodded towards their soiled clothing.

"And get something to eat?" Mitch suggested.

Hesitating at first, Ruby nodded. "I can arrange that. Follow me."

A wave of anxiety sloshed around the pit of Elise's stomach as they approached the double French doors leading to the ballroom, but she reminded herself Ruby's reluctance wasn't a setback.

It'll be nice getting a hot bath and a meal before we try learning anything anyway. In anticipation, Elise's stomach growled so fiercely, she glanced around to see if anyone else noticed. If they did, no one said anything as the group crossed the ballroom towards the main hall.

Ruby made it halfway into the hall before jerking backwards with a gasp, causing the others to bump into her. Fumbling, Ruby pushed back against them and slammed her back against the wall of the ballroom.

"What's wrong?" Elise asked before Ruby shushed her.

The princess nodded her head towards the hall.

Elise inched close enough to the doorway to see Richard and Charles speaking in the hall. She mouthed to her friends what was going on. One by one, they all crowded around Elise within earshot of the two men.

"What did she want this time?" Richard's impatient tone struck a nerve in Elise.

"She simply wanted news on the king's health," Charles replied. Richard mumbled something under his breath before his friend continued. "I did not disclose anything."

Elise glanced over at her mother, whose eyes were clenched shut as she also listened in on the lie.

"Good. Why she felt the need to come to you is beyond me given my strict instructions about the matter." Richard cleared his throat. "Did you follow my instructions?"

"Yes, Your Highness."

"You broke her heart once and for all?" Richard asked. When Charles replied he had, the prince continued. "Excellent. Perhaps now she will stay in her place where she belongs until she delivers."

Elise was brought out of her own angered state by the sound of Ruby huffing. The princess wasn't known for being patient or putting up with such blatant bigotry. Ruby sucked her lips into a tight line as her forehead creased.

She wants to interrupt. Don't, Mom. Please stay quiet. It'll only make it worse.

"I'm about to flip," Darcie whispered in Elise's ear. "They're treating her like crap for this. We need to help her."

"Now's not the time," Gavin whispered above Elise's head. "If we walk up to them now looking and smelling like we do, we'll just make things harder on ourselves."

They waited until the men's voices faded enough for Ruby to feel comfortable leading them into the hall.

"Try to be quick," Ruby whispered. "I will have the maids prepare your rooms, clothes and bring you something to eat. Richard does not need to know you are here yet, but the council members will be arriving shortly for a meeting."

"We need to be at that meeting," Elise said.

"Do not be stupid," Ruby replied. "You will not get past the door. Once you are refreshed, we will meet outside his study to speak with him afterwards."

There was no use in arguing with the princess. *At least she's willing to help us.*

Over the next hour, all four were treated to a much-needed bath, change of clothes and snack in their own respective guestrooms. Given the last few days, Elise stayed silent when the maids stepped in to help with the process. On every other occasion, Elise often felt embarrassed, awkward, and reluctant for the assistance. Perhaps it was due to the familiarity of the process that she no longer felt his way. To her surprise, Elise was able to relax and even enjoy the treatment. Not only did the hot water soothe her aching muscles, but the fresh fruit and bread afterwards were extremely flavorful on an empty stomach.

As Elise finished the offered snack, one of the maids styled her hair. *Much better.* Richard could take her seriously now. There was still the issue of what all she would say, but Elise hoped inspiration would come when she spoke with the prince. It was critical they not only learn of Derek's condition, but also of all the changes she would need to fix. As she swallowed the last bite, Elise thanked the maid with a grateful smile. It was incredible how much a bath and snack improved her mood. Except for being mildly drowsy, she felt rejuvenated and ready to take on the world.

As planned, Elise, Gavin, Mitch, and Darcie met Ruby in the main hall.

"That is more like it." Ruby smiled at their appearances. "I have been told the council is about to conclude its meeting. It should only be a moment. Good day."

"Wait!" Elise called when Ruby turned to leave. "You're not coming in with us?"

"I believe you have seen and heard enough to know it is best I am not around during these types of meetings."

"Please," Darcie said. "We wouldn't have gotten this far without you."

"Yeah," said Gavin. "Since when do you care what they think?"

Mitch nodded. "Show them they can't treat you like that."

Ruby paused a moment before she smiled. "You know what? You are right. If Charles cannot help me, perhaps there will be strength in numbers when Richard is ready to talk." Stroking her belly, Ruby paced back and forth in front of the guarded door for the next ten minutes until it opened with a swift pull.

"Are you all right, Charles?" Richard asked as he paused in the study doorway. The guard stepped out of the way so Charles could join the prince. "All you did was scribble notes in there yet scarcely spoke three words together. Surely, you are not out of spirits concerning the matter with my sister. It is only Ruby."

I'm going to kill him! What does he mean 'only Ruby'? He doesn't know we're here or he wouldn't have said that. Elise stepped closer until her movement caught Charles' attention before he could reply. A sick satisfaction twisted deep in Elise's gut while watching both men acknowledge their entire party. She was proud of Ruby for maintaining her composure despite Charles' unwillingness to make eye contact.

"Prince Richard," Elise said with a curtsy, ignoring their shocked expressions. Attempting to be as subtle as possible, Elise stepped closer to the doorway where the king stood. "We're friends of your parents. Do you remember?"

What are you hiding? Why are you acting like this?

Richard stumbled over his words before forming a proper sentence. Regaining his formal composure, he signaled for Elise to stand. "Yes, of course, welcome. Forgive me. I was not made aware of your arrival." Realization dawned on his face as he located Ruby standing near Elise's friends. A silent, yet resentful exchange passed between the siblings before Richard returned his attention to Elise. "You appear to be doing well. I should like to speak later about the purpose of your visit, because as you can see, I am quite busy at present." Lifting an arm towards the study, Richard stepped side only enough to allow Elise a brief peek into the room.

Finally! Almost immediately, Elise's excitement was replaced by sheer terror. Sitting in a chair, speaking to another council member in a matching blue coat, was none other than Vaughn himself!

Trembling, unable to speak, Elise's chest tightened when he noticed her. *What is he doing here?*

CHAPTER 6

Elise backed away from the door until she accidentally bumped into Ruby. *I need to get away. I need to hide.* She hastily looked for an escape as intrusive waves of panic crashed into her thoughts. *We need to leave. Now.*

"What is the matter?" Ruby asked.

"Nothing. I'm fine." It was almost always her default reply when questioned about an approaching panic attack despite it being the furthest from the truth. *I don't want them to see me like this. What if he walks out here? What would I say?* As the anxious thoughts tormented her, another voice ushered in. *You were the one stupid enough to trust him while he was working for Rona. You should've known he wasn't really trying to help find Gavin.*

"Elise?" Gavin's voice sounded far away yet she sensed his presence.

Ugh, and poor Gavin was being tortured while you flirted with someone else. Vaughn even kissed your neck at that farmhouse while you just stood there and did nothing. Deep down, Elise knew the stampede of insults was filled with lies, but she was unable to overcome the mental beating of each one. *You don't deserve Gavin. He's too good for you. Look what all he's done and suffered through while you blindly followed a stranger. You tried ignoring it, but now Vaughn's here* and *he saw you! Gavin will probably leave you when he finds out.*

Then came the part she always dreaded. There was often a lingering effect on some panic attacks that included having an out of body experience. It was as if she could see herself in the hallway, watching everyone's concerned expressions, yet she couldn't speak. Immobilized by the false sense of fear, all she could do was stand there reliving the last few days. *Get a grip, Elise! This is crazy. Get yourself together. You can't do this now. Everyone's watching. Even Richard. He won't talk to you unless you snap out of it!*

"Should I fetch the doctor? You look ill," Richard said, bringing Elise back to reality.

"No, I'm okay." Tapping her hand against her thigh, Elise took a deep breath. *Fake it until it's true,* she reminded herself.

"What did you see?" Gavin whispered.

Before Elise could answer, Vaughn stepped out into the hall. "I believe everything is concluded, Sire. The others wish to know if they should return to their homes or stay to continue."

He didn't bother to look over his shoulders at the travelers, but that didn't stop Elise from glaring daggers into his back. Had she not followed him for so long, she might not have recognized him so quickly. Dressed in a tailored councilman's coat, with his long hair tied back from his muscular face, anyone could be fooled by Vaughn's false status. He had even adopted the classic haughty stance to match the other members who could be heard mingling inside the study.

While Elise's friends didn't suffer panic attacks, they were also unable to conceal their own shocked reactions.

Darcie made an odd squeaking sound as if she were trying to see how long she could go without breathing. Having been the first to fall for Vaughn's charms, she remained frozen except to peek up at Mitch.

Elise suspected her best friend felt foolish for how brazen she had acted on their journey. *Especially now she and Mitch just got together.*

Mitch's blotched skin betrayed his limited self-control. If Darcie wasn't holding his hand, Elise imagined it would've already connected with Vaughn's jaw.

The reaction that surprised her the most, however, was Gavin's. The Gavin she knew would've interrupted Vaughn and the prince, stirred up a scene, perhaps even thrown a punch since Mitch hadn't. Yet, he stood there. To everyone else, he might have looked indifferent, but Elise knew him better than that. She could tell by the way his eyes shifted between the two men, coupled with his tense shoulders, that he was holding himself back from doing something stupid.

Is he mad at me? Does he blame me for what happened? Does he even know everything that happened? Elise hadn't gotten the chance to really talk to him about what they both went through, but Gavin also silenced her when she tried. His hurtful words from Joranna's house before they traveled back rang in her ears again.

"Why, so you can flirt in front of my face this time? If you're going to fall for someone else, I'd rather not be around to see it." His verbal attack was soon followed by, *"Oh, I saw plenty. Rona has her ways"*.

Sure, he apologized after, but Elise knew the truth behind what Gavin said. As traumatic as it was for *her* to see Vaughn again in person, it must be equally hard to see him this close for the first time after Rona's mind games.

"Have them stay, Rodrick," Richard replied, nodding over Vaughn's shoulder towards Elise. *Rodrick?* "I shall have our friends here stand before the council to answer any question they may have. Let them adjourn and reconvene in two hours."

"As you wish, Sire." Vaughn bowed.

"No!" Darcie cried, causing Vaughn to turn around. "You can't let him stay."

"She's right," said Elise. "You can't trust him. He's working for Rona!"

Among the anticipated reactions from her uncle regarding the accusation, laughter wasn't one of them.

The prince spluttered, doing a poor job to conceal his amusement. Only when he and Vaughn managed to contain their chuckles did Richard try speaking again. "I wasn't prepared for that. Forgive me," he chortled. "Now, Elise—"

"It's the truth!" she exclaimed.

Darcie took a step closer. "His name is Vaughn Garthorne, and he's one of Rona's spies!"

Sharing an amused glance with the prince, Vaughn cleared his throat. "Ladies, if I may—"

"How's your head?" Elise quirked an eyebrow, relieved to have found her long-lost courage again. "Any more headaches?"

Throughout their journey, Vaughn had been afflicted by recurring headaches, which—apart from invoking sympathy—were later revealed to be Rona communicating with him.

"Perhaps you ought to call the doctor after all, Sire. Nevertheless, I shall give the council your message at once." Vaughn turned his attention to the travelers. "Until we meet again." His eyes lingered on Elise before he stepped back into the study.

And there it was, flooding through her veins. The power he still had over her. With one piercing glance, he awoke all her insecurities. Elise's lower stomach cramped as if she had swallowed a brick. She didn't like the way his eyes had just roamed her body, but it wasn't because it frightened her like Brahm's leering did. It was the opposite. What scared her was the way Vaughn manipulated her without a single word. Whether he used magic to achieve this or not— and she prayed he did—Elise was left to process his effect on her.

Bombarded with memories, Elise was transported back to the farmhouse they had visited. Upon walking in on Vaughn changing, he convinced her to stay before backing Elise into a corner. She could still feel his hot breath on her shoulder as his hair tickled her ear. If that weren't enough, the feeling of his firm, experienced hands on her waist had made it extremely hard to resist. There was still a part of Elise that wondered what would've happened if Darcie hadn't walked in on them. Not to mention when Elise used her magic to prolong his life until he could receive proper treatment after a vicious animal attack. Whatever conflicting feelings she had experience at the time, Elise knew her heart belonged to Gavin.

"You'll want to tread carefully around the other members when you stand before the council," Richard said to Elise and her friends. "We wouldn't want them getting the wrong impression. Isn't that right, Charles?"

Charles nodded, still unwilling to speak or look at the princess.

"I should like to be present when they're questioned," Ruby said.

Richard chuckled. "Whatever for?"

Elise sensed her mother's anger rising.

"There may need to be an investigation amongst your council, and I have connections with a possible victim—"

"Prince Richard!" called an urgent yet familiar voice.

Elise looked up to see Ballard approaching the group. As the castle steward, he had a talent for serving the royal family and putting his nose where it didn't belong. The only reason Elise didn't completely despise him was he saved their lives when Brahm and his sister were caught committing treason.

Ballard held up a sealed envelope. "This has just arrived from King Dmitri of Lockesbarrow."

"King Dmitri?" Gavin blurted out. His voice was laced with alarm and confusion. "Did you just say *King* Dmitri? Of *Lockesbarrow*?"

Ballard sniffed before looking down his nose at the teenagers. "I don't believe I stuttered."

"What correspondence could you possibly have with Lockesbarrow?" Ruby asked, looking at her brother as if she were meeting him for the first time. "Richard, surely you aren't—"

"It'll have to wait, Ruby. I'm afraid business calls." Richard spun on his heel.

Ruby scoffed at his retreating figure. "Then you dare commit treason against your *own* family?" She made sure to call out loud enough for the nearby servants to eavesdrop, causing him to halt and turn back.

Oh no. What's he going to do? Elise cowered before her uncle's fuming figure as he approached, but Ruby's chin only lifted higher as she squared her shoulders. *Mom, don't do anything stupid!*

"What have I told you about raising alarm within the castle?" Richard spoke through gritted teeth in a tone so low, Elise struggled to make out every word. "Your *foolish* spectacles only manage to stir up *meaningless* gossip. Now, I'm trying to—"

"Be Father," she quipped.

Clenching his eyes and mouth shut, Richard took a steadying breath. "Even if that were true, I would only be helping the kingdom."

"Does Mother know about this?" Ruby asked. "Or Sarah? Perhaps Ian? I should only be too delighted to fill them in on your latest developments without Father's knowledge *or* approval."

"I'm trying to be the leader Haighdlen *needs* right now." Catching stares from the surrounding staff, Richard lowered his voice. "Be patient and you'll see. I'll be just like him."

"That's impossible," Ruby replied coldly, ignoring Charles' poor attempts from behind the prince to caution her. Keeping a steady gaze on her brother, Ruby sneered. "You may have his looks, his temper even." She narrowed her eyes. "But you'll never have his heart."

A muscle twitched in Richard's cheek as he glared down at his little sister. "May I remind you who controls your curfew?"

"I'm not afraid of you," she replied.

I am.

"Perhaps you should be," Richard answered. "Perhaps you should even restrain yourself and let the adults handle this." When she stepped closer, he nodded towards her stomach. "Careful, Sister. You would not want to do anything *else* you will regret."

Gavin grabbed Elise's arm as Ballard snickered.

I'll kill him! I'll scratch that disgusting smile off his face. No one makes fun of my mom like that!

Rage pulsed through Elise's heated body. If looks could kill, she was sure hers would shoot fire at her uncle and the surrounding onlookers who maintained a tense silence. The argument between the two siblings threatened to continue until Charles stepped in front of the prince.

"Shall I escort them to the library until the meeting, Your Highness?"

"Thank you, Charles," Richard said, keeping his eyes on Ruby. "And Ballard? Would you please escort my sister to her room? Be sure she behaves herself this evening."

Ballard offered a hand, but Ruby stomped off without him. Rolling his eyes, Ballard tugged on his vest before turning to follow the defiant princess.

"This way," Charles said, ushering Elise, Gavin, Mitch, and Darcie towards the library.

Derek is dying, Charles broke her heart, Ballard snickered, Richard belittled her, and Joranna has shut herself away. No wonder Mom felt trapped. We've barely been here an hour, and it's clear she hasn't got a friend in the world.

Elise hung her head as she followed Charles in silence. Determined to defend her mother, she waited until he stepped into the room and closed the door.

"How could you just stand there and say nothing?" she shouted. "She *needed* you!"

"Please, do not shout." Charles held a finger to his lips. "It is not that simple."

"Not that simple?" Elise shrieked. "So, you'll only love her if it's *simple*!"

"That is not what I meant. It is because—"

"How could you do that to her?" Elise cried, pulling her hand away when Gavin tried to hold it. "And then to tell her you couldn't be with her because she's not pregnant with *your* kid? I could kill you!"

"Will you please listen?" he hissed, watching to make sure the door didn't open. When he deemed it safe, he reached into his coat pocket and removed a folded piece of paper. "Would you please give this to Ruby?"

"No way!" Mitch said. "We're not doing your dirty work."

"You've put her through enough, man," Gavin said in agreement.

"We could burn it for you though," Darcie offered.

Elise felt grateful to have her friends' support. Gaining control of her emotions, she continued in a requested whisper. "And why does Richard want us to talk to the council? We just got here."

Charles shrugged. "Probably because every time you ever visited with the king, information was shared or discovered."

"We don't have time for this," Elise said, pacing back and forth in front of the fireplace. "We need to see Derek."

"I am afraid that is not possible," Charles replied. "Please wait here until His Majesty summons you."

"What're we supposed to say in there?" Gavin asked. "What happens if we don't say the right stuff?"

"I don't want to go back to the dungeon," Mitch said.

"I am sure it will not come to that," Charles assured them. "Simply tell the truth, speak only when you're spoken to, and above all else be respectful."

I still don't know what to say, but at least Charles will be in there so it's someone we know.

Relaxing her crossed arms and stiff shoulders, Elise smirked. "I see why he won't allow Ruby in then," she teased. When Charles returned a knowing smile, Elise could see the sadness behind his eyes. She pursed her lips. "You really love her, don't you?"

"With my life."

Elise hesitated, rocking back and forth in thought, before guilt got the better of her. "Fine. Give me the letter."

Holding the letter out, Charles pulled it back as it grazed Elise's fingertips. "It is for the princess's eyes only."

Elise nodded.

Charles warily gauged everyone's reactions before handing it over and walking out.

Crossing the room, Darcie pressed her ear against the door. "Okay, he's gone. You can open it now!"

How can I? Elise felt torn. Every inch of her longed to unfold the paper and devour every word. *Is Charles about to break Mom's heart again? Is he going to propose?* If this letter was what he was writing during the council meeting, it could be important. She knew he wouldn't be so secretive if it weren't. "Do y'all think I really should?"

"Yes!" the other three cried in unison.

Elise bit her lip. *Mom hates when I go through her stuff. She's so private. If she knew I was even thinking about doing this, she'd flip.*

She looked up at Darcie. "You had a good idea. Let's burn it. Maybe it's for Mom's own good not to read it."

"Elise Charlotte Laurille, you better not burn that letter! If you don't open it *right* now, I'll—" Darcie paused. Her eyes widened before she covered her mouth. Bouncing up and down, she frantically fanned her face.

"What? What's wrong?" Mitch asked.

"Spit it out," said Gavin.

Elise's brows furrowed. Darcie only did this when she was over the moon about something or petrified. Given the wide grin that ate up her friend's entire face, Elise assumed it was the former.

"Your name!" Darcie breathed.

"What about my name?" Elise asked. "You've known it for years. You use it to fuss at me. What's the big deal?"

"Your. . .*middle*. . .name," Darcie panted, finally calming down as she glanced between the other three.

"Charlotte?" Elise asked.

Darcie nodded, waiting for one of her friends to catch on. "How did we not pick up on it the entire time we've been traveling through time?"

"Probably the same way we aren't picking up on it now," Mitch countered.

Darcie rolled her eyes. "Think about it. *Charlotte*."

She doesn't mean what I think she does, does she? Gavin and Mitch wore matching blank stares, but Elise's lit up as she reached the same conclusion. "Do you think?" she asked.

Darcie nodded before clapping her hands as she resumed bouncing. "Elise is named after Charles! That means they stay in love!"

"Is that what you were trying to say?" Mitch asked, looking at Gavin, who shrugged.

"Yes!" Darcie scoffed. "Charlotte is a female variation of Charles. Both could even be nicknamed Charlie."

A hush fell throughout the room as they considered the possibility.

"That's a stretch, don't you think?" Gavin asked, tilting his chin with narrow eyes before turning to Elise. "Did your mom ever tell you who or what you were named after?"

Elise shook her head. She couldn't remember ever asking Ruby specifically, but knowing her mom, she would not have gotten a straight answer anyway.

"I'm with Gav," said Mitch. "I think you're looking into it."

"Elise." Darcie's voice went up an octave the way it always did when she was ready to prove a point. Planting both hands on her hips, she proceeded with her argument. "Do you have any relatives named Charlotte?"

Elise tried to remember before shaking her head again. "I don't think so."

"Well, that doesn't mean anything," Mitch said.

"Yeah, she didn't know any family until after visiting Joranna," Gavin said. "There could a long-lost cousin or grandma somewhere."

"Okay, *fine*," Darcie snapped. "We're in the library. There's probably a genealogy book somewhere."

It was Mitch's turn to roll his eyes as he draped himself across an armchair. "I'm not searching for another dumb book. Besides, we don't know when they'll call us. We should work on what we're going to say instead."

"He's right," Gavin said.

"Then we agree Elise was named after Charles?" Darcie asked. When Mitch tried asking why she needed to be right all the time, she cut him off by repeating the question louder. "Say it," she demanded when no one answered the second time.

"Fine," Gavin said. "She's named after Charles."

Darcie glared until Mitch reluctantly nodded. With a triumphant grin, she nodded towards the letter in Elise's hand. "There. See? Ruby clearly names you after the guy when you're born, so whatever is in that letter can't be *all* bad."

She has a point. Elise peeled the corner open before freezing again. *I can't. It's not right. I need to keep it a secret. What if I read something I shouldn't know? It could mess up what we're trying to do here.*

  "Drop it, Darcie," Mitch said. "She doesn't want to. Let's talk about the meeting."

  "Elise!" Darcie groaned as she raked her fingers through her spiky brown hair. "You're driving me *crazy*."

  Elise held the letter out of reach as Darcie lunged for it. "I want to, okay? But we can't! It's not right, and you know it."

  "I don't care. Give it to me," Darcie pleaded as she tried catching Elise off guard. When she failed a third time, Darcie stomped her foot. "If Charles really wanted to keep it a secret, he would've delivered it himself. Open it. Then we can talk about the meeting."

  Elise wanted to honor Charles' wishes. Her hand hovered over the exposed corner, feeling as if an angel and devil were perched on her shoulders. *This is wrong. I shouldn't. He didn't look like he wanted us to see what he wrote.* Then came the side of her that Darcie loved the most. *But what if it would help Mom? She needs to know someone out there loves her. Plus, if it* is *bad news, we can burn it and save her the heartache.*

  She met Gavin's eyes, secretly wishing he'd make the choice for her. When it was clear he wouldn't, she shifted her attention to Mitch, who nodded eagerly. Elise took a shaky breath, feeling the weight of the princess's future on her shoulders. *I can't. . .No, I'll wait. It's the right thing to do. I'll give it to Ruby when I see her again.* She made the mistake of looking up at Darcie, whose eyes stared at the letter with the same intense hunger growing in Elise's gut. *Do it. They all know you want to. It wouldn't be the worst thing if you folded it back correctly. Read it.*

  Knowing she'd possibly regret it, Elise unfolded the letter. Skimming the message at first, catching random words and phrases, she struggled to fully comprehend the message due to Darcie's persistent begging to let her read it as well.

  "Ugh, fine. Here!" Elise snapped, slapping the letter down on a nearby table. "We'll *all* read it, okay? Just shut up already!"

  "Thanks," Darcie beamed, unphased by Elise's outburst. "He has super fancy handwriting, doesn't he? That's so romantic."

Elise exhaled sharply to curve her annoyance. Darcie often got what she wanted by being bossy or whining until the other person cracked. *Don't make a big deal about it. It's how she is. Besides, we don't know when Richard will call us back to the study. There may not be another opportunity.*

All four hunched over the table to read Charles' words for themselves.

October 2, 1988

My Dearest Ruby,

Let it be known I am acutely aware of the inherent risks in writing this letter— particularly those surrounding my life and title— but I aim to ease your grievances by expressing my sincerest affections. It is doubtful we shall speak again before the events listed below transpire.

The first matter of importance concerns the king. Why Richard is choosing to process His Majesty's failing health with secrecy, I know not, but it is no excuse for the way I broke the news to you. Forgive me. The curse placed upon your father is a manifestation of true evil, which should never take the life of any man—least of all one of the greatest. Though he still breathes, I send my heartfelt condolences and prayers to your family for this unspeakable tragedy. I know you detest being told what to do, but be there for your mother. She will need you.

That brings me to the primary purpose of this letter. You must leave Haighdlen. Go wherever I helped send you before. Perhaps what you seek is still out there, for I doubt what lies ahead during Richard's reign will satisfy you. As my closest friend and future king, I shall not smear his good name. Nevertheless, I will caution you. Knowing your spirit, should you stay, I could never forgive myself if I sat idle to watch them kill it.

The contents of this letter are to be strictly kept with you and you alone. Richard will encourage the queen, yourself, and Prince Ian to flee the kingdom as war approaches. Preparations are underway for your sister in the case of his death in battle given he has produced no heirs of his own. While it vexes Richard that you carry the only heir to the throne at present, he has voiced on many occasions the child must be protected at all costs—even more reason to leave when he commands it.

As for the expected heir in question, any man would be fortunate to father such an extraordinary child. I am ashamed of my cruel, impulsive manner towards you this afternoon. It shall haunt me the rest of my days.

I advise you to burn this letter upon receiving it, though I know how unlikely you are to take orders from anyone, least of all myself. Protect yourself, my darling, and the child. No matter the cost. Forget me, forget what could have transpired, and be satisfied in what has been. The stolen moments we've shared will never be enough to cure our inevitable torment, but your security and aspired happiness will soon overshadow any selfish urge on my behalf.

I will end with this. Truly, there shall never be another who loves you as I do. My life's regret is never knowing you the way my heart and body desires. Whatever you may encounter in your life, Ruby, you must never underestimate your worth, for to me you shall remain as you are this day—passionate, beautiful, and vivacious, with a tenacity and brilliance all your own. This is how I shall choose to remember you.

Eternally Yours,
Charlie

CHAPTER 7

Silence enveloped the room as everyone finished the letter. Elise felt as if an elephant were sitting on her chest.

Mitch let out a slow whistle. "Man, the guy's got skills. Sure could've used some of that language on my essays."

"Poor Charles." Darcie sighed and crossed her arms. "Why can't they be together?"

Gavin rubbed his hand up and down Elise's back before pulling her into his embrace. Kissing her temple, he rested his cheek on top of her head. "Sorry."

Elise stayed quiet, finding comfort in Gavin's gesture. *I thought I would know what to do after reading the letter, but I'm even more torn.*

"Your mom's not going to want to leave," Mitch said. "Especially if someone's telling her to."

"I know." Elise scanned the letter again. "But maybe this was always supposed to happen to get them into our world. He probably found a different way to deliver it, but it would make sense of why my family left."

"Except this is eighteen years too early," Darcie pointed out. "Hadn't the rest of your family just arrived at your grandma's when we left? Why is Rona trying to take over now?"

"Do you think it's something we've done?" asked Gavin.

Elise nodded. She was sure their meddling altered the timeline more than Rona, but they still needed to find out how much. Elise had heard about Rona's prior failed attempts, and perhaps this was one of those times, but Elise was determined to make it the last. Their ultimate mission comprised of finding the spy, saving Ruby, and finding all they could about Rona to prevent her family's catastrophic fate. *Two out of three isn't bad, but it's not good enough to go home yet.*

Unable to suppress a yawn, Elise tried shaking herself awake. She caught her reflection in a nearby mirror, realizing that not even the maids had been able to cover up the dark shadows beneath her worn heavy eyes. *I don't know how we're going to do this, but we can't let everyone down. I have to be strong no matter what.*

"Lay down on the couch. Try to nap," Gavin offered.

Elise shook her head as half of her words were muffled in a yawn. "There's no time. We have to decide what's safe to tell the council." Careful to fold the letter the same way that Charles had delivered it, she placed the paper in the front of her gown since Ruby's drawing was no longer there. Her infectious yawn spread throughout the group as Darcie and Mitch walked towards one of the crimson couches while Gavin and Elise claimed the other.

"What do you think they'll want to know?" Mitch leaned back to make room so Darcie could rest on him.

"Probably the same dumb questions," said Darcie with a yawn as her eyes closed. "Why did we choose now? What do we know? They always think we're conspiring against them anyway. Why would this time be any different?"

Weren't they the ones who wanted to plan what to say? Elise agreed with Darcie though. If it was going to be another back and forth of pointing fingers with false accusations, was there any point in preparing? The truth was as farfetched as anything they could come up with. She let the moment pass when no one else answered Darcie.

Feeling the weight of exhaustion, Elise pulled Gavin's arm around her before nuzzling his chest. She idly watched the crackling fire in the grate on the only wall not lined with bookshelves. After visiting the castle so many times, this was without a doubt her favorite room. The family portraits and antique maps gave the library an aged yet sophisticated warmth. Elise realized with a heavy heart that she only recognized two portraits of her living family compared to the handful that showcased deceased members. *I still wish I knew who these people were.* As she gave in and closed her eyes, she was startled by Gavin's voice.

"What's Vaughn like?"

I thought he was asleep! Elise bolted upright. "What?"

Gavin stiffened his shoulders but managed a small shrug. "That's definitely him in there. I just want to know what he's like."

Elise sighed. "You mean what he means to me?"

A long pause passed between the two. Goosebumps prickled her arms under Gavin's expectant stare. *How do I convince him that Vaughn doesn't mean anything to me?*

"It's going to come out one way or another," he pointed out. "We may as well be honest with each other."

Elise nodded but didn't speak right away. It was difficult to say Vaughn meant nothing, because she had come to care about him—the imposter at least. Had she been falling in love with him? Never. Elise doubted she could even see a reality where she dated Vaughn. Her feelings were more complicated than that. While she couldn't deny an attraction, her feelings revolved more around gratitude. Vaughn proved on several occasions to be a leader and protector, often risking his life to save them. It may have been the actions of a fraud, but Elise doubted she and her friends would have made it half as close to Gavin as they did without his interference.

"There's something else you want to ask," Elise said. She forced the rising tide of nerves within her stomach to settle. *Spit it out, Gavin. Do you not trust me?* "You mentioned back at Nana's that you 'saw plenty'." Elise paused to see if he would react. When he didn't, she drummed her fingers on her lap. "What did she show you?" *Maybe it was a trick.*

Pulling his arm from around her, Gavin scooted away as he sat up. He leaned forward, clasping his hands together as he considered what to say first. "Rona has some of Vaughn's hair. It's how she communicates with him. It's what causes the headaches." Elise nodded before he continued. "I only saw her use it a couple of times, but. . ." Gavin cleared his throat before looking down at the carpet. "The way you touched him, and. . .the way you let him touch you—"

"Gavin, I—"

He held up a hand. "I saw the way you looked at him, Elise."

Elise frowned, unable to think of a response. *What must he think of me? He probably wants to break up. This is all so messed up. I don't want Vaughn. I want Gavin. How can I show him that?* She was momentarily distracted by Mitch's snoring on the other couch before focusing on Gavin's guarded expression. Elise folded her hands with a defeated sigh. "There was a lot going on. I was worried about you, Mitch and Darcie were fighting constantly, and Vaughn. . .well, he. . ." She shook her head to try again. "It didn't mean anything, okay? I want to be with you. He distracted me. Whether he used magic or not, I don't know. I'm so embarrassed. I don't know what to say." Warm tears stung the back of her eyes, but she managed to whisper an apology before they fell. *He hates me. He probably just wants to go home. Maybe he thinks he made a mistake coming back.*

"Don't cry. You're not the only one who needs to apologize."

His unexpected reply made her look back up. Sniffling, she swiped away another tear before asking what he meant.

"I almost gave in to Rona."

Elise felt like someone had punched her in the stomach. Whatever ill-controlled nerves were circling within her came bubbling to the surface. Wiping her cheeks and nose on her sleeve, Elise put on a brave face. *I can do this.* "What did she do to you?" Up until now, Gavin had refused to answer her burning question. Though it caused her mouth to dry and heart to flutter, she needed to know what *really* happened to him while he was missing. *Whatever happened, I can forgive him. That woman is capable of anything.*

As Gavin recalled the prison cell and field training, her heart broke with each mentioned injury. When his story took a darker turn, involving a bathtub, arousing touches, and kisses, Elise found herself twisting the fabric of her dress until both knuckles were white. Her toes curled with repressed rage, thinking of the hold this woman had on Gavin. *Have I ever made him feel that way? Probably not. I can't compare to someone like her.*

"You okay?" Gavin asked when he was done. When Elise nodded without a word, he shook his head. "No, you're not." He leaned across the couch to release her tight grip of the dress. Taking her hand, he drew circles along the back of it with his thumb. "I think we both struggled."

She nodded again, flattening her lips, but let him speak. *He had it so much harder than I did. I wouldn't blame him if he acted on his feelings.*

"I could've killed her, you know."

She looked up, unable to hide her confusion. *What? How could he do that?*

"I had this dagger." Gavin held up his hand as if still clutching the weapon but froze with his tightened fist in midair. He punched the air as he lowered it. "It was pointed against her chest, I could've—but I choked. . .just like she said I would." He rested his forehead against his clasped hands. "All this would be over."

Elise felt a lump form in her throat. She didn't know if she had ever seen Gavin so broken. It was her turn to comfort him as she returned the favor of massaging his back. *He's gotten closer than I ever dreamed of. Will I feel the same way if given the chance?*

"She was right about everything," he continued from his hunched position, making it difficult for Elise to catch every word. "I wasn't strong enough to kill her. I wasn't able to save those boys like I promised." Gavin scoffed before pulling the medallion from his pocket. "I don't even know if it was even worth it to get Tristan's medallion back."

"Who's Tristan?" Elise asked. She wanted to ask him about the medallion ever since he got it back from the fairies.

Gavin closed his fingers around the trinket, letting the chain dangle freely. "Probably the best soldier out there. Not the nicest guy, but a good friend. He deserves better. They all do."

Elise grasped his shoulders to pull him back against the couch. Taking his hand in hers, she waited until he met her gaze. "We'll get it back to him."

He shook his head. "I doubt it. I'll probably never see him again. Or any of them."

Elise pulled him into a fierce hug, clinging to him as if the tighter she squeezed, the more pain could be released. *I want to fix this. I don't want to see you hurting.*

Gavin buried his face into her neck. For several moments they held each other in a silent embrace.

I hate she hurt you.

"You can't face her," Gavin whispered.

Elise released her hold on him so he could sit up. "What do you mean?"

Returning the medallion to his pocket, he looked at her as if it were obvious. "She's *too* strong. There's nothing she won't do to get what she wants. I know you keep hearing that, but I've *seen* it. The stories I heard in that prison, the prisoners themselves, everything about that place is dangerous because of her."

She bit her tongue before proceeding. "What do you think we should do?"

With a shrug, he turned his face towards the fireplace instead of her. "Maybe leave when your mom does."

Elise blew a loose piece of hair out of her face before she stood. *Is he serious?* Pinching the bridge of her nose, she paced back and forth in front of the fireplace. Seeing Darcie stir in her sleep, Elise lowered her voice. "Look. I get you're scared. I am too. I don't know what all you saw, but I trust that she's evil. It's why I need to take care of her before anyone else can—"

"Dmitri's dead." Gavin rocked back and forth on the couch. "He's been dead for years. He's *supposed* to be dead. Did you know that?"

"Dmitri?"

"Yeah, you heard Ballard when he delivered that letter. *King* Dmitri of Lockesbarrow. He's Rona's brother. Supposedly, he's the only person she ever cared about, so when he died, she went crazy and started all this takeover crap." He wiped both palms back and forth along his thighs. "I think Rona used the diary to bring him back, and if that's the case, we're screwed."

"I don't understand." Elise shook her head as she tried processing what he was telling her. "You said the diary was blank."

"Yeah, it was," Gavin said. "It still didn't stop her from grabbing it from me. It's the only explanation for why her brother's back and Vaughn was able to get himself on that council. Not to mention your uncle's trying to pull us into one of his power trips. Don't you see how messed up everything is? We need to get out of here before it's too late."

Elise took a shaky breath. Every time she felt like the situation was becoming under control, something else came along. Although Rona grabbed the diary, deep down Elise had hoped it wouldn't give the sorceress what she wanted. She sank back down on the couch, feeling as if concrete walls were closing in on her. It was difficult to breathe, let alone try to formulate a plan. "But we can't leave."

"Why not?" he asked. His crazed stare unnerved her. "If we stay, Vaughn will eventually lead Rona here."

"She's altered too much to go home," Elise replied. "What do you think *home* looks like? Think about it. It wouldn't be what we already know. I may not even have a family in this timeline's future." Elise tilted her head back against the couch, releasing a heavy sigh. *How am I going to fix this?* "I have to put it back together."

"Elise, be serious for a second," Gavin said, twisting his body to face her. "You already decided to fight Rona. Now you're going to take on Rona *and* her brother? Plus fix every *single* change in the timeline? You can't!"

"But I have to." Her voice was devoid of emotion as she talked towards the ceiling rather than look at him.

"Then we have to figure out how we—"

"I already told you," Elise said. "*I'm* going to do it."

"How?" he pressed.

"I don't know!" she snapped after the third time he asked. Given what happened to Darcie, there was no way Elise could let her friends put themselves into any more danger. She winced as her sharp tone woke Mitch and Darcie, who stretched and sat up.

"Is everything okay?" Darcie asked in the middle of a yawn.

"Yep." Gavin pushed himself off the couch. "Elise is going to defeat Rona and King Dmitri, but don't worry. She doesn't need our help."

The sarcastic bite of his tone tugged at Elise's heart. She wasn't trying to hurt his feelings. *I have to protect y'all and this is the only way. I can't lose you again. Don't be angry with me.*

Darcie walked over to them. "Elise, why—"

Everyone jumped as Ballard swung the door open as if trying to catch them off guard. He checked the room to see if anything was out of place before informing them Richard was ready to meet.

Although Gavin's words stung, Elise knew better than to speak in front of Ballard. While he did the right thing sometimes, the steward was usually only looking out for himself. One whisper of gossip was sure to reach Richard within seconds, or worse, her grandparents, whom she had yet to see.

Give them the truth. It's all they want. Don't let Vaughn intimidate you either. While easier said than done, Elise felt an immense relief when Gavin took her hand. *Here goes nothing.*

CHAPTER 8

Elise hadn't known what to expect when Ballard led them out of the library, but it wasn't a full escort comprised of five armed guards. Being taken to the council this way felt like a death sentence. Elise's mind was filled with memories of the time she spent in the castle dungeon. *Gavin must be feeling it worse than me. He's been in two dungeons.* If Gavin was unnerved, he hid it well. Mitch and Darcie kept quiet, too. The only interaction came from the passing staff, who regarded the group with a combination of pity and apprehension. Besides a momentary glance over his shoulder, Ballard took no notice of Elise and her friends. She preferred it this way until he led them down a different corridor away from the study.

"I thought we were meeting Richard," she said. "Why aren't we going to the study?"

"Formal council meetings take place in the assembly chamber again," Ballard replied.

"Assembly chamber?" Mitch asked. "We watched the members come out of the study earlier."

The steward took a calming breath, continuing forward past a series of windows overlooking the garden. Dusk was approaching, already casting shadows throughout the courtyard below. "King Derek has held meetings in there, but the study is intended for His Majesty's private use. Prince Richard takes a more traditional approach and prefers for official kingdom business to be conducted in the assembly chamber." Spinning on his heel to face them, Ballard gestured to a closed door on his left. He knocked only once before the door was opened by a servant inside.

"Do *not* embarrass His Majesty," Ballard warned.

"Which one?" asked Mitch, to which Ballard merely rolled his eyes before stalking away.

Elise shivered upon entering the stale assembly chamber. Though not as cheerful as the ballroom, it was far grander than she initially imagined. Her eyes were immediately drawn to an exquisite chandelier centered over an elongated table that took up most of the room. Every corner boasted ornate marble columns while the remaining space was comprised of iron sconces, oil paintings of former kings, and embroidered tapestries. The elegant multi-paned windows on the exterior wall reached the ceiling and were partially covered by lush burgundy drapes that matched the velvet table runner and chair cushions.

Has this place always been here?

Richard beckoned them forward from his seat at the head of the table on the opposite end of the room. Above his hand hung a formal portrait of King Derek. Elise hesitated upon seeing her grandfather's imperial figure. Fortunately, despite the regalia, the artist captured the kindness behind his eyes. *I wonder where they're keeping him. He should be here.*

Elise took a tentative step forward while scanning the faceless sea of intimidating blue coats on either side of her uncle. She tried to concentrate on anything else besides the ringing in her ears and weak knees. Knowing she was seconds from hyperventilating, she swallowed a wave of nausea before trying to stabilize herself. Elise stilled when she felt Gavin's hand on her arm.

"You've got this. We're right here," he whispered.

Although she heard his words, she took another moment to process them until she no longer felt lightheaded. *I'm not alone. Gavin's here. My friends are here. We're going to be okay. Don't panic. Don't panic.*

"Are we to believe these children have insight into Rona's plans?" asked the man closest to Elise from the end of the table.

"We have no time for games," a younger man said from the center.

"We can!" Darcie called out over the growing rumble of disapproving commentary.

The men looked towards Richard, who nodded towards the clerk near Elise.

"This assembly is in session," announced a clerk standing by the door with the servant who let everyone in. "First order of business, introductions. Please step forward and state your name for the council."

I can't give them my name! You need to get out of here now. Elise searched for other exits, but found the only one to be how she entered, which was now blocked by guards. She ushered Gavin in front of her before finding a place behind Darcie and Mitch.

"Gavin Striess," Gavin stated.

As each of her friends introduced themselves, Richard nodded with approval until it was Elise's turn again.

"State your name, Miss," the clerk repeated.

"Elise. . ." *Say something. Anything. Lie. Make up a random last name already!* She stood frozen, unable to think of a scenario where she wouldn't have to share too much. *Why didn't I think about this part?* Elise opened her mouth, but nothing came out. *Come on, Elise! You look stupid! Smith, Johnson, Williams, Baker. Pick one!* She searched the council more carefully before locating Charles and Vaughn a few seats away on Richard's right. *They already know I'm here to help the family and have a connection. Making a false name won't do anything now. I look too much like Joranna and Ruby to get away with it. I have to face the consequences.* Twisting her hands, she looked at her friends' tense expressions. *What do I do? What do I do!* Abandoning any chance of redemption at this point, Elise closed her eyes. "Laurille."

As expected, the room erupted with gasps, groans, and the collective buzzing of inquiries amongst the members of the council demanding to know Elise's connection to the royal family.

"Did you know about this?" one member called out to Richard.

"Their unplanned, dare I say, *hasty* invitation doesn't account for such a revelation. Why are we only learning of this?" cried another.

Before the prince could reply, a third gentleman stood. "There is something sinister here, dare I even say something treasonous in our midst. Perhaps even too grave for only a crown prince. I move for Her Majesty, Queen Joranna, to be present at this hearing at once. If not, the king himself!"

A unanimous cry of approval rang out amongst the table from most of the members until Richard commanded for all to take their seats.

"What else are we not being told?" demanded a voice above the raucous.

Elise compared Vaughn to the other distressed men. Studying him, she saw the faintest of smirks cross his lips while he scribbled something down on the paper in front of him.

"I *will* have order amongst the Council of Lords before we proceed!" Richard bellowed, glaring at the most vocal of members. "I am perfectly capable of overseeing this business. My mother shall *not* be made aware of this hearing, and my father's health will not allow it. Now, I can assure each of you here that I am unaware of any possible connection this young woman has to my family. Let us add the subject in question to our interrogation and proceed beyond introductions." He waited until the room fell silent again before nodding at another clerk responsible for writing the proceedings.

"Are all those in attendance aware of the punishment for committing treason to the crown?" the first clerk asked, waiting for the majority to nod or mutter in the affirmative. "Very well."

"I should like to start, if I may," said a frail older gentleman near the middle of the table.

"Proceed, Ambassador Heathcote," said Richard.

It wasn't until that moment that Elise realized this gentleman and the elf she had seen before were not wearing the traditional blue uniform. The senior man tapped his fingers along the edge of the table as he collected his thoughts. Pursing his lips, he scanned a list of documents in front of him before examining the group of teenagers.

"According to castle records, you were present when King Derek voiced his intentions to declare war on Lockesbarrow, were you not? And that you understood Vynchia's intent to aid Haighdlen in this?"

How does he know that? She reasoned it had been months to these people since Derek was attacked rather than days.

Elise thought back to the morning they discovered Gavin was missing. The council had just finished meeting with only the elf opposing the decision on behalf of Leafbrooke. She located the elf ambassador, who keenly watched her along with the other councilmen.

"Yes, we were there," said Elise, not sure where the man was going with his question.

"Well, according to the prince," he said, gesturing towards Richard, "that was the last time any of you were seen in the castle until this afternoon."

Elise remained silent as her heartbeat quickened.

"Considering you carried such sensitive information before King Derek formally announced it the following day, please explain where you've been these last months."

Elise felt her throat constrict as she met Vaughn's gaze across the room. *How do I answer that?* Shortly after Ruby helped them leave the castle to find Gavin, Vaughn turned up instead of their arranged guide. In possession of the safe passage letters, she followed him along with Mitch and Darcie. The journey ultimately led to the shores of Lockesbarrow where Derek was injured before they were sent forward in time only hours earlier. *They're going to put us back in the dungeon for sure.*

"Answer the question," Richard commanded.

Elise looked over her shoulder at Gavin. *Help me.*

Sensing her distress, Gavin called out to the ambassador. "We didn't tell anyone if that's what you're asking."

"But how can we be sure? There are spies everywhere," the elderly ambassador responded.

"Yeah, there's one sitting in this room." Mitch said, pointing to Vaughn.

Another roar of surprise rippled down the table as the councilmen looked between the teenagers and Vaughn.

Vaughn sat motionless, unphased by Mitch's outburst. Given the twinkle in his eye, Elise wondered if he was enjoying the attention.

"Sir Rodrick, I apologize again for these baseless allegations." Richard's eyes furrowed as he addressed Mitch next. "You need to quit deflecting your answers and speak the truth."

"And *you* need to listen!" Darcie piped up. "We are telling you the truth. He's your spy. Whatever you're saying in here is getting back to Rona!"

"Enough!" Richard bellowed as he smacked the table with his fist. "I'll not have you making a mockery of this council."

A heavy silence followed until Charles spoke up. "I think we should heed their warning."

Elise watched as her own shock was mirrored among the seated gentlemen, including Richard.

"Charlie, you can't be serious—"

"Forgive me, Your Highness, but I am." Charles met Elise's gaze before turning to Richard. "We can't risk ignoring any threat, regardless of its credibility."

"Lord Fenton makes an excellent point," said the elf. He held up a pale hand when another member tried to interrupt. "We must consider this issue beyond Haighdlen's border. There have been multiple port closures, border disputes, and more unexplained kidnappings from all neighboring kingdoms. Perhaps Sir Rodrick should be dismissed until a proper investigation is conducted."

"I agree," Charles said. "After all, I was put under an investigation based on a mere rumor, and you wouldn't want there to be any discrepancies in *your* handling of council matters as Crown Prince."

Elise watched her uncle carefully. She knew Charles made a good point, yet judging by Richard's glare, the prince didn't appreciate having his authority questioned.

"Sir Rodrick has taken great care to strengthen our ranks in preparation for battle," Richard said.

"You put him in charge of *soldiers*?" Gavin exclaimed. "You're setting yourself up for an ambush!"

Richard's face reddened as he fought to keep control. "Mr. Striess, your outbursts will cost you if—"

"My outbursts are trying to save you!" Gavin said. "*I* was one of those people kidnapped. I can tell you exactly what's going on."

"Pray, tell us then," Ambassador Heathcote said.

Gavin glared across the table at the speculative gentlemen. Elise watched as he clenched both fists by his side. "Not until he's gone."

Richard made to argue, but Vaughn stopped him with a wave of his hand as he stood. "There's no need, Your Highness. I shall remove myself for the sake of the council. I hope you're able to come to an agreement as to what's in the best interest of Haighdlen. The kingdom is in excellent hands. Good day, gentleman."

Elise watched his movements carefully as he made his way towards them. She didn't know what to expect, but she froze when he winked down at her as he passed. As if that wasn't enough, Elise thought she felt his hand brush against hers before his figure disappeared into the hall. Only when the door closed behind him did she feel safe enough to speak. "He's not here to help you," she said. "He works for Rona and is very dangerous. More dangerous than Brahm."

"Rona's training all those who are kidnapped to create a large army. There are kids over there being forced to fight," Gavin said.

Richard held his hand up. "You've been gone too long. Let me inform you that Rona is no longer reigning over Lockesbarrow, nor is there any evidence of such an army or any imminent threat of war. We're only interested in building strength in the case that changes. Our priority is the king's health and maintaining good relations among the remaining kingdoms while we weed out the spies."

"No threat of war?" Elise asked with an incredulous stare. "Did Vaughn tell you that? Oh, sorry," she added with a roll of her eyes. "Did *Rodrick* tell you that? Because he's lying to you!"

"If it were a lie, then why would Lockesbarrow retreat from the prior battles that did occur?" asked a councilman. "There hasn't been an isolated attack in several weeks!"

Gavin stepped in front of Elise. "Look, I don't know why she's been quiet, but Rona wouldn't give up control. She's power hungry, manipulative, and too self-centered for that."

"Be that as it may," Ambassador Heathcote stated, "we are here to decide how to proceed with this supposed war. Your Highness, given Lockesbarrow's lack of action and your father's health, I am inclined to remove Vynchia from it."

"You can't do that!" Darcie said. "That's what she wants!"

"You're going to get yourselves killed if you do!" Mitch added before addressing the prince. "Think about the family before you decide something you might regret. You don't want to do anything else stupid to get more people hurt."

"What are you talking about?" asked Richard.

"That time you shot me in the forest," Mitch said. "Remember now?"

"Okay, okay, Mitch. We get it. Your Highness, this is what she wants," Gavin continued. "Her brother may be in charge, but he has to be a front for something. He's the only one Rona cares about, but she's trying to throw you all off the scent. The fact she got Vaughn on your council only proves it's something big."

"Sir Rodrick has been found guilty of nothing and remains innocent at this time," Richard said before addressing the ambassadors. "Now, I can understand the hesitation to engage in warfare alongside Haighdlen, but I do agree we need to remain ready for anything."

"Leafbrooke remains as it did before and will not be sending aid at this time," said the elf.

"I am disheartened to hear that, Ambassador Vailweyn, but I respect your position on this." Richard sighed, turning to the elderly man. "Ambassador Heathcote, I beseech you to please reconsider your alliance. Together we may stand a chance. Isolated, we both fall."

"I'm afraid I don't detect a threat," the Vynchian ambassador replied. "However, given the delicate situation with your father, I shall refrain from a definite decision until more evidence is presented."

Richard nodded. Elise supposed her uncle's lack of a response meant the offer was better than nothing. "Next, we need to discuss what steps Haighdlen will take to protect itself."

Elise met Charles' tentative gaze. *This is what Charles was talking about in his letter. Richard's going to try separating the family. I have to stop him.*

"Wait, before you do that, what about more help?" Elise suggested. "Are there any ambassadors from the fairy kingdoms?"

The answering chortles and laughter answered her question. Wishing she hadn't spoken up, Elise curled her shoulders inward and missed the days she felt invisible.

"That will be all from you," Richard said to Elise and her friends. "We must proceed. Now, despite your lack of propriety, I see no reason why you can't continue with your usual accommodations."

"Please don't send anyone away!" Elise blurted out. "We only want to help. Don't ignore us!"

"I suggest you get a hold of yourself, young lady," Richard said. "You are a friend of my parents. Nothing more. Don't embarrass yourself further and subject yourself to more guarded quarters during your stay."

Elise made to argue again but felt Gavin's hand around her arm. "Drop it," he whispered. "Wait."

She fought every urge to pull away from him and march up to her uncle. She knew that would be a one-way ticket to the cell he was already hinting at.

Before the guards could lead them out, a servant burst through the doors.

"Sire!" the man panted.

"What is the meaning of this?" Richard fumed. "Are we not to have a moment's peace?"

It's scary how much he looks and sounds like Derek sometimes.

"It's the king," said the servant.

The room waited with bated breath for Richard to reply.

The prince lowered his gaze. The muscles in his neck twitched as he swallowed. Suppressing his emotions, giving the illusion of the perfect leader, he softened his tone. "Is he. . .has he passed?"

"No, Sire, but the queen beckons you to his chamber." Richard sighed in relief before the servant continued. "The king is lucid as of now and wishes to speak with you."

Take us with you! What he wants to talk with Richard about? We need to get up there to talk with him too.

"I must conclude this session, gentlemen, if you'd be so kind as to stay this evening. Guards, have a maid escort these visitors to their respected rooms at once." Richard didn't wait for a response before passing Elise and her friends on the way out.

The four were not given another chance to speak to the councilmen before being ushered out of the assembly chamber. There was no sign of Richard anywhere, but Elise's heart skipped a beat when she found Ruby waiting for them in the main hall.

"Finally!" Ruby exclaimed. "I've been sick with worry ever since you left. Richard just passed in a hurry, refusing to tell me anything. What happened?"

Ignoring the flanking guards, Elise shook her head. "They won't listen to anything we tell them. Ruby, you're not safe here."

Ruby scoffed. "What are you talking about?"

Before Elise could respond, Ballard made his grand entrance into the conversation. "There you all are! I have assigned maids to take you to your rooms after dinner. Please follow me to the dining hall."

Elise bit her tongue before she got herself into too much trouble and followed the steward. Her bad mood improved along the way as the aroma of chicken and freshly baked bread reached her nostrils. She felt her stomach twist in knots and rumble no less than five times between sitting down and being served.

She was not shocked by Richard's or Joranna's absence, but she did wonder at her other uncle and aunt missing dinner. "Isn't anyone else coming?" she asked a servant.

"Only members of council who feel inclined this evening, my lady. The remaining family is otherwise engaged."

Elise frowned.

"Don't look into it," Ruby whispered. "I've eaten the last several meals alone."

"How come?" Darcie asked.

Ruby shrugged. "Sarah and Ian keep to themselves lately, and Mother never leaves Father. Eat. You must be famished."

Elise's stomach replied before she could. Giving into her hunger, she and her friends ate in silence. It was hard to get a word in with Ballard listening only feet away.

"Don't lose heart, Elise," Ruby said when they reentered the main hall. She yawned before suggesting they head to bed until any updates came about her father. "It's taking every ounce of control I have not to demand more information, but I'm a bit fed up with doors slamming in my face."

"Right then," Ballard announced when he joined them. "You'll be shown to your rooms at once. As before, I will arrange for a guard to be posted outside your doors and—"

"Oh, no, I see no reason for that," Ruby argued. "Leave them alone this evening."

"But Princess—"

"Honestly, Ballard, they've nothing to warrant such treatment, and if Richard didn't bother to order it, I see no reason to reinstate it." She held her chin high, meeting his challenging stare for several moments until he tightened his lips with a sneer.

"Very well, Princess," he said before slinking away.

"Disgusting man," Ruby muttered under her breath.

Elise chuckled in disbelief. "Wow, thank you." *I can't believe it. We won't feel like criminals anymore.*

"Get some sleep," the princess said with a smile. "You won't be scrutinized this evening. A meeting with the council is punishment enough."

They chuckled before Ruby turned to leave. It was only then Elise remembered the letter hidden in her gown. She called out to her mother before her eyes fell to Ruby's belly. *Is giving her this letter the right thing to do? She's already going through so much. I don't want her to hurt anymore.* Seeing the maids approaching, Elise went with her gut feeling and retrieved the letter. "Please read this."

"What is it?" Ruby eyed the letter warily as she took it. When Elise revealed who it was from, Ruby gripped the middle of the paper between her fingers as if to rip it.

"No!" Elise exclaimed, startling everyone in the main hall. Whispering a quick apology to the nearby staff, she nodded towards Ruby's hands. "You'll want to read it."

"Why, have you?"

Elise saw the familiar fiery rage flash across her mother's eyes. Ruby was an extremely private person. One hint of prying and the letter would be burned. No questions asked. "No," she lied. "I could just tell when he gave it to me that it was important. You should read it."

Ruby's shoulders relaxed as she considered Elise's words. The princess looked at all four travelers, assessing their reactions, before flattening the paper out. "Very well. Good night."

As they were led to their rooms and changed for the night, Elise's mind raced with all the possible scenarios that could arise from Ruby reading the letter. *I hope she reads it. Please read it, Ruby.*

Would her mother burn it after reading? Would she be convinced of Charles' feelings? Could this bring them closer together? What would happen to the timeline if they married? As usual, the other side crept in with doubts. *Knowing Mom, it could be crumpled up or in pieces. Poor Charles.* Ever since Lord Fenton vouched for Vaughn's removal, Elise's heart had softened towards the other man. Despite his questionable actions and words, she truly did believe he loved her mom. She knew Ruby loved him in return. Whatever happened later between them would be up to their own stubbornness.

By the time everyone went to bed, a storm developed nearby. As a round of thunder rolled in the distance, Elise groaned as she covered her face with a pillow. Despite everything that happened, she couldn't bring herself to fall asleep. Her mind wouldn't let her rest. *We haven't seen Derek or Joranna yet. This is so different than all our other visits. Something doesn't feel right. Vaughn is also somewhere in this castle and that scares me.*

She was startled out of her unending thought cycle by the sound of the doorknob turning. When the door didn't open right away, Elise broke out into a cold sweat as she was flooded with worst-case scenarios. *Please don't be Vaughn. Please be Darcie. Please be Darcie. Ugh, why was I so excited not to have a guard earlier?*

Elise's heart thrashed around inside her chest until she saw Gavin's face peek around the door. She closed her eyes and collapsed back against the pillows. "You scared me."

"Sorry," he whispered. "I couldn't sleep, so I came to check on you. You okay?"

Elise nodded, realizing a second later he probably couldn't see her well in the dark. It dawned on her this was the first time she and Gavin had been truly alone since reuniting. *There's no chaperones, friends, fairies, or guards. We're finally alone.* "Yeah, come in."

Despite the heavy covers, Elise shivered when she heard him turn the lock. Her breath hitched in anticipation as his dark figure crept closer to the bed. *I need you.*

CHAPTER 9

Elise slid over to give Gavin room on the bed. *Is he really here right now?*

"I didn't wake you up, did I?" he whispered. When Elise shook her head with a smile, he leaned his forehead against hers. "Good. I wanted to tell you how impressed I was earlier." Elise must've shown her confusion, because he quickly followed up with, "The way you spoke up to the council. I know that was hard for you."

She nodded. "I don't think I breathed the entire time." A breathy chuckle left her lips before she looked into his eyes. "You impressed me too, but that shouldn't come as a surprise."

"Why's that?"

Elise shrugged. "You're always confident. It makes me jealous. I mean, *look* at you. You survived being captured by Rona, and then hearing what happened to you. . .you're not afraid of anything."

"That's not true," he replied, holding up a hand when she tried to argue with him. "I've never been more scared than I was these last few days."

"You thought she'd kill you, right?"

Gavin nodded. "*That*, but. . .I kept thinking about you guys. *You* especially, and how I might never see you again." He reached down to intertwine their fingers. "I drove myself crazy knowing that Vaughn guy was so close to y'all. I kept thinking of the two of you together."

Elise felt a stab of guilt in her chest. *I hate he got the wrong idea.* "He doesn't mean anything to me."

Gavin shrugged. "It was still hard to watch though."

"I know what you mean," Elise admitted. "I worried about you and Rona. I can't compete with her beauty or power, and all I kept hearing was nobody says no to her." When Gavin didn't answer, she bit her lip. *Is that what happened between the two of you?*

"I said it before," he said. "We both messed up, and we can keep rehashing it, but that's not why I came in here."

Then why did you? Elise didn't feel the need to ask out loud, so she watched him carefully.

Gavin opened his mouth two or three times without forming any words before hanging his head with a frustrated sigh. He squeezed their connecting hands tighter until Elise could feel a thin layer of sweat forming against his palm.

Is he nervous? It wasn't often Gavin let his nerves show. At that precise moment, Elise couldn't think of *ever* seeing him so flustered. *What's going on? Did I do something wrong? Is he breaking up with me?* The longer his silence stretched, the more Elise convinced herself he must be upset with her.

"Whatever it is, I'm sorry," she apologized before more desperate words began spilling from her mouth. "I mean it. I only care about you. Please don't hate me. Let's forget everything that happened while you were missing. I can't do this without you." *You have to believe me.* She was caught off guard when his shoulders began to shake. *Is he. . .laughing?*

Sure enough, thanks to a patch of moonlight shining through the window, she could make out a wide grin across his face. "It's not funny. I'm being serious!"

"I know." Gavin took a moment to contain his amusement before looking up again. "I can't believe you thought I was breaking up with you."

Releasing his hand to cross her arms, she glared at him with an indignant scowl. "Well, why else would you be acting all weird like this?"

His voice softened. "Because I realized something while I was away." Gavin reached up to tuck a strand of hair behind her ear. When Elise raised her eyebrows expectantly, he licked his lips before taking a deep breath. "I think I'm in love with you."

What! Struck speechless, Elise unfolded her arms and searched his eyes. *Did he really just say that?* With a quavering laugh, she sat dumbfounded, feeling as if her heart would burst. A growing warmth spread along her entire body until it settled in the form of a lump in Elise's throat. *I can't believe this.* Cocking her head, she regarded him with a lopsided grin. "Really?"

Gavin nodded before his eyes widened. "I mean, I don't know why I said, *'I think'*," he added quickly, rubbing the back of his neck. "I'm an idiot."

He's so cute. Elise giggled as tears pricked the backs of her eyes. *Is this really happening right now?*

"What I should've said was. . ." Gavin inched closer until his face was a breath away from hers. "I love you."

Elise flickered her gaze between his eyes and mouth before leaning forward. "I love you, too." As their lips met, she still couldn't shake the fear that he would vanish any moment and she'd wake to find it was all a dream. Breaking the kiss, Elise dipped her head back as Gavin's mouth found the tender spot at the base of her neck.

At first, his soft familiar kisses released the usual butterflies in her stomach, but within seconds, it was as if a switch was flipped inside him. No longer did familiar Gavin's touches feel like simple caresses, but an unhinged, raw need to explore every inch of her.

Elise had never known desire like this. She didn't have a clue what she was doing. She became increasingly aware of their panting, mutual groans, and the quivering ache deep within her that pulsed like an itch waiting to be scratched.

Remembering his sensitive spot being similar to hers, she returned her attention to his neck.

'You don't want to do that', he had once warned her.

Yes, I do. Cupping a hand around his neck, she inhaled his soapy scent before nibbling the tender skin until eliciting a moan from him that awoke something within her. *I want you.*

She tugged on his shoulder until he rolled on top of her. Elise's mind ran away with thoughts of what could happen. As much as she wanted more, the risk was too high.

"We need to be careful," she said. "It feels strange to finally be alone like this anyway." When he didn't respond, she panicked. *He's going to get the wrong idea.* "I want you. You have no idea how much I want this, but. . .we should wait."

Gavin dropped his head onto her shoulder with a heavy sigh. "Yeah, you're right." He rolled over onto his back until their breathing returned to normal before pulling her into an embrace.

Elise rested against his shoulder as their legs tangled together. The thunder had ceased, and all that remained was the steady pitter-pattering of rain against the window. *This is still nice.* It may not have been how she imagined their first night alone together would turn out, but it was an intimate connection between them, nonetheless. She nuzzled her face against his chest, admiring how well she fit against him.

"Will you stay for a while?" she whispered.

"Mmhmm," Gavin hummed before adding with a chuckle, "I doubt you want us found together in the morning though."

She giggled again. "We'd never get a break from a chaperone."

He yawned. "We'd never get a break from Mitch and Darcie."

He's got a point. Darcie would whine and beg until she had every private detail. Closing her eyes, Elise focused on Gavin's heartbeat drumming against her ear. The steady rhythm, coupled with the steady rise and fall of his chest, threatened to lull her to sleep. It could have been for ten minutes or an hour. Elise couldn't be sure. They rested in their comfortable silence until Elise felt her body jerk involuntarily a couple of times. She fought against it until Gavin kissed her forehead.

"I better go."

"Are you mad?"

"No. I just wish I could stay longer. Who knows when we'll get another minute alone?"

He's right. Elise nodded, doubting he could see.

Gavin paused at the door. "I love you," he whispered.

"You too." When the door closed, Elise waited for any sounds of him being caught. Hearing none, she hugged close to her the pillow he had used and shimmied back beneath the blankets. *It still smells like him.* Although the feverish sensations were long gone, she squeezed the pillow tighter before burying her face into it to muffle a high-pitched squeal. She kicked her feet back and forth, wishing she could shout at the top of her lungs. *Gavin loves me. He really loves me!*

Despite their shortened night, Elise felt relieved when Gavin smiled at her upon entering the dining hall the following morning. *Good. He doesn't look upset.* She yearned to talk to him about the previous night but was unable due to the large party sitting amongst them, including Mitch, Darcie, and Elise's aunt and uncles. Besides pleasantries, little was said until Ruby joined them.

"Any news on Father?" the princess asked her eldest brother.

Richard rolled his eyes before stabbing a fork into his food. "How many times must you ask? He's fine."

His agitated answer wasn't good enough for Ruby, who quickly followed with, "Considering you're the only one you've allowed in his room besides Mother, I'm left with no other option." Ruby ignored Richard's glare and turned her attention to her two other siblings. "How odd to see the two of you here. I rather wondered if you both left."

"Not now, Ruby. We're not in the mood for your sarcasm," muttered Sarah.

"Speak for yourself," Ian replied with a smirk. "I rather enjoy Ruby's wit. *Someone* in the family should have an engaging personality besides me."

Will they ever get along? Elise rolled her eyes, relaxing as Gavin drew lazy circles against the small of her back. The two exchanged coy smiles before she rested her head against his shoulder.

Sitting across from them, Darcie narrowed her eyes at the sappy gesture before pointing her fork in their direction. "What's going on? Something's different."

Denying anything had changed, Elise felt the telling rush of heat seep into her cheeks.

"Spill it. Why're you two acting so weird? Do *you* know?" she asked Mitch when Elise and Gavin shrugged.

"No clue." Mitch couldn't help but smirk under the weight of Darcie's stare.

"You *do* know something!" Darcie hissed, tugging on Mitch's sleeve. "Tell me. I can't be the only one out of the loop. I'll go crazy!"

Mitch met Gavin's eyes across the table, clearly enjoying his girlfriend's momentary insanity.

Sitting up, Elise swallowed convulsively as she met Gavin's gaze. *Did Gavin tell him what we did, or almost did?* She sighed with relief when he shook his head to indicate that nothing was shared.

Darcie huffed. "If someone doesn't tell me *something* soon, I'm going to lose it." The tips of her ears had already turned red as she slumped back with her arms crossed.

She's such a drama queen. Elise couldn't suppress a smile as she shook her head.

Darcie softened her expression as she regarded Mitch before trailing a hand across his thigh. "It sure would mean a lot if you'd tell me."

Mitch froze with a mouth full of food. His cheeks quickly became the color of Darcie's ears before he swept her hand away. Once he was able to swallow, Mitch chuckled at Darcie's pouty expression. "It's not that big of a deal. I went to ask a maid for a glass of water and thought I'd stop to talk to Gav for a bit." Mitch scooped another bite of eggs on his fork with a wink in Elise's direction. "Only he wasn't in *his* room."

Darcie's eyes widened as her mouth hung open. Glancing between Elise and Gavin, she felt as if she was seeing them for the first time as she studied their body language for incriminating evidence. Checking to make sure no one else was paying attention to them, she fanned herself with both hands. "Oh my gosh. You didn't! Did you? You *did*, didn't you? I can't believe it!"

"Darcie, shh," Elise hissed, also checking to make sure her family wasn't listening. "No. We didn't."

"Liar," her best friend gushed. "You look guilty and happy at the same time. You both do."

Gavin squeezed Elise's hand under the table. *Part of me wishes we had, but we made the safest choice.* She didn't know how she'd handle any what-if scenarios while trying to save Derek *and* take down Rona. Her trail of thought wandered to Ruby. She glanced down the table at her young expectant mother, who was still bickering with Sarah and Richard. *By my age, Mom was in a strange land with a one-year-old. I can't imagine. . .*If that wasn't motivation enough to control her urges for the time being, she didn't know what was.

"Well, *something* must've happened," Darcie pressed.

"Yeah, something did." Gazing down at Elise with a lopsided grin, Gavin intertwined their fingers. "I told Elise I loved her last night."

Darcie gasped before clapping her hands. Bouncing in her chair, she nodded towards Elise. It looked as if it took everything in her power for Darcie to whisper. "*And*? Did you say it back?"

I could watch this for hours. There was something comical about Darcie's theatrics. Deciding to put her friend out of her misery, Elise nodded with her own face-splitting grin. She suspected if they hadn't been in the company of the royal family that Darcie would've broken into a song and dance routine.

"Okay, you have to—" Darcie cut off as Joranna's entrance was announced to the dining hall.

The guards and servants stood at attention as Elise's grandmother walked to stand near her children, barely acknowledging the four travelers apart from a brief nod. Joranna's bloodshot eyes were worn and sunken against her pale tear-stained face. Although remaining the epitome of royalty, draped head to toe in fine jewelry and fabrics, her mind was clearly far away from the room.

"Do you think something's happened?" Mitch whispered. "Or will happen soon?"

"Definitely," said Gavin. "I know we didn't use the diary this time, but we've always landed right where we need to be. I don't think we came to this time by coincidence, but if we don't do something soon to get to Rona, we won't stand a chance of helping."

"Mother, you look so tired." Sarah stood to hug Joranna. "Won't you join us and eat something?"

Joranna shook her head. When she spoke, her voice was hoarse and unrecognizable, as if the words being spoken were not her own. "No. I've come to. . .the doctor feels it's time for the family to. . .and I think he's right."

What is she talking about?

"You should go see him. Now," Joranna managed to blurt out as she wrung her hands together. "I fear I've have been gone too long already."

What!

"Absolutely not." Richard dropped his fork in disgust. Elise watched Ruby jump when it clattered against his barely touched plate. "Mother, I'm sure the doctor got it wrong. Again, there's no need to create havoc upon the—"

"*Richard,*" Joranna snapped, holding up a hand as he tried arguing back. The room was engulfed in a palpable silence. Even Richard appeared to yield at his mother's tone. With a shaky breath, Joranna turned to leave without waiting for anyone to follow her. "The four of you need to come with me."

CHAPTER 10

Watching her family leave without being included felt like someone punched Elise in the gut. Drawing inward, it was as if she heard herself screaming without anyone noticing.

We have to see Derek! I can't let anything happen to him.

By the time all four reached the hall, however, Ballard was already in place to apprehend them. His signature strained smile of forced politeness was firmly in place. "Well, well, well. And where would you be off to in such a hurry?" he asked.

"We need to get to the king," Elise said tersely, growing more infuriated by the second as he regarded them with a smile one might reserve for small children. She wasn't in any mood to argue with the steward, and the amusement he clearly got from preventing them access to Derek only provoked her more. When he blocked Elise's next attempt to step around him, she groaned. "You *don't* understand! We need to make sure he's okay. Tell him to let us in!" She looked around for any other staff to help, but the remaining maids and servants merely stood watching. Some even acted as if they couldn't see or hear her.

"I'm afraid you wield no power here." Ballard looked down his nose as he spoke, a gesture that made Elise want to punch the smug expression from his face. "Now, I shall be glad to escort you to the drawing room. Or the library, perhaps? Trust that the king is in excellent care. There is nothing to worry your pretty little head about."

"They're calling in the family!" Darcie argued. "We need to talk to him before anything else can—"

Ballard held up a hand to shush her. "You'll merely vex the family, which I am ordered to prevent at *all* cost." Puffing out his chest, he tugged at the hem of his vest with a haughty sniff.

Richard really is out of control.

"We're not going anywhere *except* the king's room," Gavin stated. "And you're going to lead us there."

Ballard stared at the finger Gavin pointed near his face. "My, my, how bold you've become since your capture. Nevertheless, you forget your place, sir. I take my orders from the royal family, and the last time I checked, that does not include any of you."

Elise longed to say she *was* a family member, since Ballard wasn't present during the council meeting, but she knew it was a losing battle either way. They would have to find a way to get to Derek's room without the steward knowing. *That's easier said than done. This guy's got his nose in everything.* Then it dawned on her. She could try using her magic. It worked at odd moments here and there. It was worth a try. When she was certain her voice wouldn't come out as a stutter, she stepped in front of Gavin.

"Take us to the king." Elise spoke with an air of authority, careful to keep her posture strong, while at the same time feeling as if she could become sick at any moment. Feeling her stomach churn from nerves, she regretted having so much to eat. Closing her eyes, Elise willed her breakfast to stay down before she opened them and focused on what she wanted Ballard to do. *Take us to the king.*

The steward scoffed, unable to hear the internal battle Elise was fighting to control her magic. She continued repeating the command in her thoughts, imagining a force leaving her mind and entering his own.

Ballard looked as if he was ready to hurl another condescending insult her way, but no words came out. Instead, his mouth simply opened and closed without a sound.

"Keep going," Darcie whispered in her ear. "Just focus. You've got this."

Elise felt Gavin grab her hand with a squeeze of encouragement. Their support meant more than they knew. Tightening her mouth into a flat line, Elise concentrated on a spot in the middle of Ballard's forehead so as not to lose her nerve. *Take us to see Derek. Turn around.* She watched as Ballard turned his back to them. *Yes, that's it. Now, take us to the king.*

"Come this way." Ballard's brows creased with confusion, as if he couldn't believe what he agreed to do, before ascending the grand staircase without another word. His steps were uneven at first, prompting Elise to focus all the more on the direction she wanted him to go. *Don't mess this up. This has to work. Go faster, Ballard!*

Gavin, Darcie and Mitch quietly cheered her on as they followed the steward to where the royal bedrooms were. Elise instantly recognized Ruby's bedroom door as they passed it, but she felt a twinge of concern when Ballard continued walking past all the doors without stopping. Even her grandparents' room was unattended. Fearing her magic might be backfiring, that perhaps Ballard might be deviating from her influence, Elise scrambled to form new commands. Any hope of concentrating disappeared, however, when they rounded the last corner.

A large crowd of servants, footmen, and maids were gathered outside of a closed guarded doorway.

Elise only managed to follow Ballard halfway down the corridor before a shrill cry pierced the air around them that turned her blood to ice. *That's Joranna.* She broke out into a sprint, nearly pushing Ballard out of her way. Before Elise could reach the king's door, however, it burst open as Richard stormed out. In his own haste, he bumped into a maid, knocking over a towering pile of folded linens in the startled young woman's hands without apologizing. *I can't let him see me! He'll try to stop me.* To her surprise, however, Richard *did* see her, but rather than exert his authority, he merely brushed past her without a word.

She made it to the front of the disorderly group of onlookers, who were busy griping about the spilled laundry, with half a second to spare. Only able to catch a glimpse through the crack in the door,

Elise jerked her head back as one of the guards promptly shut it, but the damage was done.

Gavin, Darcie, and Mitch caught up in time to help the maid pick up the fallen linens while Elise stood facing the severe-looking guards, but she wasn't paying attention to them. Her mind was occupied with what she saw inside the bedroom.

Upon Richard's exit, the door was left ajar enough for Elise to make out a frail-looking man propped up on the four-poster bed. While she realized now that it was Derek, he looked nothing like the strong king she had come to know. His wrinkled face grimaced weakly as his chest heaved, each breath sounding painful, and his wispy gray hair was plastered against his sweaty forehead. She couldn't make out much more. Not only due to the sickly nature of his appearance, but the drapes had been closed, giving the impression it was much later in the day. The candlelight from a nearby table cast the large room in dancing swirls of orange light and shadows. The only other person she could make out in time was Ruby standing by his head with a wide-eyed expression while Derek's hand rested against her rounded stomach.

Another round of wailing from inside, this time from Sarah, sent a cold chill down Elise's spine. She closed her eyes against the gut-wrenching sounds coming from her grandfather's room.

"Disperse at once!" Ballard hissed to everyone standing in the corridor, clearly free from Elise's powers. The crowd broke apart, many weeping themselves, until Elise, Gavin, Mitch, and Darcie were the only ones left. "Out of my way and do as you're told!" He stepped around the four teenagers and into the room. The door remained open just long enough for a guard to allow him access. This time, Elise tried to get a better look. Standing on her toes, she caught a glimpse of the rest of her family. Joranna was now draped across Derek's chest, sobbing uncontrollably as Ballard and the doctor tried pulling her up, while Ian hugged Sarah as she wept into his shoulder. The king lay motionless with his arms by his sides on the mattress. Elise gasped when she realized Ruby, who hadn't moved, caught her staring. The door slammed shut even harder than before. "You heard the orders," growled one of the guards. "Disperse!"

"Come on," Gavin said, holding his hand out for Elise to take. "Let's give them some privacy."

"I can't." Elise's voice cracked as she spoke, yet she was desperate for one more look. "There might still be time. If I could just get inside—"

"Come back!" screamed Joranna from inside the room, making Elise jump. "Derek, darling, please. Please no. Not yet." There were deep, masculine voices, but Elise couldn't make out what they were saying. "No! I won't leave him," Joranna cried. Her anguished voice sounded unrecognizable from the composed woman the four travelers usually encountered.

Elise broke out into a cold sweat as another cry was ripped from her grandmother's throat. She felt her knees buckle but caught herself in time to hear Joranna plead with the others in the room. "Leave us alone. Don't touch him! Derek, you must wake up. It's me. You must wake up. Don't leave me. I can't—I c-can't be here without you!" Her words quickly slurred into incoherent mumbling. It sounded like she might be speaking into Derek's shirt.

"Let's go," Darcie urged, pulling on Elise's sleeve. "We shouldn't be here right now. It's too private."

"I'm not leaving," Elise choked out, determined to gain any access she could. *It's my family.*

Everything around her felt as if it were paused in time. Was this how it had played out before she interfered in the timeline? Was Derek supposed to die from this curse? Elise bit the inside of her cheek to keep from screaming. Derek wouldn't have been on that beach if it weren't for them. This could've been avoided. Her mind was bombarded with flashbacks of the diner where she met Derek, to the time they spent together preparing for his and Joranna's engagement ball, before her heart wrenched at the memory of his proud smile as he shared the news of Richard's birth in the bakery during their tour of Clara. While only a few days of Elise's life had passed since then due to the diary, Derek's entire lifetime was now threatened to feel as short.

Elise was unable to move from where she stood. It sounded like Joranna quieted down as a series of footsteps crossed the room.

Elise could make out Ballard's voice, followed by who she assumed was the doctor. Feeling the adrenaline building inside her, she ignored her friends' pleas to leave, instead choosing to listen intently with bated breath. She knew in her heart what the outcome was sounding like, but she wasn't prepared for it all to become a reality. When the door opened one last time, allowing a distraught Ruby to step out, Elise felt numbness spread throughout her entire body as the doctor's voice flowed into the corridor for all who were close enough to hear the truth.

They were too late.

Derek was gone.

CHAPTER 11

The days following Derek's death were lengthy and solemn with little opportunity to interact with members of the royal household. Elise wanted to mourn *with* her family, but they were well protected, kept away from prying eyes, to grieve in private.

The only perk was that any further thoughts and attention towards chaperoning were practically nonexistent now, allowing Gavin to visit Elise's room each night in secret. While their passions hadn't resumed from the first night, Elise found herself eagerly anticipating the sound of her bedroom door creaking open after everyone went to bed. Truth be told, *he* was the only reason she hadn't completely broken. Being isolated from her newly found family, whether *they* were aware of the relation or not, was threatening to drive her insane. Gavin's comforting words were all that soothed Elise enough to sleep. He would simply talk and rest with her, sometimes for hours, as well as stretches of time when neither spoke that she found equally consoling.

On the morning of the king's funeral, even the clouded sky evoked a certain somberness as people arrived from near and far to pay their respects to the late ruler.

From the guestroom window, her forehead pressed against the cold glass, Elise watched the endless line of carriages pull into the courtyard.

So many questions still swirled in her mind surrounding Derek's death. Despite the declaration that his passing was curse-related—spurring outrage throughout the kingdom and a cry to increase war efforts—Elise couldn't shake the gnawing reminder that it could have been prevented. The king wouldn't have traveled to Vynchia if it hadn't been for them. She clenched her eyes against another bout of warm tears. How did she have any left to shed? Swiping a hand across her cheek, Elise peered over at a black dress on the bed.

At Joranna's request Edith, the fabriwitch in charge of dressing the royal household, had provided Elise and her friends with funeral attire. While lovely— probably one of the *most* beautiful gowns Elise had ever seen—she couldn't help but think how grim it looked compared to the bright luxurious ballgowns from their past visits. Stepping closer to it, Elise brushed her fingertips along the dark silken trim. It would be a perfect fit, no doubt, yet she dreaded putting it on. Wearing the gown meant admitting this was all real. She also knew, however, that if she didn't hurry, the maids would have to help her. Elise hated when that happened.

Fortunately, Elise was dressed when the maids arrived, so they only needed to fix her hair and makeup. *I can deal with that.* Those were the two areas she often didn't bother with at home anyway.

Elise's mind wandered yet again as she studied her dolled-up reflection. At some point, she would need to address her plan to face Rona with the family. There wasn't going to be an ideal time, leaving her to ponder which options were less likely to get her and the others thrown in prison.

"You ready to go?" called Gavin from the doorway.

Elise jumped. She hadn't heard him come in. *When did the maids leave?*

"Sorry." Gavin closed the door behind him before approaching her vanity table. "I knocked, but you didn't answer."

He knocked? I really was *distracted.* Elise turned back to face the mirror as he came to stand behind her.

Gavin rested his chin on the top of her head, being careful not to mess up what the maids had styled. Black suited Gavin, she mused, as she took in his polished appearance.

"Do I have to go?" Speaking scarcely above a whisper, she wondered if Gavin had even heard her when he didn't immediately reply.

"No," he finally said, kissing her hair. Meeting Elise's eyes in the mirror, he lowered his mouth near her ear. "We could stay here, but I know you. You'll hate yourself if you don't go."

He's right. The funeral would happen whether she went or not. The least she could do was be there for the family, even if they didn't know she was one of them.

It was an odd thought, she realized. After everything she and her friends had been through, Elise still didn't feel like a princess. There were often moments at night, particularly when she was alone, when Elise imagined what would've happened if she hadn't accepted her grandmother's offer. Would she have ever seen Gavin again? Were they destined to be together, or was this a coincidental fling that would die out when they got back home? Since the first night he told Elise he loved her, the words had been uttered between the two of them many times. She loved Gavin, too, but a part of her feared he only loved the idea of who she was during this journey. If she survived facing Rona and was lucky enough to make it home alive, would his feelings change? *Home.* Home, the very thing she was fighting so hard to reach, felt incredibly far away.

Taking Gavin's hand, she followed him out. That was going to be a difficult conversation, but it would have to wait. Coming down the staircase, Elise was surprised at how crowded the main hall was. Scanning the sea of faces, she met Darcie's eyes.

"There you are!" Darcie stood on her tiptoes and waved them over to where she and Mitch were standing. "Where have you been? It doesn't matter." She was talking so fast, Elise couldn't get a word in. "Bad news, guys. The funeral is over already."

"What?" Elise shrieked, causing a handful of guests nearby to jump. She would've apologized had she not been so lightheaded as a flood of nerves attacked each limb. *This isn't happening.* "W-we missed it?"

Darcie shushed her as a couple of people looked in their direction before continuing in a whisper. "Mitch and I overheard some people talking. The burial was a private event for the royal members only."

"Yeah, everyone else is here for some kind of memorial service," Mitch added while scanning the room. "Your uncle's supposed to give a speech soon."

Elise felt the blood drain from her face. Not only could she not mourn with the family, but now she had missed the burial? *I wanted to see him one last time.* Her head swam until Mitch's voice pierced through the numbness to alert them that the family had just arrived.

A bizarre sensation flooded through Elise as everyone else cleared a path for the approaching Laurille family. It wasn't until Darcie hissed, reminding her to curtsy along with the rest of the crowd, that Elise realized the feeling pulsing through her was no longer heartache or grief. In that moment, she felt nothing but pure rage.

I am family! I should've been there! Why didn't they include me?

Joranna knew they were related to some degree, so why wasn't Elise told the burial would be earlier? *I wanted to say goodbye, too. I need to tell him I'm sorry!* As the family's arrival into the hall was announced, it was as if Elise were floating above her body watching everything unfold. Countless scenarios came to mind of what she wanted to tell her relatives, but as the procession started, Elise felt her rage slowly dissipate.

They look so broken. Elise had been so preoccupied with how *she* was grieving, how betrayed *she* felt, that it was jarring to witness those closest to Derek being forced to face everyone without him.

Richard was the first to pass through. *No doubt, his idea.* Joranna came next, followed by Sarah, Ian, and Ruby. All wore matching pale expressions, bloodshot eyes, and stoic statures. Their movements were synchronous, rehearsed, and void of emotion. *Everything a royal is supposed to be, I guess.* The mere spectacle of it all made Elise want to cry all over again. She didn't know if she could ever hide her emotions like that. *Maybe that was why they didn't invite me.*

Richard's lengthy speech was as expected—assertive, cordial, yet inspiring. He told tales regarding Derek's devotion and bravery, of his wisdom and leadership, but Elise couldn't help but tune out the prince's incessant droning. She was too busy watching Joranna. The queen's eyes were glassy, distant, but more than anything, lifeless. She was a picturesque figurehead, staring at nothing while her eldest attempted to rally everyone's spirits. *I need to talk to her.*

Her wish was easier said than done. Once the service was concluded, guests were allowed to approach the family, who waited in a receiving line at the front of the room. What Elise didn't expect was that it would be over an hour before she could get even a glimpse of her relatives.

"Elise?" Joranna looked at the four teenagers as if seeing them for the first time. "How nice of you to come."

"Yes, how wonderful to see you," Sarah echoed from beside her mother.

Ian simply nodded in their direction while Ruby accepted a hug from Elise.

"So glad you could pay your respects. Thank you." Richard's curt tone sliced through what little resolve Elise had managed up until that point.

"I would have liked to have gone to the burial." Elise glared into her uncle's eyes, praying her weak knees didn't buckle.

"Family only, I'm afraid," Richard said. "You understand."

"I am fam—"

"I believe you are the final guests, and my dear mother needs her rest." Richard held a hand up when Elise tried arguing once more. "There is a delicate matter I'd like to discuss if you'd be so kind to meet me in my study in ten minutes." With a dismissive nod, Richard turned to lead the family out before Elise or her friends could reply.

Wiping a fresh layer of sweat off her hands, Elise whispered Joranna's name until her grandmother paused in the doorway. Elise closed the distance between them before peeking over her grandmother's shoulder for any sign of Richard.

"I really need to talk to you," she whispered.

"I sense what you are feeling. Richard thought it best that only immediate family attend," Joranna said. She hesitated when Darcie, Gavin, and Mitch joined Elise. "I know you're related in some way or other, Elise, but it doesn't make a difference now. Please don't press the issue any further."

"No, it's not that," said Elise with a wave. "It's about Richard. I think the king thing is going to his head. He's completely power hungry—"

"Elise—"

"And Rona did something else after hurting the king. We think she's messing with the past and plotting something. I mean, *why* would she just stay quiet for months? Wouldn't a kingdom be weaker and easier to take over if its king was sick? Why didn't she act? Aren't you suspicious? I'm telling you, something is going on!" Elise took a much-needed gulp of fresh air after finishing her hurried rant.

Joranna shook her head at an approaching guard before folding her hands delicately with a sigh. "Enough. No more, please."

She can't be serious!

"But—"

"Richard is Haighdlen's future. He will protect it."

"But there's a spy!" Darcie added.

"Children, I'm thankful for your loyalty to Haighdlen. Truly, I am, but my heart can't carry anything else at this time. I beg your forgiveness, but this needs to be put to rest and left in the very capable hands of the council."

"The spy is *in* the council!" Gavin countered.

"And the prince won't listen to us," Mitch argued.

Joranna took a shuddering breath until she could control her tone. When she spoke again, it was barely above a whisper. "Do you see these people?" She waited while Elise and the others looked around the room. "They knew what an excellent ruler Derek was. They honor us with their presence. Don't create a scene. They're here to help us mourn." Taking a step closer, Joranna held a handkerchief over her mouth before continuing. "But, one by one, they will all leave and return home. In a matter of days, they will go back to their lives, but *I* am burdened with remembering every memory, every laugh, and he won't—" She clutched the soft cloth against her face to stifle a sob.

Elise's heart shattered as warm tears streamed down her own cheeks. She regretted saying anything now.

"He won't get to see the birth of his grandchild." Joranna wiped the corners of her eyes before checking to see that no one noticed her losing control. Clearing her throat, Joranna regarded each of them one more time. "So, please forgive me if I can't humor any conspiracy theories at this time. Richard told me there have been no recent threats to the kingdom's security and I believe him. You should, too. Thank you for attending, and I wish you a safe journey home, wherever that may be. Goodbye."

"You'll see what we mean," Elise called after her. "He's not listening, and unless someone does, Rona wins." She huffed when Joranna proceeded out of the room without answering. "I am so sick of being ignored about this."

"They're grieving," Darcie said. "They're not themselves right now."

Elise nodded. *She's right.*

"We better get to Der—Richard's study," Gavin said.

I almost forgot. With a heavy sigh, Elise led the way out for what she was sure would be their final visit to the royal study.

CHAPTER 12

Elise was shocked to find her mother standing outside of Richard's study.

"I came to eavesdrop, naturally," Ruby replied with a smirk before Elise could ask what she was doing there. "Richard's hardly spoken to any of us. I'm curious what he's up to."

I bet she wants to find out if what Charles said about Richard sending the family away is true. Elise bit her tongue. She couldn't ask if that was her mother's motive. If Ruby found out anyone else read Charles' letter, she'd erupt. Elise glanced down at the princess's rounded stomach. *Nobody needs that right now.*

Ruby took a step back and pressed her ear against the door. "I can't tell who is in there right now. All I hear is mumbling."

Knowing time wasn't on her side, Elise changed the subject in hopes of getting an answer about something she had seen moments before Derek passed.

"I know now might be bad timing, but can I ask you a question?" Elise licked her lips, fighting the urge to twist her fingers together. "And if you don't want to answer, that's okay," she added quickly. *Spit it out, already!* She watched Ruby's eyebrows raise expectantly. "When. . . right before your dad passed," she began, rubbing her sweaty palms along the sides of her skirt. "I thought I saw him put a hand on your stomach." Elise flickered her gaze between Ruby's eyes and stomach, hoping the other woman got the hint without making Elise say it. "Y-you just looked scared."

Ruby's brows furrowed before realization dawned on her features. The princess looked at Gavin, Mitch, and Darcie, as if gauging whether she and Elise should be having this conversation privately. Finally, she answered, but her voice sounded hollow. "The family believes Father transferred his magic to my child."

Elise's breath hitched. *Is that why I have magic?*

"We were fortunate to see the real him for a few moments," Ruby continued. "He remembered mother first. It was—" She trailed off as her eyes became unfocused. Swallowing convulsively, Ruby blinked several times before getting control of herself. "Anyway, we all got to say goodbye."

Elise desperately wanted to know what Ruby was going to say, but judging by the shakiness of her mother's voice, this conversation was about to end whether she wanted it to or not. *I need to act fast.*

"And he died right after he touched your stomach?" Darcie asked before Elise could.

Ruby nodded. "It was the briefest of moments, but I can see it so clearly. When he reached out to touch my stomach, I thought he would admonish me, but there was silence. I felt a warmth spread through me before the baby kicked. Father smiled, and then. . .he was gone." Ruby sniffed, brushing a stray lock of hair back into place. "Sarah thinks Father's magic is what helped him live as long as he did, so when he—" She tucked her chin downward, caressing her stomach. "Anyway, Richard hasn't looked at me since. I can't help but think he blames me for what happened."

"But you didn't do anything," said Gavin.

"Yeah," Mitch agreed. "It's not your fault."

Ruby smiled. "That's sweet of you."

"Hang on. Back up a bit." Elise took a deep breath. "What happened right after he was cursed?" *We missed all of this. Maybe something can point us to where we need to go.*

The princess sighed before slumping against the wall. It was as if discussing such an idea would not only drain her emotionally but physically as well.

She looks pale. Maybe we should do this another time. As concerning as her mother's condition was, Elise knew that Ruby would be the only member of the family to share with them such intimate details surrounding Derek's death. Elise pressed her mouth into a thin line, secretly wishing her mother could humor them a few minutes longer.

"It's all a bit hazy, to be honest," Ruby confessed. She checked to make sure no one was eavesdropping, including on the other side of the door. Continuing in a whisper, she leaned in closer. "When he first arrived, he was in so much pain. There were several nights he suffered these horrific fits. Hallucinations. Nobody knew what to do. Sarah tried to heal him, and for a while it was working, but then nothing she nor the doctor did seemed to help. It became harder for him to speak. His speech, it. . .turned into these broken phrases, almost as if it took every ounce of energy to speak. And when he did, he would have lapses in memory."

"Then it *is* the same thing," muttered Gavin. "I knew it."

Elise looked up at him. "What do you mean? The same as what?"

He licked his lips before raking a hand through his hair. "When I was locked up in Rona's castle, there was a storyteller in the dungeon named Horace. I learned from another prisoner that Rona placed Horace under a terrible curse. He said it was one of her favorites."

"That's sick, man," Mitch said.

"She wanted him to suffer." Darcie shook her head. "And while he was suffering, *she* took the opportunity to steal the diary from Gavin and chance altering the time—"

Before Elise could elbow Darcie's ribs to shut her up, the door opened abruptly, making their entire group jump. *I hope Mom didn't hear any of that.*

It didn't appear that Ruby heard Darcie's slip. Ruby clenched her eyes shut, inhaling sharply as she clutched her lower belly.

Expecting Richard, Elise was surprised to see Charles on the other side of the door. He looked equally surprised to see Ruby with them.

"I'm sorry. I wasn't expecting—*Princess*! What happened?" He was at Ruby's side in a moment. Using one arm to hold her up, he took her hand with his free one. His distressed eyes searched hers, but she immediately straightened her posture.

"Don't worry, I'm not staying," Ruby said breathlessly.

"Are you ill?" he inquired. "Would you like me to arrange an escort for you? Fetch the doctor?"

"Charles? Is everything all right?" called Richard's voice from inside the study.

Ruby shook her head. "That won't be necessary. I'm perfectly—" She winced before exhaling slowly.

"Is the child coming?" Charles asked. Without waiting for a response, he turned to lead her away. "Come, we've got to get the doctor."

"*No*," Ruby insisted, pulling against him until he stopped. "The child doesn't come for at least a couple of months. I've just exhausted myself these last few days. My body needs to rest."

"Let me take you."

"And let Richard see us together? No, I'm capable of getting to my room. Now go before he comes out here." Ruby did her best curtsy before walking in the direction of her room.

Once her mom was out of earshot, Elise looked at Charles, who was still watching the princess. "You're going to get the doctor, anyway, aren't you?"

"Of course."

"You know she's not going to like that." Elise could already picture her mother's face when the doctor arrived. "But thank you."

Charles bowed before leading them inside the study.

"What on earth took so long?" Richard asked from behind the desk.

While he was unaware of Ruby's pain, Elise still felt irritated at the prince's relaxed disposition behind the desk as he perused documents. He only looked up from them when Charles turned to leave.

"Where are you going? I thought you were staying for *this*." Richard gestured between Elise and her friends with one of the letters that were folded in his hand.

Charles shot Elise a tentative glance. "Ballard asked me to oversee the room assignments for the council members while they're all here. I'm going to check in on their progress."

Richard wrinkled his nose. "Ballard's never needed help like that before." For a moment, Elise held her breath, panicking at the thought of being caught working together. Fortunately, Richard shrugged and looked back at the papers on his desk. "He's losing his touch. Very well."

Charles bowed his head once more before exiting into the hall.

The deafening silence threatened to make Elise scream while they all stood staring at the studious prince. *He's doing this on purpose.* It was taking her uncle twice as long to do mundane things—stacking papers, signing signatures, and even leafing through a reference text. According to the grandfather clock by the door, a full five minutes passed before he acknowledged them.

"Right then." Richard set the quill down so he could fold his hands in front of him, "I called you here to thank you for your service to Haighdlen. My father spoke highly of you." Clearing his throat, he continued in a stern, authoritative tone. "But now that he has passed, I'm afraid your services are no longer required."

Elise's mouth went dry as her brain tried to process what he was really saying. *He's kicking us out?* By the looks on her friends' faces, they were also having a tough time processing what Richard said.

"B-but why?" Elise managed to squeak out.

"Your longtime friendship with my parents is commendable, but I have surrounded myself with *qualified* advisors and councilmembers. We can handle any threats going forward. And out of respect for my honored father, I will provide each of you with travel pouches with enough money between you to cover any expenses to get you back to wherever you came from."

Elise didn't know what frustrated her more, the fact that they were being forced to leave or her uncle's dismissive tone. In that moment, she felt equivalent to the crumbled wads of papers that had been scattered on the floor around Richard's desk.

"You can't do that!" cried Darcie, finding a firmer voice than Elise could.

"Yeah, you need us," said Gavin. "We can help, and if the queen were here—"

"You are to leave my mother alone." Richard stood so abruptly that a book fell off the desk, making Elise jump. A menacing scowl darkened his features. "She can't bear to look at any of you. It only reminds her of him."

"We're not leaving yet," Mitch said, flailing his arm around for emphasis. "You can't discuss war one minute, and then turn around and say there's no need to worry because the threat is gone. Rona's either coming, or she's not."

"And she *definitely* is," Elise answered.

"Listen, you *little*—" The door creaked open, and Richard's face paled when Joranna entered the room.

The sight of her grandmother made Elise sigh with relief. *Maybe she does believe me after all!*

Richard adjusted his coattails before taking his seat once more. He nodded for a nearby servant to tidy up the floor. "Mother? What a surprise. You should be resting."

Joranna strolled across the room, inspecting the clutter with a raised brow, until she stopped between Gavin and Elise. "Something told me I should be present for this meeting given our history together." She regarded the four travelers warmly, though her exhaustion was betrayed by an ill-suppressed yawn. "I beg your pardon. What have I missed?"

Darcie wasted no time catching Joranna up with little thought of how it affected the prince. "He's kicking us out and won't let us help."

Joranna's eyes widened as she regarded her son. "Richard, is this true?"

"Our business with them has concluded. There's been no immediate threat from Rona—"

"But she's not dead yet, is she?" Gavin challenged. "I agree with Mitch. You can't hold a council meeting to discuss allies and then turn around and say it's peaceful."

"It is all being handled." Richard locked his jaw, refusing to meet Joranna's eyes while he drummed his fingers together.

"Is it?" Joranna questioned. "Could you share your developments?"

His mouth tightened to contain his rising temper. "Mother, with all due respect, I don't wish to threaten the kingdom's security by discussing our intent, nor do I have the time. I am scheduled to meet with the lieutenant about Sanders's murder investigation following Brahm's escape. It's been delayed for months as it is and—"

"Then what's a few more hours?" Joranna asked. "Honestly, I don't understand why you can't allow them to stay a while longer. They can give us information from the last few months."

"We don't need it, Mother," Richard all but shouted. Collecting himself, he shuffled through the pile of letters in front of him. "It is not merely the investigation demanding my reply. I have several unanswered letters requiring my attention with regards to the ambassadors' decisions to join us, coronation plans, statue placements, portrait sittings, the festival. . .take your pick."

Joranna's brows furrowed while Richard listed off his mounting engagements. She opened her mouth, closed it, then tried again. "The festival? Darling, surely you don't mean the Harvest Oak Festival." When Richard nodded, she scoffed. "In light of our loss, there's no chance we can host such a celebration at a time like this. Simply cancel it."

Richard had moved on to signing more documents while his mother protested what sounded like a fun event.

Elise was intrigued by the sound of a festival. She had attended one in Vynchia while searching for Gavin the previous week. However, she also understood Joranna's point about it being an inappropriate time for such an occasion.

"Are you even listening?" Joranna huffed.

Richard glanced up, not bothering to hide his annoyance, choosing instead to simply say, "Father loved the festival. He would have wanted us to host it. Let it be a celebration of his life." His clipped tone left little room for argument before a knock at the door announced Ballard's arrival.

Oh no.

"A letter for you, Sire." The steward made his way hastily across the room, but not before Joranna caught sight of the folded envelope.

"Thank you," said Richard, reaching for it. "Was Charles able to assist you with the room assignments?"

Before Elise could come up with a lie to cover for Charles, the queen's body stiffened as she gasped. "Is that the Lockesbarrian court's seal?"

Everyone looked between the envelope and Richard with bated breath.

I don't understand. Is he selling Haighdlen out, too? There was no way Richard could be a spy. *Why would he be in contact with Rona's court?*

"Mother, perhaps you should leave before you're taken over with hysterics." Richard grabbed a small knife from a drawer to his left before slicing the seal delicately.

But Joranna had lost all maternal warmness as she glared at her eldest. Her eyes flashed in suspicion as she awaited his answer. When he provided none, she repeated the question with a stern tone. "Is that the *Lockesbarrian* court's seal? Answer me this instant!"

Elise's blood ran cold watching the two standing at odds with one another. It was a battle of wills that ultimately ended when her uncle threw his hands in the air.

"Yes! If you must know," Richard groaned. "Let us not create a scene in front of these guests. If you wish to speak privately—"

"No, I wish to speak *now*," she hissed. "Crown prince or not, what are you thinking? Does the council know about this?"

"This protects all of us, so they need not be involved," Richard assured her.

"Please, enlighten us," Joranna scoffed, reminding Elise of the fiery young woman she met in the diner rather than the composed queen her grandmother tried to be at all times. "Surely, if it is to protect us all, there's no problem having an audience. What are you planning?"

Richard lost a fraction of resolve under his mother's intimidating stare. He, too, reminded Elise of a previous encounter, namely the scared adolescent prince who accidentally shot Mitch with an ill-aimed arrow in the forest. When the prince hesitated to reply, Joranna stomped her foot before pacing in front of the fireplace.

"Mother, there's no need to berate me publicly like this. I only wish for my plans to remain private until the right time. There's no need to raise any alarm until the details are sorted out."

"I am entitled to these details," stated the queen. "You may be taking over as King, but don't forget that it was at the discretion of your father and I. It wasn't a day I ever wanted to come, but your handling of these matters makes me second guess our decision."

"I don't wish to hear anymore." Richard slumped back in his chair, massaging the bridge of his nose. "Haven't you anything else to do? Guests to entertain?"

Elise felt as if someone wrenched her heart out on behalf of her grandmother. She wanted nothing more than to walk over and punch her uncle in the face. All Joranna was trying to do was protect everyone, including her son. Why couldn't Richard see that? *Why does everything have to be a fight with him?*

Joranna closed her eyes until her bottom lip stopped quivering. With a shuddering breath, she looked up at him with moistened eyes. Her voice was barely audible over the crackling embers in the fireplace.

"I have visited this room more times than I can count, but no matter the case or situation, I was included. I was never made to feel so unwanted until today. If your father were alive—"

"But he isn't, is he, Mother?" Richard spat. "All this falls onto *my* shoulders! Not yours, not Sarah's, nor Ian's." He scoffed. "I shudder to think what Ruby would do in my stead."

Joranna approached her son slowly, like a lioness creeping towards her prey, until her gown touched the desk. She glared down at her son. "At least they would have honored Derek's wishes to rule fairly. Furthermore, everything would be handled by now. Ruby could be married, an alliance formed—" She paused when he stood abruptly to cross the room.

Everyone watched as he bypassed an offering servant to pour himself a glass of something from a decanter. The way he tossed back the drink made Elise wish she and her friends had already left. *This is getting really serious. He has no idea what she's been through, and he just keeps adding onto it.*

Joranna took a deep breath before continuing. "Perhaps he wasn't as present with all of you as he would've liked to have been, but he knew the importance of family. He made it his top priority to provide for you and this kingdom's future."

"Which is *exactly* what I'm doing, Mother," Richard said. "I am trying to do what I think he would want me to do."

"You're putting too much pressure on yourself trying to be him. Richard, you don't have to be your father—"

"Yes, I do!" he roared, making Elise jump again. She didn't like the crazed look in his eyes as he raked a hand through his hair. It was his turn to pace. "I can be like him. I *will* be just like him. Perhaps even better."

Impossible.

Richard hunched over his desk, squeezing the edges until his knuckles were white. His shoulders and arm muscles were tense as he almost failed to control his emotions.

"If you would just tell us, dear—" Joranna began before he cut her off.

"I'm getting married," he ground out between clenched teeth. Pouring himself a refill, not bothering to aim nor caring about the overspill, he held up his glass as if to make a toast. "Are you satisfied, Mother? Have I made you proud?"

We really shouldn't be here for this, but I can't look away. Is this really happening right now?

"Hardly." Joranna wiped the corner of her eyes. "Richard, what would possess you to make such a life-altering decision while mourning your father's death? You're stricken with grief! This isn't the time to be making these sorts of choices."

"It's for the best."

Elise scowled at his uncle's nonchalant reply. "Please, let us help you."

"Like you helped my father?"

Elise felt as if the air had been sucked from her lungs. She must have looked like a gaping moron, standing there with her mouth wide open without making a sound. Her skin prickled with dozens of goosebumps as heat enveloped her face.

"Richard!" Joranna shrieked. "You are out of line. This outburst only proves you're not in your right mind. They have done nothing to warrant such treatment."

"I will not yield, Mother. Nor will I apologize. We can all agree whenever anything disastrous occurs, these four are present. Rodrick has overseen matters regarding the engagement, and the details are settled. There is a lovely maiden, Iris, from the Lockesbarrian court whom I shall wed to help ease growing tensions. Perhaps even come to some sort of peace treaty agreement with King Dmitri."

He's crazy! And what about Aunt Gwen? That's *who he married. What's going on?*

"Rodrick?" Elise exclaimed. "You mean Vaughn? The guy the council kicked out? *That's* who you've been trusting to handle your business?"

"He was the newly-appointed Ambassador to Lockesbarrow before his dismissal. I still trust his loyalties." Richard took a sip from his glass. "With any luck, I'll sire a new heir within the year, and I can avoid the scandal involving Ruby's illegitimate child ruling."

Elise felt Gavin's hand wrap around her arm before she realized she had taken a step towards her uncle.

"I can't hear anymore," Joranna said. "I wash my hands of this. You certainly don't have my blessing."

Richard collapsed into his seat, reclining until he could cross his feet over the desk. Swirling the contents of his glass, he took a long sip before meeting Joranna's eye. "Well, then it's a good thing I don't need it, isn't it, Mother?"

Elise paled as her jaw dropped open. *He did not just say that!*

A muscle twitched in Joranna's cheek. She opened her mouth, paused, and stormed out without a word.

Elise jumped as the door slammed shut behind the queen.

"You're crazy," Darcie said to the prince. "You're going to destroy this kingdom."

Again.

"It's treasonous to insult a king." Richard drained the rest of his second glass.

Composing herself, Elise sneered down at him. "Then I guess it's a good thing you're not king yet." Her stomach tightened as she willed both knees not to buckle.

Richard's eyes darkened. "Careful. I doubt our relation is strong enough to save you should you tread too close where you don't belong. Now," he pointed to the door, "as I said before. It's time for you to leave Haighdlen. For good this time."

This is worse than I thought. He's not supposed to marry someone else. Especially someone from Lockesbarrow. Now there's even more stuff to fix before we can get home. We can't leave Haighdlen now!

Elise waited until they were far enough out of earshot, and away from lingering stares, before she beckoned her friends to follow her. Once they all reached the top of the stairs, Elise broke out into a run with the other three following close behind. Praying they didn't encounter any guards, or unwanted stewards, she took the familiar path to the one person who could help them. Out of breath, time, and options, Elise bent over to catch her breath before pounding on Ruby's bedroom door.

We have to find Gwen.

CHAPTER 13

Elise continued knocking, growing more flustered with her mother for not answering.

We don't have time for this! They're going to escort us out any minute.

"Ruby?" Elise called, catching a maid's attention at the end of the hall before rolling her eyes. "I mean *Princess* Ruby? We really need to talk to you." Three more knocks and there was still no answer. Elise had half a thought to kick the door or have Mitch run into it. He probably would if Darcie suggested it.

"Elise, I don't think she's in there." Darcie pulled her away from the door into a hug as Elise released the tears she had been holding in. "This wasn't your fault. Your uncle's just being a jerk. Nothing he said was true."

Gavin came closer to rub her back. "Even if they do kick us out of there, we'll find a way to get home."

Elise eased out of Darcie's embrace to dry her face. "Don't you guys realize how hard this has made everything?" When none of the others replied, she shuddered before explaining the consuming fears circling within her mind. "Lockesbarrow now has two rulers. One is supposed to be *dead*. Not only does that mess up the timeline, but Richard is about to marry someone from Rona's kingdom. If he does, he doesn't marry Gwen. Then my cousin isn't born. Who knows how his marriage will affect my mom, aunt, and uncle? What if *none* of my cousins are born?" Elise placed her head between both hands, as if she could block out the world if she kept her eyes closed. *Is it*

115

possible for someone's head to actually explode? "I already failed to save Derek."

"Hey, you didn't fail anything," Darcie assured her.

She's only saying that because she's my friend. No amount of comforting was going to help her feel better.

"Elise, no one could save Derek," said Gavin. "I think, regardless of timelines, he was always meant to be killed by Rona. It's just how the events unfolded." He wrapped a tentative arm around her until she melted against his side.

"There's still time to fix everything," Mitch said. "Your grandma had been living in that house back home a long time before they needed to send you here, right? That means Rona attacks later if we don't stop her now. Even with your grandfather gone, there's still something to save."

They're right. Elise thought back to the first trip she and her mother made to Joranna's house after Haighdlen was overthrown for good. Ian's persistent texts caused Elise to check Ruby's phone only to find out the texts were threatening to reveal the truth about Haighdlen, something Ruby was adamantly against. In the end, it worked out for the best, since Elise probably would've never gotten the chance to see Haighdlen if it weren't for the threat Rona posed. All of this was happening for a reason, she reminded herself. While painful, she needed to accept the fact that Derek was always going to die.

However, there was still time to prevent more sacrifices. If they didn't stop Rona now, she would go on to take over Haighdlen, killing Sarah's husband Liam and. . .Charles. Closing her eyes, Elise relived her first confusing moments in Joranna's house when her estranged family arrived.

"But it wasn't my choice," Richard recalled about fleeing. *"I wanted to stay there. . .to die for my kingdom. For my people."*

Elise's aunt, Sarah, assured her brother that Liam and Charles pulled him out before he was killed.

Richard had only replied with, *"And now they're dead. They're both dead."* Although Sarah tried to convince him they were doing their duty, Richard remained inconsolable. *"They were my best friends. . .I could've been there to save them. I should have stopped Rona before she ever grew to be as strong as she is now. The people are doomed now. She finally accomplished what she set out to do all those years ago when she killed Father."*

"Y'all are right," Elise confessed to her friends. "This would've happened anyway, but it's still up to us to make sure Rona doesn't win. As bad as my uncle is acting now, seeing how he ends up is worse. I met my family when they were the worst versions of themselves. They deserve better. It's what Derek would've wanted."

"Now you're sounding like yourself," Darcie said with a beaming smile.

"Thanks guys," Elise said, joining her friends in a group hug. "We need to introduce Richard to Gwen. Then they can fall in love before he gets married. After that, we can focus on Rona."

"I wish it were as easy as it sounds," Mitch said with a playful pout.

"How can we get them to meet?" Gavin asked.

"Oh!" Darcie squealed, jumping up and down on the balls of her feet. "The festival thingy they were talking about. They can meet there!"

There's the old Darcie. Elise smirked.

"Watch out, guys. She's matchmaking again." Mitch rolled his eyes with a smile. "Is it sad I feel bad for Richard now?"

Darcie slapped his arm playfully as they chuckled.

Elise's smile dropped as a nearby door opened. Caught with no place to hide and her adrenaline spiking, she froze. As if by fate, she saw her expectant mother come out of another room followed by Sarah and Ian.

"Elise?" Ruby called upon seeing them. "What're you all doing up here? I thought you were meeting with Richard."

"We already did." Elise sighed with a hesitant glance at her mother's stomach. "How're *you* feeling?"

"Much better. Sarah and Ian kept me company while I rested. Are you all right?" Sensing Elise's unwillingness to elaborate in the hall, Ruby beckoned her siblings and the four travelers into her own bedroom.

Hurrying inside, Elise took in the familiar sight of her mother's room. She was once again captivated by the domed ceiling, painted to look like the sky. The white drapes were tied back this time, and the furniture remained as they were the day Elise first visited her mother seeking answers after Ruby's last trip through the portal.

"We were about to head downstairs for tea," said Ruby, "but you look distressed. What is the matter?"

It's now or never.

Elise spent the next ten minutes recalling the tense interaction between herself, Richard and Joranna in the study, including the prince's betrothal. The following silence only managed to spike Elise's growing anxiety. *Did I share too much? Am I making things worse?*

"Why didn't he tell us he's getting married?" Ian asked. "And to a *Lockesbarrian* woman? You're sure about this?"

Elise nodded, detecting the skepticism in her uncle's eyes, before Gavin added, "To make a peace treaty or something."

"That can't be right," said Sarah as she paced around the room. "King Dmitri wouldn't be so quick to agree to peace. Not with what Rona did to Father. It's taking too long to seek retaliation. Do you think Richard's being forced into something somehow? Blackmailed perhaps? What does the council say?"

"The council's being lied to," said Gavin. "We're pretty sure one of them is a spy."

"I can believe it," Ruby muttered.

Sarah clicked her tongue. "I wouldn't put it past Dmitri nor Rona to do such a thing." Sarah frowned. "We must tread carefully. Does Richard suspect any treason on your part?"

"I hope not," Mitch moaned. "All we've done has been to help Haighdlen, but he's still kicking us out."

"You're leaving?" Ruby exclaimed. "When?"

"As soon as the guards find us," Darcie replied with a hollow chuckle. "So, probably any minute now."

Elise crossed the room to stand in front of Ruby. "That's why we came to find you. There isn't much time left. Can you help us get to Gwen?" *Please, Mom.*

Ruby's eyes doubled in size as her gaze flickered first to Sarah and then Ian. Blushing, she shook her head. "What does Gwen have to do with any of this?"

"I. . .I can't tell you that," Elise said, biting her lip. "But if we don't, things will get worse." *A lot worse.*

"I'm afraid I don't understand. Who is Gwen?" Sarah looked at her sister expectantly.

Ruby shifted from one foot to the other under her older siblings' attentions like a two-year-old sneaking dessert before dinner. Scowling at Elise, Ruby answered. "Gwen is a girl I befriended in town. She helped me get the fairy magic to travel."

Elise blushed under her mother's scrutiny. She hadn't meant to get her mom into any more trouble, but they didn't have time to waste.

"She sounds fun," Ian said with his own playful smile.

Sarah, as expected, rolled her eyes. "I should be more surprised." She wrung her hands with an exasperated sigh before turning to face Elise. "What exactly is your plan?"

I can't tell them I'm trying to get Richard and Gwen together. They'd never help me. She had to think of something safe to tell them. "We would like to be allowed to stay for the festival and meet Gwen."

A silence engulfed the room.

"That's all?" Sarah finally asked with a raised brow, looking remarkably like Joranna as she searched Elise's face for the truth.

"We'd also like to not get arrested," Mitch added.

"If we can secure some fairy magic while we're at it, we should definitely try," said Gavin.

The other three friends nodded at his request, unable to suppress their own smiles.

"Can you take us to Gwen in time for the festival?" Elise asked Ruby. "If we can get her to give us some magic, and listen to what we have to say, we may be able to stop anything worse from happening."

Ruby hesitated. "There is no chance of Richard allowing me to leave the castle grounds, much less attend the festival."

"You've broken the rules before," Elise teased. Her heart warmed at the sight of her mother's smile. *Please take us. Please.* Deep down, she willed her magic to convince Ruby, but nothing seemed to be happening.

"Yes, but I'm not as energetic now. Staying in doesn't sound too bad these days." Ruby chuckled along with everyone else rather than appear irritated by her limitations. "But on a serious note, Gwen is not likely to acquire fairy magic for strangers. I *could* send you with a letter explaining your visit for Father's funeral and inform her that you need a place to stay during the festival. She may take you in."

"Couldn't we just stay at the inn?" Mitch asked.

With what money? We can't ask them to pay for something like this.

Sarah shook her head. "If you're planning to stay in Haighdlen after Richard's ordered your departure, you're not going to want to be caught or reported. Even more so if you're dabbling in kingdom affairs. You're sure you can help our family?"

Elise nodded.

Sarah bit her lip, clearly at odds with the proper way to handle the secretive situation. At last, she nodded towards her younger sister. "Better write the letter to your friend now, Ruby. Be discreet but include the necessary information about the situation."

This letter is better than nothing. We just have to hope Richard shows up to the festival and not catch us beforehand. Elise forced herself to remain calm as she accepted the decision.

Ruby sat down immediately at the curved writing table to draft her letter.

Fed up with pacing, Sarah walked over to the window.

It was only then Elise noticed it had begun to rain.

Sarah fiddled idly with a locket around her neck as she stared at the raindrops pelting against the window.

Elise studied her aunt's profile, feeling a sudden sense of déjà vu. It took another minute to recall why. During one of their first visits, she remembered her late great-grandmother, Queen Avalyn, staring out a window in a similar ominous fashion during a storm.

"I'm surprised Richard is hosting the festival at a time like this. I can't say I'm in a very *festive* mood. Come to think of it, it's rather vulgar, don't you think?" Sarah tossed an assertive sneer in her younger brother's direction.

Ian shrugged. "Perhaps he only wants to rally everyone's spirits. You know how much this festival meant to Father."

Sarah only responded with a reluctant nod before moving to stand behind Ruby. She stayed there for a considerable time, watching her sister write, while the rest of the room sat in an uncomfortable heavy silence.

Once Ruby had concluded the letter—careful to check that Sarah agreed with its contents—and signed it, she folded the paper and sealed it with wax.

"*No one* is to inform Mother of this," Sarah commanded. She waited for everyone to agree, including Ian and Ruby. "I've tried to not leave her alone for long periods of time already. This would surely throw her into hysterics."

"I wish we could talk to her more," Darcie said.

"That isn't possible," Ian replied. "She barely realizes when *we* are sitting with her. We try to take turns keeping her company, but she is often found sleeping anywhere but the bed she and father shared or scribbling away in her diary. I imagine it's good for her to get those feelings—"

"What did you say?" Elise interrupted.

Ian looked puzzled as he analyzed what he had just shared. "She can't bear to sleep in their bed. I mean, it's understandable since—"

"No, no. . .you said she's been writing in a diary?" Elise's heartbeat skipped a beat. *Why do I keep forgetting there's another diary that Joranna would be keeping in this timeline? Maybe if we get the fairy magic from Gwen, we can link the two diaries and get us straight to Rona instead of guessing!* "Can you get it for us?"

Her mother, uncle and aunt reacted like she feared they would. Each one looked at her as if she were crazy, even dangerous. She had to admit her question sounded suspiciously unhinged. Even her friends hadn't quite followed her line of thinking yet except Gavin.

"We can save Haighdlen," Gavin said. "We'll stop Rona and her brother, and if we succeed, Richard won't marry anyone from Lockesbarrow either. Everything can be like it's supposed to be."

Elise was thankful for his rescue and discretion.

"Richard isn't going to like this." Sarah regarded the four travelers one last time. Her usually controlled demeanor was replaced with one of fear and trepidation. She wrung her hands, much like Elise did before a panic attack, before stealing another wavering glance at the sealed envelope. Sarah's trembling fingers sought out the locket around her neck once more, squeezing it to the point Elise feared it would break. The older princess's shoulders slumped before she realized and straightened her posture. Clearing her throat, Sarah shook her head as her icy exterior resumed. "Right then. We'll contact Edith and Ruby can help have your costumes delivered to this Gwen person's house." Sarah cocked her head towards the door for Ian to follow her out.

Elise looked at the mirrored expressions of confusion on her friends' faces. *What costumes?*

Pausing in the doorway, Sarah caught their apprehensive glances before addressing her sister. "They *do* know about the festival, don't they?"

"I'll inform them," Ruby promised before her brother and sister left the room.

"Okay, please tell me *costume* doesn't mean what I think it does," Mitch whined once the door shut.

"Oh, I hope it does!" Darcie gushed as she stepped closer to Ruby. "I've always wanted to go to a real masquerade party! Please tell me that's what's going on."

Elise secretly sided with Darcie. She had always been fascinated with masquerades and ballrooms. This would be her first time, though she was surprised it was being held in Clara.

Ruby closed her writing desk and stood to push the chair back into place. She chuckled at Darcie's theatrics. "On the first night of the festival, there is a masquerade ball held in the town square."

"And. . .the royal family goes, too?" Gavin asked.

I'm glad he asked. I feel stupid thinking balls only happen at the castle.

"I've never missed it. Well, until now." Ruby looked down at her belly. "I'm sorry I won't be able to help you."

"You've done plenty. Thank you," Elise said before being startled by a knock on the door.

"Your Highness?" came Ballard's obnoxious tone through the door. Elise rolled her eyes. "The doctor is here to see you."

"The doctor?" Ruby looked warily at Elise and her friends. "I never sent for—" Realization dawned on her features before she quirked an unamused brow in Elise's direction. "Did Charles do this?"

Elise nodded, trying not to smile. "Don't be mad."

Ruby moaned and opened the door.

"There you are, Your Majesty, I—" Ballard froze upon making eye contact with Elise over Ruby's shoulder. "Ah, I see you're entertaining our soon-to-be *departing* guests. The prince tasked me with escorting them to the carriage. I'd be happy to send them on their way while helping you. I'll speak to the coachman about—"

"*I* will speak to the coachman." Ruby tucked the letter behind her back in such a way that was hidden from Ballard but easy for Elise to casually walk up and take. The exchange was subtle and quick, so much so that the steward didn't take notice.

Ballard spluttered before forcing his temper down with a frustrated sigh. "Your Highness, your brother *insists*—"

"Yes, you do so much for him, and I thank you," Ruby interrupted with a feigned smile that Elise imagined was difficult to pull off, "however, I'm perfectly capable of seeing them off on their journey. It's the least I could do. You have so much to prepare for the festival."

A tense moment passed between the two before he scowled in resignation. He pursed his lips as if tasting an overly sour piece of candy before choking out the words, "Very well, Princess."

Deep down, Elise knew Ballard was a good man. He had risked his own life to protect theirs when they encountered Brahm and his sister, Ingrid, in the castle library. However, that didn't mean he liked them. Judging by the stacked lines forming in his forehead, Elise suspected he didn't.

Ruby waited for him to leave before she rested her forehead against the doorframe with a sigh. "I suppose I better go see the doctor. Was there anything else you needed?"

"Seriously?" Gavin asked when everyone else shook their heads. "Okay, was nobody going to ask where Gwen's house is? I mean, we have the letter and that's great, but last time we were there it was the middle of the night. Does anyone know which house it was? The princess can't go this time. What happens if we pick the wrong place?"

Elise looked at her mother expectantly. *I'm glad he thought to ask before she left.*

"I'm so sorry," Ruby apologized before reopening her desk to retrieve a piece of paper to scribble down directions. Handing the note to Gavin, she bid them farewell and wished them good luck. "I'll speak with the coachman. He can take you directly. I've circled which house just there." She pointed to a circled rectangle on the drawing. "There's no need to worry."

Except there was *every* reason to worry. Although the traveling arrangement was simple enough, and the ride itself uneventful, Elise couldn't shake her growing paranoia as Gavin led their group through the residential area filled with small cottages a couple of hours later. Elise idly tapped her hand against the pocket of her cloak where she kept the money Richard provided. If this plan didn't work, maybe they could barter with a fairy for some magic or at least pay for a boat ride to Lockesbarrow.

"I think we're almost there," Gavin whispered, holding the directions closer to his face. It was nearly sunset, and if they didn't find Gwen's house soon, they'd be forced to sleep outside. The cool autumn night was already proving to be quite chilly as a shiver ran down Elise's arms. After scanning the surrounding homes, Gavin pointed to his right. "I think it's this one."

Elise followed the path of his finger to a quaint cottage. There was nothing about it that stood out from the others, but Elise couldn't remember the last time they were here well enough to pick it out for certain.

"Ready?" he asked.

Not at all. In fact, her hands were trembling, but it had nothing to do with the cold. This woman they were about to meet didn't know she was Elise's future aunt. She didn't know she was destined to be Haighdlen's next queen. Elise couldn't even share that much with her. Not only that, but Gwen was also going to be asked to help them find fairy magic while simultaneously being set up with Richard. *How did this sound like a good idea a few hours ago?*

Wiping two sweat-soaked hands along her skirt, Elise stepped in front of Gavin, and at the urging of her friends, tentatively knocked on the door.

CHAPTER 14

If it weren't for the letter clutched in her hand, Elise imagined Gwen would've slammed the door shut on them. Not that Elise would blame her. Their half story, since they couldn't very well give the whole one, was highly suspicious. Elise doubted *she* would have even opened the door at all had someone come to her door with such a proposition, yet there they stood begging for a place to stay.

Please. Elise stared back at Gwen's unamused expression, attempting to use whatever magic would work on the young woman. "I have the letter from the princess right here. You can read it." She handed the envelope to Gwen, who kept her gaze on them as she reluctantly opened it. Elise held her breath, waiting anxiously while watching Gwen's eyes scan the contents of the letter.

"Gwen? Who is that?" asked another woman who soon approached the door behind Gwen. *They could almost be twins. This must be her sister*. Mr. Archer, the falsely imprisoned farmer, and Gwen's father had mentioned he had a wife and two daughters. "What's all this? Did you tell them we have no more handouts to give today?"

"Oh, no, it's not like that," Darcie said. "We just came to—"

"To hide from the prince." Gwen sighed as she folded the letter closed once more. "They've been asked to leave the kingdom, but the princess writes to please offer them hospitality until the festival is over."

Gwen's sister looked between the two parties, obviously detecting the tension. "Well, if the princess requests it, surely we can honor her wishes." Stepping around Gwen, the younger woman smiled warmly. "I'm Talia." She pulled the small towel hanging on her apron free to dry her hands before shaking each of their hands. "It's awfully nice to meet friends of the princess. We're honored. . . however, I'm afraid there's not much room. You'd have to share one."

While all four friends eagerly spoke over one another to accept the arrangement, Elise couldn't help but focus on the way Gwen's mouth tightened into a thin line as she squeezed the letter until it crumbled within her fist. Talia had yet to stop talking at this point, already sharing their plans for the festival, until Gwen could take it no longer.

"Tal, this is absurd! Not only has Mama not given permission, but they're *fugitives*. Remember what happened—" Gwen paused as another woman carrying a rather large basket approached the door behind Elise and her friends. "Mama, there you are."

Mrs. Archer regarded the travelers with an alarmed expression, silently gauging a reaction from her daughters to make sure the situation was safe. "Is something wrong?" she finally asked when it appeared no one was in danger but remaining alert, nonetheless.

Talia ripped the letter from Gwen's grip before handing it to their mother. By the time Mrs. Archer flattened the letter back out, Talia had already shared its contents out loud with great flare and animation. Ending with a dramatic twirl, Talia slumped against the doorframe with a breathless smile. "We not only get to host guests for the festival, but they're friends with the royal family! I'm almost finished sewing my costume. Isn't it exciting, Mama?"

Mrs. Archer didn't reply until she finished reading the letter for herself. She smiled briefly at the visitors, and Elise was immediately put at ease by her presence. Giving them permission to stay, she then sent a stern maternal look at her youngest daughter. "Perhaps we should cease entertaining our neighbors for now and continue this discussion inside. Can you put on the tea, Gwen? I've got to unpack all of this." She gestured towards the food in the basket.

"Mama, I don't think this is a good idea," Gwen protested as Elise and her friends stepped into the main living area of the cottage. By the time everyone entered, there was barely room to stand. "Besides, I'm going out. Remember?"

Mrs. Archer clicked her tongue. "Oh, rehearsals are tonight. That's right. Talia, tea." She hoisted the basket onto the dining table with an exasperated sigh before emptying its contents, including bread and various vegetables. "Make it strong, please. My poor nerves need it."

Gwen locked the door before approaching the table to help unload the basket. Her brows furrowed as she examined her mother's rattled state. "Is something wrong? Did something happen in town? Come sit over here." She helped the older woman get situated on an oversized chair covered in blankets. "If I need to stay, I can—"

Mrs. Archer waved off her daughter's suggestion. "No need. It's nothing, really. I was only spooked." She paused to thank Gwen for putting the food away in the pantry and reminded Talia to pour enough tea for their guests before continuing. "As I was leaving the square, I thought I saw someone."

Elise noticed the woman's trembling fingers and pale complexion, not to mention the way she kept glancing out the windows as if someone was watching them. Unable to stifle her own superstitions, Elise also checked, but no one was there.

"Was someone following you?" Gavin asked, taking Elise by surprise. She hadn't expected him to pry, but she was also thankful that he had spoken her thoughts aloud.

"I don't think so. It looked like someone I thought I'd never see again." She reflected before correcting her statement. "Someone I never *want* to see again."

Elise felt the hairs on the back of her neck stand up as she imagined a looming figure spying on them.

Gwen kneeled by her mother's side. "Mama, you're absolutely shaken. Who did you think you saw?"

Mrs. Archer shook her head. "It doesn't matter, because there's no chance it was really him."

Him? Who would've scared her like this?

Frustrated and flustered by everyone's eyes on her, Mrs. Archer changed the subject by redirecting her attention to a different target. "Talia? Are you sure you swept in here today? The floors look dreadful."

"I did!" cried her youngest daughter from where she stood in front of a small stove. "Honest."

"She knows you did, Tal," Gwen called out, shooting a knowing glance in her mother's direction. When she spoke again, it was barely above a whisper. "Mama, what is really the matter?"

Mrs. Archer shifted under her eldest daughter's scrutiny, casting uncertain glances at Elise, Gavin, Mitch, and Darcie before deeming it safe enough to answer. "It was. . .it was that *boy*."

Elise felt the contents of her stomach churn. *Who is she talking about?*

Gwen's eyebrows rose as her mouth dropped open. "The one who stayed *here*?" When her mother nodded, sending an uncomfortable glance in the travelers' direction, Gwen huffed. "Let's not make this more complicated than it needs to be. I'm sure you saw someone with a strong likeness, but I doubt it was really him. He wouldn't come back to Clara, Mama."

"That's what I keep telling myself," said the older woman as Talia handed her a steaming cup of tea. Inhaling its rich scent, Mrs. Archer took a delicate sip. Her lips quivered as her mouth adjusted to the temperature. "Yet, I can't seem to put it out of my mind."

Gwen looked up at Elise from her kneeled position. "The last time we showed the hospitality you are seeking, our family was torn apart."

It was Vaughn after all. Elise thought back to the first night she met Vaughn, who had infiltrated Ruby's letter and pretended to be their guide while delaying their attempts to reach Gavin. During an uncomfortable cart ride, he had relayed a tale from his past. *"By the time I reached Haighdlen, I was weak and starving. I met a farmer who told me I could stay in his barn. By that point, gossip had spread about a dangerous Lockesbarrian fugitive. The farmer asked me to leave, which I did. I later heard he had been arrested, so I stayed hidden a while longer."* Yet it wasn't the story itself that bothered

Elise. It was what Vaughn had said next. *"I kept an eye on his wife and daughters—from a distance, of course. I felt I owed him that much. They're making a decent living selling their crops in Clara."* Mitch and Darcie had been in the cart with her, so this must have been news to Gavin, who had only heard Mr. Archer's account when they were all locked up in Haighdlen's prison. Derek had assured them he would look into a pardon, but Elise doubted he ever got the chance before being cursed.

"Oh, you can't go and say a thing like that without telling them the whole truth," Mrs. Archer fussed, resting the teacup on her covered lap. "But I'm sure they have better things to do than to listen to us prattle away like a bunch of gossips. But she's right. Our farm was taken from us, and my late sister took us into this cottage while we worked on local farms for a share of their crops. We manage, though. Anyway, Gwen, you had best be off."

But I want to hear more!

"Are you sure?" Gwen placed a hand on top of her mother's. "You look pale. I can cancel."

"Hold your tongue," Mrs. Archer fussed. "After the king's death, the kingdom needs this festival now more than ever. You were fortunate to be considered again this year."

Gwen rolled her eyes. "Mama, it's only a dance routine."

"Yes, but one on the opening night of the ball! That is when the most people will be in attendance, including the royal family." Mrs. Archer scowled before taking another sip of tea.

Perfect. That's when we'll get her to meet Richard. We just need to arrange it and find a way to Lockesbarrow. Elise made a mental note to speak with her friends the next time they were alone.

"She doesn't sound too excited about it," Gavin said.

Elise agreed. Gwen's movements were languid and unhurried.

"She did this to herself. I told her we were fine." Mrs. Archer tipped her head back as she finished what was left in the cup.

"What do you mean?" Darcie asked.

Mrs. Archer studied Gwen through the window. "She's been asked to join the opening dance for a couple of years but only now accepted. Gwen won't admit it, but I know she thinks we need the money. Since my husband and sister are gone, it's getting harder to manage everything."

"I'm so sorry," said Darcie, reaching into her own pocket to retrieve her portion of travel expenses. "We can pay you to stay."

Mrs. Archer waved it away as if it revolted her. "Absolutely not. We are honored to host royal guests."

"Are you sure we can't do anything to help?" asked Mitch.

Elise was surprised by his offer, and judging by the impressed expression on Darcie's face, she was as well.

"You're sweet, but there's no need." Mrs. Archer's eyes lit up. "Oh, that reminds me! Do you all have costumes? There's not much time, but—"

"The princess is sending some for us," Gavin replied.

Mrs. Archer opened her mouth but paused when Talia returned carrying a tray with four more steaming cups. The slightest blush colored the young woman's cheeks as she handed Gavin and Mitch theirs first.

Elise and Darcie exchanged a knowing glance. Thanking Talia, Elisa suppressed a chuckle inside her cup when Darcie did not do the same.

The rest of the evening passed in much the same way, with a great deal of small talk over a light supper. Unfortunately, the opportunity to speak privately didn't come until the middle of the night after Gwen returned and everyone went to bed.

"So, if we get your grandmother's diary, you'll combine your magic with some fairy magic—which we also have to figure out how to get—you want to go to Lockesbarrow and stop Rona?" Gavin's skepticism extinguished what little faith Elise still possessed.

"Don't forget she wants to get her aunt and uncle together first," Mitch chimed in.

"Gav's right. Are you sure this plan is a good idea?" Mitch whispered. "Derek just *died*. I doubt Richard will be up for being set up with anybody."

"If he even shows up at all," Gavin grumbled.

Maybe this isn't a good idea after all.

Picking up the candle holder, Darcie stood with a groan.

Candlelight illuminated Darcie's face, and Elise instantly recognized the growing, meddlesome excitement play across her best friend's features.

"Come on, y'all," Darcie whined. "Haven't you seen the movies? A ball is the *perfect* place to fall in love! Especially a masquerade! The romance, the mystery, the music. . ." Swept up in the moment, she performed a dramatic twirl in the middle of the small, darkened room the four occupied. The flame flickered violently, threatening to go out as shadows bounced across the walls, until Darcie slumped with a sigh.

"I'm thinking this is *your* fantasy," Mitch teased.

Elise nodded with a smile. "Except the part where she catches herself on fire."

"And *if* they're destined to fall in love anyway," Darcie added, ignoring them both, except to hold the candle out away from her body, "then this can't fail."

Mitch's audible yawn killed what little superficial energy Darcie had left, leaving the latter to suggest they get some sleep.

Except, Elise's anxiety often reared its ugly head the most when things quieted around her. Before everyone even got situated on their blankets, she knew she was going to have a panic attack. It started with a tingling sensation in the tips of her fingers followed a weakness in her kneecaps that made her question her ability to stand upright without falling. At least she wouldn't have to prove that one since everyone was stretching out on the floor.

Forcing her eyes closed, she focused on her breathing. Despite her best efforts, the ideal pattern of inhaling and exhaling soon quickened to a shallow rhythm that left her chest feeling constricted.

Darcie blew out the candle and the windowless room felt like an empty void imprisoning Elise's rapid imagination.

For the first five minutes or so, Elise consoled herself with the fun memories from the afternoon, but the meek attempt at preventing the impending attack only pushed her closer until she felt as if her mind were screaming. Feeling as if an electric shock bolted through her, she was on her feet in an instant. Unable to decipher where exactly her friends were, Elise decided it would be best if she didn't pace, but the lack of movement only fueled the rapidly embellishing thoughts.

I have to get out of here. How can I get out without them noticing? Crap, here it comes. I can't stop it. I can't. Stop, Elise. Stop! You're fine. Enough. What is wrong with you?

She swallowed convulsively, gripping two handfuls of the nightgown Talia had let her borrow.

What are we doing here? In my future aunt's house? This is getting too close. We are definitely messing something up with the timeline. We're meddling too much. And what if Vaughn is really out there? Could Rona be here as well? Her pleas for the madness to stop were ignored by her own crazed stubbornness. *Let's hope this works. We can't get to Lockesbarrow without magic. We can't get magic without the diary helping me. We won't get the diary if Sarah and Ian can't get it, and what if Richard doesn't allow the royal family to come? And if they don't come—*

"Stop it."

Gavin's deep, assertive voice—thick and hoarse from drowsiness—pierced through her thoughts like a needle into a balloon. The weight in Elise's mind evaporated. She lowered her gaze towards the area near her feet where she knew he was.

"What?" Elise whispered, trying her best to sound nonchalant. In that moment, she was thankful for the darkness, because he couldn't see the hot tears welling up. She wiped her eyes furiously with the back of her trembling hand while bouncing on the balls of her feet. Anything to release the adrenaline.

"Lay down, Elise."

Before she could reply, Elise jumped at the sound of Mitch snoring. She held her breath, hoping Gavin would also drift off to sleep and forget she was standing there, hyperventilating like a lunatic.

She waited.

All was quiet.

Good. Maybe he fell asleep.

Elise gasped as he wrapped a hand around her wrist and pulled her down to the floor. A pathetic choking sound escaped her lips when she felt his thumb brush across her hand, still wet from her tears, before he stilled.

"Are you *crying*?" Concern laced his voice and he no longer sounded half asleep. "Hey, if I hurt your feelings, I'm sorry. I was trying to help."

She shook her head before realizing he couldn't see. "No, it's not that."

"Then what's wrong?" When she didn't answer, he scooted closer until she felt his knees touch hers. "Tell me. What's up?"

Elise heaved a heavy, exhausted sigh and was thankful when he grabbed both her hands again. His touch grounded her, bringing Elise back to reality. She hung her head. *He shouldn't feel like he has to constantly take care of me. I feel like such a baby. I'm so embarrassed. He's going to get tired of this and break up with me. I know it. He gets kidnapped and acts like everything's okay now. He's so strong. My friends turn the lights out, and I freak out over things I can't control.*

"It's nothing. I'm fine," she lied. "Go to sleep."

"Come here." The impatience in his tone made her feel guilty. *He is sick of it, after all.* He pulled her into his lap. Immediately, she fit perfectly against him and felt the remaining energy leave her body as the panic attack finally subsided. "Are you cold?"

Elise shivered uncontrollably, an unfortunate side effect she suffered after intense panic attacks. She allowed him to ease her into a lying position and pulled her close before covering them both with his blanket. While it didn't immediately stop her trembling, she welcomed its warm embrace. They were an entanglement of limbs, giving Elise another reason to be thankful for the darkness. She pressed her back against Gavin's chest, feeling his breath against the back of her neck. The two lay there until the final tremors faded and her breath steadied.

"Better?" Gavin whispered, placing a kiss behind her ear.

She nodded.

"What happened?"

"I don't know," she replied.

"Liar."

She smiled despite herself. He really did know her better than that. "It's just that—"

They both jumped as Mitch let out a lone, offensive snore, which was followed by Darcie mumbling in her sleep. Gavin and Elise broke into fits of stifled laughter.

"A perfect match," Elise whispered between giggles.

Gavin agreed before running a hand up and down the length of Elise's arm. "Don't change the subject. Spill it."

"Okay, *Darcie*," she teased, leaning her head back as he trailed kisses down her neck. Elise stretched to grant him more access. "Let's just drop it."

Gavin moaned his disagreement before kissing her shoulder.

Although Elise couldn't see Gavin's face, she could almost hear an arrogant yet knowing smirk curving the corners of his mouth.

"Do you want me to stop?" he whispered, grazing her earlobe between his teeth.

Never. She shook her head against his chest. When he abruptly ceased his attentions, she rolled onto her back and pulled him on top of her. *I need more. Don't leave.* Elise's hungry lips sought out his as she drowned all her worries into the kiss. Only when he leaned back did she attempt speaking again. "Do you think our plan will work?"

"*That's* where your head still is? Man, I need to up my game."

She kissed away Gavin's playful pout before meeting his eyes with a sheepish grin. "Sorry."

Gavin stilled when Mitch mumbled something in his sleep before rolling over towards them.

Elise thought Gavin might continue his attentions to her aching body, but when Mitch sat up in the dark, Gavin rolled over to lay beside her.

Both Gavin and Elise shook with nervous, silent laughter. By the time Mitch resumed his snoring, the moment had unfortunately passed.

Gavin groaned into Elise's neck before he leaned over to kiss her. "I love you."

Elise smiled. *I'm disappointed, too.* Sometimes she still couldn't believe it. It was one thing to daydream in school about him loving her. It was another thing entirely for it to be a reality. "I love you, too." She brought a hand up to caress his stubbled cheek. "Since Mitch ruined the mood, I better go back to my spot, so they don't think anything in the morning."

They bid each other a good night, and Elise wasn't surprised to hear Gavin's breathing even out within a few minutes. Yet, Elise's anxious feelings didn't return. Once again, he had saved her from herself. Whatever was going to happen would happen.

She needed to be ready when it did.

CHAPTER 15

Fortunately for Elise and her friends, the days leading up to the festival passed swifter than those preceding Derek's funeral. During that time, not only had Elise received two letters from Ruby confirming the details of their plans, but she also found herself having *fun* again.

The Archers were incredibly generous hosts. When they weren't busy working on a local farm, each showered the four travelers with some sort of hospitality. Mrs. Archer was a fantastic cook and spent each night entertaining them with stories about their family and the town. Talia taught them popular local dances, and Gwen showed them all around Clara, including some shops Elise hadn't noticed during their previous visits. She enlisted their guidance with flower arrangements and last-minute details to help those organizing the festivities.

On more than one occasion, Elise was settled down for bed before realizing she hadn't obsessed about Rona that day. The liveliness of Clara was the only thing keeping her sane until the festival. In the meantime, she tried learning all she could about Gwen in hopes it would make a romance between her and Elise's uncle more feasible.

"Do you ever think you'll get married?" Elise asked on the morning of the festival as she strolled along the crowded streets of Clara with her future aunt. She held her face up towards the sun, enjoying the unseasonable heat wave that had rolled two days prior. It was all anyone in town could talk about apart from it coinciding perfectly with the opening night masquerade. The energy amongst the people was electrifying and infectious.

It's no wonder it was Derek's favorite place to be.

Gwen paused, taken aback by the question, before continuing in the direction of more shops. "I'm supposed to want to, but I can't imagine leaving Mama and Tal. They need me."

Elise understood that. If only she could share with Gwen that she'd be queen of Haighdlen. Her family would be set for life, but Elise knew to let it happen naturally. Suffocating under the growing pressure to break their silence, she steered the conversation to Gwen's ideal husband. Elise inquired what Gwen sought in a potential husband, and more importantly, what she hated.

Before Gwen could answer, the two women stepped apart as a group of children ran between them playing. She watched them with a wistful smile. "I want a family."

Good start. Richard wants an heir, and they'll have my cousin, Madelyn. Check. Elise pictured her freckled-faced cousin from her first visit to Joranna's house back home. Madelyn's small, angelic voice rang through Elise's memory.

"We don't want you to do anything you don't want to do," she had stated, *"but. . .Haighdlen is our home. We'd really love if you'd help save it."*

"A family's good," Elise agreed. "Anything else?"

Gwen shrugged. "You're asking me to create a fantasy, Elise. This is my home. A foreigner would want to take me to his kingdom, and a local man would need to support my desire to remain active in the town's growth. Not many men are like that. They'd prefer I sit idle at home, but I need a purpose."

This is getting better and better. Those are great qualities for a queen. No wonder Richard fell for her. This is going to be so easy.

"But he couldn't be arrogant," Gwen added. "I find arrogance detestable and could never give myself to someone like that."

Crap. Well, we tried.

Elise conceded it wouldn't be as simple as she hoped, but maybe Gwen would see another side of Richard.

Even she rolled her eyes at that possibility.

"So, you see I shall remain a maid." Gwen chuckled as she swung her basket back and forth by her side. "It won't be so bad, though. Talia is *immensely* popular. She'll be married soon enough and have lots of babies. Mama will get her grandchildren, and I can help focus on bringing in money so that she won't have to work anymore."

Elise's heart wrenched. Gwen's selflessness was admirable—even endearing, yet the more she talked, Elise realized there would have to be meddling after all. Her aunt wasn't going to approach a haughty prince, and Richard was close to signing a wedding contract as it was.

A silence fell between the two as they turned onto the next street near the square.

Elise's overactive brain considered multiple scenarios for her aunt and uncle to meet that night. Watching the multiple shopkeepers setting up tables and signs for the evening, she tried staging the perfect meeting place that would set the mood.

"Have I upset you?" Gwen's voice pierced Elise's focus, causing the latter to shake her head.

"No, why?"

"You've grown very quiet. That's all." Gwen looked at her expectantly, forcing Elise to put her plotting on hold.

Elise looked around for an excuse until she caught her reflection in the nearest shop window, which happened to be her favorite hidden gem. It was a simple pawn shop, yet each time Elise entered, there were always subtle changes.

Elise nodded towards it. "I was just thinking I'd like to go into that shop if we have time." It wasn't a complete lie. Elise was sure if she went in, something would pique her interest.

Gwen followed Elise's line of vision before chuckling in disbelief. "Did you not visit it yesterday? Come to think of it, even the day before?"

Elise blushed, unable to think of a proper response. She averted her eyes, catching a glimpse of Gavin coming towards them.

Gwen also spotted him. "Ah, I'll leave the two of you to it, then. Go on in." She gestured towards the basket of linens in her hand. "I must deliver these for last minute alterations, anyway. I'll meet you both at the house." Before Elise could reply, Gwen was already out of sight, lost in the growing crowds on the street.

Gavin greeted her with a quick kiss. "There you are. Talia wanted me to tell you the costumes are ready, and—" He looked up at the sign above their heads before rolling his eyes. "You're not going back into that old dump, are you?"

"I won't be long." Elise shot him an innocent smile, but his raised brow and tucked chin suggested he didn't believe her. "Come with me." Not bothering to wait, and ignoring his answering groan, she tugged on his arm to join her.

While slightly larger than Gwen's house, the pawn shop felt cramped due to its cluttered floorspace, poor lighting, and dust-covered shelves. The first thing Elise always noticed upon entering was the stale, musty fragrance of aged paper and candlewax. Reminded of a used bookstore back home, she paused to see if anything caught her eye from the door. Gavin's second attempt to leave went ignored as she pulled him over to a crooked table full of trinkets.

Elise picked up a porcelain teapot, one she had already held half a dozen times, before moving on to a comb and tarnished spoon.

"The festival starts in a couple of hours," Gavin complained. "Where *you* want to pull off this elaborate plan. . .and you're playing with a spoon."

Elise rolled her eyes. "I'm not *playing* with it." Setting it down, she brushed her fingertips across a collection of old worn shoes and quills. She didn't know what it was, nor could she explain it, but there was something enchanting about this place that stirred something within her. *So many stories.* Elise didn't expect Gavin to understand. She didn't even fully understand her own obsession with the store, but once she stepped foot inside, it was always much harder to leave.

"Back again, I see."

Elise jumped as the shopkeeper poked his head around the corner of a shelf. *I didn't even see him there.*

"*This* is why I hate it in here," Gavin whispered into her ear. "This guy's crazy."

While Elise doubted any ill will on the shopkeeper's part, the older gentleman certainly made no effort to give a good impression. Elise usually found him lurking in corners, making little eye contact, and avoiding people altogether unless he could detect a transaction worth his while.

"Y-yes," Elise stammered, watching the elderly gentleman limp across the shop to stand on the other side of a glass counter. She offered him a smile that was not returned. "I was just looking around to see what was new."

"Since *yesterday*?" Gavin hissed before she elbowed him in the ribs.

A sinister smile cracked the shopkeeper's otherwise stoic and sunken features. "I might have something. Acquired it this morning."

Ignoring Gavin's objections, Elise stepped forward as the ghoulish salesman retrieved a small velvet box from the top shelf beneath the glass. *I can't leave now.* Eager to see its contents, she fought to ignore the nagging voice screaming for her to walk away. Even Gavin was nodding towards the door. Peering over the counter, Elise watched as the shopkeeper lifted the delicate lid to reveal a bottle necklace. Elise's breath caught in her chest. She immediately recognized it as her mother's lost necklace. *Is it really the* same *one?* She had a flashback to the shores of Lockesbarrow where Rona spilled the remaining fairy magic before striking Derek in the chest. *How did it get here?*

Gavin rolled his eyes again when she waved him over. She suppressed her temper watching him shuffle his feet to take as long as possible. As he approached the counter, he looked at her expectantly with a hint of annoyance.

Elise ignored his moping and cocked her head towards the necklace. She waited for his eyes to widen, a statement of shock, or for him to say. . .*anything*. His facial expression remained neutral as he stared at the jewelry. When he didn't react the same way, she reminded herself he had only seen the necklace during the brief time Rona had it. There was no way for him to truly understand the time and dedication she put into wearing it up until that point. *Not to mention I can give it back to Mom.*

Feeling the weight of Gavin's disapproving stare burning into her cheeks, Elise chewed her bottom lip before ultimately inquiring about the cost.

"Elise! What're you doing?"

She winced at the bite in Gavin's tone.

"Twenty pieces," the old shopkeeper croaked with a toothy grin before removing the necklace from its box. Dangling the chain from a single, bony finger, he held it up in front of a nearby window for a better view.

Elise shuddered when the sunlight exposed layers of dirt beneath the shopkeeper's overgrown fingernails. The lines of his cracked wrinkled skin of his hands were equally smudged and unclean. She couldn't blame Gavin's reluctance to stay in the shop any longer than necessary. *This guy gives me the creeps, too.* Still, Elise knew this wasn't a mere coincidence. She was meant to come in and find this necklace. Her initial excitement to have it back was overshadowed by the impending realization that it could have only come from one place. *Vaughn is still here.* Mrs. Archer hadn't imagined him earlier that week.

"What'll it be?" he prompted, pulling Elise out of her thoughts.

Gavin shook his head at her, silently pleading for her to walk away. Yet, a nagging curiosity gnawed inside her to possess the necklace again. *We are looking for fairy magic after all. It would be the best place to hold it. I can give it to Mom later.* Pulling the small change purse from her cloak pocket, Elise poured the remaining coins from Richard onto her outstretched palm. *Fifteen.*

She slumped her shoulders with an apologetic smile.

"Bit short there, Miss." The shopkeeper frowned, twirling his finger so that the chain twisted and teased Elise even more.

She stared longingly at the dangling piece of jewelry. *I'd do anything to have it back.* She licked her lips. "Hey, Gavin—"

"No."

"Come on, it's just—"

"No," he whispered, keeping his eyes on the shopkeeper. "I don't want to waste any money on this junk. We need to save what we have to help get us home."

Elise wilted. She couldn't blame Gavin for being reluctant. He hadn't carried that necklace day and night around his neck, protecting it at all costs. Although he, too, watched Rona pour out the fairy magic it once carried, Gavin couldn't possibly understand the gut-wrenching wound it left within her. When Elise opened her mouth to speak again, it was towards her shoes rather than to the shopkeeper's face. "Maybe some other time."

"Pardon me?" the older man asked. "I couldn't quite make out what you said."

"She's not interested. Thanks," Gavin quipped, grabbing Elise's hand before leading her towards the exit.

"*That* is a striking piece you have there, Sir." The shopkeeper nodded towards the medallion swinging around Gavin's neck. "Might fetch a good price if you're interested."

"Yeah, right," Gavin scoffed, yanking the door open. "Not a chance."

Elise waited until Gavin slammed the door shut before finding the courage to speak. The last thing she wanted at that moment was for him to see her cry. *Don't lose your nerve.* "I only needed five coins."

"Come on, Elise. I already told you I don't want to. We might need that money later, and you're going to wish we had it."

Elise bit the inside of her cheek before pressing on. "But I really think there's something we're missing. Plus, it's not *all* your money. It's only five coins. If we could just go back—"

"Do you know what *I* think?" Gavin spun so fast on his heel she almost ran into him. "I think you're trying to juggle too much. What if this is a trap to distract us? Let's stick with our plan. We still have to introduce Richard to Gwen, find fairy magic, stop Rona, *and* get home. Going broke over some stupid necklace—"

"But it's *not* stupid!" she cried. "You don't understand. *You* weren't there when we got it!"

"And that's *my* fault?" he snapped. A tense moment of silence followed as his breathing quickened. "You think I'd rather be where I was?"

Elise's heart softened at the sight of pain in his eyes. He was practically shaking, but it wasn't out of rage. This was something else, but when she attempted to approach him, he quickly wiped his face with his sleeve and walked away.

Elise hesitated, taken aback by his rare vulnerability. *This isn't going the way I hoped. It's only getting worse, but I can't back down. I'm only trying to help, but I don't want to hurt him.* "Gavin, Mrs. Archer wasn't making it up the other day. Vaughn left this necklace. He must've picked it up that day we saw Rona, and—"

"That's it, isn't it?" He froze, casting a dark glare over his shoulder. "It's from *him.*"

"What? No!" she shrieked. *That's not what it is at all!* "I told you he doesn't mean anything to me, but if we could figure out why he's hanging around, it could give us a clue. Why would he leave it here for us to find?" *Is he even listening to me?* "He might be spying on us. I need to get to the bottom of this."

Gavin hung his head before chuckling in disbelief. "Guess I'm an idiot then. I thought we agreed to do this together."

That's not what I meant. "Don't be like that," Elise pleaded, catching a couple of people watching them as they passed. *Great. Of course, there's an audience. Why is he acting like this?* "You're not even listening to me!"

Gavin's sullen expression soured further as he dug into his pocket. Shaking his head, he silently closed the distance between them before taking her hand.

Elise watched as he placed five coins into her palm with a resigned sigh.

"Buy the necklace," he whispered. "I won't stop you."

"No, this isn't what I wanted," she argued, feeling unwanted tears welling up in the corners of her eyes. "If you'd let me explain—"

"I'll see you at Gwen's."

She watched him cross the bustling street as guilt stabbed her chest like a thousand knives.

Gavin ignored her calls until he was out of earshot altogether.

Elise dropped the coins into her purse with a huff. Her brain screamed to run after him and return the money. It would be simpler to forget the necklace and patch things up, but the gnawing suspicion of Vaughn's unknown intentions outweighed her better judgment. *Gavin doesn't understand. I* have *to figure this out. I can apologize later.*

The door creaked open as Elise entered the pawn shop again. She shuffled her feet to where the shopkeeper still stood.

Polishing a silver goblet, he cocked his head and smiled at her.

Without a word, she pinched the bottom of her purse and poured all twenty coins out onto the glass counter.

He inspected the payment. "Talked some sense into him, eh?"

Elise didn't reply except to nod towards the necklace, which was now back in the small velvet box.

He praised Elise's excellent choice before handing it to her. "Seems only fitting that you also get to wear a beautiful, exotic piece."

Elise ignored his flattery as she brushed her fingers along the ornate details of the Elven bottle necklace. She clenched her eyes shut, reliving the moment on the beach where Rona dropped it. Elise could hear her own guttural scream ringing through her ears as if it was all still happening. She saw Derek get struck over and over, crashing more violently to the ground each time. The nagging voice returned to remind her since Derek was dead, they really couldn't fix anything. Suddenly, she wasn't in the mood for a festival anymore. *This is so much bigger than us. How can we possibly hope to fix the timeline?* Not to mention Gavin was mad at her now, too. Everything was getting worse.

"Can you tell me about the man who brought this in?" she inquired.

The shopkeeper sniffed, staring warily at Elise before peering down at the box holding the jewelry. "Not much. He said it was royal business."

Royal business? What does that mean? "Are you sure there's nothing else?"

The shopkeeper declined to elaborate, causing Elise's mere frustration to escalate to rage. *He's no help.* She replied with a curt nod before hiding the box within her cloak and exiting the shop.

Gwen's house wasn't far, yet Elise felt as if she couldn't reach her friends fast enough. So many questions were swirling through her mind, and she wanted desperately to hear their thoughts on what she had found out.

In all her excitement, Elise didn't prepare herself to face Gavin following their argument. Upon entering the cottage, the air turned cold as she found him sitting at the table with his back to the door. He was listening to Mitch complain that Darcie already planned on making him dance that night, but as soon as Gavin's eyes met hers, Elise immediately regretted going back into the pawn shop.

It was the briefest of glimpses over his shoulder before Gavin turned back to Mitch without so much as a greeting.

Darcie beckoned her into their shared bedroom. *Great. Now I have a fun interrogation to look forward to as well. This day keeps getting better and better.*

"What did you do to Gavin?" Darcie pursed her lips. "He's acting weird. What did you say?"

Elise shared the details of their argument outside the pawn shop before crossing both arms across her chest.

"Can you blame him?" Darcie offered. "I see why he's hurt."

Elise scoffed. "You're my best friend. You're supposed to take *my* side. Plus, you know there's nothing going on with Vaughn."

Darcie held up both hands with a shrug, her nose pointed high in the air. "It's not me you have to convince, it's your boyfriend, and right now it sounds like you're putting that necklace and this mission before him."

Elise pinched the bridge of her nose. *Did she hear Gavin say that?* "I don't have time for this. I know you love it, but you know I *hate* drama."

"All I'm saying is you should probably apologize. He went through a lot, too."

Releasing a heavy sigh, Elise peeked out the door and saw a glimpse of Gavin's back. "I need to straighten this out before the festival."

"Good luck," Darcie said, slumping against the wall with her arms crossed.

I know we have a ton to do tonight, but if we're not on the same page, it's going to make things ten times harder. I didn't think it was such a big deal for me to get Mom's necklace back.

"Gavin?" Elise called out. She held her breath until he leaned back into her line of vision. "Can you come here, please?"

He and Mitch mumbled something to one another Elise didn't catch. The tips of her ears burned when Mitch chuckled, sending Elise's paranoia skyrocketing.

Gavin rolled his own eyes before he languidly stood to walk her way. An awkward moment of silence passed between the two girls before Elise gestured towards the door. "Out."

"But why?" Darcie whined. "I'm going to make you tell me everything, anyway."

Elise pointed a finger towards the other room until Darcie left.

As Gavin entered the room, Elise stepped around him to close the door. When he tried to speak, Elise held up a finger to stop him before leaning close to the door again. "Goodbye, Darcie," she said, waiting until she heard her best friend's footsteps fade from the other side.

Gavin put both hands in his pockets and leaned back against the door. When she didn't talk right away, he lifted his brows expectantly. A lock of dark hair fell across his chocolate eyes, momentarily robbing her of breath.

Though it couldn't be more ill-timed, Elise did her best to ignore the fluttering sensation pulsing through her stomach at his brooding appearance. Her thoughts began distracting her with what she *really* wanted to do while they were alone. Elise's gaze followed the line of his collar down to where his shirt hung partially unbuttoned. *Why does he have to look so good when he's upset? I'll never get through this.* When he called her name, she forced herself to look up at his face again.

"I don't want you mad at me." Elise fiddled with her fingers before tucking a strand of loose hair behind her ear. "The necklace doesn't mean anything."

"Oh, it means *something*," he corrected her.

She rocked back and forth beneath his heavy-lidded stare. An awkward silence passed between them before Elise realized she was chewing her bottom lip. "What I mean is. . .Vaughn doesn't mean anything. I wasn't choosing him over you or anything." When Gavin didn't reply, Elise removed the box from her cloak as a rising tide of guilt spilt from her mouth. "I wore this the entire time we searched for you. It carried fairy magic. I kept it safe and protected, hoping to use it to get us home. When Rona dropped it. . ." Elise's eyes glossed over as she stared at a tile in the floor, but her mind once again played out the events on the beach. "We found out who Vaughn really was, and I thought I lost everything." She sucked her lips into a thin line as she awaited his response. *You have to believe me.*

The silence between them grew so intense, Elise felt as if she would collapse from the weight of it. *What's going through his mind?*

Gavin looked as if he *wanted* to say something, but before he could utter a single syllable, the door opened and pushed him forward.

Elise gasped from the sudden intrusion, and only calmed when Mrs. Archer poked her head in.

"Oh, I'm sorry to interrupt. I didn't realize anyone was in here." Mrs. Archer bustled about the room before burying her head inside the closet. "I need to sew a small tear in Talia's sleeve. She's practically inconsolable. I believe I put it in here somewhere. . ."

Gavin and Elise shared an aching stare while the older woman muttered to herself about the unusually warm weather outside, not realizing she was causing the palpable unspoken tension between them to mount.

"Aha!" sang Mrs. Archer, holding the sewing kit up in the air like a trophy. Her triumphant smile faded when she looked between the two teenagers. A flustered, disapproving scowl colored her features as a line formed between her brows. "My goodness! Don't you know what time it is? You both must get dressed! The sun is nearly set, and Gwen's already left. Her performance will be early.

Hurry, hurry!" She tugged on Elise's sleeve with an offer to help with her hair.

Casting a disheartened glance back at Gavin, she mouthed an apology before Mrs. Archer once again closed the door.

CHAPTER 16

"Are you sure it's a good idea to wear this thing tonight?" Darcie asked as she clasped the bottle necklace around Elise's neck. "I thought we were trying to be discreet."

Elise centered the bottle against her chest. "Vaughn wanted me to find it, and if he shows up, I want him to see that I'm not afraid anymore."

"Is that true?"

Elise shook her head. She was terrified, but she would have to conceal her fear if their plan was going to succeed.

"Are you and Gavin good?" Darcie glared when Elise nodded. "Liar."

Elise fidgeted in her chair. "We're as good as we're going to be for now." She and Gavin hadn't made up the way she wanted to yet, but time was slipping away from them. Using a finger to adjust a smear of lipstick, Elise inspected herself in the mirror.

Edith's design was more daring than Elise was comfortable with, but she had to admit it suited her curves. Turning towards Darcie, Elise peeked back over wavy shoulder straps to inspect the low-cut back of her sparkling emerald gown. Goosebumps swam along Elise's naked arms as she trailed a trembling hand up the equally revealing front until she grasped the bottle necklace for comfort. *I can do this.*

As it turned out, Mrs. Archer was a skilled hairdresser like Darcie—who wasn't offended, but who also didn't pass up the chance to tease Elise about being replaced.

Elise tilted her head, admiring her elegant updo from all angles. She was thankful Mrs. Archer was able to incorporate the matching silk ribbon that arrived with the gown. The color stood out as it weaved in and out of her dark red hair. Settling her gaze on the necklace again, quavering doubts churned in Elise's lower gut as she ran both clammy hands down the fabric of her gown. "It's time to go." Readjusting the accompanying ornate mask for comfort, Elise turned around to see Darcie tying her own. "Wow. You look great!" *How does Edith make these so perfect?*

Darcie's plum-colored gown hugged her form like a glove except for a billowy feather skirt. Oversized matching feathers lined the top of her solid velvet mask. Against the lush, deep purple fabric, Darcie's pale skin practically glowed.

Elise chuckled when her best friend was unable to resist the urge to twirl.

A huge smile split Darcie's face as she squealed. "Thanks, but shouldn't we wait for the guys?"

Elise shook her head. "Gavin promised he'd find me since Mrs. Archer asked the boys to stay back and escort her once she's ready. I don't even think *they're* ready yet."

"And they complain about *us* taking forever."

Their excitement only grew as they followed Talia to the town square before the latter excused herself to join another group of friends. Although Elise had spent the better part of a week in town, nothing could have prepared her for its finished transformation.

According to the Archer family, the Harvest Oak Festival was a highly anticipated event, and Clara took its hosting duties very seriously. Nothing was left to chance and no detail went unnoticed.

Countless torches and lanterns lit the unseasonably warm night, sending an array of shadows dancing along the busy streets. Stringed flags and banners bearing Haighdlen's crest waved from shop rooftops and carts. It was nothing short of impressive, and Elise struggled to take it all in.

Proud vendors lined the main square with their most successful fruits and vegetables of the season on full display. Vibrant colors and scents attacked Elise's senses as she soaked in the rich sight and aromas of plump pumpkins, onions, fresh corn, sweet potatoes, apples, carrots and plenty more. Other carts showcased jewelry, wine, spices, perfumes, and painted canvases. Laughter, shouting, and buzzing conversations overlapped with lively music coming from a band of musicians playing near a makeshift dance floor.

Above the crowd, half a dozen performers dressed as masked scarecrows paraded by on stilts. As one passed, Elise stepped out of the way before gazing beyond the dance floor where a guarded dais awaited the arrival of the royal family. She dared to hope after counting the empty cushioned chairs. *There are five seats. Maybe Mom will get to come after all!*

"Elise, look at this." Darcie pulled Elise over to a lone decorated cart beneath a flower-covered arch. In the middle sat a magnificent crown-shaped corn dolly centerpiece. Around it lay intricate straw-woven hearts atop a bed of hay and fallen petals. Beside the cart stood an easel supporting an oversized oil painting of Derek.

Elise's breath caught in her chest. Taken aback by its likeness, she studied her late grandfather's eyes, marveling at the artist's ability to capture both Derek's assertive features and compassionate stare. *The people loved him, too.* Elise could still hear Derek's voice the day he led them through Clara as a young father.

"'I hope my children grow to love it here as I do. As you can see, we enjoy most of these products in the castle and have come to know these wonderful people well.'"

Elise swallowed convulsively when Darcie asked what she thought of the display. Without taking her eyes off the canvas, she whispered, "It's perfect."

Darcie wrapped an arm around Elise's shoulder before pulling her into a hug. "I know you miss him, but let's try to have some fun."

Elise pulled away to survey the crowd. She couldn't shake the feeling they were being watched. "Where are the guys? They should be here by now."

Darcie rolled her eyes. "They probably stopped at the first food cart they came to. Let's go back there and check."

Shifting her eyes, growing more unnerved by the minute, Elise licked her lips. *Something is wrong. I feel it. I need to get Darcie away from here until I can figure it out.* "You go ahead. I'll wait here in case my family shows up."

Before Darcie was out of sight, Elise was well on her way to having a panic attack. Anxiety was already a crippling endeavor but experiencing it in public was like wearing a mental straitjacket. Every nerve in her body pulsed with anticipation while her mind fought to sedate the swarm of unwanted thoughts. Nothing about her surroundings gave Elise cause for alarm, yet the hair on the back of her neck rose, nonetheless. Instinctively, she reached up and squeezed the bottle necklace as her head swam. The once roaring crowd was now muffled as if she were underwater. *Where's Gavin? I need him. I need to know everyone is safe. Something's definitely wrong.*

Her thoughts cycled through the same erratic pattern until an offending trumpet silenced the crowd and her thoughts to announce the arrival of the royal family. Elise smiled, relief washing over her as she took in their masked faces. Among them, Joranna's handheld mask was the most impressive. Even the stick it was attached to was covered in jewels and pearls. Elise suspected the mask alone was worth more than anything she had ever worn. Cheers erupted as each member entered the dais and acknowledged the people. Wiping the sweat from her palms, Elise stepped closer to get a better look. *I wish I could join them.* Her smile dropped, however, as the applause dwindled.

Gasps and murmurs rippled through the crowd when Richard took the largest seat in the middle, leaving Joranna the place next to him.

Why isn't she in the middle?

Sarah and Ian hesitated before following their mother to fill the remaining seats at Richard's left.

Elise's heart fell as she stared at the lone seat to Richard's right. Rather than Ruby, Charles entered the dais to join the family. Elise didn't bother listening to Richard's welcoming speech. The few triggering words that did manage to reach her ears left her fuming. *Family, gratitude, honor, loyalty, dedication, love. . .* She couldn't help but think his speech was written *for* him rather than by him. The prince's recent behavior certainly did not model these ideals. Elise hoped to catch Joranna's or Sarah's attention with a subtle cough, even going as far as to bounce on the balls of her feet, but it was no use. Richard finished speaking so another performer could approach the dance floor and Elise still went unnoticed.

The Master of Ceremonies thanked the royal family before introducing a masked young maiden. Though she wore a bold, voluptuous white gown, reminding Elise of a delicate swan, the singer's shoulders slumped as she awaited the musicians to play. The maiden fidgeted with her hands as her credentials were read aloud, including her popularity across borders, namely Lockesbarrow.

Elise craned her neck to see over the other bystanders as the woman initially sang towards her feet. At first, it was difficult to hear her, but as the song progressed, the singer's voice displayed incredible range. Her raw, natural talent and ethereal tone mesmerized the crowd, the royal family included, and Elise couldn't help but hang on to every lyric.

> *Hold steadfast,*
> *Dear lover,*
> *For the thrills of life lay ahead.*
> *Dwell not on the past,*
> *Dear lover,*
> *For time chases no immortal bed.*
>
> *Cease fleeing this moment,*
> *This one aching moment,*
> *Alas, it is all we may share.*
> *Seize your moment,*
> *Our lone stolen moment,*
> *Kiss me now while I am still fair.*

As the song reached its climax, the young woman switched to simply vocalizing. *This sounds like something out of a fairy tale.* During one particularly high note, Elise felt her chest swell as tears pricked the corners of her eyes. This voice was hauntingly beautiful, as was the singer herself, and for a few precious seconds, Elise's worries vanished.

Until she felt someone watching her. Elise barely managed a clap as the young woman finished before gazing into the sea of masks around her. Cheers and whistles erupted as another jig began. Within seconds, couples reappeared, and skirts once again swept across the dance floor. Elise stepped back, putting as much distance between her and the dancers as possible. *I want Gavin. And where is Darcie? She should've found the guys by now.*

With one last desperate search, her heart fluttered at the sight of him. *Gavin!*

A masked figure emerged from the crowd with a subtle wave and made his way towards her. Elise's breath hitched as heat rushed to her face. *Wow, Edith's outdone herself again.* Elise didn't know why she continued to underestimate the fabriwitch's good taste in fashion. Gavin's costume was certainly tailored for his body only. She couldn't tear her eyes away from the way the solid black fabric hugged his athletic frame. Even the satin mask Edith chose, which covered almost his entire face, was complimented with a stylish hat. As if the fit wasn't perfect enough, the final embellishment was a dapper cape that hung over one shoulder.

He looked incredibly dangerous. . .and it excited her.

Gavin paused to let a group of people cross in front of him, giving Elise another moment to admire his mesmeric physique. She chuckled at the fact that even the way he rested a hand in his pocket got her hot and bothered. Her abdominal muscles tightened beneath her gown as he resumed his steps. All she could think about was ripping his costume off in a secluded alleyway somewhere away from prying eyes. *I'll happily let him return the favor.* Blushing from the direction of her own thoughts, she chuckled as he closed the distance between them with a series of goofy steps timed with the music. *Oh, good. He's forgiven me.*

"I didn't think you liked dancing," Elise said as the musicians finished another piece.

He replied by offering his hand before leading her towards the dance floor. As Gavin pulled her body against his, awaiting the next song, Elise felt a shiver course down her spine. As if their embrace wasn't sensual enough, he trailed a gloved hand along her jaw, tipping her chin up towards him. Goosebumps trailed along the exposed skin of her arms. *I love him so much.*

The first soft notes from the band sent the surrounding couples in motion around them, causing Elise to look down at her feet before Gavin lifted her chin once more. He tightened his hold, guiding her back and forth until she felt comfortable with the rhythm. Melting against him, she closed her eyes to soak in this fleeting moment. She doubted there would be any masquerades once they returned home. *Never in a million years could I have imagined a night like this.*

All her anxieties vanished when his hand slid further down her lower back. When Elise lifted her head from his chest, she saw the playful smirk that sent an exciting rush of adrenaline through her.

"Kiss me," she whispered, snaking a hand around his neck before crushing her lips against his.

It took only a second for Elise's excitement to come to a screeching halt. She could no longer hear the music over the deafening sound of her heart beating in her ears.

This wasn't Gavin.

Elise ripped the mask from Vaughn's face, inwardly screaming and berating her own ignorance. *How could I not know?*

Then came the stifling guilt. She thought back to the erotic dream she had experienced involving Vaughn during their journey to save Gavin. Deep down, she was convinced Vaughn manipulated her dreams with some sort of magic. It still didn't make it any easier to stomach the amused smirk on his lips.

What have I done? Gavin's going to kill me!

"What are *you* doing here?" she hissed.

She made to pull away, but Vaughn grabbed the mask before holding her flush against him. "Now, let's not draw attention to ourselves, shall we? Besides, *you* kissed me."

Gaping in horror, Elise watched him readjust his mask. "I-I thought you were Gavin!"

"I still can be if you wish." Feeling as if her knees would buckle from his arrogant smile, she composed herself long enough to stomp a pointed heel into his foot.

He bit his lip to stifle a groan yet kept a firm grip on her arm. "Play nicely," Vaughn warned, almost songlike, into Elise's ear before inhaling the sweet scent of her hair. His appreciative, primal moan vibrated against her own cheek. "I've missed you."

Elise attempted to jerk away again but was held still. She fought against the seductive effect his voice had on her body, but he was right. If she screamed and created a scene, it would do more harm than good for their already jeopardized plans.

"What do you want?" Elise's mind became keenly aware of the lazy circles he drew on her exposed back. *Stop it, Elise. Ignore it.*

"You look stunning," he said, ignoring her question completely before nodding towards her chest. "I see you found my little gift."

Elise glanced down at the bottle necklace. *I knew it was him.* She bit her tongue to control her nerves before grounding out her next words. "What're you planning?"

He clicked his tongue three times with a shake of his head. "All in good time," he purred before twirling her. "The night is young, and *you* are breathtaking."

Sucking her lips into a thin line, Elise increased her self-awareness, desperately searching for a familiar face or an escape.

"Word on the street is you've befriended the Archer family." Vaughn's breath tickled Elise's ear as he pulled her close.

Elise felt her blood turn cold.

Vaughn's eyes flashed from beneath his mask. "I often consider paying them a visit. They were such gracious hosts, as you know."

Elise pushed against his chest enough to meet his gaze. "Stay away from them!" she spat. "Tell me what you're planning. Why plant the necklace where I might not have found it?"

"I knew you'd see it." He threw a casual shrug in her direction. "Like all Laurilles, you couldn't satisfy your curiosity if you tried. After spending these last few months at the castle, I have found it to be a family trait."

"I'm warning you," Elise said, feeling the initial terror in her veins melt into a searing rage. She dug her fingers into the back of his arms when he prevented her from backing away again. "Stay *away* from my family. They're on to you."

He had the nerve to chuckle, sending what little gumption she possessed plummeting. "Is that so?"

If he weren't holding her up, she might have stumbled. *Focus, Elise! Don't let him see you weak.* She cocked her chin up at him. "You were already kicked off the council."

"Dismissed for an *investigation*," he corrected. "An investigation, I might add, that has yielded no evidence against me. In a matter of hours, I'll be restored and carry on with business."

"Which is?" Elise asked. She gritted her teeth when he didn't reply. "And why return the necklace at all? Is Rona here?" *Only hours? What's he planning to do?*

Vaughn used the climactic swell of the music to catch Elise off guard and spin her one final time. Feeling him release her hand, Elise caught her balance and whirled around, but Vaughn was nowhere to be found. As the other couples stepped away to mingle, she stood there, dumbfounded, convincing herself she hadn't imagined the whole exchange. When the initial shock wore off, only one clear thought remained in her head.

The family's in danger.

Elise ran frantically towards where her relatives sat. Gritting her teeth, she was convinced the population in Clara had doubled since she arrived. Elise lost count of how many people she pushed past, and even gave up apologizing when her own frustration piqued. *Can anyone move? I'll never reach my family at this rate.* At one point, all she could do was stare at the wall of people ignoring her attempts to get through. *If Richard sees me, I'll get arrested, but if I don't warn them, Vaughn or maybe Rona, might attack. Something is about to happen. I can't just sit here and wait!*

Out of time, and options, Elise peered around for a way to get Sarah's attention. Her aunt was positioned in the seat closest to Elise, but the eldest princess was invested in a hushed conversation with Ian. Reaching down, Elise picked up a small pebble near her shoe. She checked her surroundings to make sure no one was watching before nonchalantly tossing the pebble towards her aunt's feet. Elise stomped her own foot helplessly when it bounced off the edge of the dais.

Four stones later, one finally skipped along the wood panels before landing on Ian's shoe.

Close enough.

Elise crouched with bated breath as the prince inspected the stone before warily surveying the crowd. The moment Ian's gaze roamed close enough, she lifted her mask only long enough to wave him and Sarah over. Ian whispered something into Sarah's ear before the princess also glanced in Elise's direction.

Now to just get them here without too much attention. Richard had thankfully missed the subtle interaction, bouncing between conversations with Joranna and Charles, giving Sarah and Ian ample time to use discretion by excusing themselves one at a time.

Elise beckoned them away from the guards.

"Did you get it?" she whispered, feeling breathless as her uncle retrieved the diary from his vest and offered it to Elise. It took everything in her not to snatch the book from Ian's hands. Elise scanned the worn cover, brushing her fingers across it. She toyed with the corner, itching to open it. *I want to go home and forget about what I'm supposed to do.* "Does anyone else know about this?"

"Just Ruby," Sarah replied. "Ballard almost caught us, but Ian was able to escape using his invisibility."

Elise chuckled. She had almost forgotten her uncle's unique superpower. At the mention of her mother, Elise twisted the bottle necklace between her fingers. Checking over her shoulder, Elise asked Sarah to hold the diary momentarily while she unclasped the chain from around her neck. She held it out towards the princess. "Please give this back to Ruby. Tell her thank you."

Before Sarah could take it, however, Elise froze. There it was—that nagging, tugging feeling—the same one that prevented her from following Ruby through the portal that she couldn't explain before. It wasn't a panic attack, yet it left Elise paranoid all the same.

Whether it was magic, or plain intuition, she had learned to listen to it. Ignoring her aunt and uncle's inquisitive stares, Elise took a step back as an unnerving barrage of thoughts swarmed within her mind.

Vaughn put this where I would find it. He knew I'd get it back. What if he did something horrible to it? It could be tracking our location. I can't put Mom in danger, too. Quick, think of something!

"On second thought, she wanted me to keep it. I don't want to hurt her feelings."

While Sarah nor Ian looked completely convinced, neither questioned her decision apart from sharing a dubious glance.

"What will you do now?" Ian asked.

"Stop Rona," Elise said, hugging the diary close to her chest. *Open it. Open it right now.* Heat rushed to her cheeks as she idly stuck a finger between the pages before pulling it out again. "For good this time."

Ian lifted a skeptical brow, but Elise couldn't blame him. Her plan did sound farfetched, particularly coming from an outsider.

"And Mother's diary is going to make that happen? Is it charmed or something? Perhaps Sarah and I could awaken its magic."

Elise stepped away from his reach. *If they open it while I'm this close, who knows what will happen?* "No, really. I've got it from here. Thanks for your help, but there's more."

Ian scoffed before cocking his head towards Elise. "Why do I feel like we've just made a grave mistake?"

Elise scanned the crowd as if Vaughn could appear out of thin air. She squeezed the necklace in her fist, praying he wasn't eavesdropping somehow through it. She curled her toes before forcing herself to stand taller. *Spit it out! You look stupid.* "There's a man here. A spy. His name is Vaughn Garthorne, and he's going to—" She and the other two jumped as fireworks erupted above them. The cheers from the crowd were so deafening, Elise's warnings could not be heard until she repeated herself a moment later.

Sarah stared intently into Elise's eyes, as if trying to gauge if she were telling the entire truth. Over the whistles and applause amidst another booming display above them, the princess shouted, "I'll only ask you this once more. You're absolutely sure you can use *that?*" She nodded towards the diary. "Because if Mother finds out we—"

Before Sarah could finish, Elise was pushed aside by other guests making room for Joranna, who made her way off the dais towards the decorated carts for a better view of the illuminated sky. Sarah and Ian used the opportunity to wish Elise luck before excusing themselves back to their seats undetected.

Cursing the bad timing, Elise dug her foot into the ground and bit her lip to stop from screaming. She felt her frustration evaporate, however, after watching Joranna congratulate a few vendors before slowly approaching Derek's portrait. The queen stared at the gifts atop the hay and flower petals in silence. Despite the merriment around her, Joranna remained somber and introspective. Elise didn't know what was going through her grandmother's mind, but the mourning widow painted a truly heartbreaking scene that few even bothered to notice apart from her attending butler and the Master of Ceremonies. Hovering behind the queen, awkward and eager, the second gentleman approached with a jovial greeting and bow.

"How do you like our festival, Your Majesty? I believe the late honored king would've approved."

Elise held her breath at the mention of her grandfather. *I don't know if she's going to like that.*

Joranna, ever the perfect model of a queen, took a moment to compose herself before offering him a poised smile. "I believe you are correct. You truly have outdone yourselves this year. Derek would have certainly enjoyed himself. Please take care to return this to the castle after the festival." Lowering her mask, she gripped the stick and pointed towards the canvas. "I expect it to be in the same condition as it was loaned."

"Of course, Your Majesty," replied the Master of Ceremony with another bow.

Casting one last longing glance at her husband's portrait, Joranna nodded and excused herself to visit other vendors and members of court.

She's so broken. I still don't understand why he had to die. Why couldn't we save him? Maybe I could find a way to talk to her.

"There you are!" Darcie's voice was a welcome interruption from Elise's wistful thoughts.

Elise's excitement was short-lived, however, as Gavin and Mitch appeared beside her best friend. Her first thought was how handsome Gavin looked in his similar black costume, which sent another crushing wave of guilt pulsing through her body. *I can't believe I didn't know it was Vaughn before. Gavin won't understand. I really thought it was him.*

"You okay?" Gavin's brows furrowed as he studied her distressed state.

Elise swallowed convulsively. *He knows me too well. Even with a mask, I can't pretend I'm okay. Here goes nothing.* She shuddered under her friends' scrutiny.

"We need to get close to Richard. . . a-and tell him Vaughn is here." She let out a steadying breath, careful to speak to the ground rather than their faces before feeling cramped by the surrounding crowd. Elise led her friends behind the dais, careful to put enough distance between them and the guards as not to raise any alarm. They allowed a few stragglers to step in front of them while remaining close enough to overhear the royal family.

"So, you *actually* saw Vaughn?" Darcie whispered.

Elise finally met Gavin's eyes, feeling her throat constrict from his darkened stare. Eager to suppress her returning paranoia, she turned to Mitch before holding out the diary. "Here, hang onto this, will you?" She waited for him to hide it beneath his vest before nodding at Darcie.

"But why bother Richard? He's been brainwashed by Vaughn. Will your uncle even care that he's here?" Mitch asked while fidgeting with his shirt. "I get the feeling he'd be more pissed off that *we're* here."

"Maybe we tell Joranna," suggested Darcie.

Elise shook her head. *I can't bother Joranna right now.*

"Did you talk to him?" Gavin asked.

His abrupt question cut through any attempt Elise might have made to change the subject. Hesitant to anger him, she nodded.

"What did he say to you?" When she didn't answer right away, he stepped forward with more urgency. "*What* did he say?"

Elise winced at the bite in his tone. Seeing equally expectant expressions play across her friends' faces, heat rose to the tips of her ears. *How can I tell them the truth without sounding unfaithful?* After three attempts to speak, she faltered.

"Can you guys give us a minute?" Gavin's request, while soft and reserved, sent an icy chill plunging down Elise's spine. There was nothing in his voice to warrant her response. . .

It was his eyes.

Whether from the flickering torchlight or the costume, there was a subtle shift in their depths. Though masked, his fierce brown stare bore into hers, and she felt every silent dagger pierce her skin. Again, Elise questioned how she could ever mistake the effect they had on her.

Rather than wait for privacy, Gavin grabbed Elise's hand before pulling her away from Mitch and Darcie.

His swift stride made her stumble to keep up until he swiped a discarded lantern off a cart and led her into an alleyway between two shops. Elise gasped when he guided her to stand against the stone wall.

"Okay, what's going on with you?" Gavin asked, setting the lantern down near their feet.

Elise imagined her eyebrows getting lost in her hairline as she stared at him, dumbfounded. "*Me?*" She scoffed, not bothering to hide her disbelief. "*You're* the one leading me into an alley!"

"*You're* avoiding the question. Just please be honest with me. What happened with Vaughn?"

"Nothing!" Elise fidgeted with the necklace she still carried. When he noticed it hanging from her hand, she cleared her throat. "Okay, you were right. I should've left the necklace in the store. It *was* from him." She ignored his feigned surprise. "He wanted me to find it and knew I wouldn't be able to control myself."

Although he made every attempt to hide any reaction, a twitching muscle in his jaw betrayed him. "Then what?"

She shivered when he took a step closer. "What are you talking about?"

"You heard me," he said softly. He untangled the chain from her fingers and dangled it in front of her face. "How was he able to get so close to you? Did he hurt you?"

Elise shook her head as hot tears threatened to spill beneath her mask. *He's going to kill me.*

"What aren't you telling me?" Gavin groaned at her continued silence as he clutched the necklace and backed away from Elise. "Who knows what he did to it? He could be spying on us right now!" Without warning, he chucked it into the lantern.

Both jumped as the dancing red and orange flames spat and fizzled, burning bright green before burning out completely.

Elise gaped at the smoke, feeling as if she had swallowed a brick.

Gavin lifted the lantern up between them, but there was no sight of the necklace inside.

Vaughn really did use magic on it. I almost gave that necklace back to Mom. What if something had happened? I'm an idiot.

She glanced towards the square at the end of the alley to make sure no one else witnessed what just happened. In that respect, it appeared they were safe. Elise knew the only thing left was to tell Gavin the truth. He deserved that much. Coughing to clear her lungs, she willed her heart to steady and found the nerve to meet his gaze.

"You're right," she whispered. "I should've listened to you. About everything." She flattened her lips into a thin line. "I've been so blind to everything, and I understand if you're done with me."

Gavin rolled his eyes. "Done with you? Elise, you can tell me any—"

"I kissed him!" she ground out.

CHAPTER 17

Gavin set the lantern down carefully before lifting his mask off. He quirked an inquisitive brow.

"You kissed him?"

Elise licked her lips with a tentative nod. "I didn't mean to."

He scoffed before tossing the mask back and forth between his hands before glaring down, giving Elise the impression he might kick the lantern.

"I thought he was you."

Gavin didn't bother hiding his confusion.

Elise continued. "You said you would find me, and while I was waiting around, he came up to me."

"So, you assumed it was me and kissed him?"

"Well, he didn't tell me he wasn't," said Elise, realizing how lame her excuse was.

"Must have been difficult with your mouth on his." Gavin crossed his arms and leaned against the wall beside her.

Elise wished there was something she could say to make the weight of his stare lighter. The last thing she ever wanted to do was hurt him, but every word out of her mouth made the situation worse.

"I'm so sorry. But as soon as I did it, I knew it wasn't you and tried to get away," Elise offered, knowing it was a weak argument after the fact. When he didn't reply, her voice cracked as she pleaded for him to say something. His disappointed silence always broke her more than words ever would. Pretending to pick some lint off her dress, she continued. "He's expecting to get back on the council, and

165

there's definitely something else going on, but I couldn't figure it out before he disappeared."

"What a shame."

Elise rolled her eyes as she stepped away from the wall to face him. "It was an accident, and I said I was sorry! I would *never* cheat on you. Now, I'm going to find out what he's up to and stop it before we try using the diary. You can stay here and pout if you like." As she made to walk away, Elise's empowerment was cut short as Gavin took her hand. In an instant, she was flush against him, pinned between his body and the wall.

"Careful," he warned, gazing at her mouth. "I'm not the same guy I used to be."

Elise's breath quickened as his hands wrapped around her waist. Although impossible, Gavin appeared taller as he towered over her. The heat of his body created its own sense of danger that concentrated itself in Elise's stomach. The power he had over her body was electric, plain, and simple. He tilted his forehead down to meet hers.

"I definitely messed up," Gavin whispered.

It was Elise's turn to be confused. *How did* he *mess up?* He turned to replace his mask as a drunken group of people passed by the alley.

Elise pulled him into a hug. Caressing his back, she felt Gavin relax against her until the two silently swayed to the distant music. She didn't know how long they held one another, but when he made to speak again, Elise placed a finger over his lips and kissed him.

Easing back, Elise felt rather than witnessed his eyes roam across every inch of her trembling body. Feeling naked beneath his gaze, she secretly longed for Gavin's hands to follow the same path. The familiar trail of goosebumps lined Elise's arms. What frightened—no, *excited*—her most was not knowing what he would do next. A lump formed in her throat as she accepted that her childish crush was over. She knew what he said was true. Gavin wasn't the same boy now, but a man. Something happened when he was taken from her, and now she hardly recognized him at times. . .or his touch. Yet, she craved more.

"If you don't know what you do to me, then I've definitely messed up," said Gavin.

Before she could respond, Gavin cut her off with a searing kiss. It was as if her thoughts were washed away by a storm. Elise buried a hand in his hair, but he quickly gripped her wrist. She gasped when both of her arms were pressed up against the wall as his lips began their journey down her neck.

"Are you still confused about who can make you feel like this?"

His breath was hot against Elise's collarbone.

Clutching a handful of her skirt, he paused until she managed to nod her head. Satisfied with the silent invitation, Gavin lifted Elise's gown enough to hoist her legs around his waist and swallowed her gasp in another kiss.

Elise's arms wrapped around his neck to support herself as she eagerly found his mouth again and deepened the kiss. It lasted another moment or two before he pulled away.

"You drive me crazy," he purred into her ear. "Do you know that?"

Her legs quivered as she hung onto his every word.

"All those nights we were separated, this. . .*this* is all I could think about. D-did you think of me?"

"Yes," she panted.

"And no one else?" He paused for her answer, making Elise whine with need until she met his eyes.

"Only you. I promise," she gushed against his soft experienced lips. She craved his kiss like oxygen and was rewarded when his tongue met hers.

"Good," he said, "because if I'm going to keep risking my life for you, you better not confuse me for someone else. Got it?"

Shuddering, Elise tilted her head back, this time giving him easier access to place kisses down her throat. Her thighs tightened around him as she used her heels to bring Gavin closer. The cold brick wall scraped against her exposed back, but there was no way she was going to make him stop now. Elise never knew love could be like this. Gavin somehow managed to freeze and scorch her skin all at once.

Each time she thought her breathing was returning to normal, he found a new place to touch that stole it again.

"I have to know you want this," he said. "That you want only *me*. Do you?"

Maybe it was the menacing edge in his voice. Perhaps it was the masks or the distant music and risk of being caught. Whatever the reason, Elise was absolutely consumed by her love for Gavin. Never in her life had she felt this way about anyone. Her desire for him was insatiable. How could *one* person simultaneously make her so elated yet frustrated? It made no sense, but she was determined to chase it until the end. She wondered if Gavin truly comprehended what he meant to her. If not, she feared he never would.

A layer of sweat broke out across her body, making her shiver wherever his breath touched. She softly raked her nails across his own heated skin and managed to choke out a response. "O-only you. There's only you. I only want *you*."

Elise heard the piercing, shrill calls of Mrs. Archer nearby in the square. Next came Talia's voice before her mother continued fussing.

"Have you seen Gavin or Elise? They're going to miss Gwen's performance. Help me find them!"

Gavin's hold on Elise faltered and she felt herself slip down as he sucked in a sharp breath. Gripping the fabric of his coat, Elise lowered her feet to the ground before they parted. Gavin muttered something indiscernible under his breath and slammed his fist against the wall while Elise adjusted her gown with unhinged frustration.

When their breathing and tempers calmed, she searched his equally aggravated eyes for the hundredth time. Would there ever come a day where she didn't find herself hypnotized in their depths? Tracing the edge of Gavin's mask, Elise moved her fingertips to his lips again before caressing the side of his face. As eager as she was to satisfy his body, Elise knew it was more important to soothe Gavin's mind and heart.

"One day we won't be interrupted. . .Again, there's no one else I think about." Elise rested a hand against Gavin's chest until his breathing evened out. "For the last two years, I've only wanted you. I convinced myself before all this that you'd never know who I was. There's still a part of me expecting to wake up. I'm really sorry for everything that's happened, but I'm in love with *you*," she whispered, desperate to hear it back. It didn't matter he had said it before. She needed to hear it *now*.

Gavin regarded her in silence before adjusting her mask with a playful smirk. Elise wondered if he stalled as long as he did to purposely unnerve her. He already knew how flustered she was.

"Okay, you can say it back now!" Elise pushed him until he stumbled back with a laugh. She couldn't stop a chuckle from escaping her own lips. Digging a heel into the ground, she crossed her arms with a playful pout. "You're enjoying this. Aren't you?"

"Only a lot." He shrugged before interlocking his hands with Elise's. His expression grew serious once more as he leaned down to kiss her. "I love you, too. You're forgiven."

Lifting Gavin's hand to her mouth, Elise kissed his knuckles before the two walked back into the square.

The royal family was seated once again, including Joranna. Everyone faced the Master of Ceremonies, but it wasn't until they got closer that Elise heard him introducing Gwen's group. A movement out of the corner of her eye caught Elise's attention before she noticed Darcie and Mitch waving them both over behind the dais.

"You guys good?" Mitch whispered as they approached.

"I'd say they are." Darcie chuckled as she fixed a loose strand of Elise's hair. A nearby lantern illuminated a bejeweled bracelet dangling from her wrist.

"Is that new?" Elise asked with a knowing smile.

Darcie blushed, smiling at Mitch over her shoulder. "I told him not to, but he caught me looking at it and used his coins."

Elise suppressed a chuckle when Mitch tried hiding a red mark with his collar. "I'd say you thanked him enough. Looks like we weren't the only ones who needed a minute."

Both girls giggled as Gavin nodded in approval.

"Have we missed anything?" Elise asked once she composed herself again.

"Your family's not saying much. Especially Joranna. Gwen should be coming out, though." As soon as the words left Mitch's mouth, the abrupt bang of a drum and crash of cymbals cut through the crowd's chatter.

They craned their necks in time to see two lines of masked, scantily clad women approach the dance floor amidst lewd whistling and calls from the surrounding audience.

Though their identities were hidden, Elise recognized her aunt's infamous red updo and loose twisted tendrils. Oddly enough, Elise noticed Gwen was the only one wearing gold bands around her upper arms.

Ignoring the carousing onlookers, Gwen led the second line forward before pausing in a practiced pose to await the music. Gwen's glassy eyes, coupled with a lackadaisical posture spoke volumes until a fellow dancer snapped her fingers. Gwen straightened her posture before blowing out a slow breath as the first lone whining note left a violin.

"She needs to watch herself," said a voice behind Elise, causing her and the others to jump until they saw Talia standing behind them with Mrs. Archer. The older woman chastised them for worrying her sick about their whereabouts before rambling on that at least they made it in time for the dance. Talia apologized on behalf of her mother with a hearty chuckle before turning their attentions back to the dancers. "As I was saying, this is the opportunity of a lifetime, not to mention good money, and she's going to throw it all away! I would've been such a better choice." Talia clicked her tongue, shaking her head as she continued critiquing Gwen's performance. "Why didn't they stick her in the back?"

"She'll do fine, Love. Just watch," Mrs. Archer said.

Elise had a suspicion Gwen's selection had everything to do with her beauty, which was certainly a sight to behold. Not only was she the only red-haired woman amongst the dancers, but her fair complexion and long limbs made her stand out. It was even more impressive since each of the women wore the same crisscrossed halter top with dangling beads and exposed midriffs. Though their skirts swept across the floor, the high-cut slits and sheer fabric left little to the imagination. Elise rolled her eyes. *A man designed these costumes.*

As she studied her aunt's provocative movements, Elise couldn't help but be proud of Haighdlen's future queen. If put into Gwen's position, Elise would have skipped the whole event altogether. She smiled to herself as she remembered the time Gavin experienced the same scenario when he didn't initially show up to Derek and Joranna's engagement ball, leaving Elise alone on the dance floor. Given all that had happened since then, it felt a lifetime ago.

The sound of laughter broke her reminiscing as she turned to see Charles and Richard clinking their glasses together from a few feet away. Elise took care to stay out of their sight but inched as close as she could without drawing attention from the guards. It was almost impossible to hear over the music, but fortunately for Elise, there were moments when the drums weren't pounding in her ears.

"I imagine the princess would have enjoyed the festival," Charles muttered into his cup before taking a long sip.

Richard sighed. "Think not of her, Charles. There's plenty of beauty in front of you. Besides, I will not have my sister's *situation* paraded around as if we condone it. The funeral was enough exposure for her."

Elise fumed. *Was he always this hateful or did something change after we meddled?* A small, yet spiteful part of her considered *not* setting him up with Gwen. Her aunt deserved better than this pompous, unsupportive hypocrite. *Why is it okay for* him *to end up with someone from the town but Charles can't be with Mom? Mom's shut away like a criminal while he parties and flirts with anyone he chooses. Is being queen worth putting up with a man like that?*

She knew better than to jump to conclusions, since there were times when even Derek came across in a bad light despite good intentions. Deep down, she knew Richard was only looking out for Ruby's well-being. . .but it didn't change the fact she wanted nothing more than to wring her uncle's neck.

"Don't do anything stupid," Gavin whispered in her ear, making Elise jump. She hadn't realized he followed her. "Just ignore them."

Elise was thankful when he squeezed her hand. It was difficult, but she was finally able to tune them out and focus on the performance again. The music swelled, and the slow steady rhythm of the hypnotic drum created a sensual beat as most of the dancers performed a series of choreographed steps. Elise hoped she was the only one to notice when Gwen fell out of sync two or three times behind the other ladies.

Elise could barely suppress a laugh at the sight of Darcie's glare. Not that Elise could blame her. Mitch was practically drooling. Gavin would be stupid not to join him. Despite Gwen's reluctance, Elise couldn't argue how talented she and *all* of the dancers were.

As the song neared its climax, the performers pulled matching sheer scarves from their tops and completed a series of synchronized twirls.

"What I wouldn't give to have a man look at *me* like that someday," Talia said with a dream-like sigh.

Puzzled, Elise followed the young woman's line of vision to the royal family. Ian was mesmerized, of course, but it was Richard who looked the most invested.

"Who is *that*?" he inquired with a nod. "The red-haired woman in front." He peered over the brim of his glass as he took a long sip. Sure enough, his feral, brooding stare followed Gwen's every move across the floor before he summoned the Master of Ceremonies to the dais to inquire about her.

"That is Ms. Gwendolyn Archer, Your Highness. Her father was a prominent farmer before his scandalous arrest. This is her first performance, I understand."

"It appears *you* are quite captivated," Charles told Richard with a drunken smirk as the music ended. "Not that I blame you. She is exquisite."

Elise looked between both men and the dancers as Gwen led the other ladies away from the dance floor amidst whistles and applause.

Gwen was soon joined by Mrs. Archer, who had slipped away from Elise's group and pushed through the crowd.

Charles chuckled at his friend's darkened, possessive stare. "Do you see something you like, Sire? Shall I summon her to your chamber tonight?"

I doubt she goes for that, but at least he's interested! We need to keep his attention on her no matter what if they're going to fall in love.

Elise stared at her uncle's face, hoping maybe her magic would extend to him. Although details of Richard and Gwen's original meeting were still unknown to her, a little magic couldn't hurt to push him along since it was clear he liked her. *It's not meddling if it was meant to be.* At least that's what she told herself to justify her actions. Crouching lower to avoid being seen, she focused on Richard's tense expression.

Ask her to dance. Talk to her. Charm her. Come on, ask her. All he needed to do was ask Gwen to dance and then they would fall madly in love. Their engagement would work itself out and they could convince Richard to help them get to Lockesbarrow. He wouldn't be mad at them being there once he knew they were friends with Gwen. Everything would be perfect. It was simple. *Ask her to dance.*

Richard stood. *Yes, good. Keep going. Talk to her. Sweep her off her feet.* Yet, as he took a step forward, Charles rested his hand on the prince's shoulder.

"Are you so eager?" Charles' knowing smile widened. "You'll be devoured by the mob of eligible maidens if you go out there unattended. Allow me to go or send one of the servants. Surely, there could be no objections from a farmer's daughter."

Richard shook his head as if to clear thoughts that were not his own and nodded. "You are right, friend. Have her brought to me." The prince called for his glass to be refilled before taking his seat once again.

This ought to go well. Elise held her breath as the same footman trotted down towards where Gwen and her mother were talking. *I've got to get down there.* She motioned for Gavin, Darcie, and Mitch to follow closely behind her, careful to avoid Richard's line of vision. Glancing back over her shoulder, Elise noticed only the prince and Charles remained in their seats. Joranna, Sarah, and Ian were nowhere to be found.

Hoping the others could keep up, Elise weaved in and out of the bustling crowd. She kept a close watch on the footman ahead of her since numerous couples were approaching the dance floor after the musicians began another set. The group of friends were detained at least twice by clusters of people moving in the opposite direction, not to mention the double take Elise did upon seeing Ian flirting with not one, but two dancer girls beside Derek's portrait. By the time Elise got close enough to Gwen and the footman, Richard's invitation had already been extended.

"This is a tremendous honor, Dearest," Mrs. Archer whispered to her eldest. "To be singled out by the Crown Prince himself? Many a girl has dreamed of such an invitation."

"Mama, you cannot be serious," Gwen replied, locking eyes with Richard. She swallowed convulsively. "Our situation is not so dire that we need to move this way to advance our status. My reputation—"

"Will only be questioned if you refuse," warned her mother. "Seldom does a woman in your position deny a future king."

As tempting as it was to push the timeline along, Elise did not even dare use her magic on Gwen for a decision. This was too personal, and her future aunt had the right to choose for herself without any interference.

Elise watched as Gwen checked her surroundings before continuing in a lower voice. "Mama, what if I were to become with child? His Majesty could already have any number of illegitimate heirs running around this festival he does not acknowledge. Do you honestly encourage me to satisfy this sinful invitation?"

"Of course not!" Mrs. Archer hissed. "But what if more could come of it? If he only got to know you—"

"Forgive me, Mama, but it's out of the question," Gwen said, meeting Richard's eyes again over the crowd. "I doubt he took the time to know those who previously accepted his advances." She turned her attention to the footman. "Please thank the prince for his offer, but I must decline."

The two women waited for him to leave before speaking again.

"You are right." Mrs. Archer sighed. "Forgive me. I just fear for you and your sister since your father's arrest. I'm not getting any younger, you know. I only want you two taken care of."

Gwen leaned forward to hug her mother. "I promise I will always care for you two. We will be fine, but there must be a different way than being used and cast aside by the prince." Glancing back towards the dance floor, she waved her sister over. "But it is getting late. I think you should take Talia home before she gets into any mischief of her own."

Mrs. Archer's reply was lost amidst the applause that followed the end of another song, but it appeared she took her daughter's advice as she waited for her youngest to approach.

However, Elise was too preoccupied watching the footman return to the dais. She held her breath as the servant leaned down to whisper the news to Richard.

"Do you think he'll be mad?" Darcie whispered, making Elise jump.

I forgot they were following me. Elise watched her uncle's expression darken before he stood up. "I'd say so."

Richard made his way off the dais. Except for a momentary delay created by a swarm of eager, eligible ladies, he never took his eyes off Gwen, who had already left her mother to browse the food carts.

"Something tells me he's not used to hearing the word *no*," Mitch muttered with a low whistle.

"Should we distract him?" Darcie offered. "Or get Gwen out of there?"

Elise's breath hitched again when Richard reached Gwen. "Too late," she choked out.

"Gwen's pretty tough," said Gavin. "I think she'll be able to handle him."

Let's hope so.

Darcie clicked her tongue. "Look at how he's looking at her. It's not Gwen's fault the costume is so revealing." She shook her head. "I can't *stand* his arrogance. If it wouldn't get her arrested, I'd tell her to slap him across the face. Am I right, Elise? Elise?"

It took two more attempts from Darcie for Elise to hear her name. She was too invested in studying her uncle's primal expression as he conversed with Gwen. Throwing Darcie an apologetic smile, Elise inched closer to the whispering couple. *At least I have a mask to help. If I'm not careful, they're going to see me, but I have to know what's happening!*

Elise held up a hand to keep her friends at a distance before sliding behind an adjacent cart. It was a tight, awkward fit, but as soon as she picked up Richard's deep voice complimenting Gwen's dance, Elise stilled with her eyes closed. It wasn't until Gwen thanked him that the prince continued.

"I will not insult you by pretending you did not understand the meaning behind my invitation." Richard paused, and though she couldn't see the two, Elise imagined Gwen nodded. "Yet you declined?"

"I did, Your Highness." Gwen's voice was steady, much more confident than Elise could ever hope to achieve if put in the same situation.

"Do you not think I deserve an explanation? Any other woman here would accept without question."

Elise chanced a peek around the curtain shielding her from view. She had to admit, despite her aunt's objections, the two shared unmistakable chemistry with one another. She could cut the fiery tension with a knife, yet Gwen squared her shoulders with a defiant chin.

"I certainly meant no offense, Your Majesty," Gwen said with a brief curtsy, "though it sounds like it will be the only time. You will no doubt succeed with your next choice, and *if* your men are unable to advise you, I would be happy to make a few suggestions."

"Do you deny me on purpose?" Richard took a slow step forward, but Gwen stayed put. "Does it excite you to make men chase you?" He brushed the back of his knuckles down the length of her arm. "I detect you are well worth the pursuit, so I will ask again."

Gwen's gaze followed the same hand as he lifted a finger to trail a path from her lips to the center of her exposed cleavage.

"I can guarantee you the most *erotic* pleasures." His finger continued down the center of Gwen's body before pausing at the waistband of her skirt. "A night to fulfill your darkest fantasies. The way you tremble at my touch, for example, betrays your aching need to be satisfied. You will not be disappointed."

This time, Gwen stepped back from his touch. Although her breaths came quicker, she found the courage to meet his eyes. "*That* is where you are mistaken, Majesty. I seek to satisfy my heart first, not to mention have a man's affection continue longer than a single night. Since I am convinced you can provide me neither, I will repeat my offer to point out a replacement. If not, then I bid you goodnight." With another curtsy, she turned on her heel and proceeded to disappear into the crowd, leaving a rather disgruntled Richard to stomp his way back to the royal dais in silence.

Elise remained in place a few more minutes to insure she would not be spotted before finding her friends.

"How did it go?" Darcie asked first.

"We've got work to do," said Elise with a sigh. "Honestly, I'm frustrated at what's going on, but I'm also proud of her for sticking up for herself. He definitely didn't like that."

"Should we go find Gwen and ask her about the fairy magic then?" Gavin offered. "Maybe she and Richard can get together some other time."

Elise reluctantly nodded before furrowing her brows as the Master of Ceremonies was summoned back to Richard. "What's he up to now?" she asked.

Before Elise and her friends could get closer, the Master of Ceremonies raised his hand to demand everyone's attention and request the royal family take their seats.

"It is my honor and privilege to continue the evening's celebration with an exciting announcement concerning His Majesty, Prince Richard."

The restless, carousing crowd pushed forward, eagerly prattling away about the upcoming declaration. While most focused on Richard, who straightened in his chair, Elise studied Joranna, who appeared as confused as everyone else.

"I must say how thrilled I was upon receiving the prince's letter yesterday," continued the Master of Ceremonies, pulling on his jacket fondly, "that I have scarcely rested in anticipation. Could we have our lovely songbird join us on the dais please?"

Elise gritted her teeth as the drunken crowd blocked the view. She caught a brief glimpse of the singer from earlier in the evening as she made her way up to the dais with the help of the footman.

What is going on? Why is she up there?

Elise's blood froze when Richard stood to greet the woman with a kiss on her hand. She immediately turned around to see if Gwen was watching. Elise found her aunt standing by the jewelry cart with crossed arms and a wary expression towards the beautiful swan-like stranger beside Richard.

"This lovely young nightingale, who blessed us with an angelic performance, is none other than the one who has captured our own prince's affections!"

What? But he was just trying to get Gwen into bed with him. Is this who he was talking about when he mentioned getting married? Who is she?

There was a collective gasp amongst the group before whispering and gossip started to radiate throughout the onlookers.

Richard intertwined his fingers with the lady's before facing the town.

The Master of Ceremonies took a glass of champagne off a nearby tray. "Let us toast to the future king and his future queen, Iris Brahm!"

CHAPTER 18

"Did he say *Brahm*?" Elise shrieked. "As in Brahm, the spy?"

"They have to be related." Mitch's face twisted in disgust. "Does he have a daughter? What woman would want to—"

"I doubt *he* has a daughter," Gavin said, "but his sister, Ingrid, does." Gavin described one of his encounters with Rona when Brahm mentioned Ingrid and her daughter. "There were arrangements after they escaped prison for Brahm's sister and niece to go back to Lockesbarrow."

"Then that has to be her," said Elise. "Ingrid kept her family name, too, it sounds like." She released a heavy sigh, surprised that a rush of anxiety did not follow. This sort of news would normally have sent her spiraling, but she was pleased with her ability to remain calm. "We'll have to add this to the list of messes to clean up on the timeline."

"But there's no way Joranna's going to accept this," Darcie argued. "Look at her trying to hold it together for the crowd. She's furious!"

Sure enough, Joranna wore a trained, plastered smile as she greeted the young songstress.

"I thank you," Richard announced, holding up a hand for the town to quiet down. "My beloved Iris and I are thrilled to be able to share this wonderful news." There was a hushed set of whispers amongst the crowd. "I sense your uncertainty, but I can assure you that such an alliance will only benefit Haighdlen."

"An alliance with who?" called a man standing ahead of Elise. "Is she Lockesbarrian?"

The gossip increased as many began shouting disgraceful objections towards the young woman. The remaining outbursts accused the prince of everything ranging from insanity to treason.

"How else do you explain such a slimy union? What exactly is her connection to our former Captain of the Guard?" called another, igniting a passionate uproar until the guards advanced on the townspeople.

Richard looked to his mother, but Joranna offered no response. In fact, Elise wondered if the queen was having the same thoughts. The prince locked his jaw and silenced the men with threats of imprisonment. "I will not hear of anyone besmirching my betrothed's honor or ruining our engagement. It is our wish to avoid war, and I am certain such an alliance will smooth any further entanglements with Lockesbarrow."

Elise glared at her uncle, uncomfortable with Iris's silence. *He's had this planned, so what was he doing chasing Gwen? We can't trust him. He could be working for Rona.*

"Let us celebrate. It is why we are here. I also wish to take advantage of our gathering to announce we are to wed in two days, prior to the coronation where we will *both* be crowned. Preparations have been underway for quite some time. That is all. Congratulations on yet another productive harvest," Richard said before leading Iris away amongst an explosive outcry from the crowd.

Two days? Why so soon? That's crazy! It doesn't make any sense.

"Did you sign our death warrants along with your marriage contract?" a third man accused.

The Master of Ceremonies tried to intervene, but he was drowned out by the distressed partygoers.

"Let's get out of here!" Mitch shouted. "This is going to get ugly."

"Wait, look over there!" cried Elise, frantically pointing to the side of the dais. "There's Vaughn! He's still here."

Richard and Iris stepped down to greet him, further increasing Elise's suspicions about her uncle's motives.

"I don't like this, guys," said Darcie as Vaughn nodded and bowed before the couple walked out of sight. "Something dirty is going on."

"Vaughn is definitely orchestrating everything," replied Gavin. "But he isn't the one we need to be worried about." Checking over his shoulder, he led the others away to a more secluded area. "Rona has a lock of Vaughn's hair. Whenever she wants to spy, or see what he sees, she uses it to create a connection with him," he reminded them.

"Which causes his headaches, right?" Mitch asked.

Gavin nodded.

"Then there's no doubt she's sitting back watching her little puppet manipulate Richard into practically handing the kingdom over," said Darcie with a sneer.

"While making it look like a peace treaty." Elise sighed. "There won't be a need to wait years to take over the kingdom like before. She'll be able to do it now if we don't stop this."

"Mitch is right, though." Gavin scanned the crowd before ushering them forward. "We need to get out of here."

Spotting Gwen, Elise called out multiple times, but the other woman continued without stopping. *Can she really not hear me?*

"Should we be yelling her name if we're trying to lie low?" Mitch asked.

I guess he has a point.

Elise felt heat rush to her cheeks but pressed on. "We need to follow her. She's our only hope to get magic and use the diary."

She checked over her shoulder once more in time to see the royal family being ushered to their carriages while the Master of Ceremonies worked to ease the crowd by calling for more music.

Before Elise and her friends could make their way through the sea of restless onlookers, a familiar voice called out to them. She froze when Charles walked into view. Feeling her heartbeat quicken, Elise searched for anyone else in her family who may have followed him. *What is he doing here? How did he see us?*

"Do not be alarmed," he began, "I have not shared your attendance this evening with His Majesty."

Elise leaned away from the offensive scent of ale on his breath. *How drunk is this guy?*

"Were you able to deliver the letter?" Charles hesitated, failing to suppress a smile when Elise nodded. "Good. Thank you. Please tell her I miss her, will you?"

The five of them stood in an awkward silence another moment or two before Elise took advantage of his inebriated state.

"Charles?" She waited for his eyes to focus on her. *Here goes nothing.* "Why was Vau—Sir Rodrick here tonight?"

Tensing his shoulders, Charles' features darkened at the mention of Vaughn's fake name. "It was not by my influence, I can assure you. In fact, it would seem my advice has gone *unnoticed* as of late. It would not be surprising if I were soon dismissed altogether."

"Why is that?" Elise asked.

"It is no matter. Forget I spoke of it."

Elise clenched her teeth as she focused on his face. Willing her magical energy forward, she proceeded to ask again. "*Why* is Sir Rodrick here?"

Tell us. Now.

Charles furrowed his brows as he leaned against the nearest cart for support. "There was. . .a meeting."

"What kind of meeting?" Darcie asked.

"Who was there?" Gavin pressed.

Charles shook his head with a shrug. "I do not know."

What else do you know? What do *you remember?*

"Richard. . .His Majesty, forgive me. He and I stayed up late one evening about a fortnight ago," Charles mumbled. "We both had incredibly too much to drink, but instead of going to bed, he called a meeting."

"A council meeting?" Mitch shared a confused glance with Gavin. "In the middle of the night? Does the prince even remember doing that?"

"It is difficult to say," said Charles before belching. "Forgive me. What was the question?"

"Well, weren't *you* there? What did he say?" Elise hissed. She bit the inside of her cheek to avoid screaming and grabbing his collar. His intoxication made this even more difficult.

"I. . .I was not invited."

What? But he just said it was a council meeting.

"But you're part of the council," Darcie said, echoing Elise's thoughts. "Why weren't you invited?"

Charles looked at all of them before clearing his throat. "I never said it was a council meeting, yet even then I doubt he would have had me join. I am not exactly in good standing with His Majesty."

Elise thought she would explode when Charles grew silent again. *Then what? Keep going!*

"Elise, maybe we should talk to him later," Gavin suggested.

"No!" Elise snapped.

"But he can barely stand," he continued. "He probably doesn't know anything."

"He does," Elise said, glaring at the royal advisor. "He's just not trying hard enough. Why else would he have risked coming to talk to us?"

"He already said," Mitch replied. "He asked if we got the letter to Ruby. That's it. Let him go already."

Elise felt that there *was* something else. She could not put her finger on it, but Charles was hiding something. Perhaps he did not want to keep hiding it, and that is why he followed them. She pondered his motives during another stretch of awkward silence.

"Are you going to ask him about Vaughn?" Darcie whispered.

"Not yet," said Elise, gauging Charles' ability to follow the conversation. "But his guard's down. This is the only time we're going to find out anything he might know. Charles?"

"He looks like he's going to be sick any minute," Mitch muttered to Gavin. "You better ask him quick, Elise."

Elise contemplated her list of questions before proceeding to wear Charles' resolve down further.

"Why did you come up to talk to us?" she asked.

"It. . .it is imperative the princess read my letter," he said.

Elise waited to see if he would continue on his own. When he did not, she pushed forward more energy as she stared deeply into his broken eyes. It took a moment of studying his countenance before Elise relaxed her shoulders and changed strategies. Unclenching her teeth with a deep breath, she could see him for the lost, lovesick man he truly was. Demanding anything from him would be useless. This would take a softer approach. *You can tell us. It's okay. We only want to help.*

"She received your letter," Elise whispered slowly. "Ruby is fine, but how is Richard?"

She flattened her lips into a tight line. Feeling her heart swell, Elise willed the rest of her resolve to convince his mind. *What do you really want to tell us?*

Charles opened his mouth, but no words came out.

Tell us.

"I fear. . .I fear he is in danger," Charles choked out. His face twisted in agony as if the words were spoken against his will. He wiped his face with the back of his hand before making eye contact with them again. "I warned him. I warned him not to make this announcement. I advised him to reconsider the decision." Charles grimaced as if his confession made him feel nauseas. "I told him as a friend that it would only bring about rioting and protests, or worse, attempts on his life!"

"And he wouldn't listen to you," Darcie said, gazing at Charles as if he were a wounded puppy in need of rescuing.

"Did that Rodrick guy put him up to this?" Gavin asked. "Was he in the meeting?"

Charles nodded before belching again. He swayed a moment before Mitch propped him up.

"But if he's so mad at you, why were you allowed to sit with him tonight?" Elise asked.

"To keep up appearances," Charles slurred. "He did not want the princess to come, but anyone else would have looked more suspicious."

Before Elise could ask any more questions, Charles cut her off with a piercing stare that broke her heart into a thousand pieces. *What is it? Tell me. What do you want from me?*

"Please," he whispered.

Please what?

"Please save him," Charles managed to choke out. "Please save the prince. He is not himself. That man is not my friend. I do not know what has come over him, nor how to stop him, but something occurred in that meeting that forever changed his course of action."

Darcie glanced over her shoulder at Elise. "I'll give you one guess."

"Do you think Vaughn cursed Richard? Or hypnotized him somehow?" Elise asked. "Could he be doing all of this without knowing it?"

"The prince is in his right mind. That much is certain," Charles said. "But he is closing himself off from his family, which is not like him. I suspect it to be a threat or ultimatum."

"Like what?" Elise asked.

"I know not," Charles said, "but if anyone can find out, it is you four."

"Well, let's just tack that onto our to do list," Mitch groaned. "It's not like we're strapped down with anything else."

"Please," Charles said, "Do not mention we have spoken, for I fear of who to trust any longer, but I will do what I must to protect my friend. . .and the princess."

Elise took her focus away from his face, removing any pull she still held on him. *He's exhausted.*

Charles blinked a few times as if waking from a dream before he looked at all four of them with a peculiar expression. "Have you seen my drink?"

"I think you've had enough," Gavin said before he and Mitch each took one of Charles arms to guide him towards the carriages. Keeping a distance, they watched and waited for Charles to stumble his way back to the dais before a guard helped him into a carriage.

"Once he sleeps that off, I doubt we get that kind of confession again," Darcie said. "What do you think happened in that meeting?"

Elise shook her head, scanning the crowd until she spotted Gwen tasting an assortment of delicate bite-sized cakes. "I don't know, but I think it's time to get us some fairy magic."

Waiting for a crowd of people to walk past, the friends made their way over to the dessert cart before standing around Gwen.

She looked warily at them, with a mouthful of cake, before shaking her head. Only when she swallowed did she walk away. "Whatever it is, the answer is no."

They caught up to Gwen at the end of the street. After the fourth or fifth time Elise called her name, Gwen finally turned to face them.

"No more, please," she begged, holding out a hand until they stopped approaching her. "I have been humiliated enough for one night."

Elise understood her future aunt's frustration. Not only was she not comfortable in her clothing, but she also turned down the offer to spend the night with Richard. Despite Gwen's wishes, Elise and the others could not afford to waste any time. Throwing caution to the wind, Elise took a direct approach.

"I'm sorry about how things turned out tonight," Elise began, taking Gwen's hand to lead her away from the crowd, "but there are bigger things happening right now. Can you get us some fairy magic?"

Gwen's mouth opened, as if she were already ready to argue or toss out a witty response, but Elise's unexpected question made her pause. Her expressions fluctuated so quickly that Elise had difficulty sensing what Gwen's reaction might be.

"Why on Earth—"

"We know you helped the princess all those times," Elise blurted out. "And I have magic, but not enough for what we need to do."

Gwen collected herself before steadying her voice. "And what might that be?"

The teenagers took turns filling Gwen in on everything that had happened they deemed safe to share.

"And fairy magic is the only way we can make it to Lockesbarrow," Elise finished. She knew the other woman was not entirely convinced given the tightness of her shoulders and guarded nature.

"I wish I could help you, but—"

"*Please.*" Elise's voice broke as she desperately tried to wield her magic again, but it was weakened from forcing Charles to confess only moments earlier.

"Come on, Elise," Gavin whispered, gently pulling Elise away. "We can try by ourselves in the morning when we have daylight."

Elise reluctantly followed her friends away, suddenly too tired to put up a fight. *Gavin's right. We're not getting anywhere here.*

Mitch clicked his tongue. "As long as we don't run into that Horanis guy again, I'm good."

I agree.

"Did you say Horanis?" came Gwen's voice from behind them. Her entire body froze as if she would be enveloped in pain should she move. "As in, the King of the Fairies?"

"You know him, too?" Though they were isolated, Mitch scanned the area for any bystanders. Fortunately, they were well out of earshot of anyone else.

The muscles within Gwen's neck quivered before her unfocused gaze met theirs. "I. . .I *belong* to him."

CHAPTER 19

Elise parted her lips but made no sound. Silenced by a strangling numbness that managed to seep down to her fingertips, she studied Gwen as if meeting the other woman for the first time. An odd, aching sensation tugged at Elise's heart. All this time, she felt proud of the progress being made regarding growing closer to her family. Yet, as she stared into Gwen's glassy, fearful eyes, it was as if facing a stranger again.

The urgency of their escape halted as they processed the confession.

Looking at Elise, Mitch patted his vest and released a long, deep whistle. "I take it *that* didn't make it into your grandmother's diary."

Elise took a tentative step forward and felt relieved when Gwen did not move away.

Things just got way more complicated. At least ten questions popped into Elise's mind—all vying to be answered—yet in the end, she decided on one. "Does anyone else know?"

Gwen shook her head.

Let's keep it that way.

The same rational approach did not apply to Darcie, who—after finding her own voice—paced around Gavin, Mitch, and Elise. "But when? And how does *nobody* else know? Not even your mom or Talia? How exactly *does* King Horanis own you? What does that mean? Do you know where to find him? Is he close by right now?"

"Darcie, breathe." Mitch planted both of his hands on Darcie's shoulders to calm her. "Relax, will you? This is probably why she hasn't told anybody."

"Indeed," Gwen replied. "If *you* are in hysterics, imagine how my own family would receive the news."

Gavin joined Elise's side. "How does that work? I mean, how can a *fairy* own you?"

Grabbing a lantern from the nearest vacant cart, Gwen nodded towards the forest. "I suppose there is no use trying to deny anything, but we should move somewhere more private. Come this way."

"But it's the middle of the night!" Darcie objected when Gwen pointed towards the vast wall of trees ahead of them. "We can't risk getting lost out there again."

"You will not get lost," Gwen assured them.

"That's what *you* think," said Mitch. "We have a natural skill for getting ourselves in trouble. Especially in the forest."

"And the one time we *did* have a guide, he was purposefully leading us the wrong way," Elise added, reliving the moment they found out Vaughn was sent to prolong their journey to find Gavin.

Gwen dropped her shoulders and smiled. The type of patient smile one might give a small child. "This time will be different," she promised. "This time you have *me*."

The confidence with which Gwen spoke should have reassured Elise, but it only made her more hesitant to reenter the forest at this hour without protection.

Nevertheless, Elise and the others reluctantly followed Gwen away from the festival. Within minutes of entering the forest, wandering down the winding path, the only visibility came from Gwen's lantern. The flickering light bounced along thick trunks and overlapping vines, creating fleeting shadows that only lit a few feet ahead.

Elise's paranoia ran rampant, tricking her into thinking she could see movement in the darkness. Even the breeze whistled in ways that sounded like someone whispering. A cold sweat formed along her brow, making Elise grab hold of Gavin's arm as she became acutely aware of Mitch's breathing behind her. The four took turns jumping at random animal calls, crackling leaves, and insects flying too close. The chirping of crickets and frog croaks were deafening in Elise's sensitive ears. Yet, Gwen never slowed or faltered as she led them forward.

"How far are you taking us?" Gavin asked. "Do we really need to go this far?"

"I guess we could look on the bright side," replied Mitch. "At least it's not raining."

Darcie made a strange squeaking noise. "Did you *really* just say that? That's like people saying things can't get any worse! I swear, Mitch, I'm going to kill you if it starts raining."

For a brief moment, it felt as if things were back to normal. Hearing Mitch and Darcie bicker playfully back and forth lightened the mood for a short period of time until it became too difficult to ignore how deep into the forest they truly were.

Okay, I think we're far enough from people. She can tell us now. . .why are we still walking? I can't see a thing.

Elise cried out as she tripped over an overgrown tree root, but Gavin caught her.

"Are you okay?" Darcie asked. "Maybe we should stop now. We're nowhere near the town."

"And something just crawled across my foot." Mitch whimpered. "Can you please tell us what we need to know so we can get going, Gwen?"

Gwen took a few more steps forward before wincing and turning abruptly to face them. The lantern she carried swung back and forth, creating a haunting effect as it lit their pale shadowed faces. Each of them had discarded their masks at different times along the path, and all but Gwen wore the same petrified expression.

"I do not need to remind you how dangerous King Horanis is," Gwen replied with a grimace. Staggering, she looked down at her arm before regaining her balance. "Are you sure you want to face him again?"

Is she okay?

"No!" Mitch cried. "We can talk to another fairy. Any other fairy. Call one of the small ones."

Why is he doing this now? We're all scared, but we need to get moving. There's no time to stand here and argue like little kids!

The teenagers began to overtalk one another as the argument heated.

"I understand if you would rather go back," Gwen replied.

"Uh. . . hello? Did you hear me?" Mitch asked. "*Something* crawled across *my* foot, and we're walking around in the *dark*. Why would we have followed you into this creepy forest to turn around and go home? Just get one of the small ones out here already."

When the disagreement continued, Gwen huffed before setting the lantern down by her feet. Her voice rang above the others. "I thought you were in a hurry."

"We are," said Elise, giving Mitch a pointed look to quit arguing. "How do you contact the fairies? We've always found them by luck."

Expecting Gwen to call out or gesture, Elise watched as the other woman reached for one of her armbands.

Gwen's lips tightened as she pulled against the snug fit, but as the accessory loosened, they could make out a mark on the inside of her upper arm. In the weak lighting, it looked nothing more than an oddly shaped bruise that had not completely healed, perhaps a birthmark, but as Gwen lifted the lantern again, it proved to be something else altogether. The tender flesh was blemished with a combination of blue, green, and yellow swirls woven together like a knotted rope.

"It's called a Fairy's Kiss," Gwen informed them. "And if I am caught being marked, I could be exiled from society."

"So, it's like a curse?" Gavin asked, sharing an anxious glance with Elise when Gwen nodded.

"But it's only a mark," Mitch pointed out. "What's the big deal? Especially when you can hide it like you do. Tell everyone it's a tattoo."

Gwen's trembling hands forced her to set the lantern down again with a solemn expression. "Being marked by a fairy allows me to communicate with them at will, but it is often associated with a loss of virtue. Horanis spared mine, but the town would never believe me if word got out."

Communicate at will? Loss of virtue? "So, that's how you were able to help the princess get fairy magic so easily," Elise replied.

Again, Gwen nodded. "The princess happened upon me speaking with Horanis one evening. The price of her silence was access to magic when she requested it."

Blackmail. Elise shook her head. *Yeah, that sounds like Mom.*

"Horanis found out and forbade me from giving her anymore. Not to mention the visit from Lord Fenton."

"*Charles* came to you?" Elise's breath hitched. Every inch of her body froze as if drenched in an ice bath. *I never knew about this.* Rendered speechless, she was thankful when Darcie inquired as to why Charles visited.

"When pressed, Princess Ruby disclosed everything to him before his brief dismissal from court. Lord Fenton tracked me down and urged me to stop helping her, but it was too late. The princess was already with child and restricted to the royal grounds. I suppose I was fortunate both protected my involvement from spreading any further. After my father's infamous arrest, I believe another scandal would have killed my poor mother. Not to mention tarnished Talia's reputation by association."

One detail plagued Elise's mind more than any other. "You said it's associated with a loss of virtue, and that he spared you. I'm glad he didn't force you into anything, but do you know why he did that?"

Gwen let out a hollow laugh. "It is so odd to be speaking of it after all this time." She paced back and forth, caressing the mark as she walked. Gwen did not meet their eyes as she began to finally tell her secret. "He said I was to remain pure for another but would not disclose a name. My purpose was to be much greater as I would play an important role in a secret prophecy."

The feeling of Gavin's hand grabbing hers was the only thing that thawed Elise's stiffness, allowing her to think clearly once more. She squeezed his hand back, remembering why they had sought out

Gwen in the first place. She darted her gaze to Mitch's vest where the current diary was still hidden.

"What kind of prophecy?" Darcie asked before Elise could find the words.

When the other woman spoke again, her voice sounded distant and dreamlike as she recited the message by heart.

"My lips shall mark you,
'til I see fit,
Retain thy virtue,
Shield this secret.

Come, lure those here,
Who first speak my name,
Reveal to them your kiss.

Though danger be near,
A coveted game,
Be crowned in forgotten bliss."

Watching Gwen come out of her reverie, Elise wondered how many nights the other woman must have mulled over the prophecy's meaning.

"So, Horanis knew we were coming?" Gavin asked. "Then why not tell us when we met him before?"

"It wasn't time I guess," Elise said.

"Yeah, he wanted us led here like bait." Mitch glared at Gwen as he spoke. "Did you know when you met us?"

Gwen took a long, deep breath but did not cower. Holding her chin up, she met his gaze. "Not at first, but over time, I grew suspicious of your secrecy and involvement with the royal family. It was not until tonight that I knew for certain." Gwen rolled the sheer fabric of her skirt between her fingers. Chewing on her bottom lip, she studied each of them in turn. "And now here you are, speaking the name I've held in my heart all this time, but is it enough? Can I be rid of this shameful curse? Can I stop lying to my family?"

Elise sensed her future aunt's uncertainty. The questions weren't directed at them, but she knew Gwen longed for the answers. "I promise we're going to fix all of this and help your family. Go ahead and call Horanis."

"Elise!" Mitch stepped between Gwen and Elise. "Are you crazy? He kidnapped Darcie! Why would you want to face him again?"

"We need strong fairy magic to travel," Elise argued back. "Why *not* go directly to the source?"

"No!" he ground out. "I can't go through that again."

"Mitch, I know he's scary, but—"

"I *won't* let him near her!"

The desperation in his voice tugged at Elise's heart as she met Darcie's gaze behind Mitch's towering figure. She did not want to risk any of their lives, but Gwen was their only ticket to getting fairy magic to find Rona and end all this. It was a risk they would have to take. "Mitch—"

"You're really okay letting your friend get taken again?" he challenged.

Wiping the sweat from her palms, Elise lowered her gaze before responding. "I understand why you don't—"

"No, you *don't* understand," Mitch hissed, taking an involuntary step back when Gavin moved between them. Yet, he continued. "I've been shot at, nearly drowned, and chased across this awful place more times than I care to remember. . .but nothing, *nothing*, has been as bad as thinking I lost Darcie. I would take all those other scares fifty times over if it meant I didn't have to relive believing she was dead. Do you want *her* marked, too?"

Elise opened her mouth, but no words came out.

A stifled, agonizing silence followed that was only broken when Gwen cleared her throat. "She may already bear the same mark if she was taken once."

"Yeah, well, believe me. She doesn't!" he snapped.

Even in the near pitch-black darkness, the flickering light was enough for Elise to catch Darcie's blush and embarrassed smile.

Mitch's expression softened as he sent her an apologetic smile.

Elise chuckled in spite of herself. *Looks like Gavin and I are not the only ones sneaking off.*

"She'll be okay, Mitch," Gavin promised, meeting his best friend's glassy stare.

Looking between Gavin and Elise, a muscle twitched in Mitch's cheek as his hands curled into fists. "You don't know that. Besides, Sage is the smallest fairy, and he was able to send us before. Why bother with Horanis?"

"Because I want to know what he knows," Elise said. "He's the only reason we found out about the timeline and the prophecy. He made sure Gwen led us to this exact spot. I think there's more he's not telling us."

Mitch jumped when Darcie touched his shoulder before turning him to face her. Cradling his face between her hands, Darcie searched his eyes. "This is the only way. It will be okay. *I'll* be okay. . ." She kissed him gently before resting their foreheads together. Pulling him into a tight embrace, Darcie met Elise's eyes over Mitch's shoulder with a reluctant nod.

Elise took a deep breath, squeezing Gavin's hand tighter to keep her own nerves calm before addressing Gwen. "Call him."

Gwen raised her arm high enough to kiss the discolored skin. As her lips made contact, the mark began to glow with a searing light that nearly blinded them. With a brilliant flash—eliciting a cry from the teenagers—all went dark, including the lantern by Gwen's feet.

Elise scanned the void in front of her as she tried to gauge what happened. If not for her hold on Gavin's arm, coupled with the aroma of smoke from the extinguished lantern, she would question their whereabouts. Yet, there was no sign of fairy lights anywhere.

"Are you sure you did it, right?" Gavin called out. When there was no response, he asked again. "Gwen? Gwen?"

"She's passed out!" Darcie shrieked.

Elise's heart thrashed so rapidly within her chest that she could hear it drumming in her ears. Releasing Gavin's arm, she staggered blindly towards Darcie's voice. "Are you sure?"

"Yes!" Darcie cried out. "I heard something hit the ground over here."

Elise crouched down, sensing rather than seeing where Darcie was.

"This is bad," Mitch said. "I told you not to call him. Now he's killed her."

Elise ignored him. She could not bear to consider he may be right. Crawling on her hands and knees, Elise rummaged through the fallen leaves and twigs until she felt Gwen's soft hair. Elise trailed her fingers until she felt the lines of her aunt's nose and chin. "Gwen?" she whispered, sliding both hands down to shake Gwen's shoulders. "Gwen, wake up."

"Let's get out of here," Mitch whispered.

"Mitch, we're not leaving her here!" Darcie hissed. There was a rustling sound as she slid her hands amongst the forest floor. "I can feel her breath on my hand."

"Then maybe it's like what they did to you," Elise said to her best friend. "So, she's not dead."

Mitch groaned. "Yeah, but there's no one here to wake her with a true love kiss. Do you think Richard's just going to appear out of nowhere and save the day?"

Elise wished there was such a chance of that happening, but the longer they sat, the more paranoid she grew of Horanis's tricks.

"I can carry her on my shoulders," Gavin offered. "Help me lift her. We can try again later."

"That will not be necessary," echoed a familiar, silky voice around them.

Elise leapt to her feet, eager to find the fairy king, only to be met with the same confusing darkness. Turning in slow circles, she tensed her muscles in anticipation of him possibly jumping out at them. "Does anybody see him?"

The other three replied they did not.

"How fickle you are," Horanis chuckled, before Elise heard his voice lower to a mere whisper that tickled her ear. "Can you not sense my presence?"

Elise gasped, turning in the direction of his voice. She was suddenly aware of her own breathing as a layer of sweat formed along both palms. Taking tentative steps backwards, she cried out when she bumped into something.

"Hey, relax. It's only me," Gavin said. "You okay?"

"He's *here*," she whimpered. "He-he's talking. . .can't you guys hear him?"

If they shook their heads, she could not see them.

Mitch mumbled from somewhere to her right. "Isn't this what you wanted?"

"Shut up, Mitch," Darcie snapped. Her voice indicated she was still on the ground by Gwen. "Everyone, keep your eyes and ears open."

If there was one thing Elise truly feared, it was hearing voices others could not. First the scarf, and now this. Both tied back to the fairy king.

Panicking won't solve this. I've been through too much to let my anxiety control me any longer. I need to get a grip and face him. It's the only way we'll find out anything. You've got this, Elise.

Elise straightened, dried her palms along the fabric of her skirt, and took a steadying breath before calling out into the void. "We're here about the prophecy. We don't want any tricks. Now, come out!"

The surrounding crickets and frogs provided the only sounds with no sign of fairies.

They must think I'm crazy. Maybe I finally have lost my mind.

"I didn't make it up," she whimpered. "I really did hear him." Elise felt Gavin pull her into a warm embrace as tears stung the edges of her eyes. She replied with a sniff when he kissed the top of her head. An amused chuckle, accompanied by a bright light, made the hairs on the back of her neck stand.

"No need to appear so crestfallen."

Before them, gallant and enticing as ever, was King Horanis. Floating above Gwen's sleeping form, he gazed down at them from an illuminated orb that only went out once he touched the ground. Rather than be cast into darkness once again, dozens of small hovering fairy lights proceeded to dart out from every direction until Elise could see clearly again.

Mitch locked his eyes on Horanis, remaining silent and pale. Darcie gaped at the giant fairy while bringing herself to stand.

Looking up at Gavin, Elise saw his shoulders tense as he squeezed her hand while also staring at the king.

Good. They see and hear him this time.

Elise wiped her eyes with her free hand. "Let's get this over with."

"My, my, and skip the formalities? Very well. You are here to fulfill the prophecy, are you not?"

Elise bit the inside of her cheek, willing herself not to lose what bravery crept beneath the surface. "That depends." She paused to swat at a fairy flying too close to her face. "Have we heard the whole thing?"

A smirk snaked across Horanis's lips as he knelt beside Gwen. His wings curled as if to cradle her on either side. "She is stunning, is she not?" He trailed featherlike touches along her arm, ribs, and hip. "Poor little thing was on a horseback ride through the forest, no doubt troubled by her father's infamous arrest. So much anger and pain for such a fragile heart to carry. Vulnerable to my advances yet declined my offers to help."

You're trying to distract me. I doubt help is what you really offered.

"Why did you mark her?" Darcie asked. "And why—"

"Not *you,* too?" the king replied wryly.

Darcie's features grew small and the zipping lights around them betrayed her tinted cheeks.

Horanis stroked Gwen's hair. "You were merely a ploy to pass the time, but *she*. . .she was my masterpiece." The long fingers of his hand curved around her head as he turned Gwen's face towards him. His other hand grazed the mark on the inside of her arm. Without another word, he lowered his head and placed his lips atop of it as Gwen had done.

An audible gasp left Gwen's mouth as she arched from the ground, yet her eyes remained closed. A blue light, similar to the magic Elise once carried around her neck, danced along Gwen's skin, outlining the mark. Only when Horanis separated his lips from it did the light skip about the surrounding trees before disappearing altogether. Twinkling laughter rang out amongst the floating balls of light. The king scanned every inch of Gwen's face with sheer adoration before placing a chaste kiss on her lips. "You have done well."

"What will you do now, Father?" came a familiar, raspy voice as Hemlock landed on the king's shoulder. "Does she come live with us?"

"No." The king's indignant expression softened as he beckoned a group of fairy lights to come closer. "She has served her purpose. Erase all memories of us."

"*All* memories?" Thicket, the king's eldest, landed on his other shoulder. "Must it be all?"

"It is best," Horanis replied with a sigh, watching the lights close in around Gwen's body before it was magically lifted higher and higher.

"You're not going to hurt her, are you?" Elise asked warily.

"Certainly not," he replied, rising to his feet so that Gwen floated near his chest. Waving a hand across the length of her body, a bluish smoke encircled Gwen's head. A crease appeared between his brows as Horanis eased her gently onto the grass with a forlorn gaze. "A deal is a deal. She is free."

"And what exactly was the deal?" Gavin asked. "What is she free from?"

"Simply to play the messenger in my plan to vanquish Rona once and for all. No one should be allowed to mess with the fabric of time, let alone rise one from the dead. I knew I needed to intervene." The four teenagers remained silent. "Do not think for a moment you are the only ones out to see her demise."

It had not occurred to Elise that others were plotting as they were. Perhaps that made her foolish, but at least Horanis was including them.

"Can this not be the last time we speak to them, Father?" Thicket's whiny, mouselike voice droned as she sneered down at Elise. "She has that stupid look on her face again."

Elise was not sure what look Thicket referred to, but she attempted to change it, nonetheless. Scratching at the back of her neck while avoiding eye contact, Elise inquired whether Sage was nearby.

"Ah, yes, her favorite. No wonder she's curious," Hemlock grunted with an impressive rolling of his eyes. "She always gets her way when it comes to him."

"Do not get any ideas!" Thicket snapped at Elise. "There are to be *no* deals this time."

"Now, where is the fun in that?" Horanis inquired.

"Father, you can't!" Thicket continued. "It's one thing to part with the *one* human who means something to you, but it's another to—" The tiny fairy cried out as Horanis flicked her off his shoulder into the nearest bush.

Elise fought hard not to laugh at the high-pitched squeal that followed. Meeting her friends' eyes, it appeared they were struggling to do the same.

Quirking a brow at his son, Horanis waited for Hemlock to fly away on his own. "Let them not speak for me," Horanis continued as one of the hovering lights lowered to his shoulder, revealing Sage's poised, dignified face.

Feeling her chest swell, Elise wished she could be alone with him. The most level-headed of them all, Sage saw something in her that often led to assistance of some kind.

"But how can Gwen's part be done?" Gavin asked. "She hasn't married the prince yet."

He's right.

"Tell us the prophecy again," Elise requested. When Horanis obliged, ending at the same place as Gwen, she scrunched up her face in confusion. "And that's all?"

"Of course not." He chuckled. "But it was all Gwendolyn needed to know to be of service. Apart from being influenced by a spoiled princess, she proved quite useful."

Elise ignored the slight against her mom, not wanting to take the attention away from the prophecy. She asked again for the rest of it.

"She must know, Father," Sage replied. "It is time."

Horanis regarded Elise, looking her up and down several times before stroking his chin.

She watched his wings flex on either side of him and swallowed. Her throat grew dry under the watchful eyes of the remaining fairies and her friends.

He's wasting time on purpose and getting a kick out of it. Enough with the theatrics!

Once it appeared Horanis was satisfied, he nodded when Sage offered to recite the remaining portion.

Elise held her breath as his small mouth parted.

"For time moves on,
Masked in deceit,
If left unchecked,
Will not repeat.

Among those led,
A blooming descendent,
The bond estranged,
One must mend it."

"There you have it," said Horanis, applauding his son before turning to face Elise with a renewed solemness. "One cannot argue your lineage with the royal family. You all have two days to put an end to Rona and correct the timeline. For if another queen is crowned, this shall be our only reality."

"What does that mean exactly?" Mitch asked.

Elise took a deep breath. "It means if we don't stop Rona before Richard's wedding and coronation, Haighdlen will be attacked for good. . .and *we* won't exist anymore."

Mitch spluttered before finding his voice. "But we're not from Haighdlen, and *you're* not Gwen's kid. So, how does another queen affect you being born?"

"It's not that," Gavin replied, his eyes darting back and forth as he put the pieces together. "If Richard doesn't marry Gwen, the family history automatically changes."

"Makes sense," Darcie agreed, catching on. "And if, for some reason, Joranna doesn't bring Ruby and Ian to our world in time. . ."

"Then *I* won't be born there, and *we* never meet," Elise concluded, gesturing between them. She could no longer imagine a lifetime of not knowing the other three as she did now. Especially Gavin, whose gaze bore into hers with the same unspoken truth. "It's a chain reaction. Rona and her brother will destroy all of this if their plan works."

This is more than avenging Derek, saving Mom, or getting back home. Everything we know is at risk of not existing.

"I won't let that happen," Elise vowed before stepping forward in front of the fairy king. Lifting her chin, she narrowed her gaze and quieted the unwanted thoughts creeping below the surface. "We're ready to face Rona in Lockesbarrow. Just tell us what to do before you send us."

CHAPTER 20

"You will not be going to Lockesbarrow. Not yet."

Horanis's unexpected response left Elise and the others floored in confused silence.

"But why not?" Darcie finally asked. "You spent all this time telling us it's Elise's destiny to stop Rona, but now she can't go to her?"

Horanis hummed. "I said *not yet*." His languid, carefree way of speaking unnerved Elise. With every drawl and nonchalant movement, the king demonstrated a sense of boredom.

Is this honestly his idea of fun?

"We only have two days," Elise pleaded. "I'd like to get there as soon as possible."

"You will not stop the wedding if you are in Lockesbarrow," Sage replied, his voice the same lifeless tone it had always been, only now it made Elise grit her teeth. "Besides, the Lockesbarrian armada is sailing towards Haighdlen at this very moment."

"*What?*" they cried.

"Sage, you meddle too far!" Hemlock bellowed, flying to his brother's side. "You treasonous git! Father, rip the wings from his body this instant. Denounce his actions, dismiss him from your court, and let him be publicly disgraced!"

"Calm yourself, Hemlock," Horanis commanded.

"Father, it is known he is a favorite of yours, but—"
Hemlock's words were silenced as Horanis clutched him out of midair

within his grasp. "*That* is enough." The king released his son when he was certain no more arguments would follow.

Elise and the others watched a resigned Hemlock fly off without a word into the same bush Thicket had disappeared into.

Horanis's relaxed, unphased demeanor made Elise conclude that this sort of behavior must be commonplace on his part. None of the other fairies made a sound as Horanis turned back to address the teenagers.

"Is she really sending an army here?" Mitch's strangled voice mirrored the tightness in Elise's chest.

Elise waited with bated breath as Horanis shared a hesitant look with his youngest son before nodding.

"Then go tell my family that!" Elise shrieked, sending many of the fairies hurling backwards from the sheer force of her outburst. *I'm going to be sick. I'm definitely going to be sick. They're all sitting ducks.* Her strained voice cracked as it left her burning throat. "People are going to get hurt!"

"It is not for *us* to warn them." Horanis brushed a fallen leaf from his shoulder. He spoke of the impending attack as if it were nothing more than a minor account of the weather. "They have lookouts and such. Word will get out soon enough." His wings flexed as he yawned with a wide stretch, reminding Elise more of an alley cat than a fairy. "We tend to side with the Elves on these matters and stay to ourselves."

"The cowardly way," Gavin spat. "It's just a sick game to you."

Horanis had the nerve to laugh, but he did not deny it.

"Maybe, we can prevent it," Elise muttered, more so to herself than the others.

"How?" Darcie asked, her own voice already an octave higher. "We don't have a clue of how to stop Richard's wedding, let alone an entire armada!"

Elise looked back up at Horanis and Sage.

"Your family can do nothing," Sage chimed in. "That does not mean all hope is lost."

Elise made to argue but paused before words left her mouth. It occurred to her Sage always found a way to help her figure out difficult decisions. *He wouldn't say something like that without a reason.*

Gavin, who had not made the same connection, kicked at a pile of leaves with a frustrated groan. Mitch declared their situation hopeless, and Darcie slid her back down the nearest tree until she sat in a huddled ball of despair on the forest floor near Gwen.

"Why. . .why did you word it that way?" Elise asked, staring knowingly at the tiny fairy.

"You really must learn to censor yourself." Horanis glared down at his son but showed no sign of forcefully removing him as he had the other two. Elise thought she even detected a hint of a smile on the youngest fairy's lips.

"Magical creatures are not limited to land."

"Yeah," Mitch scoffed before the color drained from his face, "but that would only leave—no, no way. You can't be serious."

Merpeople.

"I believe you have helped enough, Sage. You had best be off now." Horanis nodded before the youngest fairy followed his father's orders and flew off.

Elise watched Sage's light drift until it went out altogether once he got too far away. *Does he even know what he's suggesting?* So many conflicting thoughts filled her mind until she felt lightheaded.

"You're seriously expecting us to get help from mermaids?" Gavin gaped at Horanis's stoic expression. "They don't trust anyone!"

"Neither do we, and yet we find time to strike deals with humans often enough. You should give them more credit," the king replied.

"No way. There is *no* chance I'm stepping foot near another lake. I'm not getting pulled in again," Mitch vowed.

Darcie had likewise paled, and Elise suspected she too was remembering the time they almost lost Mitch to the merpeople in Lake Mirage. She could not blame either for being against such a plan.

Elise chewed on her bottom lip, mulling over everything she had learned about the secretive creatures.

Then it occurred to her.

"Maybe we won't have to." Seeing confused expressions from the others, she clarified. "The bowl. Remember the crystal mermaid bowl? I saw it at my Nana's house, and we even went with Derek to pick it up for her when Richard was born. Queen Eugena said Joranna could use it to communicate with her."

Understanding dawned on their faces.

"That's right!" Darcie's face split in a beaming grin as she clapped her hands together. "So, we only need to convince Joranna to use it and ask the mermaids to stop the attack! What're we waiting for?"

Mitch shook his head with a scoff. "Why are you saying it like it's an easy journey? Let alone an easy task? What happens if Richard sees us first?"

"Mitch is right," Gavin agreed. "All it takes is for one guard to recognize us, and we're back in the dungeon. For good this time."

"We'd be safer in Lockesbarrow," Mitch grumbled.

Both boys had valid points. The odds of them waltzing up to Joranna were slim, but this was their best chance to stop an attack by sea. Elise doubted Rona herself was on one of the approaching ships, but the sorceress would be sure to send a deadly number of soldiers. Haighdlen would be surrounded and overtaken in no time if not properly warned. Elise felt deep down Rona could even find a way to sneak in undetected. There was no telling what the limits were to her magic. She herself had only encountered Rona in person for mere moments, yet it was enough to instill the same fear that plagued everyone else who met her.

Elise looked down at Gwen's sleeping form sprawled out across the forest floor. Her peaceful expression made it easy to see how much Elise's cousin, Madelyn, favored her mother in the future. Madelyn's innocent plea replayed in Elise's memory from her first night at Joranna's house upon meeting her extended family and learning about Haighdlen.

"We don't want you to do anything you don't want to do," her cousin had said, *"but. . .Haighdlen is our home. We'd really love if you'd help save it."*

An entire generation could be wiped out if she failed. All her cousins, not just Madelyn, deserved to live without fear of fleeing their home. Horanis was right. They were not needed in Lockesbarrow.

They were needed here, in Haighdlen. The biggest obstacle was going to be convincing her family of that. Not only did Elise possess magic, but she was also the fulfillment of a prophecy sent here to complete this very task. She would be naïve to ignore that. All of Gwen's suffering would be for nothing if Elise fled now. Clearing her throat, she squared her shoulders and faced the fairy king.

"Elise, what are you doing?" Gavin whispered, but she ignored him.

"Give us enough magic to go to Haighdlen Castle," she demanded. "My blood will get us through the protective barrier."

"Whoa, slow down," Mitch warned.

"Yeah, be careful," Gavin piped in. "You can't say something generic like that. What if he plays one of his games and drops us into a dungeon himself?"

Horanis failed to hide an impish grin, yet Elise stood her ground.

"We have to take that chance. Mitch, pull out the diary. We're lucky the fairies have helped us this far. Are you with me or not?" she asked.

Darcie took her hand, gesturing for Mitch and Gavin to do the same.

Elise understood their unwillingness, but ultimately, it would take a risk to pull this off. She searched Gavin's eyes, begging with her own for him to agree with her plan. A sigh of relief escaped her when she felt his fingers intertwine with hers. Not one to remain the odd one out, Mitch pulled on his collar before placing a hand over Darcie's. He used his other hand to retrieve the diary from his vest. Elise felt her heart swell with affection and hope.

If they failed, they failed together. If they succeeded, they would succeed together. Nothing could change that.

"Please also change our clothes!" Elise squeaked, realizing how conspicuous they would be arriving in their formal festival clothing.

Darcie nudged Elise before nodding towards their feet where Gwen remained asleep.

"Oh, right. And send Gwen with us! We need Richard to see her again. Gavin, grab her hand so she gets through the barrier, too." Elise and the others adjusted their footing so he could bend down to take her hand.

In all the commotion, she had almost left her aunt stranded in the middle of the forest with a possessive fairy king. That would haunt her for a long time, she mused. Elise mouthed a quick thank you to Darcie, feeling heat envelope her neck and ears. *Here we go.*

A little less than a minute passed before Elise realized the king had yet to move.

Horanis's impish grin only widened. "You are forgetting one important fact. *I* am not Sage."

I don't understand.

The fairy king chuckled to himself. "I am not swayed by human emotions and trials. It will take more than a sentimental drawing to gift you with magic."

"You can't be serious!" Gavin argued. "You set all this up so Gwen would bring us here. You're really going to make us pay?"

So much for Thicket's no deal approach. If Sage were still there, Elise and the others would already be on the castle grounds.

He is wasting our time. "What will it take?" Elise ground out.

"That is more like it," he replied with a melodic drawl. The only thing more menacing than his smile was the glint in his eyes as he focused on Darcie. "*Such* beauty."

"Forget it!" snapped Mitch, returning the diary under his vest. He stepped between Darcie and Horanis.

"Calm yourself, hero," Horanis replied with a condescending click of his tongue before nudging Mitch aside. The other three released each other's hands as the king lifted Darcie's with his own.

The bejeweled bracelet dangling from her tiny wrist glistened in the surrounding fairy lights. "This should do nicely."

"No!" Darcie quipped, yanking her wrist away from his grip. She caressed it with her free hand. "It's special."

"That's exactly why he wants it," Gavin pointed out without taking his eyes off Horanis. "He knows it'll hurt. It's part of his fun."

Elise proceeded carefully. "Darcie. . .maybe you should—"

"No!" Darcie repeated, clutching the bracelet against her chest. "Mitch spent all his money on it. He was so charming and thoughtful to do it. I even got to pick it out. I've only had it a couple of hours. No, I won't give it to you! Find something else."

Elise sucked in a breath, looking between Darcie and Horanis. Expecting the king to respond with wrath, Elise was once again blindsided when he answered her outburst with a calm smirk.

"Something else. . .or *someone*?" He let the threat hang over their heads before continuing. Darcie visibly gulped under his scrutiny but did not reply. "Five is rather a large party for traveling, indeed. Unfortunately, the balance of time has deemed it impossible for me to claim my beloved Gwendolyn or your precious savior here." He looked pointedly at Elise before returning his attention to Darcie. "And I have no use for these sidekick gentlemen. But you. . .as I have stated before, *you* would make a perfect wife to one of my lords. . .or myself." He cocked his head as he regarded her warmly. Darcie's eyes welled up with tears, prompting Horanis to click his tongue once again. "A mere bracelet is not so difficult to part with *now*, is it?"

Mitch closed the distance between himself and Darcie. Tipping her chin up to look at him, he wiped a tear away with his thumb. Both looked down as he reached to unclasp the bracelet, eliciting a sob from Darcie.

"Come now," Horanis called with a dramatic roll of his eyes, "It is not as if I am requesting a wedding ring or life of servitude. Show some dignity. Honestly, humans are exhausting."

Although the temptation was palpable, Mitch said nothing to Horanis. Instead, he handed the bracelet to a fairy waiting nearby. He and Darcie watched as it was carried to Horanis, who inspected it fondly.

"Listen to me," Mitch whispered to Darcie, waiting until she met his eyes. "I don't care how many bracelets, diaries, or vials we lose while we're here. . .I'm not losing you. Do you understand?" When Darcie nodded, he leaned down to kiss her before pulling away with a lopsided grin. "It was Richard's money anyway, so it's kind of his loss."

Darcie chuckled through her tears. "He does deserve it at this point, huh?" Taking a deep breath, she wiped her eyes and thanked Mitch.

Mitch replied with a kiss to the inside of her now bare wrist.

"How touching," Horanis said. Tossing the bracelet into the air, the four teenagers watched as it disappeared into a cloud of the same bluish smoke as before. He feigned disappointment by placing a long, bony finger against his chin. "However, *one* small bracelet is not sufficient payment for such a request."

He's joking, right?

"After all, you asked me for three favors—travel, garments, and a companion." He considered each teenager before focusing on Mitch. The king narrowed his eyes. "Give me the diary."

How does he know about the diary?

"What!" Elise shrieked. "You can't take that!"

"Collect yourself, you silly girl," he admonished. "I have no need for the entire book. . .I desire something much more important."

There's no way I'm letting him anywhere near the diary.

"Give it to him, Elise," Gavin whispered. "It's not the original. Maybe the one Rona has will show up later. We can afford to gamble with this one."

"He's right," said Darcie. "We don't even know if this one works."

Then why would he ask for it?

Elise weighed their options carefully. Unable to think of an excuse or counteroffer, she sighed with a resigned nod.

Mitch scoffed with a few whispered words of his own before holding the book in question out for Horanis, who swiped it with one dramatic sweep.

The pages, filled with all the memories and events Joranna deemed important enough to document, flipped before Elise's eyes as she swallowed a cry. It never became easier to watch others flip through the diary, something she had been unable to do since first accepting her family's mission.

By the time Horanis came to the end of Joranna's eloquent writing, less than a handful of blank pages remained. The king's eyes glinted with a hint of amusement when he reached the final entry. Expecting him to make a spectacle of the written words, Elise's jaw dropped at the gut-wrenching sound of paper ripping from the spine.

"What are you doing?" she cried, watching him tuck it away after folding it eloquently as Gavin blocked her with his arm. Elise did not even realize she had taken a step forward. Feeling as if her heart would leap from her throat, she grabbed Gavin's arm but remained still. *Something made him tear out that particular page.* Every nerve in her body ignited. "What did it say?"

"That is for me to know."

"But you can't do that!" argued Elise.

"On the contrary," he calmly pointed out, his even tone a stark contrast to her unhinged one.

A heat spread across her skin as she contemplated pushing Gavin out of the way to reach the king. Knowing she would never stand an actual chance of reaching him, she concentrated on his face, willing him to reconsider. The familiar electric sensations warmed her fingertips. *Read us the entry. Tell us what it says.*

The smaller balls of lights bounced with glee as Horanis laughed. The alluring sound reminded Elise of musical notes as it skipped about, echoing throughout the blackened forest. The muscles in her stomach clenched when he met her feeble gaze.

"Your weak magic is no match for mine, child," he said between breaths. "It is inexperienced at best, but I admit your meek efforts have livened up the mood."

Gavin lowered his arm to squeeze her hand. "There has to be something on there that makes it valuable to you," he countered. "Just tell us what it is."

"Come now, enough of this nonsense," Horanis announced with a clap of his hands. All hints of mirth vanished from his features, and though impossible, his youthful handsome face looked tired and worn somehow. "Time to get to work." With another grand sweep of his hand, Horanis pointed in the opposite direction from which they had come. "I need not remind you the importance of utmost discretion as you move forward."

Elise nodded.

"But we don't know what to say," Mitch interrupted. "We came out here to get magic to Lockesbarrow. How are we going to convince Joranna to use the mermaid bowl when everyone there knows we were sent away? We won't get through the front doors."

"Not without a disguise," Darcie added.

Elise looked expectantly at the fairy king. "We can trust you to help with that, can't we?"

Rather than a twinkling laugh, Horanis chuckled deep in his chest as he shrank to the same size as the others with a brilliant flash. The diary, which he had been holding, fell open onto the dirt path. The pages flipped wildly as his voice radiated around them. "Never trust a fairy."

As he hovered above their heads, the same blue smoke rained down onto each of them, prompting Elise to act quickly. "Grab onto me! Gavin, hold Gwen's hand. Mitch, get the diary! Take us to Haighdlen Castle!" An intense, warm wind picked up, whistling at a fever pitch as it circulated leaves and twigs around them until it felt as if they were in the middle of a vortex. Elise watched each fairy light extinguish one by one, with Horanis vanishing last before she succumbed to darkness.

CHAPTER 21

An incessant knocking pulled Elise from her already unsettled sleep. As reality hit, she sprang up in a cold sweat and assessed her surroundings.

Are we in the castle?

She did not recognize this room. It was by no means as grand as the guest room she normally slept in when visiting her family. It did not even have a window. The only light came from a mostly melted candle on the dresser. Elise looked over at two more beds close to hers where Darcie and Gwen slept.

Where are Gavin and Mitch?

Standing up, she also noticed she no longer wore the elegant emerald gown. It had been replaced with a simple, unflattering brown dress. Elise clutched a fistful of her skirt at the sounds of distant voices and footsteps outside.

Where did Horanis send us?

Leaning down, she shook her best friend awake. While Darcie reacted in much the same fashion as Elise, both of theirs paled in comparison to Gwen, who awoke seconds after.

"What is going on?" Gwen's voice lifted an octave higher than usual as she sprang from the bed. Planting herself against the wall, she looked between Elise and Darcie as if they were ghosts. "Where am I? What is happening?"

Elise took a deep breath, unsure of where to start. "That depends. . .what's the last thing you remember?"

"We were at the festival. I danced, spoke with the prince, and left." Gwen's lower lip quivered as her face paled. "Where have you taken me? And what are we wearing?"

All three jumped when an assertive female voice boomed from the other side of the door, ordering to be let in. More knocking ensued.

"Elise, look! It's the diary!" Darcie kneeled to pick it up off the floor. "What do you think this means?"

"Hide it!" Elise turned to Gwen. "We'll explain everything in a minute, but just play along and stay quiet until we can."

"What are you saying?" Gwen hissed, watching with an apprehensive eye as Darcie shoved the diary beneath a pillow. "What happened at the festival? Did you—"

"Fine. I have no choice. You had your chance," grumbled the voice. Upon hearing the jingling of keys, the girls stared in horror as the lock clicked before the door sprang open.

Light from the hall leaked into the tiny room, causing the girls to shield their eyes until they could focus on the woman looming in the doorframe.

"*This* is what I have to work with." The woman clicked her tongue, muttering under her breath while bustling around the room. "You will call me Ms. Persimmons. I am one of the housekeepers for the royal family. I will oversee all your duties during your stay." Collecting three aprons and bonnets from the dresser, she threw a set towards each of the girls. "I was told Lady Iris would be accompanied by her own staff, but I was not told they were such a lazy bunch. You couldn't even be bothered to snuff out your own candle. Were you planning on burning the castle down? Honestly."

She doesn't seem to recognize us. So, that's a good thing, I guess. A hint of guilt tugged at Elise's heart. With everything going on during their visits, she never took the time to get to know the servants. Perhaps it worked in their favor in this instance. If Ms. Persimmons did recognize her, she said nothing.

"Lady Iris?" Darcie asked, sharing an anxious glance with Elise. Gwen's own dubious expression only managed to make them look further ignorant.

"The prince's betrothed. You *are* here to tend to Lady Iris?" Her mouth tightened as she raised her eyebrows expectantly.

Elise stammered on the spot, suddenly feeling as if she were back in high school under the discerning stare of her chemistry teacher. *They even look alike.* Enough silence passed that Elise could feel the housekeeper's suspicion growing. She needed to act fast. "Of course," Elise finally choked out, locking eyes with Darcie and Gwen. "We are here. . .to tend to Lady Iris."

Darcie nodded fervently, and after a moment of hesitation, Gwen did the same.

The housekeeper hummed with disapproval. "Count your blessings you are not on *my* staff. If I ever caught such laziness, you'd all be flogged immediately. Now, there's a tray of biscuits and tea just outside. Ready yourselves, have a bite, and report to Lady Iris's bedchamber before the steward makes his rounds this morning. I'll not receive a lecture on your behalf. Get on now."

Yikes. Yeah, we don't want to see Ballard. He'll recognize us right away.

Half an hour later, the girls were washed up and fed. Fortunately, Ballard had not crossed their path, but Elise did not want to press their luck. It unnerved her further they had not seen or heard from the boys yet. *I hope they are safe.*

"We're going to be arrested," Gwen repeated over and over as they wandered the third-floor corridor. "Why did you bring me here?"

Having been watched and followed all morning by Ms. Persimmons, Elise had yet to fill Gwen in on everything. Peeking over her shoulder, Elise pulled Darcie and Gwen into a corner.

I can't mention the fairies, but I can tell her enough to keep us out of trouble. "I am close to the royal family, and right now there is a fleet of ships headed this way to attack Haighdlen." Gwen's eyes widened in horror, but Elise pressed on before her future aunt could interrupt. "The queen has a way to communicate with the mermaids. We have to convince her to ask them for help."

"B-but. . .why am I here?" asked Gwen.

So, you and Richard can fall in love. Elise cleared her throat, desperately searching for an excuse.

"In case Ruby sees us," Darcie piped in. "We're less likely to get in trouble if you're with us since you are both friends."

"We can only trust Ruby, Sarah, and Ian at this point," Elise continued. "Maybe Joranna and Charles, but it will depend on what Richard's been up to."

"Not to mention we need to stop the wedding," Darcie added.

Elise inquired if Darcie brought the diary with her just in case. Darcie replied by tapping the pocket of her apron with a smile.

"But why?" Gwen's brows furrowed. "Why can't the prince marry the singer from last night? If the prince has forgiven her family's connection, I do not see why we should interfere."

Elise and Darcie shared another strained glance.

"Are you lost?" asked a meek voice. They turned to see another maid carrying trays. Elise inquired where they could find Lady Iris before the maid replied, "Her room is just there. Second door on the left. This one is for her."

"They're not eating in the dining hall?" Elise had always had breakfast in the dining hall with the family during all her visits.

"Prince Richard is in with the council and requested no formal breakfast this morning," said the maid.

Darcie took the tray and thanked her.

The three girls waited for the other maid to round the corner before proceeding to the correct room.

"I do not like this," Gwen whispered. "We will be found out immediately. I will end up like my father! What will happen to my mother and sister?"

"Calm down!" Elise whispered. "The only way we get through this is if we act like we belong. I'm freaking out, too, but if we panic, we're dead. Now, we need a game plan. She will need to get ready. What do they normally do for us when we're here?"

"They help us dress, do our hair, and make our bed," Darcie offered. "They do so much more, so I don't know."

"Then we'll start with that," said Elise. Her heart pounded, hoping their attire would be enough to shield them from being found out. "Gwen, you help her dress. You're more familiar with the laces and corsets. Darcie, you'll do the hair since that's your area of expertise."

"I don't know if I can do it as intricately as they do here," said Darcie.

"It will have to be good enough," Elise said with a sigh. "I'll make the bed. Let us hope that is enough for us to slip out undetected and start looking for the guys and Joranna."

Pulling on the bonnets to cover their hair, the girls lowered their heads and knocked on the door. When they were granted entry, they found Iris sitting up in a four-poster bed.

"Good morning," muttered Elise before opening the drapes to allow a flood of sunshine into the luxurious room. She held her breath, feeling as if she were walking on eggshells. *Get in, get out. Get in, get out.*

"Good morning," answered Iris with a delicate yawn.

Elise suppressed a smile when Darcie set the tray down onto the bed, narrowly avoiding a spill as a spoon fell onto Iris's lap. When Darcie returned, blushing, to her side, Elise took a moment to study the young woman.

She certainly was a natural beauty, like her mother, Ingrid. Fair skin, soft cheeks, and impeccable manners. It was going to be tough to talk Richard out of marrying this one.

After an excruciating wait, Iris finally finished her breakfast and requested to be dressed. Darcie removed the tray, setting it on the nearest dresser with a clatter before waiting with Elise while Gwen stepped forward.

Elise was relieved Gwen was with them. She would not have stood a chance fastening all the hooks, buttons, and laces involved in the voluptuous gown Iris selected from her wardrobe.

Everything is going smoothly. Now, just make the bed and get out.

All was going according to plan until Iris sat down at the vanity table. As Darcie took her place behind Iris's chair, a soft knock at the door announced Ingrid's arrival.

"Good morning, dearest," she practically sang before her eyes flashed with disappointment towards the three maids. "Are you not yet ready for the day?"

Elise squeezed her hands into fists as her cheeks grew hot, yet she kept her face lowered. All the memories came flooding back from the night Ingrid and Brahm were arrested, and yet, here she was. Parading around like the queen herself. Elise could kill her uncle for allowing such an embarrassing display to happen in front of her family. *If Derek were here. . .*

"Almost, Mother. The maids are helping. They were only a few minutes late. Do not be angry."

"We shall see," Ingrid mumbled, entering with a great flourish. Her classic beauty reminded Elise of an old Hollywood actress. "There seems to have been much confusion over the staff I requested. I hardly recognize half of them."

Thank you, Horanis. That certainly was the fairy king's doing to gain them access. Elise knew they would not have stood a chance to blend in otherwise.

Elise busied herself with making the bed while listening intently to the mother and daughter.

"You sang magnificently, my dear," praised Ingrid, looking over Darcie's shoulder at her daughter's reflection. "No doubt your little prince will be ill in love this morning."

Iris looked down at her lap, fiddling with her fingers. The only sound came from the brush Darcie held as she tried to gently untangle the girl's soft dark hair. "I'm afraid his attentions may be pulling elsewhere. I was told by a footman he was quite friendly with one of the dancers last night."

Gwen froze by the door and met Elise's gaze. Elise shook her head. *Not now. Don't say anything.* She sighed in relief when Gwen collected herself long enough to prepare the makeup on the vanity.

Ingrid waved off her daughter's comment. "He is a man. *And* a king. Do not expect any different."

"Was his father not loyal to the queen?" Iris's voice was so quiet, Elise questioned the young woman's desire to marry Richard at all. "Every account I hear is that theirs was a passionate love."

Gwen proceeded to put on Iris's makeup, and Elise could not help but see the irony of the two women sitting so close to each other, secretly foes. Fortunately, Iris barely gave them two glances. She was too completely distracted by her mother.

"A rarity, to be sure," continued Ingrid, pacing back and forth, "but I'm afraid the prince is not favoring his father as of late. Best to take his faults with the strengths. So long as you quickly produce an heir, it matters not whose bed he shares."

Iris frowned but did not reply.

Elise found it odd to feel pity for someone she was supposed to hate. Deep down, Iris struck Elise as any normal girl with ideas of marrying for love. Perhaps she was not the villain, but Elise knew she needed to remain firm in their plan, nonetheless. She also prayed the subject would change, as the idea of her uncle's bedroom habits was enough to make her want to gag.

"Your itinerary is quite full." Ingrid beamed with pride. "There is the cake testing, your dress fitting, not to mention the flower arrangements and color scheme." Inhaling deeply, Ingrid released her breath with a blissful smile. "It is so good to be back." Not one to be caught too long in an awkward position with everyone's eyes on her, she diverted everyone's attention away by fussing at Elise, Darcie, and Gwen. "Are you not finished yet? How long does it take to dress someone anyway? My daughter will be queen tomorrow night! Enough of this nonsense. You are dismissed. Go clean something."

Already eager to leave, the three girls shuffled out of the room and down the staircase to the second floor where a group of servants searched the corridor.

"It is not here," one called.

"Not over here, either," said another.

"I've checked all the bedrooms. There's nothing," replied a third.

"That is unacceptable!" snapped a familiar, strict voice.

Elise tensed as Ballard, the overbearing castle steward, walked into view. While he had his moments, like saving Elise and her friends from Brahm and his sister, he also found pleasure in getting them into trouble as well.

"Her Majesty requests her diary. It shall be located and returned immediately or else," he barked.

Elise swallowed convulsively, watching his every move to avoid being spotted. She ducked into an open doorway, pulling Darcie and Gwen with her. "Leave it on a table or something. Then, let's get out of here."

"But they'll see me," Darcie argued.

"Let us cross the corridor to that other room," Gwen whispered, nodding ahead. "There is a table just outside of it. Elise and I will cover you, so you can set it down without anyone noticing."

Darcie bit her lip, unconvinced, but nodded and waited for Elise and Gwen to step out first. Hyperaware of Darcie's crouched, careful steps beside her, Elise stared forward and tried not to bring any attention to the group. Her paranoia spiked as others commented on the missing diary. Whispering ensued, even a couple of laughs, until Ballard ordered everyone to keep searching.

Almost there. Keep your head down. Elise's heart skipped a beat when Darcie retrieved the backup diary from her apron pocket. *Drop it. Drop it, now. Just drop it.*

As soon as they were close enough, Darcie tossed the diary onto the table. At once, the three quickened their steps into the room and waited with quivering breaths.

"Here he comes!" whispered Darcie. "Duck!" She closed the door only enough for them to peek around.

"Who is coming?"

Crying out, all three girls whipped around to see Queen Joranna behind them.

I didn't know she was in this room! Why didn't we pay more attention? She wanted to find Joranna, but she did not want to be found by Joranna. Elise's breath hitched as four guards burst into the room in response to the commotion.

"Step away from the queen!" one barked.

The sound of swords being pulled made Elise's blood run cold. Clutching her bonnet tighter, she avoided Joranna's eyes.

Elise, Darcie, and Gwen stared at the floor as they pressed their backs against the nearest wall.

"Show your faces," came another order. This time from Joranna herself.

Once again, they obliged.

A pool of dread settled in the pit of Elise's stomach when Joranna's face fell. This was not how their plan was supposed to go, and now they would be arrested and end up in the dungeon.

"Are you hurt, Your Majesty?" a guard asked.

"No," replied Joranna, her tone reflecting disappointment rather than fear. "These young women are no threat to me. You may stand down. Thank you," she added when they hesitated.

After a long silence, the guards sheathed their swords and filed out of the room just as Ballard appeared breathless in the doorway.

"Why are they leaving? I heard shouting," he panted, looking back and forth. "Are you quite all right, Your Highness? Is there anything I can—"

He caught sight of Elise first, then Darcie, and finally Gwen. Ballard's shock ran so deep, it looked as if he had been bewitched to remain frozen. At long last, his expression did change—this time, to rage. "The *insolence!*" Inching closer to the ladies, he practically spat through his teeth. "Never, *never*, would I ever expect you to be so stupid as to return after direct orders from—"

"Ballard," Joranna called, waiting for the steward to look at her. "That is enough. I shall handle this."

"But Your Majesty, this cannot be allowed—"

"Except by *me*," Joranna corrected. "Leave us, please."

While she feared for her own fate, Elise was always amused when Ballard got put in his place. This time his face resembled a deflated balloon as he stalked out into the hall. He perked up, however, when he saw the diary sitting on the table. Inspecting the cover, he lifted a suspicious brow at each young girl.

Elise gulped.

"I believe you were looking for this, Your Highness." Ballard held out the diary for the queen to take. After she thanked him, he sent one last sneer in Elise's direction before closing the door behind him.

Slumping against the wall, Elise, Darcie, and Gwen sighed in relief.

Joranna, however, wasted no time berating all three for their reckless behavior. "You know you are not supposed to be here," she added at the end of her lecture. "I expect a good explanation, and quickly, for he is probably reporting to Richard at this very moment."

Gwen and Darcie pushed Elise forward.

Glaring at her friends, Elise took a deep breath and met her grandmother's concerned gaze.

"Rona and her brother. . .are about to attack Haighdlen. There's an armada on its way, and we need to stop the wedding from happening."

CHAPTER 22

As soon as the words left her mouth, Elise wished she had found a different way to share the news. Had she bothered to look at her grandmother closer, she would have seen the queen was already pale and thinner. An assortment of used handkerchiefs and empty glasses with lipstick stains littered the table. Random pillows were discarded on the floor and the drapes remained closed, allowing only a sliver of sunlight to peek through. A pitcher and basin rested on a dresser in the corner, and an oversized blanket was thrown across a lone chaise positioned in the center of the room.

Has she been sleeping in here?

"This is grave news, indeed." Joranna spoke barely above a whisper. "You are absolutely sure?"

Elise nodded.

"I do not need to remind you what a serious allegation this is, Elise. You still stand by what you say?"

Again, Elise nodded.

Joranna walked over to the window, pulling the drape only far enough to peek out of it. "Where did you hear of this?"

"A fairy," Darcie said, ignoring Elise's tight-lipped glare in Gwen's direction.

Gwen doesn't have any memories of the fairies anymore.

Joranna's bewildered expression matched Gwen's as they both stared at Elise and Darcie.

"A fairy?" Joranna asked. "Honestly, Elise, you could not have picked a more unreliable creature."

"You both dragged me here because of a fairy?" Gwen asked incredulously. "I'm risking my life here today on a wild goose chase started by a *fairy*?"

You were the one who led us there. Elise held her tongue, although every fiber of her being wanted to lash out at the allegations. Yet, she waited for the women to finish.

"And who are you?" Queen Joranna asked Gwen. "I do not recognize you."

Gwen introduced herself, adding she was nothing more than the daughter of a farmer whose family housed Elise's party for the festival. She made no mention of her friendship and dealings with Ruby, which Elise agreed, was best for everyone. Especially the princess.

Joranna scrutinized each girl before shaking her head. "I must alert Richard immediately."

"Wait!" Elise cried out, blocking the door. "Not yet!" Sucking her mouth into a thin line, she searched for the right words to say. "We have a plan."

Joranna raised a skeptical brow. "*You* have a plan to aid in warfare and stop an entire armada?"

Elise paled at the sound of it. *Well, when you say it like that, no.* Licking her lips, she stammered on the spot.

"I thought not." Joranna attempted to sidestep Elise but was stopped again.

"Eugena!" Elise blurted out, wincing as the doorknob pressed against her lower back. "Ask Eugena."

Joranna took a step back, allowing Elise to alleviate the pressure from the door. Looking at Darcie and Gwen, she nodded towards Elise. "And you two are in on this plan?" Once the other two girls reluctantly nodded, Joranna took a deep breath. "That is out of the question."

"But *why*?" Elise pressed. "Is it because they live in a lake? Because I always assumed with their magic they could visit any area of water—"

"It is not that," Joranna said. "While you are correct, this sort of request simply is not done. Perhaps you do not remember visiting, but they are not known for their hospitality, nor do they cater to the favors of others—least of all, humans."

Elise opened her mouth, but Darcie beat her to it.

"Yes, but *you* are different," she said. "They gave you a bowl to communicate with them whenever you needed."

A crease appeared in the center of Joranna's forehead. "How do you—" Realization dawned on her face. "That is correct. I forgot you were there the day I received it." She wrung her hands before pacing back and forth in front of the chaise. "But what does all this have to do with Richard's wedding? Apart from the reports of protests occurring throughout the kingdom?"

Protests! This was more serious than Elise even realized. Even the people of Haighdlen were not going to sit around and accept a traitorous alliance. Maybe it would work in their favor.

"We can't let him marry her," Elise said, shooting Gwen a quick glance. *Spin the truth.* "Iris isn't the one for him."

"I agree with you there," Joranna said, heaving a sigh. "But it is out of our hands. He will not be convinced otherwise."

"What if we could prove it to him?" Darcie asked. She waited until all eyes were on her. "Her mom is here, and she was helping Brahm. What if we tricked Ingrid into giving away their plan? Richard might be brainwashed, but we all know she's probably acting for Rona."

"That's true," Elise said. "There's no way that woman wants to make peace. Not after she was thrown in prison here."

"She even escaped and is walking around freely in front of your faces. You know she's laughing at this whole thing," Darcie finished.

Gwen's eyes widened.

"You share my thoughts exactly," Joranna said. "In a matter of days, Richard has stripped most of our legacy from us. He is going to run this kingdom into the ground one way or the other."

"Which is why he must be stopped," Darcie finished.

It was Joranna's turn to widen her eyes.

"She doesn't mean kill him," Elise jumped in. "We think he's been hypnotized. I bet if we could get Iris alone, we could break her down for information. Part of me doesn't think she's completely on board with everything."

Gwen and Darcie nodded their agreement. If they were not successful in convincing Joranna, at least they provided a united front. Elise was surprised when Gwen spoke up.

"She's the weak link. In the short moments I saw her, there is room to infiltrate for sure, but it will be dangerous."

Joranna scrutinized each of them for the fifth or sixth time, as if waiting for them to admit this was all a ruse. Deducing their sincerity, she scratched the back of her head and began pacing frantically again with a huff. "Do you honestly realize what you are asking me to do?"

Elise felt it best to remain silent as her grandmother processed their plans. She herself had drafted multiple mental lists of pros and cons, but everything led to following through with contacting Eugena.

Only when Joranna slumped across the chaise, her eyes glistening, did Elise choose to join her.

"Hey," whispered Elise, waiting for her grandmother to meet her gaze. "You can talk to me. I know I'm asking you for a lot."

Gwen and Darcie stepped closer to the doorway to provide them privacy, but Elise lowered her voice, nonetheless, as she encouraged her grandmother to speak.

Joranna pulled out a fresh handkerchief from a nearby drawer, wiping her eyes delicately. Her voice was distant, sorrowful, and so incredibly meek it tugged at Elise's heart. "I am wondering how we got here. Everything Derek and I built together, everything we instilled in our children, and it is all about to be taken away in a matter of hours." She sobbed into the handkerchief as Elise rubbed her back. "I miss him so much."

Elise never knew a sound could destroy her as deeply as the sound of her grieving grandmother weeping.

"Forgive me," the queen said with a steadying breath. "No one should see their queen this way. If only Avalyn could see me now. She would call me an utter disgrace."

Derek's mother was always a stickler for the rules. Elise only spent a matter of days with her great-grandmother. Joranna spent years being coached how to be a queen with her as a mother-in-law.

"If Derek were here—" Joranna continued. "None of this would have happened. I blame that toxic council. Derek always hated holding those meetings. They will waltz my boy straight to his own grave."

Elise wilted. *Was there anything else we could have done to prevent this from happening? Was this always supposed to happen in one form or another?* Things did seem dire. Whether Rona attacked at this moment or in eighteen years, was the kingdom always meant to be overthrown regardless of interference? She shook her head. *No, I can't think that way anymore.*

"That's why we have to do this," Elise reasoned. "It might not work, but we have to try." She waited until Joranna dried her face and looked at her. "Yes, to save Haighdlen, but we need to save Richard, too. Even if it's from himself. Isn't he worth it?"

Joranna sniffled, but ultimately nodded. "Always. I would do anything for my children." She paused, scanning the room as if seeing the mess for the first time. "Good gracious. I have been withdrawn. My children also lost a father, yet I have only thought of myself." She stood to collect the handkerchiefs around the room. "If we are going to contact Eugena, I will not have her see me living in squalor."

Elise perked up, beaming at Darcie and Gwen across the room. "You'll help us?' she asked Joranna.

"Absolutely. I want to thank you girls. While I will never stop mourning my beloved Derek, I still have a duty to my family and this kingdom. Both of which Rona is planning to steal from me, and if I do nothing, I am essentially surrendering everything to her." Smiling warmly, she hugged Elise and nodded towards Darcie and Gwen before crossing the room to the door. She pressed her ear against it, listening for movement, before continuing in a whisper. "I do not want to trust anyone with the bowl. I shall retrieve it and return. You three stay here where it is safe."

Nodding, Elise added, "If you see Gavin or Mitch, could you let them know we're in here?"

"You got separated *again*?" she asked. "Are you sure they are here?"

Darcie shrugged. "Well, not exactly, but we hope they are."

Joranna frowned. "Let us address one problem at a time. I shall be back shortly."

Twenty minutes later, Elise concluded she and her grandmother had different definitions of the word *shortly*. It did not help the queen left the diary sitting on the table nearest to the chaise where all three girls sat. The temptation to rip it open, regardless of if they had a plan, was tantalizing. Surely, if needed, she could find some magical object to help boost her own powers like before.

"I have always wondered what the castle looked like on the inside," Gwen said, breaking the painful silence. She scanned the entire room, admiring the details down to the subtle woodwork. "I never actually thought I'd get to see it. It is incredibly beautiful."

You'll live in it one day. . .if we don't fail.

"I'm sorry we got you caught up in this," Elise apologized. She meant it. Now that things had slowed down, she felt selfish to forcing Gwen to tag along in hopes of falling in love with Richard. Maybe it was a mistake rushing it this way. He certainly was attracted to her, but Elise did not even know if Gwen felt the same way about him.

They shared a collective sigh of relief when Joranna entered the room, but stared in horror when Sarah and Ruby followed her inside. Only when the door was secured did Joranna pull the bowl out of her sleeve.

"What's going on?" Elise asked, looking between her mother and aunt.

"Should anything happen to Richard, Sarah is next in line," Joranna shared. "I summoned for Ian, but he appears to be out at the moment. No one has seen him. We could use his invisibility powers right about now."

That's right! I forgot he could turn invisible. It was a trait Elise envied, but at the same time, joked that she already possessed.

Gwen and Ruby stared at each other but said nothing.

"And I am not going to keep Ruby in the dark," Joranna continued. "She carries an heir of her own should the worst come to pass."

Elise never considered the possibility of ruling on the throne, and hoped she never would. It was one thing to know she was a princess. It was another to play the part formally. She loved Haighdlen, and prayed there would be a chance to visit should they fix the timeline, but she could not imagine a scenario of leaving her world. . .of leaving Gavin. She considered a world without not only him, but without Darcie, her mom, and even Mitch. The thought alone lit a fire under her to fight no matter the cost to preserve all their futures.

"Mother, should you not be resting? And are you sure striking a deal with the merpeople is the safest plan?" Sarah inquired.

"It is the *only* plan," replied the queen, setting the bowl down on top of the diary.

"Shall I open the drapes for better lighting?" Ruby offered.

"Best to leave them closed, dearest. We never know who to trust or where they may lurk." Joranna cleared her throat and asked Gwen to carry over the pitcher on the dresser. Thanking the young girl, the queen poured water carefully into the bowl. Setting the pitcher down on the floor, she touched the engraved crystal mermaids one at a time.

"Isn't that the coolest thing you've ever seen?" Darcie whispered in Elise's ear.

Nodding, Elise watched in amazement as the carved mermaids stirred and swam around the outskirts of the bowl. Small ripples appeared followed by rapid bubbles that splashed over the rim onto the floor. Joranna set the bowl on the diary once more and urged everyone to stand back.

All but Joranna gasped when the water took on a life of its own. It swirled, lifted, and threaded like clear ropes before coming together to form not one, but two individual heads. The heads were followed by shoulders and torsos. One male and one female. While their features were completely comprised of water, they were detailed enough for Elise to recognize them as Queen Eugena and her intimidating right-hand-man, Erumann. Despite the number of times she had heard of and seen them, Elise was no less mesmerized by their regal presence.

"Queen Joranna." Eugena's voice was distorted as the water that formed her mouth sloshed in time with the words. "This is an unexpected summons."

"Yes, I am so sorry to disturb you." Joranna's hand twitched against the side of her gown as she fought to keep her resolve. "But there is news of a Lockesbarrian armada headed this way. I thought perhaps that—"

"That perhaps you would sacrifice *our* queen instead of yourself?" Erumann accused, causing water to drip along the table as he lifted a fist.

This was a bad idea.

"I assure you that is not it," said Joranna.

"Why do you not send your own ships?" Eugena asked, echoing Erumann's thoughts. "Do you think us more prone to violence?"

"Of course not," replied Joranna. "I fear I have put off this request too long. I should have sought aid long before now. There is reason to believe Haighdlen is under a severe threat."

Eugena looked to Erumann before nodded. "We have received similar reports." Eugena's form rippled as she leaned to the side and stared behind Joranna. "Is that the girl? The one who accepted this bowl on your behalf?"

Elise froze. *Why does she always look at me? She's not even really here, and she's singling me out.*

"Indeed," said Joranna. "Do you wish to speak to her?"

Elise waved both hands in front of her, mouthing several objections as the stares of everyone standing nearby heated her skin. Darcie nudged her forward until Elise stood in front of Joranna looking down at the miniature water mermaids protruding from the filled bowl.

"She is weak! Let us leave her out of this!" Erumann growled, the water sloshing against Elise's dress before Eugena placed a hand on his shoulder. The water instantly calmed as she turned back to Elise.

Talking to heads made of water unnerved Elise in a way she could not put into words. Let alone being insulted by one.

Is this really happening right now? Why does she want to talk to me? It's not my bowl. Elise gulped, suddenly regretting her idea to contact them.

"What is your plan?" Eugena asked calmly.

"Me?" Elise squeaked. "Why me?"

"News reaches my ear one way or the other," replied the queen, "and *you* always find a way to be in the center of it."

Elise blushed.

"The king's recent passing, followed by a scandalous engagement *and* an incoming armada?" The queen's water form shook her head. "These are not by coincidence, and I am not a fool. Neither are you. So, I ask you again, what is your plan?"

Can I trust them? Elise glanced over her shoulder at Darcie, who nodded back with encouragement.

"Enough of this," Erumann bellowed. "My Queen, she is as ignorant as the rest of them. There is no plan, and they are willing to put everyone in danger on a whim!"

"Silence, my love," Eugena muttered before looking back at Elise. "Speak, girl."

Elise's body flared into a full hot flash as every inch of her burned under the pressure. She asked for this, and yet, in that moment struggled to even form words. Looking at each member of her family, Gwen, and Darcie, Elise settled her gaze on Ruby's stomach. *There's too much at stake to chicken out now.*

"I want to stop the armada before it reaches Haighdlen. I want to stop the wedding. Maybe even the coronation," she added. "And then I want to find Rona myself."

A deadly silence followed as Elise's answer was processed by everyone. *I hope I can trust all of them not to share it with Richard or anyone else.* It was too late either way.

At long last, Eugena nodded. "Quite ambitious. . .and noble. However, what you described is not a plan, child, but a mere goal."

Looking at Erumann, who shook his head, Eugena ignored him and nodded once more. "However, my army will locate and put a stop to that armada." She paused while everyone in the room smiled and cheered. "However, I caution you about seeking out Rona."

"I know she's dangerous," Elise said. "But I can't let her keep threatening everybody I love."

"And while that is commendable," added Eugena sternly, "it is worth noting that she is protected beyond her stolen army."

What is she talking about?

Erumann lifted a watery fist to his chest. "Whoever takes the life of Rona is also doomed to a most painful death."

What! Elise stammered on the spot, looking helplessly at her family's equally shocked faces. *Did they really not know, either?* Suddenly, Elise's lungs felt closed, her throat too tight.

"So, I ask you again," Eugena continued carefully, "Do you still believe in carrying out your mission?"

Elise did not know how to respond. There was always a chance she would not survive facing Rona, but it had also come with an opportunity to succeed and go home.

Now, everything had changed.

In that moment, Elise felt separate from her body. She heard whispering behind her, but she could not focus on who was speaking. Numbness spread throughout her body as the price of their mission came down to her willingly sacrificing herself.

Possibly dying is scary, but knowing *I would die. . .how can anyone expect me to be okay with that? Did my family know this before they sent me?*

Whether the present-day Laurilles knew or not, Elise felt utterly betrayed. *What will happen to my friends? Will they even be able to get home if I die?* Meeting Darcie's eye, the girls seemed to be sharing the same line of thought. This time, Darcie did not nod.

"We cannot ask her such a thing," Joranna argued. "She's just a child!"

"Rona's army is comprised of children," Eugena countered. "There will be unfortunate casualties regardless of our decision here today. What I need to know is if she will do what is necessary when the time comes, for no one else has been brave enough to take on the task."

"Elise, don't do this," Darcie pleaded. "We can figure out another way. We'll find the boys and do more research. There has to be a loophole somewhere."

While tempting, Elise knew deep down someone would have to be willing to kill Rona and *be* killed in order to save everyone. Never in her life had Elise stood up for anything, nor did she think she would ever have to. Rubbing the rough fabric of her skirt between her fingers, Elise took a tentative step forward.

"What are you doing?" Joranna asked. "Elise, you cannot—"

Elise shook her head to stop Joranna's interference as warm tears spilled down her cheeks. She faced the two water figures again. "So, if I agree, you stop the armada and save Haighdlen, right?" The queen nodded. Elise licked her lips and stared at the ceiling, unable to bring herself to look anywhere else. Short of breath, she curled her hands into fists. *This is worse than any deal with a fairy, but Richard could never get a ship there in time.* "Could you use your magic to send me to Lockesbarrow afterwards?"

"All four of us!" Darcie called over Elise's shoulder in spite of not having located the boys yet. "She's not going without her friends."

There was nothing Elise wanted more than to protect her friends, but Darcie's immediate support meant more than she would ever know. *Thank you.*

Elise waited with bated breath as the two mermaids whispered. Several droplets spilled along the cover of the diary, yet Joranna did not make any attempts to disturb the bowl.

After an excruciating period of deliberation, Eugena nodded. "You have my word. *If* all goes according to plan, and the armada is defeated, we shall meet you near Lake Laulie at sunset."

Wow, their magic is *fast.*

"Let us hope your bravery remains intact," Erumann sneered.

Eugena moved her attention to Joranna. "I would advise you to ready soldiers along your eastern border to be safe."

"Of course," Joranna answered.

Both dipped below the surface and the water calmed as the crystal bowl froze in place once more.

All was silent.

What have I gotten myself into?

"I did not expect that," Sarah whispered breathlessly. "Mother, surely there has to be another plan."

Joranna opened her mouth, closed it, and repeated the motion before shaking her head in shock.

"You don't need to say anything," Elise said. "I know what I have gotten myself into. I had to do it to save Haighdlen. An armada could kill so many *and* start a battle on your land. If we can get to Lockesbarrow in time, I can try to stop her."

"Doubtful," Ruby muttered under her breath.

Elise fought the urge to roll her eyes. *Thanks, Mom.*

Joranna admonished her youngest daughter before addressing the room. "We have until sunset to know for sure. You will need time to travel to the lake."

Wiping another falling tear, Elise sniffled and cleared her throat. "What will you do?"

Joranna squared her shoulders. "Well, after your selfless act of heroism, I can hardly stand to mope around here any longer. You will need reinforcements."

"But, Mother," Sarah quipped, "I commend her bravery as well, but you heard Richard earlier this morning. The Ambassador to Vynchia denied aiding Haighdlen after the protests began."

Joranna poured the water from the bowl back into the pitcher. "Then I will not speak with the Ambassador. I shall write to Queen Arymei herself. Between her magic and Eugena's magic, they could get the Vynchian fleet and our fleet to Lockesbarrow's shores by tomorrow."

"So soon?" Ruby asked solemnly. She crossed her arms. "The perks of magic, I suppose."

I need to tell her what happened with the fairies in case she tries to talk to Gwen about it.

Judging by the looks on Sarah's and Ruby's faces, neither had much confidence of their mother's chances.

"We keep this between us," Joranna said, settling her eyes on Gwen, who had paled during the whole mermaid conference. "Do I have everyone's word?"

Despite palatable doubts, each person nodded.

"Good. Sarah, would you fetch me my stationery? Be discreet."

Sarah nodded and left the room.

Joranna pressed a hand to her chest and began pacing again. "There is so little time. Magic will be as necessary as complete discretion on this matter. Richard cannot know until the letters are already sent out."

Sarah returned with the stationery before sitting beside her mother.

As the room quieted, it dawned on Elise that Gwen was still in the room, no doubt confused and filled with questions.

There was still the matter of what to even do with Gwen before Elise could leave for Lake Laulie. They could not simply send her home as if nothing had occurred. Elise took advantage of Joranna's involved conversation with Sarah to warn Ruby. "The king of the fairies wiped Gwen's memories. I don't have time to explain everything," she whispered into the princess's ear. "Gwen still knows you, but she won't remember giving you fairy magic. Keep it that way, please. Can you keep an eye on her? Keep her safe while I'm gone?"

Easing back, Ruby shuddered and nodded her understanding. It was apparent the princess's head was rapidly filling with questions but she remained silent.

"Yes, I'm sure you're lonely. A princess should be allowed to have friends," Elise said louder with a knowing smile, before continuing in a whisper so that only Gwen and Ruby could hear. "No one has to know when you two met."

"Well, that is ironic, because I am not sure I even know myself," Gwen chuckled. "I feel like it has been forever though. It all blends together really."

Ruby nodded with a bittersweet smile. "We have shared many talks, often late into the night." Cradling her rounded stomach, she raised her voice. "I would be honored to extend your visit here as my close friend if you accept. I could sure use the company during this time."

Gwen smiled. "I should like that very much, but I will need to write to my mother. Am I able to?"

Joranna paused her conversation to nod. "I see no reason why not, but we must proceed with caution. Please avoid any details you have overheard here today. Simply inform your mother the princess has invited you here for companionship. News will reveal itself in time, I am afraid. It will be best to let it occur naturally."

Gwen agreed before Ruby took her hand and led her out. "But first, we must get you some finer clothing." Their laughter carried into the corridor before Sarah suggested they also disperse to avoid suspicion.

"This is great!" Darcie whispered into Elise's ear. "Now, Gwen will be here and have more chances of running into Richard!"

At least something good might come out of this. Elise wanted to be happier. The idea that Richard and Gwen were under the same roof would normally be enough to put Elise over the moon. However, she could not bring herself to feel anything but existential dread as the plan was set into motion.

The following ten minutes passed like an hour.

Joranna drafted a letter for the current Captain of the Guard and one for Queen Arymei. She was able to make jokes about the legibility of such hastily written notices, but Elise did not join in the anticipation.

You wanted this. You asked for this. You can't be so surprised it happened this way. While logical, Elise could not get on board with her rationalizing train of thought.

Darcie did her best to comfort Elise on the chaise while they waited, but Elise was not paying attention. Her mind was far away from this room. All voices were muffled as she stared ahead in a daze. It was as if she were wandering lost around in a dense fog. The world continued turning, but she was immobilized within the confines of her own mind.

Trapped.

Paralyzed.

It dawned on Elise as she recounted the many panic attacks in her life, that she never truly understood fear until that moment. She was thankful to be sitting as the thought of standing made her knees weak.

Everyone here was willing to depend on her, but when the time came to act, could she rely on herself?

How am I going to tell Gavin?

She needed to find him, and Mitch, yet it was only when Joranna finished the letters that Elise was pulled out of her reverie.

"Sarah, take this letter to the captain." Joranna handed a piece of paper to her eldest daughter before turning to Elise and Ruby. "We need to get Arymei's copy to her ambassador."

"I thought you said you wouldn't talk to him?" Darcie questioned.

"I simply meant to try and negotiate. Only he will have magical access to communicate with her instantly, but Richard would never allow such a thing from our family." Tapping the letter against her chin, Joranna pondered how they would transfer it safely.

Darcie's eyes lit up. "What about Charles?"

"Richard's closest friend?" Joranna released a hollow chuckle. "Are you mad?"

Elise came to her friend's rescue. "No, she's right. I think we could trust him with this. He's made it known Richard hasn't been himself. He would want to do everything he could to make things go back to the way they were."

Joranna sighed. "We have no choice and are losing precious time. Let us hope you are right."

Before they could leave, however, shouting could be heard coming up the corridor.

"What on earth?" Joranna stepped closer to the door before Ballard knocked and entered.

"Forgive the intrusion, Your Highness, but there is a groundskeeper in the main hall who requests an audience with you. Prince Richard is not seeing anyone at present and there is a growing concern around Lady Iris's *staff.*" He glared at Elise and Darcie. "What shall I tell him?"

"For goodness' sake," Joranna huffed. "Richard wants to take over, yet will not take care of simple staff disputes." She instructed Darcie and Elise to stay with her as Ballard led them down the staircase.

All thoughts of hiding her identity were far gone when they entered the main hall to find Gavin and Mitch standing behind a shaggy, disgruntled-looking man.

Elise's breath caught as her heart threatened to stop beating.

Darcie had the same reaction as both girls ran past Joranna into their respective boyfriends' arms.

Elise tightened her embrace as tears streamed down her face. *Thank you, thank you, thank you. Thank God you're safe.* Ignoring the stunned audience, Elise kissed and hugged him once more, inhaling his scent.

"You probably don't want to do that," he chuckled. "We've been in the stables."

"I don't care," she wept into his neck. "I don't care. I'm just glad you're here. I love you."

If she were going to die, moments like this were sacred and numbered. The pure joy on his face and hearing him tell her he loved her back was what she wanted to remember. He would find out when the time was right.

For now, she was content with holding him.

CHAPTER 23

"Are you going to allow this?" complained the groundskeeper to Joranna. He sneered at the two couples. "Like I told Mr. Ballard here, these two are the most *incompetent* stable boys I've ever seen. They should be dismissed immediately!"

Joranna fought to suppress a smile as she folded her hands delicately in front of her. "I hear your concern, and I shall handle it personally. Thank you."

Whether or not he believed her, the groundskeeper bowed and stalked away muttering under his breath.

Once he was out of earshot, Joranna addressed the steward next. "Mr. Ballard, please arrange for any further disruptions or issues to be handled during court. I should like it if others do not get the idea to parade their problems through the main halls on a whim. We do have a level of decorum to protect."

"Understood, Your Excellency, but Prince Richard has suspended court gatherings."

"Honestly! He is being such a child." Joranna pursed her lips with an impatient stomp.

Ballard regarded the reunited teenagers. "Will *they* be remaining on the staff?"

The queen chuckled. "Goodness, no. I have business with them. See that proper garments are prepared for them before we go to the dining hall."

Stumbling over his words, Ballard pinched the bridge of his nose. Elise noted his eye also began twitching. "With the utmost respect, Queen Joranna, the prince has made it quite clear that they are not to be on castle grounds and—"

"And yet here they are," Joranna pointed out with an overly sweet smile. "*My* guests. Have five place settings added. Princess Ruby also has a guest who will remain with us for some time. Please also instruct Ms. Persimmons to have a room prepared for her."

Ballard bit the inside of his cheek. "Shall any other rooms be required for tonight?" He stared point blank at Elise, who glared back with the same level of disdain.

"No, one will be all. Thank you. You all stay with me while we wait for everything to be prepared." Joranna ushered them towards Richard's study.

"Your Highness!" Ballard squeaked, sweeping a strand of oily hair across his forehead. "Prince Richard was *most* insistent he be left alone this morning. I should caution you—"

"Ballard, that is enough," Joranna quipped. "Now, open the door."

The steward grimaced, his skin a sickly shade of green. Hanging his head, he opened the door and stepped out of the way. "Yes, Your Majesty."

Elise shivered under the steward's disdainful sneer. His eyes narrowed as she passed him, making her pause as Joranna stepped up to the doorway. "Maybe this isn't a good idea." She fiddled with her fingers. "We can wait out here. This really doesn't concern us."

Joranna smirked. "Since when has that ever stopped the four of you?"

She has a point. Elise held her breath as they filed into the familiar study.

Not once had Elise entered this room with enthusiasm. Often, she resembled a dog with its tail tucked. Goosebumps lined her arms as she caught sight of her uncle behind the desk. There would never be a time where she did not initially mistake him for Derek. The resemblance was uncanny, making her miss the late king even more. Richard was now the third generation of Laurille rulers she had encountered. If they did not get through to him soon, he would be the last.

Ballard cleared his throat. "Your Majesty—"

"Are you familiar with the word *privacy*, Ballard?" Richard groaned without glancing up from a document. "Perhaps we should discuss the definition of *dismissal* next."

Joranna cleared her throat, making Richard lift his head at last. "Mother! I was not expecting you."

"It appears not," Joranna agreed, narrowing her eyes on the empty glasses that had yet to be collected. "I thought we might discuss—"

Elise felt her knees buckle when Richard's demeanor stiffened and witnessed the seething fury behind his eyes.

He rose from the chair, sweeping his hand along the desk's edge. Inhaling sharply, he blew out an exasperated breath. "I do not have time for this. Ballard, dispatch the guards to arrest them this moment. They will be dealt with after the coronation."

"Not so fast," Joranna argued. "They are my guests."

Richard had the audacity to roll his eyes with a hollow laugh. "*They* have been your *guests* my entire life and yet have not aged a day. *They* claim to come in peace yet wreak havoc wherever *they* go. What a coincidence *they* should return prior to my being enthroned. I take it *they* have a problem with it?"

"Not at all," Joranna replied before Elise could answer. "I do."

Elise did not hide her surprise at Joranna's bluntness. All thoughts of the plan vanished as the air in the room chilled. She met Gavin's equally tense gaze, wishing they could return to the hall. *I thought she was just coming to fuss at him about not meeting with the groundskeeper. We shouldn't be in here right now.*

Richard smiled politely. "Perhaps we should speak in private, and if I recall, you gave your blessing for me to be crowned early before secluding yourself in mourning." He checked the clock. "Is it not a bit early for you to be out and about?"

Joranna did not take the bait but remained composed, something Elise knew she could not have done so easily herself. "At one time, I trusted it was in the kingdom's best interest for you to be crowned. However, in the past weeks, you have become quite corrupt."

"Careful," he warned.

Yet, she pressed on. "How long has it been since you held court? I had to handle a minor grievance in the main hall, of all places, because you are not receiving anyone. If this is to be the common practice, then we may as well leave the front gates open."

Richard closed the distance between them and took his mother's hand. "You are upset. Naturally, it will take time to grieve father's death—"

"*That* is another point I wish to make," Joranna added, pulling her hand away. "*You* have not taken the time to mourn *at all*. You have all but barricaded yourself in this study, avoiding your responsibilities—"

Rolling his eyes again, Richard turned on his heel and walked over to the window. "I am taking respon—"

"Oh, really?" she challenged. "Then where is Ian? Why are there reports that you have ceased your morning briefings? I even caught word from the servants of violent protests occurring in Clara following your announcement last night. Richard, do you not understand the severity of this decision? There could be attempts on your life! Have you even sent out guards to address it?"

Richard opened his mouth, reconsidered, and closed it again. His eyes flashed with calculation as if withholding information.

What is it? Spit it out!

"Are you finished?" he asked her before nodding towards Elise and her friends. "You have created quite a spectacle to undermine my authority. Spreading false narratives of my corruptness will not prevent the ceremony from proceeding."

Joranna held up a finger when Mitch tried to interrupt. Glaring at her son, the queen browsed the letters on his desk. "This group seeks to protect Haighdlen and learn the truth. Something that has been elusive as of late."

Richard shook his head. "I knew I would have those who doubted me. I feared they even sat on the council. Never would I have guessed my own mother would have such little faith in me." He asked her to step away from the desk, waiting until she finally obliged. "Allow me to put your conspiracy theories to rest. Tomorrow night,

Lady Iris will be crowned Queen of Haighdlen. *You* will lead the family in welcoming her *and* her mother. A united front is the only way to prevent war, which is all I seek to do."

"You can't prevent it. It's already here," Elise blurted out. "Everything we've warned you about is happening now."

Richard continued as if he did not hear her. "The council can continue speculating, but once we are wed, Lockesbarrow will be an ally."

"Yeah?" Darcie challenged. "Then why do they have an armada headed this way?"

I don't know if we should have told him that yet.

Hearing it for the first time along with Richard, Gavin and Mitch wore matching shocked expressions.

The smugness faded from Richard's face. Narrowing his gaze warily, he looked between each of them as if waiting for a practical joke to come to light.

"Perhaps you would have known if you received your morning report," Elise offered with a quizzical brow.

Rather than respond to her, he bent over his desk in a panic, shuffling the disorderly pile of documents. "I must meet with the captain."

"It is already done," Joranna replied calmly. "The situation will be resolved by sunset."

The prince stared at his mother as if she spoke a different language. He scoffed in disbelief, as if convinced their entire exchange was a satirical prank. "You have been so incredibly sick with grief that you can barely lift a spoon. I hardly think you need to have a hand in foreign policy. What is next, Mother? A coup against me?"

"Enough!" Joranna snapped. "You will not belittle me or your siblings any longer. If a rebellion occurs, it will be self-induced."

He slammed his fist against the desk. "*I* am being a strong leader!"

"*You* are being a spoiled tyrant!" she corrected. "You have completely abandoned your late father's priorities."

"Such as?" he demanded.

"What about investigating the prison?" Darcie offered.

Joranna made to calm Darcie, insisting she could handle the matter, but Elise felt compelled to support the argument.

"That's right! Gwen Archer's father is in there, and he's completely innocent. King Derek promised to look into it before he was cursed. Her family has even lost their farm over it."

"Who?" asked the prince.

"From last night," Mitch reminded him. "The dancer who turned you down."

"I can't blame her," Gavin added.

Elise suppressed a chuckle as she met her boyfriend's eyes.

Realization dawned on Richard's face before he shook his head. "How do you know—"

"We are getting entirely off the point," Joranna announced. "What I want to know is how you could collude with Brahm's family after what he and his sister did. Who initiated this arrangement?"

Elise bit the inside of her cheek so as not to scream when there was a knock at the door before Richard could reply. Ballard poked his head in long enough to announce breakfast was awaiting them in the dining hall. He bitterly added that enough places were set to accommodate every guest.

Richard looked down at the floor as the door closed. "Let us not quarrel, Mother. We both know this kingdom needs strong leadership, particularly during this vulnerable time. That is all I seek to provide. You need to join me and convince the people this is the right path forward. It is that simple."

Joranna sighed with a shuddering breath. Shaking her head with a glassy stare, she turned to face the door. Glancing over her shoulder, she added, "A strong leader would know the simple path is not always the correct one." Without waiting for a reply, she beckoned the teenagers to follow her.

The door was opened for them by a guard, and Joranna waited until they were all in the main hall before retrieving a handkerchief. She took a moment to compose herself. "I must agree with you. That is not my son. The difficult decision will be how to rescue him in time."

Luck, perhaps fate, was on their side, however, as Charles rounded the corner at that precise moment. Elise suppressed the urge to cry out as he greeted them with a mixture of surprise and ingrained manners.

Beckoning him to her, Joranna retrieved the letter from her sleeve and whispered important directions into his ear.

"It's to Arymei. Don't say anything. I'll explain later," Elise said when Gavin asked her what the letter was about.

"I need that delivered before he sets back for Vynchia today," Joranna finished.

"The Ambassador has planned to stay until after the ceremony," Charles replied to Joranna. "However, I do not believe any of the councilmen will be dining with the family. They have requested an emergency session with Richard, but I will deliver this immediately." Charles bowed before retreating up the staircase.

"Does someone want to tell us what's going on?" Mitch asked.

Elise and Darcie were prevented from informing the boys yet again as Joranna suggested they all freshen up for breakfast.

Ballard approached and ushered them upstairs to be bathed and dressed.

"How are you always around, man?" Mitch whined. "For someone so busy, you sure know how to pop out at the right moment."

Agreed.

Ballard tilted his chin haughtily. "The family relies on me to be available and oversee daily operations. Not to mention, just this morning, you four impersonated staff to gain access to the family and have added to my duties. I have been instructed to tend to your needs rather than your deserved arrest. You have no one to blame but yourselves."

I can't believe this guy actually saved us once. Sounds like he would've been happier letting Brahm win. I guess I should be happy he's so loyal to my family.

By the time they were ready and entered the dining hall, Ingrid, Iris, Gwen and the royal family—save for Richard and Ian—

had already begun eating. Elise and her friends took the seats opposite of Ruby and Gwen.

"Why are the maids eating with us?" Iris asked her mother, who had not yet looked up from her plate. "I thought I recognized one sitting with Princess Ruby, but now all three of them are sitting here."

Without the bonnets to conceal their identities, Elise and Darcie were instantly recognized. Ingrid's eyes widened as she choked into her glass before subsequently giving way to a coughing fit.

Joranna studied the woman before smirking at Elise and Darcie. Her voice was calm and unbothered. "Are you quite all right, Lady Ingrid?"

Ingrid looked between Elise, Darcie, and Joranna, opening her mouth repeatedly without actually speaking. At a loss for words, she finally dabbed the sides of her mouth with a cloth napkin and released an awkward set of polite giggles. "I am q-quite well, Your Majesty, thank you."

Suppressing a laugh around a mouthful of food, Elise chewed in silence. She basked in the opportunity to watch the other woman squirm in her chair. Given the devious glares she sent their way, Ingrid most likely recalled Elise and Darcie pinning her to the floor the night of her arrest. Elise still longed to know how Brahm and Ingrid escaped prison that ultimately led to Gavin's kidnapping. As her mind ventured down that unwanted path, Elise reached out and squeezed Gavin's hand under the table.

From that moment, any exchanges between Ingrid and Iris were whispered, further fueling Elise's suspicions. The only part of breakfast more frustrating was the series of looks Darcie kept sending her to speak to Gavin.

If she winks or clears her throat one more time, I'm going to kill her.

"You got something in your eye, Babe?" Mitch finally asked, prompting Darcie to roll her eyes.

"I think she wants Elise to tell me something," Gavin said with a laugh before turning to her. "So, what's up?"

Not here. Not like this. Instead, she kept it brief. "When the mermaids return, they're going to meet us at Lake Laulie and send us to Lockesbarrow."

"Does it have to be mermaids?" Mitch groaned. "I hate mermaids."

"I can't say I'm excited to get back there," Gavin confessed. "But at least they're helping us. Why do you sound so uneasy?"

When the doors were opened for Richard to enter, Elise watched the prince stride across the room to his seat at the head of the table without so much as a nod towards anyone. When his food was plated, he proceeded to stab at the contents with a fork, unbothered by everyone's stare.

Joranna played off his rudeness with an uncomfortable chuckle. "You must excuse my son. There are many preparations to attend to. He forgets himself."

Only when Joranna cleared her throat, did Richard look up and notice Gwen's presence. His eyes darted between her and Iris before he leaned back in his chair.

"Were you not supposed to meet with the council?" Joranna inquired.

"I cancelled it," he snapped, irritably whipping his cloth napkin loose on his knee rather than unfolding it.

Joranna offered the others at the table a polite smile before carefully proceeding. "Do you think that wise?"

Richard ignored her.

Determined to ease the tension, Lady Ingrid switched the topic of conversation to wedding preparations and the lace on Iris's gown. As Ingrid and Joranna prattled on, and everyone else settled into their own conversations, Elise ignored Darcie's insufferable attempts to get her to tell Gavin the whole truth by watching her brooding uncle.

Expecting him to be annoyed with the idle gossip, Elise watched as he feigned interest in what Iris was saying. Humming politely during pauses, he stroked his chin and nodded at whoever was speaking.

However, his eyes frequently landed on Gwen, who was too engrossed in her own talk with Ruby to even notice.

"I am told you excel in horsemanship, Your Highness," Ingrid said, nodding towards her daughter. "I am constantly encouraging Iris to improve her own skills, but I am afraid she would prefer to tend to her watercolors and singing. In those areas, you will not find anyone as accomplished."

"Yes, Iris, we were quite taken with your beautiful voice last night," Joranna agreed. "Like an angel. Is that not right, Richard?"

The prince redirected his attention away from Gwen as Elise met Sarah's eyes. The eldest princess looked between her brother and Gwen before realization dawned on her features.

"I must extend a compliment to Ms. Archer as well," said Sarah, nodding towards Gwen. "Your performance was quite captivating. Would you all not agree?"

Ingrid straightened up and wiped the sides of her mouth with a frown. "I must confess I found it a vulgar display. Is that what they are trying to pass off as art these days?" Shaking her head, Ingrid tittered into her glass.

Richard cleared his throat as he swallowed a bite of food. "I was not aware you were a renowned critic of the arts, Lady Ingrid. Perhaps you can enlighten us to a suitable art form that would insure Ms. Archer's protection against future scrutiny."

Joranna frowned at her son's impertinence while Iris hunched forward to make herself appear smaller.

"I should have liked to have seen it," said Ruby.

"It was nothing special," Gwen said to Ruby before looking at Richard. "And I require no protection but thank you."

The prince's eyes lingered on her long after everyone else returned to their meals.

Ingrid drained her glass before groaning. "A fierce migraine has come over me, I am afraid. Perhaps I should rest. Iris, will you not join me?"

Elise shared an anxious glance with her friends.

How convenient. She is up to something.

"Is there anything we can give you? A glass of wine perhaps?" Joranna offered.

Ingrid declined the kind gesture and ushered her daughter out of the room.

Another tense silence followed before Richard realized his family's eyes were watching him.

"What?" he asked.

"How long do you plan to act in such an impetuous manner?" Joranna demanded. "I am not in favor of this misalliance, but your mistreatment of those ladies cannot go unnoticed."

Richard rolled his eyes and popped a grape into his mouth. "What mistreatment?"

"You all but ignored poor Iris, who is meek as it is," Joranna explained. "And as for her mother—"

"Lady Ingrid insulted a young lady's reputation," Richard said.

"Please do not consider my reputation," Gwen interrupted. "I am perfectly capable of taking care of myself."

"I would not be doing my duty to you as your future king if I allowed such slander against your name."

Gwen scoffed. "It would benefit everyone if you did your duty at all."

There was a collective gasp around the table—except by Ruby, who laughed—but before Ballard or anyone could address Gwen's insult, the doors burst open. Charles ran in accompanied by another young man with blood splattered across his face and shirt.

"Lord Fenton! Honestly, what is the meaning of this?" Joranna demanded.

"Prince Ian was just attacked at one of the protests in town!" Charles informed them.

"What on earth was he doing there?" Joranna stood abruptly and made her way towards him. "Where is he? Is he alive? Who is this? He is also injured." She regarded the man beside Charles.

"The prince is alive, Majesty," Charles replied. "He was rescued and safely delivered here by guards and this young man."

"I am greatly indebted to you, sir," Joranna said. "You have saved my son's life. What is your name?"

The man in question bowed before the queen, wincing as he clutched his ribs. "Liam, Your Highness. Liam Faerse."

The blood ran out of Elise's face. *Liam? That's Sarah's future husband.* She chanced a look at her aunt, but Sarah had already made her way over to Joranna, who met Richard's eyes across the room.

"Well, Richard, here is the result of your peace treaty." The queen gestured towards the injured man before turning towards Charles. "Please take me to Ian at once and have Mr. Faerse treated by the doctor as well. Sarah, come with me. You can begin healing their wounds while we wait." Without another word, the two women exited with Charles and Liam.

Gwen cleared her throat, staring between the door and Richard. "Are you not going to go with them?"

Richard shrugged. "My mother and sister are capable of tending to my brother's needs. He hardly needs me to add to the chaos."

Gwen scoffed before looking at Ruby. "Is he serious?"

"Sadly," Ruby muttered miserably into her cup.

"Do you not want to go see him yourself?" Gwen inquired.

"And leave you?" Ruby asked, sending Richard a disapproving glare. "Unlike my brother, I possess a fraction of manners."

"I will manage. Go," Gwen urged, standing as Ruby stood to leave.

The doors opened before Ruby reached them as Charles returned. Sharing a tense silent exchange, he stepped out of the way to allow her into the hall.

"I think that's our cue to leave, too," Darcie whispered.

Gavin, Mitch, and Elise agreed and excused themselves as well.

"We can wait in the library," Mitch suggested. "They usually don't mind us hanging out in there."

"You guys go ahead," Elise said. "I'll be there in a minute."

Gavin paused and turned around. "Are you okay?"

"Yeah," Elise said. "I just want to hang around and make sure Gwen's okay."

Gavin hesitated but nodded when Mitch tugged on his arm.

By the time Elise hid behind the dining hall door, Richard was standing with Charles in a hushed discussion about what happened. She could only make out what he was saying once the prince called out to Gwen as she passed them.

"Would you care to take a turn around the courtyard with me, Ms. Archer?" Richard asked.

Gwen shook her head.

"Is that all the reply I get?" He smiled at Charles. "I suppose I should not expect more from a commoner."

Did he really just say that? What a jerk!

The men's laughter subsided when Gwen approached them.

"This commoner has plenty to say about His Highness," she corrected him. "Whether you are capable of hearing it is another matter entirely."

She appeared unfazed to their mockery and jeers.

"By all means," Richard laughed, regarding her with amusement. "Let us hear it. Do you worst."

Uh oh. He should not have said that.

Gwen narrowed her eyes at the arrogant prince.

"The crown may influence others to shield you against such censure, but I believe it will benefit Your Highness to hear the truth from someone who lives outside this castle." Gwen tipped her chin up towards him, a menacing flash in her eyes. "King Derek put his family and this kingdom first while you are busy pandering to a known enemy. In the few minutes I just spent at your table, it was made clear you ignored the wishes of your mother, the council, and ultimately the welfare of the people protesting by proceeding with such an engagement."

"You think I picked the wrong bride then?" he chortled, nudging Charles to join in before letting his eyes roam over her body.

Elise swallowed convulsively, debating whether she should step in with a diversion.

However, Gwen remained unimpressed as she squared her shoulders and stepped closer, careful to maintain a safe enough distance as to not alert any guards. "Until you can think of someone other than yourself, your subjects will sink into poverty, and Haighdlen will be vulnerable to attacks similar to the one made on your own brother." It was her turn to look him up and down. "Not a promising start for a king. Now, if you will excuse me, your sister is expecting me."

She spun on her heel and stormed off, not taking notice of Elise standing speechless gaping behind the door.

That was awesome! He needed to hear that.

Peeking through the crack in the door, Elise suppressed a laugh at Richard's stunned expression.

"Why does she keep doing that?" he asked Charles. "That is twice now she has berated me and stormed off."

"Why do you allow it?" Charles challenged with a knowing grin. "You have arrested others for less offense."

"I do not know." Running a hand along the back of his neck, Richard sighed. "Intoxicated as I was, I could not sleep last night from thinking of her. Now, she is a guest in my own castle. What have I done to deserve such torture?"

Charles shrugged and patted Richard on the back. "Would you like the short list or the long?"

Both young men laughed and walked out, leaving Elise to wait until the hall was clear to join her friends in the library.

CHAPTER 24

When the doctor allowed Ian to have visitors outside of family, Elise and her friends found Joranna holding her son's hand. The prince was asleep, and Ruby—who sat on the other side of the bed—informed them he had lost a lot of blood, evident from his deathly pale complexion tainted by various cuts and scrapes that accompanied a black eye. Sarah stood at the foot of the bed trying to heal large bruises on his calves with her magic.

"Did you find out why he was out there?" Elise asked.

Sarah nodded grimly. "I have been talking a great deal with Mr. Faerse, who is being treated in the nearest guestroom. Ian snuck out first thing this morning to join the protestors."

"But why?" Mitch asked. "Why be a part of the violence against his own family?"

"Supposedly, it was scheduled to be peaceful," Sarah continued with a skeptic shake of her head, "but it got out of hand and quickly escalated into a full riot."

"And Ian is not one to lie down and quit," Ruby added.

"It was foolish of him to be out there in the first place," Joranna snapped, wiping Ian's hair out of his eyes. "Completely reckless."

It must be so hard to see her son like this after just losing Derek.

"Did that Liam guy say anything else?" Gavin asked. "Anything about Rona or how they escaped?"

Sarah shook her head.

"The important thing is that he is home with his family," said Joranna with a sad smile. "After tomorrow, I fear I will not recognize our family any longer."

"What do you mean?" Elise asked.

"We may be separating for a while," she mumbled. "Richard spent the better part of an hour explaining it was for security reasons. Sometimes, I think he just likes to hear himself talk."

Crossing her arms, Elise scoffed and leaned against the wall. "Yeah, well, Gwen found a way to shut him up." Encouraged by their curiosity, she went on to share what was exchanged outside the dining hall.

"I love her." Ruby chuckled. "I wish I could have seen his face."

Despite her best effort, Sarah failed to suppress a smile of her own. "I cannot say he did not deserve it."

The lighthearted humor vanished, however, when the door opened to allow Richard and Iris entrance.

"How is he coming along?" asked the prince.

"Ah, Richard," Joranna tossed over her shoulder. "So good of you to finally visit."

Iris remained behind the prince with her head lowered. A silken purse Elise had not noticed at breakfast dangled from her gloved hands. As lovely as she was, the young woman stood like a porcelain doll that would potentially shatter.

Sarah cleared her throat. "I must check on Mr. Faerse now. Ruby, would you please join me?"

Ruby stood. "You go ahead. I should like to find Gwen."

As the princesses exited, the room was enveloped in a suffocating silence until the door closed again.

"Lady Iris, it is kind of you to visit my son," Joranna said.

Iris merely nodded her head, prompting Richard to clear his throat. "My darling Iris actually requests a private meeting with the travelers."

"Oh?" Joranna stared at Elise, Gavin, Mitch, and Darcie, who shared the same shocked expressions. "Whatever for?"

"I believe that would fall under the perimeters of *private*, Mother. Could you give us a moment?"

Joranna scoffed and met Elise's apprehensive gaze.

Elise shook her head. *Please don't leave us alone with them.* There was something brewing between the prince and his grim fiancée, who looked equal parts skittish and ill. Despite her wishes, Elise watched her grandmother exit the room.

"Tell them, darling," Richard said. "Whatever it is."

"Before you tell us whatever it is you came in here for," Elise said with a bite to her tone, "answer me this. Does your mother get those headaches often?"

Iris paled even more, which Elise did not know was possible. At this point, she was ghostly white. "Y-yes. I have urged her to be seen by a doctor, but she refuses." Seeing their unconvinced expressions, Iris lowered her eyes to the floor and cleared her throat. "However, that is not why I came. My mother cannot know I am here. Not yet anyway."

Spill it! Elise could not stand the building tension in the other woman's unspoken message.

Iris lifted the small purse and removed a velvet-lined box.

Gavin inhaled sharply, taking Elise by surprise.

"What is it?" she asked.

"I've seen that box before," he answered, keeping his eyes glued on it. "Rona used it to connect with Vaughn."

Elise's brows drew together. "Where did you get that?" she asked Iris.

"It was delivered to me this morning," Iris said before retrieving a folded piece of paper from her purse. She held it out for Elise. "Along with this."

The note simply read, *Deliver this to Elise. She will know what to do with it. Do not open outside of Lockesbarrow.*

Iris handed Elise the box. Despite the warning, Elise tried to open the box anyway. When it would not budge, she groaned. *He spelled it.* As irritated as that prospect made her, Elise considered the risk he took to get it to her.

"Can you hold onto this for me?" she asked Gavin before approaching the frightened young girl. "I want to know what you're really doing here."

"I-I just told you," she stammered. "I wanted to deliver that to you. Now, I'm done. I can go."

Darcie and Mitch blocked the door.

"You're not going anywhere," Elise said.

"This is treason," Richard argued. "Guards!"

"She has you under a spell," Elise continued. "I'm sure of it, and I want to hear her confess as to why." Elise targeted Lady Iris with her thoughts. *Tell us why. What is really going on? Why are you here?*

Trapped against the wall, it took less than three attempts from Elise's powers before Lady Iris fell to her knees in hysterics. "I cannot take it anymore. I w-was sent to marry the prince for a forced alliance. Rona said she w-would kill my mother if I didn't. . .and me."

"So, you have no desire to take over and be queen?" Gavin asked.

She shook her head and looked at Richard. "I am sorry, Your Highness. I have tried to play the part, but I am not strong enough. I cannot take the guilt any longer. I am a mere singer tainted by the wrong family line."

Keep going. How do we end the curse? Elise put all her strength into keeping Iris talking.

"I am an embarrassment to my mother and uncle," Iris wailed, "and now to Rona, too."

Vaughn must have known she would do what she was told and hand over the box without question. I still question his motive.

Elise repeated her request for the curse to be broken. "End whatever control you have over him. Turn him back to his normal self."

Iris stood, sobbing, and tugged on a ring she wore. "Richard was given this during the contract meeting. It was tampered with beforehand, cursed, so that Richard would be convinced to give it to me and make me his bride." She placed it into Richard's palm and closed his fingers around it. "Use your magic to destroy it, and you will see the truth."

Richard looked from Iris to his fist. Hesitating, he squeezed it until a light appeared from his powers. When he opened his hand again, it vanished, and he fell to his knees unsteadily. Before anyone could help him, he was able to stagger into a standing position while using the wall to hold himself upright. When the effects of the spell completely left him, he was able to correct his posture.

"There, you are back to normal now," Iris whispered, sniffling without meeting his eyes. "I am so sorry."

"I have to go," was all Richard said, waiting for Mitch and Darcie to move before opening the door and slamming it shut behind him.

What do we do about Iris? Elise's question went unanswered as the young woman fled the room in a fresh bout of tears.

"That was crazy," Mitch said, looking at Elise. "Did you make her confess or did she give up that information on her own?"

Elise sighed. "Honestly, I think it was a little of both. She never wanted to be a part of any of this. I believe that."

The doctor returned at that moment, insisting they had stayed long enough and to let Ian sleep in peace.

Now, we just have to wait until our meeting with Eugena.

A few hours later, Elise lounged at a table with her friends in the back courtyard just outside the ballroom. Invited to play croquet with Joranna, Gwen, and the two princesses, Elise and her friends opted to watch instead. It was a perfectly decent way to pass the afternoon, given they had no other plans, yet every chime of the grandfather clock inside the castle reminded Elise of what was coming.

"Do you think we'll even make it to Lake Laulie?" Mitch asked out of the blue. He tore a piece of cake off his plate and plopped it into his mouth. "I'm just wondering. Mermaids hate humans after all. Who knows if that was really Eugena you talked to. It could have been bewitched separately or something."

"It was really her, Mitch," Darcie groaned, pinching the bridge of her nose. She tilted her head back on the chair. "Is it sunset yet?"

Gavin squinted up at the perfectly positioned sun as its rays warmed their faces. Not a cloud appeared in the bright blue sky. "I'd say not," he replied sarcastically as birds flew in and out of the garden ahead.

Elise sat upright in her chair as Richard walked towards the ladies' game. "Guys! Guys, look!" Shielding her eyes to get a better look, she ushered them out of their seats. "Come on. Let's see what's happening."

Royal etiquette thrown aside, Elise sprinted down to the lawn with the others on her heels.

Joranna was taken aback by their hastiness. "Elise, my goodness. You should really slow down, my dear."

The other ladies, engrossed in a whispering exchange, giggled excessively until Richard approached.

"I did not realize so many of you would be out here. Do not pause your merriment on my account," he pleaded. Clearing his throat, Richard paused to collect his thoughts. "I have done a great deal of thinking about what you all have shared. In light of the recent acts of treason, I have ended my betrothal and wedding to Lady Iris. I will not have her defamed in all this, but I thought it best to send her and her mother home. It was a mutual decision between Lady Iris and myself. Her mother's temper I cannot vouch for."

He shifted from one foot to the other and folded his hands behind him. "First, I should like to apologize to you, Mother. Ever since Iris was kind enough to withdraw her control over me, memories keep flooding back of my latest actions, and I cannot help but be appalled by them. You of all people deserve the utmost respect, and I will do whatever is needed to remedy that." He kissed his mother's hand and faced Sarah and Ruby. "I should next direct my apology to my siblings. Ian will need to hear this later, but you— come to think of it, Elise, the four of you as well—all tried to warn me about the path I was taking. I would not listen. It appears my stubbornness was present before the curse, so it only intensified its effects. It was still not fair to—"

"Is that my mother?" Gwen interrupted, squinting to gaze across the courtyard.

Following her line of vision, Elise was also shocked to see Ballard was indeed escorting Mrs. Archer and Talia towards them. *What are they doing here?*

"Ahh, good." Richard nodded. "Right on time." He ignored Gwen's confounded expression and greeted the two women upon their arrival. "Thank you for coming on such short notice."

Mrs. Archer blushed as Richard kissed her hand. "The honor is ours, Your Highness." She darted a motherly side glance at Gwen. "I do hope Gwendolyn has been conducting herself accordingly."

"Of course," Richard assured her. "In fact, the kingdom could do with more strong women like her."

Talia tossed an unconvinced glare in her sister's direction as Richard continued. "I am afraid I may have offended your daughter last night at the festival, and to my utmost embarrassment, this morning as well. My manners were abhorrent, but her quick wit challenged my arrogant ideals and put me in my place, rightfully so."

Talia broke out in an unflattering fit of laughter. "She told him off. Now, that I can believe."

Mrs. Archer sighed hopelessly at Gwen before addressing the prince. "Your Majesty, please excuse any impertinence on my daughter's part." For good measure, she also slapped Talia on the arm to silence her, too.

Richard chuckled. "There is no injury to report, madam." At this, he met and held Gwen's gaze. "But I am disgusted to have given such a poor first impression that I believe only a most sincere, grand gesture can atone for it." He checked over his shoulder before returning his attention to Gwen. His eyes softened with a brief smile. "I only hope this is enough of a token to prove how truly sorry I am and to beg your forgiveness."

Richard stepped aside, and in the distance six guards were escorting someone behind them. Only when they entered the clearing could the group see a frail older man shuffling to keep up, his clothing reduced to rags that hung off his bony frame. His hair, gray and stringy, blew ever so slightly in the breeze as a layer of sweat formed on his brow.

"Is that. . ." Talia trailed off, her eyes widening in shock. "Is that *Papa*?"

Mrs. Archer and Gwen grabbed each other's arms with a gasp.

"I have issued him a full pardon," Richard informed them. "Not that an innocent man, which he clearly is, needs it. However, he is the first in a long line of false arrests made under the last Captain of the Guard." He held out his arm.

Mrs. Archer, unable to wait a second more, lifted the front of her dress and hurried towards her husband. Gwen dropped her mallet, grabbed Talia's hand, and the two trotted closely behind their mother.

I don't believe it. After all this time.

Elise choked back a cry when she watched Mr. Archer lift his head and recognize his family running towards him. He quickened his step as fast as his feet and legs, though weak and shaky, could carry him. Mr. Archer hunched forward with outstretched arms as his openly weeping wife threw herself into them. They rocked back and forth in the tightest of embraces, only parting long enough to envelope their daughters upon their arrival.

"Thank you," Richard said to Elise's group as he watched the sentimental reunion. He smiled as the crying elderly man placed kisses on his wife and daughters' heads and equally soaked cheeks. "For not giving up on me."

Elise wiped away a tear of her own and leaned into Gavin's embrace. "I'm so happy for them."

The reunited family slowly made their way back to the royal family and teenagers. After bowing to Richard and the others, all but Gwen chatted happily with Joranna and her daughters while Gwen stepped aside to approach Richard.

Swiping a hand across her face, she could not help but break out in the most genuine of smiles. Her voice broke in a choked sob and her smile widened. "I cannot believe you did this."

"Indeed, Mr. Archer is a free man," replied the prince. "You will also be contacted about reclaiming your lost farm, including compensation for wages lost for the duration of your father's imprisonment. I hope you will find this to be enough to forgive me."

Closing her eyes, Gwen tightened her lips to suppress another sob as more warm tears streamed down her cheeks. When she opened them, it was as if to see the prince for the first time. "More than enough," she whispered. "Thank you."

Kiss her. Come on, kiss her.

From where Elise stood, her uncle and future aunt were certainly close enough. The sun's rays bouncing off the castle could not have created a more romantic ambience, and yet neither gave in to the temptation.

"Are you feeling well?" Gwen inquired. "I imagine being cursed to have your free will removed could be quite taxing."

He chuckled. "My pride is wounded, as expected. I have not only disgraced my late father, but nearly ruined the legacy of my family, and almost waltzed my kingdom into a hostile takeover."

Gwen rocked back and forth, her lips drawn into a thin line. "That is quite a long list of achievements."

"Indeed," he replied. "I only wish I can gain the respect and trust of my kingdom before it is too late."

She stared at his profile while his attention was on her family. "I know you will do the right thing. It appears you have a heart in there after all."

His chest rose and fell with a laugh.

Catching herself staring too long, Gwen cleared her throat and pretended to straighten out her dress. "I must tell my family the good news."

"Please extend my invitation for dinner this evening to your family. I hope they will accept." He lifted her hand and planted a tender kiss.

It's better than nothing.

The sappy, lopsided grin returned to her face. The sun lit her eyes perfectly as she regarded him warmly. "Thank you."

He stayed a moment longer, watching the family laugh and cry together before another guard rushed up to him out of breath.

"There is news, Sire," he panted. "An armada was reported not far off our coast. It was intercepted by the merpeople, but not without casualties on both sides. Erumann has been slain. Eugena has sent word she will still meet with the travelers." The guard sent a pointed stare at Elise, who looked back in shock.

"Poor Eugena," Joranna said. "What a devastating loss. I shall need to reach out to her."

"Can you contact Edith first?" Elise asked. "It is almost time for us to go. I'm worried we're already going to be late, and we'll need something we can run in." She whispered for Gavin to make sure he kept track of the box even after changing his clothes.

"I can help you get to Lake Laulie in time," Richard promised.

Joranna ushered Elise, Darcie, Mitch and Gavin inside to be properly fitted prior to their meeting with the mermaid queen.

CHAPTER 25

One key advantage of having Richard on their side again was his ability to transport them to Lake Laulie faster. Not only did they get the luxury of a carriage, but his willingness to use magic easily cut their travel time in half. Elise was particularly thankful for that last part, since they managed to arrive shortly before sunset.

"I don't like mermaids," Mitch said as the carriage lurched to a halt on the path. His face fell as he gazed at the water through the thin line of trees. "Have I mentioned that before? I *feel* like I have."

Pecking him on his cheek, Darcie pulled Mitch out of his seat.

Elise could not blame Mitch for his distrust of the merpeople. He nearly died at the hands of mermaids, and every encounter usually carried some form of a threat. Despite that, Elise had no choice but to trust them. Especially after all they sacrificed just that afternoon to help her family.

Six guards followed them to the lake while maintaining a safe distance. Already, the drifting clouds had taken on rich red and orange hues. The water itself, quiet and still, resembled a sheet of glass as it mirrored the breathtaking sight.

It would be difficult to look Eugena in the eye after losing Erumann. Deep down, Elise knew the relationship between the two was more than the queen let on. However, when the time came to call them, and Elise stirred the waters as Derek previously modeled, the queen was not present among the dozen or so who did rise above the surface.

A familiar mermaid, Lanai, beckoned them into the water. Gavin, Mitch, and Darcie ventured only as deep as their ankles while Elise stopped when the water reached her knees where Lanai waited.

Elise wished it could have been Eugena who greeted them, as planned, but with Erumann's death, she could not blame the queen for seeking solace in private.

"Please tell Eugena I'm so sorry," Elise whispered. "I never meant for anyone to get hurt, I. . .I was only trying to protect Haighdlen."

Lanai gave a solemn nod and held out a folded wet blade of seaweed for Elise to take. "As promised."

Elise paused, her gaze flickering between Lanai and the slimy offering. *What am I supposed to do with that?* Nevertheless, she reluctantly took it from the mermaid. Once her fingers touched the thin layers, freshly coated with grains of sand, Elise felt something moving inside. She tilted the clump of seaweed until what resembled four small oyster pearls rolled onto her palm.

As Lanai watched her expectantly, Elise's bewildered demeanor resulted in an awkward silence. Chewing her bottom lip, Elise tried seeking a response from Gavin, who only sent back a slight headshake.

"Eugena promised to send us to Lockesbarrow. What are these supposed to do?" Elise massaged the pearls around with her thumb.

Laughter and whispers spread among the surrounding merpeople, causing Elise's face to immediately flush.

What did I say? Is this a riddle I'm supposed to figure out? I don't get it.

Lanai's widening grin further intensified Elise's humiliation and bafflement. "We travel fastest *under* the water."

"You mean. . ." Elise touched her lips as her brain processed what had to be done.

Lanai nodded.

"No," Mitch called out. "Absolutely not. This falls under what they taught us in health class. There is *no* way I'm taking drugs from a mermaid."

Darcie scoffed. "No one is offering you drugs, Mitch."

"Well, what do you call it?" he challenged her. "They look like pills, don't they? Plus, I'm not good at swallowing pills. I can barely manage a vitamin."

"They're pretty small," Gavin reasoned. "It sounds like it's to help us not drown. Would you like to drown?" He waited until Mitch finally shook his head. "Then let's get this over with."

Wading back to the water's edge, Elise placed a pearl in each of their hands. Blowing out her cheeks, and releasing a breath, she counted down from three. They took turns swallowing, chasing the pearls down with a swig from a nearby guard's canteen.

Bracing herself for an immediate transformation, perhaps fins or even a tail, Elise could not help but feel underwhelmed standing and staring at her circle of friends while nothing happened.

"Have I mentioned I hate mermaids?" Mitch grumbled. "Not to mention, look around. It's a secluded lake. It doesn't lead any—" He trailed off, his voice growing hoarse. Mitch took a couple more shallow breaths before clawing at his throat.

"Are you choking?" Darcie shrieked, leaning down to check his face from where Mitch was bent over. "He's choking! Somebody do—" She lifted a hand to her own throat. Panic flooded her eyes.

Then Elise felt it.

What first felt like a tickle at the base of her throat soon grew until it felt like a wire comb scraping the sides of her esophagus. The sensation moved downward, clawing its way into her lungs until she was wheezing. She watched as Gavin fell to his knees beside her, splashing water against her leg. Mitch and Darcie also fell, gasping and shuddering to breathe. Somewhere within the depths of Elise's mind came a strange, instinctive plea, urging—no, *demanding*—she go underwater. She submerged herself, and within seconds, her friends also responded by dipping below the surface.

Going against human nature, Elise took the risk of inhaling a much-needed breath of water. Rather than drown her, it soothed the burning and tearing of tissue, and she felt her lungs swell to accommodate and filter the water rather than trap it. Bubbles scattered in all directions as she released another breath. Once her brain processed what was happening, convincing the rest of her body she was safe, Elise was able to fully open her eyes.

Despite its murkiness, she was able to see several feet in front of her. Not only could Elise make out her friends, who floated close by, but she could also see a distant light glowing below. Waving her friends on, she kicked hard enough to propel herself downward. Gavin passed her within a matter of seconds, and Elise kept him in sight. Darcie stayed at a similar pace with Mitch bringing up the rear. Water rushed in her ears, and all sounds were muffled. She was faintly aware of nearby merpeople passing by to guide them. One in particular waved impatiently for them to quicken their pace.

I'm so glad I'm not in a dress. I'd never make it. I'm not sure I'm going to make it. She briefly wondered if Mitch experienced anything like this when he was taken under before. Lake Laulie was much deeper than Elise ever imagined. There was no telling how deep Lake Mirage was when they saved him. The light grew brighter, closer, and compelled her further. Elise was not a particularly strong swimmer, and her heavy limbs ached by the time she reached the bottom where the light was coming from.

It was Eugena's staff, and Elise gasped when she realized the queen herself was waiting for them. She had come after all. Next to her, two enormous shells—Elise questioned if they belonged to some sort of magical sea turtle—rested, overturned, for them to board like underwater chariots.

This is insane! There is no way any of this is real. Elise opened her mouth to apologize, but Eugena held up a hand to silence her. The heartbroken queen nodded towards the shells, ushering them in. It was an awkward climb, but Elise and Gavin managed to board one shell while Mitch and Darcie took the second.

Elise turned around to attempt speaking one more time, but Eugena shook her head. The light from her staff brightened until all four of them had to shield their eyes from an intense flash.

All at once, the shells quaked beneath their feet, and a rumbling sound shook and disturbed the water. Surrounding fish scattered away in fear. Elise grabbed Gavin's arm with one hand while the other gripped the shell. Bits of broken rock and swirling sand further clouded the water around them before a deafening crack pierced their ears.

Crying out, Elise witnessed a whirlpool trail form ahead of them as the rocky barrier parted.

It's a portal!

Gavin wrapped an arm around her waist as they were pulled forward by a powerful current.

With one last desperate attempt, Elise opened her mouth, but all that escaped was a horrific scream as the queen pointed her staff forward. The two shells, illuminated in the same light, lunged forward into the spiraling path as if from a slingshot.

Elise did not know if it was water or wind rushing across her face, muffling all sounds except a deafening roar. Everything grew hazy until they were plunged into darkness, yet the shell twisted and turned as if they were on a rollercoaster. A sudden dip made Elise scream and reach out for Gavin again. The two clung to each other while trying to stay inside the surging shell. It moved at such a high speed that Elise struggled to move. She did not know how they would survive this. A high, screeching sound reached her ears next, reminding her of a train whistle, and within moments she felt the shell lurch out of the swirling current. Tremendous pressure built in Elise's ears as she watched Mitch and Darcie get spit out of the portal next. With only a minute to gain their bearings, the shells lifted upwards.

Higher and higher they climbed, until at last, there was a hint of shimmering light above them.

Is this thing speeding up?

They were indeed gaining speed, and the surface was approaching at a rapid pace. She could hear Mitch and Darcie yelling behind them.

"Brace yourself!" Gavin gargled into her ear, covering Elise with his own body.

With only half a second to respond, Elise ducked down as the shell broke through the surface with the force of a breaching whale. A wall of ocean spray burst all around them, landing in the shell and submerging their feet.

She and Gavin bobbed up and down on the choppy water, unable to see anything except what little light the full moon above provided. Pulling him forward, Elise crushed her lips to his, clinging desperately until it felt like they were joined. They parted when Darcie's and Mitch's shell erupted into view with a similar gust, creating more uneven waves.

"Is everyone okay?" Gavin called out, wrapping his arms around Elise.

Darcie hollered back from their own rocking vessel.

Elise breathed a sigh of relief until she realized Mitch was leaned over the side, retching into the water. *Poor thing. I'm surprised we all didn't get seasick after that wild ride.*

A sinking sense of dread settled in her stomach as Gavin and Darcie quickly followed.

What's going on? No sooner had the thought crossed her mind, Elise also lurched over the opposite side as Gavin. Initially, she could only dry heave, praying for whatever was causing the excruciating cramps coursing through her body to exit. *I don't want Gavin to see me like this.* She winced at the sound of him expelling the contents of his own stomach. Longing for the same release, her wish was granted when her muscles seized, and she vomited into the water. Out popped the pearl, still fully intact. It plopped into the water with a brilliant glow before sinking into the depths of the sea in which they found themselves stranded. Elise spluttered and wiped her chin with her sleeve before falling to her knees in exhaustion. Gavin followed suit, and both sat with their backs rested against each other.

"I'm with Mitch," panted Gavin, his voice weak and hoarse. "I hate mermaids."

"Can't blame you. That was miserable," Elise mumbled, tipping her head back against his shoulder. "Do you still have the box?" She felt him adjust behind her as he checked his pocket.

"Yeah," he said. "Do you want to try to open it now?"

Elise inhaled a fresh breath of air, held it, and blew out over several seconds. "In a minute. If it requires magic, I don't have the strength yet."

They continued riding the gentle waves in silence. Elise drifted in and out of sleep, losing track of time. Given the gentle rhythm of Gavin's breathing when she did open her eyes, he had also fallen asleep.

"Hey!" cried Darcie from the other shell, startling them both. "Look over there!"

Gavin and Elise rose to their knees. While difficult to see very far, they managed to follow the direction of Darcie's voice and finger pointing to a massive spread of mountainous land. Tiny lights, emitting from lanterns and shops, sent a surge of adrenaline through Elise's fatigued body.

Leaping to her feet, Elise bounced with excitement, causing the shell to rock back and forth unsteadily. "Gavin, look! She's right. That's Lockesbarrow, isn't it? It didn't take as long as I thought. We won't have to float in the middle of the ocean all night." When he did not reply, she did a double take over her shoulder and kneeled in front of him. "Gavin?"

"Yeah, great," he snapped, raking a hand through his sopping-wet hair. "Can't wait."

"Should we jump out and swim to the shore?" Mitch called.

Elise watched Gavin close his eyes and lean against the edge of the shell as if to make himself smaller. Crossing his arms, Gavin's chest rose and fell in quick succession until he was practically hyperventilating.

I know that look.

"Just a second!" Elise answered Mitch without taking her eyes off Gavin. Elise was then careful to make her voice as soft and soothing as possible. "What's going on?"

"Nothing."

"Gavin, it's *me.* You've talked me through more panic attacks than I can count, so I know how to spot one."

He flinched when she first took his hand but slowly yielded to her touch. Releasing a series of shallow breaths, Gavin managed to find his voice again. "Sorry."

"Don't be," Elise whispered. "Just tell me what's wrong. Are you hurt?"

He shook his head. "I can't explain it. S-seeing the coast, being back here. . .something flipped inside me. I d-don't know if I can go through it again."

She wilted. Never had he appeared so broken, or scarred, like a little lost boy. Elise empathized with the fear, having learned it was always worse inside the sufferer's mind than outside of it. Knowing words would not be sufficient, she pulled him forward into a hug.

He melted against her, squeezing Elise until she was short of breath. Rubbing small circles along his back, she waited for Gavin's heart rate to regulate, supporting him until he felt calm enough to let go of her.

It occurred to Elise in the five minutes or so it took to calm Gavin down they had not moved any closer to shore.

Did we stop?

The ocean swayed around them, but it was as if an invisible shield prevented the shells from floating closer.

"Guys, we're not moving anymore, and the waves are getting rougher!" Darcie yelled out at them. "I don't know how much longer we can stay in these shells before they capsize!"

Gavin scrambled to his feet. "Okay, we have to go. I think this is as far as Eugena is willing to help us."

"Yeah, but what about you?" Elise asked as he scanned their surroundings. "I can't ask you to go back if it's scaring you this much."

He scoffed with a forced smile. "Don't worry about me. Darcie's right. We're close enough now to swim and let the tide carry us in."

Gesturing for Mitch and Darcie to follow, Gavin grabbed Elise's hand as both leaped into the dark water.

If there was a protective shield, it vanished once they all plunged into the water. Almost immediately, many approaching waves doubled in size, rising and falling around them. Every time Elise could get a deep enough breath, another wave would crash and send her reeling in the dark underwater. More than once, she crashed against the ocean floor. Clawing at the sand, she kicked off and steadied herself again and again while barely managing to suck in enough air above water.

When the waves calmed long enough for her to tread water, Elise was relieved when the others popped their heads up as well.

Thank goodness, they're still alive. I don't know how much longer we can survive out here.

"We're almost there!" Mitch yelled over the breaking waves. "We've come too far to get eaten by sharks now."

Beaten, exhausted, and heavy under the weight of the tide, Elise floated on her back while there was a reprieve to conserve her energy. Would they ever catch a break? Why did everything have to be life-threatening, one right after the other? It was enough to make giving up more tempting than ever.

"We can't quit," Gavin warned her. "You have to keep trying. Rest when we get washed to shore. It's not that far now."

Alternating between swimming and treading, they finally approached the shore. Elise said a prayer of thanks when her feet touched the ground and she could walk.

Dragging themselves from the ocean, the friends choked and spit up the water they ingested before collapsing in a heap on the sandy beach.

Elise checked on everyone, unsure of her own ability to stand now that she was resting. She wrinkled her nose as she bit down on grains of sand between her teeth. Numbness spread through her sand-covered arms and legs. Yet, an even bigger part of Elise was just thankful to be on land again.

Once recovered, she asked for Gavin to hand her the velvet-lined box. "Please tell me you still have it."

He fished inside his pocket and retrieved it, looking as shocked as her that it remained intact. "Vaughn said wait until we were in Lockesbarrow, so let's hope it still works."

Elise took it from Gavin, gasping when the lid opened with ease. *He must have spelled it to only work here.* Her brows furrowed when she gazed down at the light brown locks of hair. *It's completely dry inside.* Pinching pieces of hair between her fingers, she looked expectantly at Gavin. "How did Rona use this?"

He hummed in thought as he tried to remember. "She talked to it."

"Excuse me?" Elise asked.

"No, not like that. Like an incantation. Then it started to glow and showed a sort of live feed in Vaughn's head. I couldn't make out what she said, but you could probably use your powers to activate it."

"It's worth a shot," Darcie said. "We've come this far. It's our only chance to make it work."

"We didn't go through that portal of death for nothing," Mitch added. "And you got that other diary to work."

"Yeah, but I had fairy magic to help me," Elise countered.

"Vaughn wanted you to have it for a reason," Darcie pressed on.

Elise shook her head. "Which doesn't make any sense. Whose side is he on?"

"Who cares?" Darcie snapped irritably. "Now, hurry up. It's driving me crazy!"

Elise lifted the hair near her lips and focused on finding Vaughn. *Where is he? Show us.* This went on for ten minutes, all the while making Elise feel more foolish with every attempt.

"Ugh, it's no use!" she growled, tossing the hair back into the box.

"You're not trying hard enough," Darcie accused. "Vaughn wouldn't make it easy in case it got intercepted. Now, try again."

Elise glared at her best friend with an indignant huff. *Who does she think she is? How would she know what it takes? I don't see her with any powers.* "I'm doing my best!"

"Guys, relax," Gavin said. "We're all exhausted but turning on each other isn't going to help. Now, Elise, please try again."

After apologizing, both girls quieted as Elise sat up straighter and brought the box up to her mouth. *Show me Vaughn. Take me there. What does he want me to see?*

She jumped when the hair began to glow. In her mind, Elise was immediately transported into a throne room with four figures talking in secret. Gasping, she opened her eyes and relayed it to the others.

"It's working!" Gavin leaned closer. "Keep it up."

"You can do this, Elise," Darcie encouraged.

Elise clenched her eyes shut, willing the vision to show more. This time, a different light flickered from the hair, creating a winding trail towards the ocean. Crawling closer to the water's edge, enough for sea foam to wash over her hands and knees, Elise gasped as the light hovered over a small collection of shells. She brushed the shells away to make a hole. As the water washed into it, the same vision came to life before them in the small pool. At first, only the dark figures could be seen.

"Concentrate, Elise," Gavin groaned, waiting eagerly for the rippling image to focus.

Elise pinched the hair again, forcing her mind to think of nothing but finding out where Vaughn was. It mentally took a toll on her, but she could not let her friends down after what they all risked to get there. With a brilliant flash, more details came into view, including another approaching figure.

"Who is that guy?" Mitch asked, watching as a man entered into view.

"That has to be her brother," Gavin said. "We're seeing what Vaughn is seeing—or saw. Who knows when this actually happened."

"Okay, I see Rona!" Darcie exclaimed. "Who is she talking to?"

"Why can't we hear anything?" Mitch also questioned.

Slowly but surely, the figures grew closer as Vaughn moved throughout the room. As he neared, Elise's heart sank when Iris glanced at him over her shoulder.

"This happened today," groaned Elise. "Iris is wearing the same gown she was this morning. I'm guessing that's Brahm and her mom with her."

"What?" Mitch shrieked as sat up on his knees. "How does Iris and her mom get an instant trip while we had to be dragged through Poseidon's butt to get here?"

Elise covered her nose as an unexpected snort escaped while laughing. Darcie tousled his hair with a giggle of her own before pointing at the scene for him to pay attention.

"Mitch, you're not helping," Gavin laughed. "We had to make it without being detected."

"Forget being detected." Mitch dusted the sand off his hands. "That settles it. I'm about to work for Rona. If nothing else, for the benefits."

As Rona came closer into view, following Vaughn's movements, Darcie shushed the others. "Wait, I think I can hear something!"

They crouched down closer to the small pool.

Elise heard Vaughn groan, assuming she had tapped fully into his head, creating the inevitable migraine.

"Are you ill?" Rona called out to him.

Vaughn hesitated. "N-no, My Queen." His voice took on an echo as the rest of his message came in the form of his thoughts. *"Stay silent. Do not speak, no matter what happens."*

Elise shivered in response, exchanging an anxious glance with her friends. She knew better than to ignore Vaughn's warning. *He knows something is going to happen.*

"Forget him, Rona. What do you mean the engagement is cancelled?" Dmitri demanded of Ingrid.

"The crown prince had a change of heart, Your Majesty," Ingrid informed him. "I can assure you, there is nothing wrong with my daughter."

Elise noted with a grateful heart that Iris remained silent about her involvement.

"Well, there is something bloody the matter with her!" Dmitri snarled. "Has she been compromised?"

Straightening her posture, Ingrid placed hands on Iris's shoulders. "Certainly not!"

"My niece's honor remains intact," Brahm assured the king. "We are still investigating what caused the sudden shift."

The king paced back and forth before facing his sister. "Rona, this man and his family came highly recommended. You assured me keeping the Brahm family close would secure an alliance between our kingdoms. The prince's public display of forgiveness and the peaceful union was to call Prisha out of hiding. I was promised all these things!"

"Careful of your tone, Brother," Rona warned. "For it was *I* who disrupted the fabric of time to deliver you to the throne." She took a step closer to him, her voice falling to a whisper. "You have missed much over the years, Dmitri, including all my hard work to claim this kingdom for us."

"I wish to rule with Prisha by my side," Dmitri argued. "You promised me she would reign as my queen."

"Forget your childish fairy tale life, Brother!" Rona hissed. "She is old, lost, and forgotten—conceivably dead, as you once were. I said what I needed to forward our plans." The sorceress spun on her heel to glare at the three onlookers. "And all was going according to the plan until this morning. *Why!*" Her voice echoed around the chamber, making Iris visibly jump. "Was it you? Did you suddenly grow a brain and try to sabotage me?"

"I can assure you, Highness, my daughter would never interfere in your plans."

Rona rolled her eyes. "I am getting quite tired of you speaking for her. Is she mute?"

"Leave the girl alone, Rona," Dmitri growled. "We have our own business to settle."

Rona's face split into a wide malicious grin. "I believe I stated our business is concluded, Brother. We will go on ruling as we are."

"You killed her. Is that it?" he accused. "Did you murder her as you did her parents? All for the sake of some pathetic power trip?"

Rona pinched the bridge of her nose. "I forgot how insufferably righteous you could be."

"If I may," Brahm spoke up, "in light of the recent defeat of your armada, and the return of the travelers—Elise in particular, perhaps the cancellation is a blessing in disguise. Erumann's death is a victory in and of itself that speaks volumes of your power."

"But it is not enough!" Rona huffed, her veil of composure dwindling as she turned her temper on Iris. "All this idiot had to do was distract the prince long enough for Haighdlen to begin destroying itself from the inside."

Silence followed.

"That reminds me," offered Ingrid timidly. "The youngest prince was critically injured during one of your desired protests. Does that not count for something?"

"But he did not die, did he?" Rona challenged. "If nothing else, without his eldest brother under our control, their insipid little family is stronger than ever since Derek's death. Considering how meddlesome those parasitic travelers are, they were involved in this somehow. I know not Elise's full relation to the Laurilles, but Laurille blood flows through her veins, nonetheless. Speak girl!" Her cold, severe stance towered over Iris's cowering form. "I demand you tell me what you did to ruin this."

Tears spilled from Iris's eyes. She looked between her mother and uncle.

"She's only a child," Ingrid reasoned. "Iris could hardly bring such ruin upon your Highness's legacy."

Rona took a step back and regarded Ingrid with indifference. "I thought I made it quite clear to let this spineless excuse of a woman speak for herself."

"But she—"

Whatever Ingrid planned to say was cut short as Rona gripped her neck. A jolt of light shot out of Rona's fingers, rendering Brahm's sister speechless. When the sorceress released her, she was already dead before her body collapsed on the floor.

Brahm and Iris cried out, falling to Ingrid's lifeless form with desperation and shock.

"How could you?" Iris screamed, attempting to lunge for Rona before Brahm grabbed her arm.

Rona quirked an unimpressed brow. "Oh, now find your voice. I confess, I preferred you silent."

"My Queen," Brahm spluttered, releasing Iris to hold his sister's hand. "After all my loyalty. . .everything I have done. . .what threat did she pose to you?"

"None, whatsoever," Dmitri admonished. "Rona, cease this tantrum, immediately, or—"

"Or what?" Rona chuckled. "You are not the brains nor the power behind this war. You are a puppet, brother, meant for nothing other than to bait the other leaders."

"You do not mean that," replied the king. "Love is in your heart, despite what your sinister mouth spews."

Rolling her eyes, the sorceress ignored her brother and sneered down at her feet. "Save your blubbering, Brahm. She served no real purpose." Advancing on the two mourning souls, with Iris's weeping nearly drowning out the queen's words, Rona glared down with contempt. "I want this to serve as your warning. A great deal rides on your unwavering allegiance. I have no doubt the Laurilles are concocting a plan, and I will not be a sitting target when they strike. Now, get up. We have work to do."

"I cannot," Brahm sobbed, watching his niece cover Ingrid's body with her own. "Oh, sister."

"Brahm, honestly, this is path—" Rona stiffened, sniffing the air suspiciously. Ignoring the bizarre looks the rest of the occupants gave her, she spun slowly around and scanned the room. "Someone is watching us."

Elise's blood ran cold when Rona's eyes landed on Vaughn. Panicking, she thrust a hand into the pool, disturbing the connection until it vanished completely. She asked Gavin to put the box back into his pocket.

The teenagers sat staring at one another in stunned silence.

"Do you think she knows it was us?" Darcie asked.

Elise shook her head and shrugged. *I don't know. I hope Vaughn is okay.*

"Poor Iris," Elise said. "I didn't like Ingrid, but having to watch her mom die like that. . ."

Gavin groaned and stretched his neck. "At least some good came out of watching that. It doesn't sound like Rona and Dmitri are as close as we assumed they were."

Mitch scoffed. "Yeah, the guy actually has a conscience."

Darcie clicked her tongue. "But he's still alive at a time he shouldn't be. That complicates things. I mean, it's one thing for Elise to want to save Charles and Liam from dying in the future, but Rona just plucked Dmitri out and placed him randomly on the throne without making sure everything else was stable."

"Yeah," Mitch agreed. "I doubt she considered him opposing her methods."

"She stopped his death, but not what led up to it." Gavin massaged his eyes. "If we don't stop her, then we risk the same thing happening. Even if we manage to protect Charles and Liam from dying during a future attack in our present time, every day Rona rules increases the odds of it happening sooner. We can't leave Lockesbarrow until she's stopped."

Elise's heart sank as she realized they were out of time. When the moment came for her to kill Rona, she could only hope her friends would not interfere.

"I don't think we're leaving Lockesbarrow anytime soon," Mitch whimpered.

Elise and the others gasped as a group of hooded figures surrounded them with swords and bows pointed in their direction.

CHAPTER 26

Elise's heart thrashed wildly inside her chest. Blindfolded, her wrists bound, she stumbled aimlessly at the mercy of their captives. Would they be taken to the castle? Or worse, prison? Elise's intrusive thoughts spread through her mind like a virus, conjuring up gruesome images of torture and warfare.

She did not know how long or far they walked, but when the blindfolds were removed, Elise, Gavin, Mitch, and Darcie saw that they were deep inside a forest at a campsite. All the soldiers were young, similarly dressed in torn, ragged uniforms, and many were crowded around the fire talking. Others trained with swords in the distance. As they were led forward, Elise sensed more and more eyes on her by the second until the surrounding soldiers all but trapped them in a large circle.

"Is this where you were?" she asked Gavin. "In one of these camps?"

Gavin shook his head. "No, this is different. This is something else." He scanned the area. "There aren't any officers and not nearly enough tents or weapons."

"We captured some prisoners for the captain," announced one of the soldiers flanking Elise and her friends.

A lone figure emerged from the assembled bystanders. He could not have been much older than Elise, yet she felt intimidated by his muscular presence. With a struggling mustache and overgrown shaggy hair that fell past his shoulders, the young man narrowed his eyes at them one at a time.

"You're a captain?" Gavin asked, eyeing the same rips and tears on the young man's shirt and trousers.

"Honorary captain." The boy shrugged with a menacing smile. "What do we have here?"

"We found them by the ocean's edge, sir," reported the soldier holding Darcie. "We think they're royal spies."

"It's been a long time since I've seen a girl this close." The captain leered at Darcie until Mitch pulled at his restraints. He laughed. "Taken, I see."

Elise scoffed. "We aren't spying for Rona."

"What little we did hear says otherwise," said the boy holding a fistful of her tunic. "They were deep in conversation about the queen's plans."

A disapproving murmur radiated through the crowd of soldiers with many calling for their deaths.

"That's because we're trying to stop her and save the boys in her army," Gavin said over the commotion. "It's the only reason I'd ever come back here. Believe me."

"Wait a minute," said the captain, raising his arm for silence. "Bring me a torch." Flexing his hand impatiently, he snatched the nearest one offered. Lifting his arm, the captain inspected Gavin closely. So close, in fact, that Gavin had to lean away and still the torch remained mere inches from his face.

What is he doing?

Elise watched as the captain's expressions transitioned from skeptic to shocked, and finally jubilant as recognition dawned on his face.

"I cannot believe it," said the captain. "Is that you, Gavin?"

Gavin's brows furrowed as he regarded the other man. "Do I know you?"

"I certainly know you," the captain laughed before addressing the crowd. "How fortunate we are, men! Gavin Striess is among our number again!"

The once hostile crowd erupted in cheers and shouts, taking Elise off guard. "What's going on?" she asked.

Gavin shrugged. "I don't know."

"'I don't know', he says." The captain laughed, amping up the other boys around him.

"Are you famous or something, Gav?" asked Mitch, wary of the surrounding soldiers pressing in around them.

"He's more than that, mate," jeered the captain. "Gavin's a legend among our ranks. He could barely hold a sword, but I have yet seen anyone stand up to Rona the way he did. A true hero, he was, and vowed to save us all. Now, he's returned among us vigilantes."

"Vigilante?" Gavin surveyed the campsite. "So, you're not part of Rona's army?"

"Some may call us runaways, deserters, or rebels." The captain winked at Elise, who stepped behind Gavin. "I prefer defiant militia. Long live Queen Prisha!" Chortles and murmurs rang out amongst the group, escalating to shouts of allegiance and battle cries as the captain pumped his fist in the air.

"Quite the poet," Darcie quipped.

"Call me Drebson," said the captain. "I was also a member of Isaac's unit while you served here." He shook Gavin's hand and clapped him on the back.

"Isaac?" Elise asked.

"He's one of the commanding officers," Gavin informed her.

"*Was*," Drebson corrected. "He was killed in a local raid about ten miles from here."

Elise paled as she studied Gavin's unreadable expression.

"What about. . ." Gavin swallowed a lump in his throat. "What about others from that unit?"

"Many of us belong here now," boasted Drebson. "We have lost a few, but that's the price of war. Am I right?"

Gavin's face fell, and Elise wondered if he was thinking of specific members. Yet, he did not ask for them by name. Perhaps he did not fully trust the captain.

"Forgive my manners, mate," continued the captain. "Release them. Any friends of Mr. Striess are friends of ours, and you must stay with us tonight. I can offer you no better protection or company in all of Lockesbarrow."

There was little reason to turn down a hot meal and a place to sleep while they formulated a plan. Within the hour, the four friends were given seats closest to the fire to get warm and dry.

Mitch poked at the contents of his dinner. "I don't want to be rude, but what's in this?"

With a polite smile, Darcie took a tentative bite. "It's very chewy."

"Leftover squirrel stew," said a boy about thirteen years old.

Darcie released what was in her mouth back into the bowl.

"It's an acquired taste," agreed a slightly older soldier beside him. "Sometimes we get spare potatoes and biscuits from sympathetic locals. Our supply is low, I'm afraid."

Elise fell into despair, trying to find joy with her company, but all she could think about was facing Rona. Magic would not be enough. She needed fighting experience. Regardless of Rona's unspeakable atrocities, there was still the matter of Elise having to willingly take someone else's life. Elise groaned with nausea as she forced herself to eat. Choking down the stew, her attention was drawn to Gavin, who absentmindedly twisted the medallion between his fingers as he stared into the fire deep in thought. "You're thinking about your other friends, aren't you? The soldiers."

Gavin nodded, his own stew forgotten. "If Isaac could get killed so easily, anything could have happened to them."

"They could be here," Mitch offered as someone brought him a second helping.

"We had a large enough introduction," Gavin argued. "They would've heard or seen us. I've lost sleep over it—seeing their faces at night. . .I promised to help. It was the one duty I took seriously."

Elise ran her hand along his back. "You can't beat yourself up, Gavin. Whatever happened is not your fault."

"She's right," Mitch said. "And you did something right. These guys hold you on a pedestal. If we don't make it home for some reason, you could have a future here."

Gavin drummed his fingers together and hung his head. "You joke but being stuck in this place made me start taking my life more seriously." His eyes glassed over as he stared into the flames. "I've decided when we get home to go talk to a recruiter."

What!

"That's deep, man," Mitch replied. "Your dad will be proud."

What about me? Elise silenced her selfish thoughts. She had no right to be mad at Gavin for not disclosing his plans to her sooner. After all, she still had not told him the truth about what would happen to her when she killed Rona.

Sensing the growing discomfort, Gavin shifted the conversation to include the others. "What about y'all? What are you guys doing after graduation? Darcie, I know you're getting your license for cosmetology."

Elise only half listened to her best friend list the places she was thinking of applying to with plans of opening her own salon one day. It wasn't that she didn't care. She had already heard it from Darcie several times already. Instead, she watched Gavin, who she felt like was avoiding her gaze on purpose. Did he expect her to be upset? Hurt? The truth was that his news was painful to hear, but not one part of Elise wanted to dash his dreams. She could not expect him to choose her over a lifetime of security, duty, and honor. In fairness, hearing the way he spoke made her respect him all the more.

"Mitch?" Darcie asked. "Did you decide yet?"

Mitch shrugged. "For the longest time, I assumed I'd go into engineering, but the last year or so I started considering culinary school."

"You'd be a great at that." Darcie smiled. "I bet my dad could let you shadow him in his bakery this summer. Maybe even an intern."

"I'd like that," said Mitch, taking her hand before looking at Elise. "What about you?"

Elise normally shied away from discussing futures. Truth be told, the future frightened her. Since it was only her and Ruby, she often felt obligated to stay near home to help out. She had held little jobs here and there to bring in some extra money, but the idea of college and careers always seemed limited. Now that she knew Ruby had family closer to home, including Joranna and Ian, and hopefully a brighter future if their mission succeeded, it broadened Elise's possibilities. Taking a moment of reflection, she considered what she wanted to dedicate her life towards.

"I don't know, really," she confessed, drawing lines in the dirt with the toe of her boot. "I want to help people and make a difference, but I don't have the stomach to do anything in the medical field."

"That's okay. What are some hobbies you enjoy?" Mitch offered.

She thought long and hard about her life back home. "I really like working with people. I volunteered in Darcie's mom's classroom a couple of times and really loved it. Something about being with the kids and seeing them learn was really fun."

"Sounds like you'd be a great teacher," Gavin suggested with an encouraging smile.

Mitch nodded around a bite of stew.

"And you have the patience for it," Darcie praised. "I know I sure don't."

If things were different, I think I could really like teaching. She feigned excitement about her career choice, not having the heart to break the news to Gavin despite Darcie's pointed look across the fire. At least Darcie was playing along for now, but Elise knew it was a matter of time before the truth came out. She did not want to spend what was most likely her last night alive fighting or persuading. Elise just wanted this—to sit with her friends and laugh. More importantly, to trick herself into thinking this is how things would always be.

They continued talking late into the night. At one point, a group of soldiers and Gavin helped teach her to hold a sword along with some basic moves. Elise's favorite part, however, was snuggling and making out with Gavin alone by the fire after many, including Mitch and Darcie, had gone to bed. Elise studied every curve of his face, each freckle, and made sure she told him every chance she got that she loved him.

"We should probably get some sleep," he murmured against her ear from where they lay spooning.

She opened her eyes and stared into the fire, much like Gavin had done earlier that evening. Never in a million years did she think they would get as lucky as to have this chance together to relax and enjoy one another's closeness. Being invited to spend the night in a safe campsite with a fun crowd was not on her radar for the evening, yet it was precisely what she needed. Elise nodded at his suggestion and stretched as Gavin planted soft kisses along her neck. After all, the real world had to come first at some point. She prayed Gavin's dreams would come true and accepted the harsh reality that she would have to give hers up.

He deserves a happy life, even if it's not with me.

A tent was pitched for the girls and one for the boys. Stopping by Gavin's first, he rolled his eyes as the sound of Mitch's snoring was already protruding from inside.

Elise giggled. "I love you."

"I love you, too."

They bid one another good night and crawled into their tents.

The night passed peacefully enough, but it felt like only five minutes passed when cries and warnings pulled her out of sleep. It awoke Darcie as well, who pulled the flap of the tent up and peered out. The fire was extinguished, apart from smoking embers. "What's going on?"

A soldier stopped in front of their tent. "Our watchmen just delivered the news. There are approaching fleets with Haighdlen and Vynchian flags. We are dispatching some of our members to greet them, but we've lost contact with a few rebels and the Masked Lady was spotted in the forest."

"Masked Lady?" Elise asked.

The soldier nodded. "She looks after us, leaving food and weapons, but no one's met her. If she's been seen, it means there's trouble from—" He lurched forward as an arrow pierced his back.

Darcie and Elise screamed as he fell to the ground. As they exited the tent, they witnessed a horrific sight. Pots and pans were thrown and kicked, tents burned, swords clashed, and cries filled the air as young formally uniformed soldiers ravaged through the camp.

It's an ambush!

Clamoring out of the tent, Darcie and Elise came face to face with Gavin, Mitch, and Drebson.

"Get away from here," said the captain, who already had blood running down the side of his face. "Head into the forest! Go as deep as you can!"

Whirling around to follow orders, they halted as a group of soldiers carrying swords and Lockesbarrian flags entered the burning campsite. Elise and the others stared in horror as Rona and King Dmitri followed with Brahm and Vaughn flanking them. Even further back, one of the uniformed guards gripped Iris's arm. The young woman was dragged forward with a petrified stare, bound and gagged.

We need to save her.

Elise's breath hitched when she met Rona's stare. Gavin squeezed her hand, which was the only thing keeping Elise from passing out.

Rona remained poised, as if unaware of the mayhem occurring around them. "Elise," she said sweetly. "I wish I had known you would be here, dearest. So good of you to visit. Have you met my brother, King Dmitri?"

"He's not the real king!" Drebson snarled. "A brother and sister both trying to be king and queen at the same time is disgraceful. Prisha is the rightful queen and always has been."

Rona nodded at the closest guard standing by her, who closed the distance and skillfully disarmed Drebson with little effort. A true assassin. Elise turned her face into Gavin's chest as the soldier slashed the captain with his own sword.

"Are these the travelers?" the king asked casually, as if they were nothing more than spectators at a sporting event. "The ones you told me about?"

Elise paled, recalling the scene she witnessed the night before.

"Yes, brother. They are the ones I told you about. The ones responsible for Prisha's disappearance."

What? "We had nothing to do with that!" Elise shrieked. "We haven't even met her!"

"Quite sad how they lie so easily. Especially Elise." Rona shook her head and feigned disappointment. Clicking her tongue, she clapped her hands together. "Do you not see, Dmitri? She will not be satisfied until she takes the throne for herself. We cannot allow that."

As Gavin, Mitch, and Darcie were apprehended, and forced to watch, Elise was left standing helplessly alone as the king's face hardened with rage. She found his eyes devoid of emotion as he nodded for Vaughn to step forward. *He's going to kill me. I can't breathe.*

CHAPTER 27

"Kill her," Dmitri ordered.

Gavin fought to free himself from the guard's hold, but it was no use. Also held against their will, Darcie and Mitch cried out, too.

"Elise, use your magic!" Darcie insisted.

"Yes, use your magic," Rona mocked with a chuckle before encouraging Vaughn to follow the order.

Elise's head swam as she swayed off balance, watching Vaughn saunter forward to kill her. She suspected his aid was only a ploy to lead them here. This is how she would die. Everything they had worked towards would all end here. Rona had won. Elise braced herself, inwardly spiraling at the thought of never seeing Gavin, Darcie, or Mitch again. Of never seeing her family again. It was all for nothing. The prophecy, Derek's untimely death, her family's estrangement. . .none of it would change. Rather than succumb to an expected panic attack, Elise took a shallow breath and met Vaughn's eyes. *Will it hurt? Will it be quick?* All these questions raced through Elise's mind along with memories as her adrenaline spiked. Try as she might, Elise was unable to sustain her external resolve. Warm tears burst through her brave facade, cascading down her cheeks without any sign of stopping. Elise made a few feeble attempts to muster her magic without success before falling to her knees.

A cry caught in her throat. Through burning eyes, her vision blurred, Elise could make out his boots inching closer. Hanging her head, she jumped when the toe of one of his boots lifted her chin. He gestured with his gloved hands for her to rise. *He's really going to draw this out. I am going to suffer so much. It's going to hurt so badly. I want it over with. Please get it over with. I can't take it.*

Without an ounce of hope, she pled with bloodshot eyes for him to spare her. Rather than reach for his sword, Vaughn took a few steps back. His gaze darted back and forth.

He looks distracted. What is he staring at?

Elise did not bother to hide her confusion, nor did Dmitri and Rona, who shared a wary glance behind him.

What is he going to do?

Releasing an embarrassing sniveling sound, Elise wiped tears away with her sleeve. Her arms were anvils, every muscle ached, and her legs felt unsteady as she willed herself to stand.

Facing her killer, Elise took a deep breath and closed her eyes. And then. . .

Nothing.

Elise peeked to find Vaughn still watching her. Only when she opened both eyes did she see his mouth form one single, silent word.

Run.

Was he really trying to save her? *What about my friends?* Knowing she could not help them if she were dead, Elise did not stop to ask or focus on anything except getting away. Turning on her heel, she raced toward the forest amidst cries from her friends to run as fast as she could. A blast of magic shot to her left. Dodging right, she headed deeper into the cover of trees.

"You fool!" Rona shrieked.

Elise chanced a look over her shoulder as Vaughn blasted similar magical blasts at the guards holding Gavin, Darcie, and Mitch, who all took off running in the same direction as her.

"Out of my way!" Rona commanded, slamming Vaughn into the nearest tree with a burst of magic. However, as she reached the forest's edge in pursuit of Elise and her friends, a series of arrows shot from the top of the tallest tree at the guards. The closest ones ran to shield the king, who cowered under their cover. One by one, they were struck, until the final arrow came from the ground level, striking Dmitri in the back.

"No!" Rona cried, running back to her brother. The sorceress threw herself over him, repeating his name, and urged him to look at her.

Elise paused until her friends caught up.

"What are you doing? Go!" Mitch bellowed.

Is he really dead? Though she had gained a sizeable distance, Elise peered through hanging vines until she could faintly see Rona. Brahm was once again by her side.

"Show yourselves!" Rona demanded to the open silence around her, scanning the area for the slightest movement.

Dmitri's body staggered, redirecting Rona's attention before landing heavily at Brahm's feet.

Brahm kneeled to check his pulse, hesitated, and met Rona's gaze with a grim expression.

Throwing her head back, Rona let out a shrill, piercing scream. The unnerving sound echoed throughout the forest, disturbing birds and creatures who fled, and affecting all others who could hear. Surrounded by other dead bodies of her guards, she gave attention only to her brother. Reaching down, she lifted trembling fingers to close Dmitri's eyes before glaring at Vaughn, who limped into view. "Gather more guards. Find the travelers! I will make them suffer for this! I will deal with you after. Now, get out of my way!"

Gavin tugged Elise's hand to keep going. She heard Vaughn cry out, but there was no time to go back. They needed to get away.

Who attacked them? She searched the trees as they ran but could see no movement.

"Keep going!" Darcie screamed. "Someone's chasing us!"

Her cry made Elise check over her shoulder in time to see two soldiers appear from behind trees. They were gaining, yet all Elise could do was concentrate on not tripping and giving them an easy target. She became acutely aware of the wind in her ears as both knees threatened to buckle. It was no easy feat trying to keep up with Gavin, who now led the way past the jagged forest trees. Her chest burned, begging Elise to stop for air, but she did not want to be responsible for stalling them. It was difficult enough dodging sharp thorns and low-hanging branches without her slowing everyone down.

She gasped as a third lunged out of the bushes, taking Gavin down with him. "Gavin!"

The two men struggled, rolling around at her feet as Mitch and Darcie caught up. In less than a minute, Gavin was pinned to the ground.

Please, don't hurt him! Elise's breath hitched as Gavin braced for an attack.

"Is that really the best you can do?" the soldier asked with a lighthearted chuckle.

Gavin scoffed in disbelief as the other young man removed his helmet.

Elise stared at the soldier, who appeared to be similar in age to her and Gavin. She noted the disheveled forest green uniform and fresh cuts against his light brown skin.

"Everett?" Gavin asked.

"We feared you dead." Everett smiled with ease before leaping to his feet and helping Gavin to stand. "Looks like I just won a bet."

"Then that means. . ." Gavin trailed off, watching as the other two soldiers removed their helmets. One was noticeably shorter, and younger, with a mop of unkept hair, while the other was tall, poised, and more athletic despite a pale, sickly complexion.

Elise furrowed her brows, watching an initial calamitous moment descend into what she could only describe as some sort of reunion. *How does he know these guys? Who are they?*

"This is insane. I've been trying to find my way back here to help you guys." Gavin took the time to introduce Elise, Mitch and Darcie to his friends from when he was recruited into Rona's camp. Everett, Erick, and Tristan greeted them in return. "I can't believe you found us."

"The other rebels told us of their meeting with you," Tristan said. "We've been tracking you all morning with help from the Masked Lady, of course."

So, that's *Tristan.* She remembered Gavin telling her he was the best soldier, though not always the friendliest.

"It paid off," Erick beamed, raking a hand through his unruly dark hair.

"Masked Lady?" Mitch asked, sharing an uneasy look with Darcie. "Why don't I like the sound of that?"

The boys chuckled.

"She is a true legend here," Everett explained. "Rescuing soldiers, such as ourselves."

"How did you escape?" Gavin asked.

"You are not the only defiant soldier," Tristan replied with a smirk.

Elise marveled at the way Gavin's entire demeanor changed around these young men. It occurred to her that it had only been days for Gavin, but months had spanned in this timeline. She had no idea what they went through, but it clear to anyone with a pulse that there was a bond that ran incredibly deep. Not wanting to interrupt, she took a step back to stand beside Mitch and Darcie. When Gavin noticed, she waved away his offer to join them, but took the opportunity to point at Gavin's neck.

Understanding dawned on his face.

"Oh! I have something for you," said Gavin, pulling off the medallion and holding it out for Tristan to take.

Elise watched an array of emotions play across the soldier's face.

The little color that Tristan did possess vanished from his face as he froze. His mouth parted, but no sound came out. His eyes glistened with memories as his mind wandered far away from the forest. At last, he finally accepted and donned it around his own neck. "I did not expect to see this again." Twirling it between his fingers, Tristan cleared his throat and nodded at Gavin. "Thank you."

Warm tears pricked the edges of Elise's eyes as the two young men shared a brief hug and handshake.

"How sentimental." Rona's sarcastic, droning voice cut through the heartfelt moment.

Elise's heart stopped as she whirled around to see Rona, Brahm, and Vaughn flanked by a handful of new guards. Thankful to see Vaughn still alive, she was surprised to see him still standing given his haggard, beaten appearance.

Tristan pulled his sword from its sheath, prompting Everett and Erick to do the same. As the tips of their blades met Vaughn's and Brahm's in midair, Rona chuckled in spite of herself.

"Good of you to finally show some skill, but it is too late."

"Stand your ground, men," Tristan growled, digging the toe of his boot into the dirt.

"Cowards," Brahm spat. "All of you."

"Dishonorable they may be, but cowards they are not." Rona hummed with impressive interested, placing a fingertip on Erick's blade as she examined all three of Gavin's friends.

A bright, sudden flash of light made everyone jump. Elise doubled over and covered her eyes, afraid of what she might see if she looked. *Did Rona kill one of them?* Feeling her breath begin to return to normal, Elise finally opened her eyes when Darcie tugged on her sleeve.

Between Rona and the soldiers now stood Arymei, the Queen of Vynchia.

Elise stared incredulously at the magnificent presence of the queen, whom she had not seen since the day Derek was attacked. Three guards stood around her.

Joranna's letter worked! We're saved!

All felt right in the world for precisely two seconds until Brahm and Vaughn began backing away. Vaughn took it one step further, bolting out of sight into an even thicker area of the woods.

Elise fumed. *He's the true coward.* Surprisingly, Brahm remained still by Rona's side rather than chase after him. She also did not seem fazed by his absence as she crossed her arms.

"Queen Arymei, to what do I owe this honor?" Rona asked, her gaze fixated on the other woman's face.

"Let these children go, Rona," the queen commanded.

"Oh, but they are not children. Simply ask them," Rona replied, winking at Everett, Erick, and. Tristan, who glared as they brandished their swords towards her. "They're *real* soldiers now. In death, they may even earn the title of heroes."

Elise gulped at Rona's calm, collected tone. This moment called for anything else. Goosebumps trickled down her arms as she failed to see a way out of this scenario alive.

"You can give up now, Rona," Arymei announced. "You are no match for Haighdlen's *and* Vynchia's fleets, both of which are on your shores. You are outnumbered."

Rona answered with a shrug. "Let our armies face off. I anticipate a decent war." Rona smirked. "How many months has it been since we have seen each other?"

"This will not work, Rona," Arymei countered. "You will not distract me."

"Several months, at least," Rona resumed, ignoring the Vynchian queen's response. "Oh, I remember. We have not been in each other's company since the day I cursed the late king Derek."

Arymei did not reply.

Elise's stomach tightened at the mention of her fallen grandfather. Gavin stepped in front of her as if he knew she wanted nothing more than to charge at Rona herself.

How can she talk about it so lightly? Her brother just died, and she's already playing mind games. She's a psychopath!

"I relished watching you sob over his injured body, though." Rona circled Arymei as she spoke. "How humiliating it must have been returning with his cursed, aging mind to Queen Joranna." She stopped abruptly, inching her face closer to Arymei's before bringing her voice to a whisper. "The guilt alone must have been positively dreadful. Enough to drown you, I imagine."

Drawing his sword, Brahm joined Rona's side. "Shall I strike her now, my queen?"

Rona feigned a pout. "Do not be ridiculous, Thaddy."

Brahm grimaced. "Not here, Your Highness. Please."

Rather than oblige the disgraced captain, Rona rolled her eyes and nudged his blade away like a child. "Put away your silly sword, Thaddy. It is beneath you." She stared back at Arymei. "No, Queen Arymei came for a worthy fight, and a worthy fight she shall have."

The following moments were chaos. Elise, Darcie, the boys, Brahm, and even Arymei's guards were reduced to mere bystanders thanks to a barrier shield created by Rona to separate them. Although they all wanted to step in and aid the Vynchian queen, the soldiers going so far as to use their swords against the wall, they were forced to pray Arymei would prevail against the evil sorceress.

Magical blasts erupted from both women's hands. Back and forth, shots were fired. It was difficult to determine who was winning or losing as the queens appeared equally matched. They took turns delivering and receiving hits, yet neither was willing to yield to the other.

Helpless to break through, Elise focused on Arymei's tactics. She longed for her magic to make some sort of difference. The Vynchian queen was skilled in attacks and stealth. At one point, she even looked to teleport into the trees, sending a shower of leaves and branches down below.

Rona dodged, however, and the cat and mouse chase continued.

Arymei narrowly missed an incoming blow, ducking down and sweeping a leg under Rona's feet. Her victory was short-lived, however, as Rona's hands closed around her neck from behind.

I need to help her! She might not know about Rona's protection spell. If Arymei succeeded in killing Rona, she, too, would die.

Arymei arched backwards, twisting and trying to free herself. Rona's hold only tightened. Wheezing, Arymei clutched at Rona's fingers before teleporting again. Reappearing behind the sorceress, Arymei quickly connected her foot with Rona's spine, sending her forward onto the ground.

Rona rolled over in time to block Arymei's next attack. Their energies met in midair and clashed. Holding steady, the battle stalled as it took all their energy to keep their magic going strong against the other.

Rona finally gained the upper hand as Arymei tripped and stumbled over a root. The magical connection ceased, pushing both women further apart. Arymei landed against the trunk of a large tree.

With a wave of her hand, the sorceress caused the thick trunk of the tree to split with a loud crack. It creaked and twisted before toppling over.

Crying out in horror, Elise watched as Vaughn ran out from hiding and leapt to push Arymei out of the way, narrowly missing death himself as it shook the ground with a crash.

No one moved.

Elise's heart raced when she noticed Arymei's eyes were closed. Biting her lip, she waited for Vaughn to examine her.

"Don't worry," Darcie called. "Her chest is moving. She must've hit her head is all."

"You need to be more worried about yourselves," Rona replied from behind them as the wall barrier vanished. However, in the blink of an eye, Elise watched her friends, Vaughn, the guards, and Gavin's friends freeze as if tied by invisible ropes from the neck down. A second later, Elise felt as if her entire body was wrapped in chains that squeezed to the point of painful. Yet there were no signs of actual restraints.

Rona and Brahm inspected each of the captives.

"I am through with distractions. You have robbed me of the only person that matters in this world. I will handle you once and for all."

"But we didn't kill your brother!" Mitch called out.

"Shut it, will you?" Brahm spat before kicking Mitch in the leg.

"We clearly do not have much time," Rona said, flickering her gaze back and forth between those on the ground and the trees. "I need to act now."

Elise licked her lips and decided to address the sorceress herself. "You're afraid, but you don't have to do this, Rona!" Elise took a steadying breath. "I know fear. I *know* what fear can do. Not just in my head, but within my own family." Desperation tugged at Elise's heart, her eyes glossed over, and she used what last minutes she possibly had to look at her friends. "But it's a lie! You can't be controlled by fear. It won't last, but lo—"

"Do not say it!" Rona roared. She spat each word with disdain as she closed the distance between herself and Elise. "Do *not* say love will. It is overdone, pathetic, a *true* lie in and of itself. *Love* is what has failed me, and I will not be fooled again!"

"Rona—" Elise pleaded.

"Silence!" Rona's crazed eyes raked over Elise. A manic chuckle radiated from deep within her. "Save your little rehearsed, self-righteous speech. I have heard enough. Let me tell you about your precious love sentiment." She twirled a finger before poking the air in Elise's direction.

A searing, hot pain pooled through Elise's arm, as if the blood itself were on fire. Elise cried out, gripping the afflicted arm.

"What ultimately killed King Derek? What was he willing to die for? *Love*." Rona jabbed the air again, sending a flash of magic into Elise's other hand that cradled her arm.

Elise fell to her knees as Rona moved closer.

"What is currently ailing the great, mourning Queen Eugena this very moment? Again, love. Or loss of it, rather. Take it from me, life is best when no one loves you. Only then can you know true strength."

"But you have someone who loves you," Gavin interrupted. "Brahm loves you, and he's been willing to do anything for you!"

"Hang Brahm!" Rona bellowed, ignoring the man in question, who frowned and remained silent. "He is no more use to me now than my dead brother."

She is completely detached of all emotion. How can she say these things? There's no way she actually believes what she is saying.

Welling up the courage, Elise kept her eyes fixated on Rona's every move. "From where I'm standing, you're the only thing those stories have in common. Love didn't cause those deaths. *You* did." She waited for the inevitable panic attack that normally arose when she spoke her mind, yet it didn't come. In fact, a quiet sense of calm steadied Elise's breath, and she relaxed her shoulders as best she could muster.

"And *you*, their weak-minded, anxious little savior. Behold what I have reduced you to, my dear, without a single touch. What has brought you here today? *Love*." She spun her hand around until Elise limply floated inches above the ground. "But, unlike your doomed little family, I refuse to lie to you." Rona dark red lips split into another grin as she sent Elise reeling in pain once more. The more bystanders, including Elise's friends, begged for her stop, the longer Rona watched.

I can't survive this. She's going to kill us all.

Writhing in agony, Elise screamed. Hot tears soaked her face. Her veins felt as if they would burst, her bones heavy and useless. She could not think. She could not move. Again, Elise desperately pushed for her magic to work. *Leave me alone. Let us go. Let us go.*

"Is that you doing that?" Rona chuckled. "Are you really trying to win? You see how well that worked for the queen."

Elise managed to turn her head enough to see Arymei's unconscious body on the ground.

"Do not waste your time," Rona purred. "My life lesson to you is simple. The root of all pain is love." She stroked a strand of hair out of Elise's eyes. "And I mean to cause you a lot of pain as love has given me."

Yanking Elise's hair, Rona forced her head back to look at Gavin, Mitch, and Darcie.

Elise gasped when Rona made the diary appear out of thin air. "Have you missed this?"

Elise longed to snatch it from the sorceress, but her scalding, hanging limbs prevented it. *Please don't.* She weakly uttered the same sentiment.

"Oh, but I must," Rona sang. "You see, I have spent many an hour with this blasted book, trying to uncover its secrets. Your own lover failed to help me, yet I prevailed in saving my brother with it. That is. . .until today."

The blistering, scorching pain swimming through Elise's veins all at once ceased. She felt her toes touch the ground, yet she remained frozen and breathless. Her brain remained numb with shock as was her ability to speak.

"Let me finish this story for you," Rona said, pointing the diary at each of the other three teenagers. "You shall not die today, dearest. For that would mean sacrificing your own life. I suspect you knew that."

Elise looked hopelessly into Gavin's eyes.

Rona followed her line of vision as understanding darkened his eyes. "Is your family worth all this trouble? Is *he* worth it?" she whispered into Elise's ear.

"Elise, don't," Gavin called. "Ignore whatever she tells you. I won't let you die! We can figure out another way."

Rona shook her head. "There is no need. Elise here will watch as each of you die one by one instead." Her chest swelled with pride as she fed on the panic, watching the blood flood from their faces. "Afterwards, Elise, you will open this diary and be sent back to whatever hole of a world you came from. Perhaps, their dead corpses will even follow you. Carry the burden of that loss." Pushing Elise to the ground, she advanced on Elise slowly as a lioness would her prey. Rona's soft, alluring tone then took on a terrifying, guttural hiss as she began speaking through gritted teeth. "Then, and only *then*, will you even get a taste of what I have been through!" Her words echoed around the forest. A flock of birds fled the trees around them as all parties gaped at the unhinged woman.

As Rona raised her hand to strike, Elise winced, clenching her eyes shut. *The pain is going to start again. I won't be able to handle it. It's too much. We've already lost.*

"Release the girl, Rona."

Elise opened her eyes in time to see an approaching hooded figure. The command was quiet, yet forceful, and when the hood lowered, Elise saw a masked middle-aged woman peering down at her. *She can't be much older than Joranna.*

The woman then removed her mask.

"Queen Prisha!" rang out the whispers from the surrounding guards and soldiers, including Vaughn and Brahm. Many hung their heads, lowering their weapons to kneel.

"Get up, you fools!" Rona whirled around. "You all answer to me! Me alone!"

"It is done, Rona," Prisha stated. "You have no power here."

Rona tipped her head back with a chuckle that made Elise's blood run cold. "Is that so? Pray, tell me who was it that fled in the first place, leaving her citizens to perish?"

"I intend to answer for my own crimes later," Prisha replied, careful to keep her voice even. "You, however, will answer for yours now."

"Do your worst, Prisha, but these are *my* subjects now. Lockesbarrow belongs to me. Now, if you do not mind, I am in the middle of something."

Turning her back on Prisha, Rona rolled her eyes when the rightful queen continued to push back.

"Release these children, Rona. *All* the children, in fact, that make up your so-called army."

"I do not take orders from you," Rona growled. "May Dmitri's soul haunt you until your death and beyond."

Elise grimaced as Rona shot another invisible force to immobilize Prisha, who remained calm with a stoic expression. It was Rona's turn to stalk towards Prisha one slow step at a time.

"You betrayed your people!" Rona exclaimed, her outstretched hand tightening into a fist. Her face split into a satisfied grin as the forcefield around Prisha squeezed harder. "And a traitor must *always* suffer in the end."

Prisha winced and hung her head. Her lip twitched as she released a distressed sigh. Composing herself, she met Rona's eye. "I apologize for Dmitri's death, Rona, and the pain it caused you. You may choose not to believe me, but I loved him, too. He was a good man, but the people deserved justice. The first time was a mistake, but the second was necessary."

Understanding dawned on Rona's face. "*You?*"

"Whatever version you chose to resurrect for yourself was not your brother. Altering time itself cannot truly bring him back. Deep down, you must know this. He was but a shell of his former self."

Rona glared into Prisha's eyes with such intensity, Elise felt it radiating off the sorceress. If looks could kill, Prisha would not be standing.

"This is my kingdom," Prisha continued. "I should have fought harder for it rather than be convinced otherwise by advisors. You have no power here. . .and it is time to stand down. Surrender."

"Says the woman who is currently captured," Rona pointed out. She leaned in until her nose almost touched Prisha's. "I commend your efforts, even admire your spirit, but you are too late." Rona turned back to face Elise with a dramatic turn. "It is also too late for you and your family. Now that I do not have to split the kingdoms with Dmitri, I can rule them both. You two ladies may have broken my heart, but you will never be strong enough to defeat me."

"You're wrong." The words left Elise's mouth before she realized what was said. "We are strong enough. Even if you kill us, we're strong enough because we tried." She felt adrenaline rushing through her where the pain once ran. Rona could kill her any moment, and probably would, but Elise held her head high, nonetheless. "The root of pain is not love." She held Gavin's gaze as she spoke. "Love is made up of too many elements to be the single root of anything. It can be whatever you make of it."

Gavin mouthed the words *I love you.* Elise did the same.

Rona clicked her tongue, staring between Elise and Gavin. "How poetic." Her sarcastic, mocking smile melted into a thin, strict line as her eyes narrowed. "What sentimental last words. Brahm!" she quipped, walking over to where Brahm and Gavin stood. The blade of Brahm's sword still rested against Gavin's neck. "Kill Mr. Striess first."

"No!" Elise wriggled and writhed against her invisible binds. *This can't be happening. This can't be real!* She could hear her heart beating in her ears. It pounded against her chest. There was so much she wanted to say to Gavin yet could not find words at the same time. Staring hopelessly, her own cries mixed with those of Darcie and Mitch. Prisha demanded Rona cease her theatrics and surrender, yet all objections were ignored. "Please, no! You can't. Don't kill him," she sobbed, thrashing against her holds. *He can't die. I can't lose him!*

Brahm lowered his sword before standing between Gavin and Rona.

Elise watched as every ounce of color drained from Gavin's face until even his lips turned white. His forehead glistened and his breathing was uneven. She desperately willed Brahm not to kill him, hoping a fraction of magic would leave Rona's forcefield. Brahm's inaction proved it did not, fueling Elise's manic attempts to free herself as the two men stared at one another. Brahm lifted the blade and rested it against the skin of Gavin's chest. *I've got to get to him!*

Then Brahm looked at Elise.

Every time Brahm put his eyes on her, Elise instinctively distanced herself. The hairs on her neck would stand and her thighs would clench. Elise did not trust this man or his intentions. He had done so many vile things.

Yet, this time was different.

Rather than repulse her, it stopped Elise's heart. It was as if she were seeing Brahm for the first time. He studied her face, clutching the hilt of the sword by his side, before inhaling deeply. Brahm bowed his head in Elise's direction before squaring his shoulders. "Forgive me."

Elise closed her eyes. *I can't watch.* "Brahm, don't!" she screamed, straining every muscle, before choking back a sob. Against her better judgement, she opened a single eye to peek.

In one swift motion, Brahm twirled the tip of the sword from Gavin's chest and sank it deeply into Rona's. Elise gasped, along with everyone else, as the sword pushed through her completely before protruding out of her back.

It was as if time stopped. The diary fell to the ground with a heavy thud. Rona's shivering body lurched over Brahm's shoulder, her expression one of genuine shock and disbelief. Her mouth hung open, quivering. "Thaddy. . .*Brahm.*" A look of utter betrayal flashed across her eyes as she regarded his own anguished expression. Perhaps, Elise suspected, even an ounce of regret.

All at once, the invisible shields disappeared, and Elise could move again as well as everyone else.

As Rona's body fell limp, Brahm pushed her onto the ground before falling to his knees with a painful groan. Panting, he clutched his heart.

"What is happening to him?" Prisha asked. "Did she strike him?"

Elise shook her head, rushing to Brahm's side along with Vaughn, who inspected Rona. "Whoever kills Rona also dies. It's how she's protected herself all this time. Brahm. Look at me." She took his face between her hands. "Brahm, stay with me. We can get you help."

"No," he wheezed. Doubling over, he gasped for air. "It has to be t-this way." With an awful rattling sound, he met her eyes with the same soul-crushing expression. "A traitor must *always* s-suffer in the end."

Brahm's eyes closed, his mouth drooped, and finally he fell forward, draped across Rona's lifeless body.

Elise looked at Vaughn, who nodded. *They're really dead.*

Nobody moved.

Nobody spoke.

The only sound came from the distant gulls, canons, battle cries, and the clashing of swords. As numbness spread over her like a blanket, Elise felt like she was watching and listening from underwater. The faces around her became distorted as she succumbed to the aftermath of everything. Before her brain could comprehend what was happening, Gavin scooped her up into an embrace. Inch by inch, Elise felt the numbness shatter until she could breathe again.

"Excuse me." Vaughn cleared his throat until Gavin and Elise parted. "I believe this is yours."

Thanking him, Elise reached out to take the diary, running her fingers over the aged cover. *I didn't think we'd ever get this back.* She smiled before looking up at Vaughn. "Were you really on our side the whole time?"

He shrugged with a charming, innocent smile. "Guess you'll never know, will you?" Winking down at her, Vaughn turned his attention to Gavin before holding out his hand. "The best man won. Take good care of her."

Gavin hesitated, looked at Elise, and finally shook Vaughn's hand. "It would have been more satisfying to punch you."

"Understood." Vaughn nodded before offering his arm to Prisha. "Might the rightful and beautiful Queen of Lockesbarrow have any openings in her court for a handsome, aimless philanderer?"

"That remains to be seen," Prisha chuckled, linking her arm with his. "Something tells me you will cause a great deal of scandal in my court amongst the ladies."

Elise and Darcie shared a knowing look.

"However," Prisha added, "I am in search of a new captain."

Vaughn accepted without hesitation.

"That reminds me," Gavin said to her. "I met a few inmates while I was kidnapped who are innocent. Now that I think about it, you may want to examine the whole prison."

Hopefully, Richard is doing the same for the remaining Haighdlen prisoners.

"Consider it done," said the queen. "That is, after I get this army dispersed and sent to their homes. I should like to recruit a proper army."

"So, what do we now?" Mitch asked, squeezing Darcie's hand.

Watching as the Vynchian guards helped Queen Arymei recover and stand, Prisha beamed. "We spread the word that war is over. Rona has fallen."

CHAPTER 28

Only after Prisha was restored as Queen of Lockesbarrow did she fulfill her promise by ordering the return of all surviving adolescent soldiers to their homes. They, as well as those who had fallen, were honored for their service. The next phase of her reformation plan consisted of investigating the prison, a task delegated to her newly appointed Captain of the Guard, Vaughn Garthorne, who—according to a letter sent to Joranna from Prisha—*"wears the uniform and title well, with the utmost dedication, and answers the call of duty in hopes of atoning for past wrongdoings"*.

Elise giggled in spite of herself as she finished the letter Joranna shared back at Haighdlen Castle. *There's a twist. I never would have pegged Vaughn for enforcing the law.* While his character was often shifty, this was an amazing opportunity for him, and she was thankful he was given a second chance after all his help.

"What are you reading?" Gavin asked as he, Mitch, and Darcie joined her in the library.

Elise held the letter out for him to take. "She sent Joranna some updates, mentions people she's hiring, and says she's sorry she can't make it to Richard's coronation with everything going on."

"That makes sense," said Darcie, reading the letter over Gavin's shoulder. "Anything about your friend? Travis or something?"

"Tristan," Gavin corrected her before his face lit up. "Actually, yeah. It says here she offered him the job of Ambassador to Leafbrookc. That had to have meant a lot to him."

"Why do you say that?" Mitch asked.

"When we were in the training camp, he told me lots of stories," Gavin explained. "But one of them involved his dad being the Ambassador to Leafbrooke and them traveling together. Rona killed his dad when she took over. It'll be a good fit for him."

It was Darcie's turn to giggle. "Not to mention that'll keep him in court to see more of Iris. Joranna said she's now one of Prisha's ladies-in-waiting. I doubt she'll be waiting very long."

Mitch rolled his eyes with a scoff. "You just can't help but meddle, can you?" He laughed at her feigned pout. "You're matchmaking across kingdoms now!"

"Hey, don't be jealous of my skills," Darcie teased. "*Someone* had to introduce them before we left. You could cut their chemistry with a knife."

"Well, if the hairstyling gig ever gets old, we know you'd make a great living planning weddings," Elise suggested with a playful smile Darcie quickly returned.

The door opened abruptly, interrupting their friendly banter, for Joranna to enter with a small white box in her hand.

"Oh, good, Edith has already dressed you all," she said, taking in their formal garments. "The coronation is about to commence. The last of the guests are arriving now."

"Yep, we're ready," Darcie piped up before nodding at the box. "Did someone bring you a gift? That was nice."

Joranna looked down at the box in question, turning it over in her hands. "Yes, rather unexpectedly. It was found among Richard's gifts, but no one saw who delivered it." Holding it up to her ear, she shook it lightly back and forth.

Elise prayed it was nothing dangerous and sighed in relief when Joranna lifted the top without any surprises.

The queen gasped as she lifted a silken pink scarf out of the box. "Oh, how beautiful!"

Elise's smile fell as her eyes widened. *Horanis's scarf!* She remembered the story of the fairy king gifting Joranna the scarf, but Elise never realized it was part of a coronation gift. "Let me see. There is a small note here." She lifted a piece of paper with elegant writing on it. *"To the mother of the new King of Haighdlen—may this scarf serve as protection wherever you reside. Sewn by the hands from my kingdom, may its magic cover you in yours and beyond. - Horanis.* Horanis? What kingdom is he talking about?" Joranna asked.

"King of the fairies," Elise replied.

Joranna looked back at her as if she had swallowed an ice cube whole. "I always thought he was a myth. The type made up to keep children from messing with fairies." Speechless, Joranna scanned the letter, rereading it many times. "But why would he reach out now? The wording he uses. . .it is as if he knows I am planning to leave, but I have not shared that. How would he know?"

"You're leaving?" Elise shrieked. "What do you mean you're leaving? The war is over. There's no reason to leave."

Joranna waited until Elise calmed herself before folding the letter with a sigh. "I was going to wait until after the ball tonight to share the news."

"I don't get it," Darcie said. "Rona's dead. Why leave now?"

The queen sat down on the nearest chair, careful not to wrinkle her gown, and rested the box on her lap. "Richard and I met with the council about our plan forward. Although the war is over, there may still be those loyal to Rona. Uprisings, those seeking revenge—all are possible. We have been too careless in the past, and we must move forward with a plan. As painful as it is to leave, it is also the best course of action to ensure our family's survival."

"Who's all going?" Mitch asked.

"We have not shared with everyone yet," Joranna replied cautiously, "but we will resume our previous plan for me to take Ruby and Ian. As I come from that world, it is in our family's best interest that I accompany them."

Elise scooted closer to the edge of the couch. Draping herself over the arm, she gazed at her grandmother. "Are you sure you want to leave?" She focused on Joranna's silent form, willing her magic to compel her grandmother to tell the absolute truth.

"I have done a great deal of thinking," Joranna assured her. She smiled at her lap. "If we take some of my jewelry and treasures, we can surely live comfortably. Ruby can deliver quietly there, and Ian is adventurous enough he will not fight such an opportunity. It will increase our chance for a safe future." She stared at the map on the wall depicting the four kingdoms. "It is funny. . .I have lived in Haighdlen far longer than I ever lived in the other world. You and your friends have longed to return, but it took a great deal of convincing on my part. In the end, it came down to be providing for my grandchild."

Again, Elise felt as if Joranna was not telling her something. She was quiet as she pondered her family's move. *It would make sure they are back in our world. If I'm born there, and Mom stays, I'll grow up and meet my friends. Everything will occur the way it's supposed to. . .but why do I feel so sad about it now?*

It was not that she wished things to happen differently. Elise certainly wanted to be sure she would meet her friends again in the new timeline. She shared a glance with Gavin, but her smile didn't reach her eyes. If all went according to plan, and the timeline was truly fixed, would he still be in love with her?

Gavin took her hand.

"Do you think Ruby will be okay?" Elise asked quietly.

"I do," Joranna said with confidence before her shoulders shook with laughter. "She has done enough visiting that world. Now, she will not have to sneak around anymore. Let us hope she has learned to be a bit wiser." When Elise did not reply, Joranna smiled. "She will be safe, and she has you to thank for that. I overheard her talking with Sarah that if she has a daughter, she is considering the name Elise. Is that not thoughtful? Such a wonderful tribute to you."

Elise laughed, but it was a hollow sound underlined with nerves. Unable to meet her grandmother's eyes, she still felt the uneasy weight of Joranna's knowing stare. *Maybe she's figured out who I am.* If she knew, Joranna did not hint or say anything. Elise looked up when Joranna hummed in surprise, claiming that there was something else in the bottom of the box.

"I seem to have missed something." Joranna lifted another folded piece of paper before her eyebrows rose in surprise. She pursed her lips before holding it out. "It is addressed to *you*, Elise. How odd."

Elise paled and glanced at her friends. *Why would he send* me *something?* She hesitated before finally taking the paper. Her name was written on the outside with the same elegant writing as Joranna's letter.

--Well done. The prophecy is fulfilled. Replace this and your involvement will be erased from their memories as the restored timeline resumes.

It was difficult to unfold the paper with her hands shaking like they were, but she finally managed and gasped when she recognized what it was. *It's the final entry he ripped out of Joranna's diary.* She was careful to hide it from her grandmother to avoid suspicion. Elise's eyes scanned across Joranna's original writing.

October 19, 1988

Dear Diary,

I am determined to write no more of my grief. The last several pages have served me well enough. As I enter another restless night, my thoughts have wandered again to the visiting travelers. Namely Elise. She is the most fearless young woman I have ever met. Despite the odds against her, I honestly think she is the key to saving our family. I know not her exact relation, but I am inclined to think we are closer than she lets on. If only Richard would take her more seriously. She has done so much already and shows a fierce loyalty. Even if we are forced to flee, and the worst occurs, Derek was right about her. She is a true Laurille, and we are indebted to her.

"What does it say?" Joranna asked.

Elise took a moment to compose herself as both of her eyes stung with approaching tears. "He wanted to tell me to take care of you all and make sure everything turns out okay."

For the first time in her life, Elise was thankful Ballard interrupted at that moment to inform Joranna that Queen Arymei had arrived. Elise waited for her grandmother to follow the steward out before she let out a trapped sigh.

Gavin scooted closer and wrapped an arm around her shoulders. "What happened? What did he say? Is something wrong?"

Elise shook her head before holding out the letter for him to take. Mitch and Darcie also took turns reading it from their stance behind the couch.

"That's deep," Mitch said an appreciative whistle. "I wonder why Horanis tore it out."

Darcie rolled her eyes and kissed his cheek. "Because she had to learn that for herself. Even if Brahm was the one to actually kill Rona, Elise was willing to face her and do what she had to do."

"Yeah," Gavin added, smiling at Elise. "If she hadn't shown so much stubbornness—" He referenced the torn entry with a wink. "I mean, '*fierce loyalty*', we would have quit a long time ago."

"I know I would have," Mitch muttered playfully. He patted Elise on the shoulder. "But you stuck with it, Elise, and now your family is closer. Only you could've done that."

It was difficult for Elise to take the compliment. She had not given much thought or energy to self-worth in the past, often seeking invisibility over notoriety. However, her friends were right. Since her return from Lockesbarrow, Elise also noted how close her family was becoming. While she could not say she was the one who ended Rona, Elise could accept that she helped end her family's estrangement.

"Thanks, but I couldn't have done it without you guys," she admitted. "And I don't know about you, but after this coronation and ball tonight, I just want to find a way home for good."

As soon as the words left her lips, they jumped as a puff of smoke appeared from the chair Joranna previously occupied. As the smoke cleared, Elise leaned closer and gasped at the sight of the diary—the *original* diary.

"Oh, finally!" Mitch exclaimed as he lunged for it before Darcie's arm stopped him. "Come on, I want to go home!" He tried again, but she prevented him once more. "Rona's dead. The family loves each other. Let's go home before something bad happens."

"And we will," Darcie answered with a laugh, "but we're all dressed up for a fun night, probably our last time at a ball like this, and I'm not going to waste it. Plus, you promised me a dance." The rest of Mitch's protest went unheard as Darcie pulled him out of the room to join the other guests.

Gavin and Elise shared a laugh.

"Poor Mitch," Elise teased.

Assuring her that Mitch would get over it, Gavin intertwined his fingers with hers before resting their joined hands between them. "That was really nice of Joranna to write down what Derek said about you."

Folding the entry into the front of her gown, Elise nodded.

"You got everything you wanted," he added before lifting their hands to kiss her knuckles. When Elise's smile did not reach her eyes, he inquired what was the matter. She tried to wave it off, but Gavin persisted until Elise chewed on her lip and sighed.

"I should be excited," she began, "because you're right. I did get everything I wanted." Elise squeezed his hand. "But, now that things have slowed down, I keep thinking about you wanting to join the military."

She felt him stiffen but continued in a small voice. "I wanted to be mad at you for not telling me, but that wouldn't be right since I didn't tell you what could've happened if I had been the one to kill Rona. I'm so sorry."

"I understand why you didn't tell me." He kissed the top of her head. "And I'm sorry, too, but please don't ever feel like you can't come to me with stuff."

Elise nodded and requested he do the same. "I hate you'll have to leave." She coughed to disguise a cry in her throat. "Will it be soon?"

That's a dumb question. We're about to graduate. Did you expect him to hang around while everyone else moves on with their lives?

He rested his head on her shoulder. "Sooner than later, probably. I have to talk to a recruiter first."

Don't cry. This is a great opportunity for him. At least you can enjoy the summer together. Rather than share her insecurities, Elise leaned her head against his and asked what made him decide to join.

Deep down, Elise wished she listened better. As he explained his upbringing, including his father's career, her thoughts wandered to the inevitable day when he would have to break up with her. *I can't expect a long-distance situation. He has to know what this decision means.*

She was not upset about the choice itself. The military was a highly respectable path. Realizing he was still talking, Elise forced herself to focus and return to reality.

"To be honest, I never really understood my dad until I was in Rona's training camp," Gavin confessed. "I know it was only a few days, but being out there with the other guys—let's just say my dad's old stories started making more sense. . .Is that stupid?"

Elise nudged his head up with her shoulder before kissing him softly. "Nope. It makes perfect sense." She attempted to stand up, but he pulled her back down to the couch.

"What is it?" he asked. "You're not telling me something."

Elise pretended to pick a piece of lint from her gown, taking a moment to admire Edith's flawless work yet again. She was going to miss these gowns and the royal treatment when all was said and done. Feeling Gavin's expectant stare on her, she forced herself to smile. "It sounds like your dad is going to be really proud of you."

He once again pulled her down as she tried to escape again. "And what about you?" His eyes searched her entire face before landing on Elise's lips. "Will you be proud of me?"

She detected a hint of uncertainty in his tone, which tugged at her heart even more. "Of course!" Elise intended to say more, but it became increasingly hard to concentrate when he trailed a finger from her lips down to her collarbone. The path continued until the same finger lowered the strap of her gown. Before she could react, he replaced the finger with his lips, tracing the same path back to her lips.

"Good," he whispered huskily in her ear before turning his attention to the sensitive skin behind it. "I thought you'd be mad at me."

"No." She moaned when his other hand cupped her bottom, which was a challenge given the volume of her skirt. "I'm just dreading when you have to leave." Clinging to him, she warned herself to enjoy every moment they had left together.

"Yeah, boot camp will be tough, but after that. . .Well, I kind of hoped you'd come with me."

His words cut through the desire pooling into Elise's lower belly, and she jerked forward as he slid down to kneel in front of her.

"Elise?"

What is he doing? Goosebumps covered Elise's entire body as he took her hand. She wanted to say something profound but was unable to speak as he drew small circles on the back of her hand.

He lifted his other hand to lift her strap back into place. The corner of his mouth twitched before he smiled and looked at her. "You look so beautiful. . .plus I'll never be able to plan anything more romantic than this. . .being dressed for a ball and everything."

"Gavin—"

Shaking his head, he cleared his throat. "I-I've thought about this a lot. I know I don't have a ring yet, and maybe it's too fast for you—"

"Do you know what you're saying?" She squeezed his hands. "Are you sure you want to do this?" Elise's thoughts swirled rapidly, her heart fluttered, and she laughed in spite of herself. Never in a million years did she think something like this was possible for her.

Despite the euphoric high she felt, a nagging part of Elise's brain reminded her of the challenges they could face, but she pushed them all away. Those could be dealt with later. She was not set on a particular college, and if she did pursue teaching, it was a career that traveled well. Marrying a military man would also come with many hurdles, but there was nothing she wanted more than to face them by Gavin's side.

"Let's do it," he said before breaking out into a smile of his own. The same charming smile that made her weak in the knees. "Will you marry me?"

Elise closed her eyes and sucked in a breath. Dreaming of marrying Gavin was one thing—she lost count of how many times she had scribbled *Mrs. Elise Striess* in her notebooks back home—but being asked to marry him was an entirely different situation. It did not feel possible. Things like this did not happen to invisible girls like her, and yet, here he was on one knee awaiting her answer.

"People are going to think we're crazy," she whispered, unable to control her smiling. *Or that I'm pregnant*, she added in her head. None of that mattered, however, and it was the first time Elise disregarded the opinions of others that she could remember. All that mattered was the two of them together in this moment. Feeling her eyes water, Elise nodded fervently and met his gaze. "Yes, I will."

Leaping to his feet with a childlike energy, Gavin scooped Elise into a tight hug before twirling her around. Before she could say anything, he crushed his lips against hers with such eagerness, the two shared a series of small kisses before Elise felt like she could breathe properly again.

"I love you," she whispered into his ear as he hugged her again. When he repeated the words back to her, she tightened their embrace. *I can't believe I'm engaged!* She suppressed the urge to squeal, choosing instead to clear her throat. "We should probably keep it quiet for now with everything going on, and it's probably better to have a long engagement."

He nodded in agreement.

"Not only for college, but maybe let us have some regular dates first." They shared a laugh before hugging again. She proposed a movie or dinner date when they returned home.

"That sounds pretty boring compared to fixing a magical timeline and saving the royal family together," Gavin whispered against her shoulder. He pulled back long enough to kiss her. "But a long engagement it is."

Pulling away to pick up the diary, Elise tossed a teasing smile over her shoulder at him. "Well, maybe not *too* long." She beckoned him to follow her. "You can go ring shopping if you want." Holding out her hand, Elise wiggled her fingers as if imagining one. Elise melted against him as he wrapped an arm around her. "After all, once I tell Darcie, she'll have the entire ceremony planned in a day."

Taking the diary from her to tuck into his vest, Gavin scoffed. "Probably an hour."

Wrapping her arms around his neck, Elise quirked a brow as she eased back. "You sure about this? I'm kind of a mess."

He shrugged with ease as his smile returned. "Yeah, I know. I've met your family." He laughed when she slapped him with a playful pout. "But just wait." He winked at her with a smirk. "You still have to meet mine."

Lowering her arms to link their fingers together, Elise's face grew serious as she searched his eyes for any sign of doubt. Finding none, she leaned forward and kissed him deeply before whispering against his lips. "I can't wait."

There was something thrilling about carrying a secret. Having Mitch and Darcie question their joyful smiles as they arrived to the throne room was worth every ounce of keeping their news quiet a little longer. Elise particularly relished catching Darcie glaring knowingly at her throughout Richard's speech. *You'll find out soon enough.*

The coronation proceeded as planned, with Richard officially being crowned King of Haighdlen in a lavish ceremony amidst cheers, applause, and fanfare. While the attention stayed on Richard, and rightfully so, Elise was especially moved watching Joranna, who was ever the vision of a proud mother and queen.

As the occupants of the throne room transitioned to the ballroom to celebrate, Elise reflected on the journey that led them to this moment. How many times had she feared the worst? How many tears and panic attacks occurred for Elise to finally find her self-worth? Watching everyone go through the motions of a toast, dinner, and later dancing, the evening felt as if it were passing in slow motion. Longing to bottle up the insatiable energy in the room, Elise committed the elaborate details of the music and merriment to memory, knowing it most likely could be her last time there.

Spotting Richard and Gwen sharing a dance as the Archer family happily observed from a nearby table, Elise thought back to the first ball she attended in the same ballroom when Derek and Joranna were engaged. Given the similarities of the two couples, if she squinted, Elise could almost see her grandparents again on the dancefloor.

With a heavy sigh, Elise rose and made her way to the royal head table. *I have to say goodbye sooner or later. I can't put it off any longer.*

Only Joranna, Ian, and Ruby were still seated. All three greeted her as she approached with Joranna asking if she was enjoying herself. Elise carried on with pleasantries longer than necessary as the pain of leaving felt too much to bear. . .and they would not even remember her visiting.

It's better this way.

"Where is Sarah?" Elise asked.

Ian nodded at the sea of couples dancing. "She is dancing with my friend Liam. I invited him, and it seems they have grown rather close since he saved me."

"I could not be happier," Joranna commented. "I have never seen Richard so happy either. Let us hope some good news comes out of these attractive pairings."

That takes care of Richard's and Sarah's futures. Ian will meet Aunt Morgan in our world at some point. That only left Ruby to be dealt with. Surely, their meddling planted a seed for a happier future. Scanning the crowd, Elise frowned. "Where is Charles?"

Ruby took a sip from her cup as Joranna wrung her hands. "I am afraid Lord Fenton is busy assisting Ballard with our traveling arrangements."

"That's too bad," Elise said. "I would have liked to say goodbye. It's time for us to leave."

Joranna stood from her seat and embraced Elise in a warm hug. "We are forever grateful for your help. We will not forget all you have done for us."

Unfortunately, you will. Elise inhaled her grandmother's sweet perfume. *I wish you of all people could remember me. I'm going to miss you so much.*

As they parted, Elise moved on to her uncle. "You healed up nicely. I hope you have a safe trip."

Ian winked with a smile. "You as well. Thank you for everything."

Elise nodded politely and paused in front of her mother.

Ruby met her eyes but said nothing as she stroked her stomach in lazy circles. *I know you can't say it, but I'm going to miss you, too. Hopefully, whatever future I return to is happy for you as well. You deserve it, Mom.*

Before Elise could say anything else, Ian asked his mother if she would like to dance. Joranna appeared shocked at the offer. After all, Elise suspected she had not done much dancing since Derek returned home ill. Staring wistfully at the dancefloor, Joranna smiled at Elise as her son escorted her away.

Now that it was only her and Ruby, Elise stepped closer to the table. "Good luck with the baby and your new home." Ruby nodded and wished her a safe trip. Yet, something still felt off to Elise. The spark had left Ruby's eyes. Elise could not imagine what anxieties preyed on her mother's mind about moving away and entering motherhood all at once. Licking her lips, Elise nodded toward Ruby's stomach. "Your child is lucky to have you for a mother. I know you're going to do great in the other world. You are strong enough, Ruby, even without magic. Don't forget that, even if things get tough."

Ruby looked taken aback by Elise's forwardness but thanked her and wished Elise well.

As difficult as it was to say goodbye to Joranna, it was twice as hard to walk away from her mother. Feeling a cry form in her throat, Elise caught Gavin's eye across the crowd and waved him, Mitch, and Darcie away from their table to follow her into the courtyard.

Given the crowd of people standing outside, Elise led them into the garden for privacy.

"Are you sure you're ready?" Gavin asked.

Elise sighed. "As ready as I'm going to be. To be honest, guys, I don't know what we're returning home to."

Darcie grabbed her hand. "It's going to be great, and no matter what, we'll always remember the truth of what happened."

Sucking her mouth into a thin line, Elise thanked her and pulled the piece of paper from her gown while Gavin did the same with the diary in his vest.

"I know this is emotional for you and all," Mitch said to Elise, "but I can't wait to get back and never look at another diary ever, ever again."

"I can't blame you there," said Elise as they all laughed. When Gavin handed her the diary, she took in one more view of the picturesque castle and braced herself. "Are y'all ready?" When her friends nodded, Elise slipped the final entry behind the other pages before fully opening the diary and welcomed the suffocating portal, for what she hoped would be the last time.

CHAPTER 29

Elise questioned the diary's magic when she woke up in her own quiet bedroom. Drowsiness consumed her, lulling her in and out of sleep. She watched the blades of the ceiling fan rotate at full speed eight or nine times before movement to her left made her scream and bolt off the bed. The sight of familiar red hair made Elise blow out a steadying breath. "Mitch, you scared me!"

"All I did was sit up." Mitch yawned and stretched from his position on the floor. As Gavin and Darcie stirred as well, he took in the details of the room. "Where are we?"

"Why did the diary bring us to your house?" Darcie asked Elise, who shrugged.

"Hey, what about my car?" Mitch scrambled to his feet and pulled on the blinds to peer out the window. His shoulders sagged in relief. "Oh, good. It's here."

"Do you think something went wrong?" asked Gavin. "Why wouldn't it have taken us to Joranna's?"

What business would the diary have to bring them back to her house? A diary, she realized, that was no longer with them. She could think of no reason her house would hold anything special. Nothing looked out of place or different. . .until she caught sight of the photo collage on the wall.

There used to only be four photos there.

Stepping closer, Elise counted eight photos strung together with clothespins on a makeshift board. Only now, instead of all being photos of her and Darcie, Elise saw a handful contain candid pictures of herself and Ruby. Some were recent, while others were old trips and birthdays. *Mom is smiling. Look how happy we look.* Elise pointed to one showing members of her family from Haighdlen. "What's going on?"

"Elise?" Ruby's voice called from downstairs.

Elise froze, looking anxiously between her friends. "I don't know if you're all supposed to be here. I'm not even sure which version of *here* this is." Grabbing Gavin's hand, she urged them all to follow her. "I doubt she'd want boys in my room. Let's go into the spare guest bedroom before she catches us." Tiptoeing down the hall, Elise led them to the next door and slipped inside. "Sorry for the mess. This room always gets used for storage, so—" Elise did a double take of the once cluttered space. Where stacked bins once rested against the wall, there was now a computer desk. The lumpy old mattress in the corner was now a full bookshelf. Various framed pieces of art hung on the walls and both windows now had matching curtains.

"Whoa," Darcie said, doing a full spin and whistling in appreciation. "If we fixed nothing else, your mom's improved interior design was worth it. This office is awesome!"

Elise said nothing as she approached the computer desk. Her attention was drawn to the framed college degree hanging above it. She smiled in disbelief at the decorative lettering spelling out her mother's name. Hearing her name again, Elise jumped when Ruby poked her head in before entering the office cradling a steaming cup of tea.

"Is everything all right in here? I heard screaming." Her eyes widened when she noticed the other three. "Oh, I am so sorry. I did not realize you had friends over. I would have made more tea."

Mom? This could not be her mother. Instead of a worn, wrinkled dress and stained apron, Ruby sported dress slacks and a silk blouse. Rather than a tangled mass of hair clipped on top of her head, smooth voluminous shoulder-length curls framed her slender face. She easily looked ten years younger and her once permanent scowl was replaced with an amused smile.

"Why are you all staring at me like that? Do I have something on my face?" She dabbed her cheek with the back of her hand before blowing on the tea in the other.

Yeah, makeup!

"I do not believe we have met," Ruby said to the boys. "I'm Ruby, Elise's mom."

Gavin and Mitch exchanged an anxious glance at one another.

Elise apologized as the boys awkwardly greeted her mother. "Mom, this is Mitch, Darcie's boyfriend." Licking her lips, she hesitated. "And this is Gavin. . .*my* boyfriend." *I can't introduce him as my fiancé yet.* Bracing herself, Elise stared in shock when Ruby beamed.

"You did not tell me you were dating someone! And Darcie, I am surprised you kept a secret that long," she teased before nodding towards the boys. "Well, you two ladies have done quite well for yourselves. I trust you are both respectful gentlemen?" There was a strict undertone in her voice that both Gavin and Mitch knew well enough to take seriously. Once both nodded, Ruby's cheeriness returned. "I wish we could all sit and talk more, but I am afraid I need to cut your visit short. Elise and I have some last-minute items to purchase for the party on Saturday."

Ruby set her cup down on the desk and shuffled through a pile of envelopes.

Furrowing her brows, Elise looked at her friends with a blank stare. She shrugged when Darcie mouthed the same question playing on repeat in her own brain. *What party?*

Gavin took the bait. "What party?"

They tensed when Ruby spun around. "Elise, you and Darcie didn't invite your boyfriends to your graduation party? We have been planning it for over a month!" She turned her attention to Mitch and Gavin. "You boys should come if you can. There will be plenty of food. Oh! That reminds me." Ruby took a delicate sip of her tea before addressing Darcie. "Am I still good to receive the family and friends discount at your father's bakery? I placed the order over a week ago, but I forgot to ask."

What is happening right now?

Darcie bounced on the balls of her feet with an uneasy smile. "Sure?"

"Thank you. Again, I'm sorry to ask you to leave for now. After we run our errands, Elise, I'll also need your help tidying up before the family comes."

The family? They're actually coming here?

"The whole family?" Elise did not hide her confusion. "Coming here?"

Ruby finished the rest of her tea before replying. "Well, they will stay at Nana's house, since we do not have the room, but yes. You do not think they would miss your graduation, do you?" She checked her watch. "I have to make a few calls before we leave. Darcie, always a pleasure. Boys, it was nice to meet you both. We will talk soon. Goodbye!"

As the door closed behind Ruby, a deafening silence filled the room as the group of friends stared at each other. The last five minutes had occurred at a whirlwind speed. If Gavin, Mitch, and Darcie were not there, Elise would question her own sanity. Shaking her head, Elise scoffed and pointed towards the door. "Okay, who was *that*?"

The oddities continued well after Elise and Ruby returned home from dinner and shopping. Not only did Ruby ask her questions throughout their outing, but she *listened* and seemed to care about Elise's responses. There were moments throughout the evening while her mother talked when Elise caught herself marveling at Ruby's transformation. It was simply incredible that this was the same woman.

Later that evening, while Elise lay on her bed texting Gavin, her mother's cell phone rang from the other bedroom.

"Elise?" Ruby called. "Can you please answer that? I am in the shower."

Elise pursed her lips and rolled off her bed. *Not sure that's a good idea considering what happened the last time I checked Mom's phone.* She would never forget learning about Haighdlen in the first place after reading a series of texts on Ruby's phone. Shuffling into her mother's bedroom, she peeked down to see Joranna's name and face on the screen.

Upon hearing Elise answer, Joranna excitedly went into a two-minute storytelling spree, sharing how excited everyone was to be planning a visit. Elise had to hold the phone away from her ear for the more animated parts. "I am tempted to go meet them at the portal."

How strange it was to hear Joranna speak of the portal so openly. Daydreaming while her Nana continued updating her on the other Laurilles, Elise absentmindedly fiddled with random items on her mother's nightstand. *I can't wrap my head around all these changes. Is this even real?*

"Elise? Elise?"

Hearing a pause, Elise realized she had yet to string two words together since answering. "Nana, I'm sorry. What did you say?"

Joranna chuckled on the other end of the call. "Can I get you to write down a message for your mother to call Ian at work tomorrow? Do you have a pen nearby?"

Hearing the shower still running, Elise agreed and sat down on Ruby's bed before opening the nightstand drawer. She shuffled through old papers and receipts before locating a pen. After scribbling down Ian's work number, something in the back of the drawer caught Elise's attention despite Joranna's continued talking in her ear. Checking one more time to make sure the water was still running, Elise pulled out a wrinkled piece of folded parchment. *Is this what I think it is? Would she really have kept it all these years?* The worn discolored edges gave away its age, yet Elise remembered seeing it—reading it—when it was new. Holding her breath, she unfolded and reread Charles' love letter to Ruby.

With every heartfelt word, her heart broke in much the same way as the first time reading it. Time was never on their side, yet something caused Ruby to keep this. Elise's mind immediately traveled back to Haighdlen Castle. The secrecy, the anxiety, and the urgency were so fresh in her mind. Since returning, Elise could not help but feel as if she were in two places at once. The idea that life was going on in Haighdlen at that very moment while she did mediocre things like go to the store with her mom and plan for a party felt unnatural.

Hearing her name repeated, Elise apologized to Joranna again.

"You sure are distracted this evening. Is everything all right?" Joranna waited until Elise replied before continuing. "I meant to ask you, is there anything specific you would like for a graduation present?"

Elise glanced down at the letter again. Running her thumb across Charles' signature, she cleared her throat. "Are you able to communicate with the family on short notice?" Elise knew she must sound incredibly suspicious, but her grandmother did not sound bothered and replied it was possible.

"Why?" Joranna asked. "Do you need to get a message to them?"

"Not *them*." Elise froze as the sound of Ruby's water stopped. She hurried to stuff the letter back into the drawer. Once it looked buried again, she slammed the drawer. "Hey, I have to go, but there *is* something I would like."

It was a stretch. Charles may have moved away or gotten married. Elise hardly doubted he spent the last eighteen years alone. Yet, it was a chance she was willing to take to give the one person who deserved it most her own chance of love. She had just enough time to make her request before ending the call as Ruby emerged from the bathroom in pajamas.

"Who called?" Ruby inquired.

"Ian wants you to call him at work tomorrow. The number is written down there. Goodnight, Mom." Without waiting for a reply, or a chance to lose her nerve, Elise returned to her room.

Please, she thought as her head hit the pillow. Within minutes, Elise was surprised to find herself already drifting off to sleep. *Please let this work out. . .Please, for Mom.*

The few remaining days leading up to her graduation passed in a blissful blur that included a real first date with Gavin. Elise's initial fears of him growing bored of her in their world vanished soon after she was invited to meet his parents. After that, the two of them were practically inseparable. There were moments Elise wished their graduation would not come, because that would mean time was passing and he would be leaving soon. She vowed to make the most of their summer. Yet, despite her wishes, time marched on and graduation day arrived.

Part of Elise felt silly knowing her entire family was attending. Her small high school graduation was nothing compared to a royal coronation or ball. Surely, her uncles and aunt knew that. Yet, there they were, waving and cheering for her as Elise crossed the stage to receive her diploma while her mother took pictures. She still considered them an odd group of characters who stuck out in this world, but Elise wanted to keep it that way.

The sight of them all lined up, her cousins included, on the school lawn to greet her following the ceremony filled a void inside Elise she did not know was there. Smiling down at her feet, she wove in and out of the crowd to join them.

"You did it!" Ruby exclaimed, handing Elise a bouquet of flowers. "I am so proud of you!"

Elise blinked away approaching tears as she hugged her mother. "At least I didn't twist my ankle in these heels. I was sure I'd fall on my face."

"I keep waiting for your mother to do the same," Ian teased, nodding at Ruby's own heels. After chastising his twin daughters for playing tag around groups of people taking photos, he turned to give Elise a hug as well. "I wish I could stay longer. Morgan also sends her apologies for not being here."

"Well, considering she just had a baby, I think I can forgive her." Elise laughed, thanking him for coming, and requested he send Morgan her congratulations.

"I will tell her, thank you. Congratulations yourself." He checked his watch. "I better get back home. It sounds like Mother will be driving the grandchildren to the party, so the girls will stick around here with you all."

Elise nodded, watching her other cousins Paul, Eric, and Madelyn joking and laughing near their parents. Richard and Sarah held their spouses' hands, and without realizing it, Elise had a wide smile spread across her face. *This is how it should be*. She said goodbye to Ian as Gavin walked up to her.

"Hey!" she exclaimed, wrapping her arms around his neck. "Where are your parents?"

"They're getting the car," Gavin said. "Dad can't stand to get stuck in traffic."

"Can you still make it tonight?" she asked. "Your parents can come, too."

He nodded and leaned in to kiss her as Ruby snapped a photo of them.

"Mom," Elise teased.

"Do you want me to get a family photo of everyone?" Gavin offered.

Without missing a beat, Joranna accepted the request and called out to Ian before he got too far out of earshot. Instructing Ruby to give Gavin her camera, she gathered all the children and ushered everyone into place with Elise in the center.

Once Gavin handed the camera back to Ruby, the family dispersed loudly, chattering over one another until Ian offered to drop off Richard, Gwen, Sarah, and Liam at Ruby's on his way home. Elise offered Gavin a sheepish grin. One by one, the adults wished her well and planned to meet up later until only Ruby, Joranna, and the cousins remained. "Sorry. They can be a lot."

Gavin waved off her apology and pulled Elise closer. "Don't worry about it. In fact, maybe the next time there's a family photo taken. . .I'll be in it."

Elise's heart threatened to leap out of her chest, and she kissed away his lopsided grin.

"Hey, get a room," Mitch called out as he walked up holding Darcie's hand. "This is a family friendly event."

Elise made to hug Darcie but stopped short when Ruby called out for them to pose together.

"Mom, come on," she laughed. "I think we have enough pictures."

"You will thank me later," Ruby replied.

"We will be here forever waiting for Ruby to take her photos. You poor dears are ready to get out of here, I am sure, but I would be happy to take one for you," said Joranna.

Darcie held out her phone to Joranna before posing with the other three. Once the last photo was taken, Mitch and Darcie said their goodbyes and planned to see them later that night.

"Oh, that reminds me," Joranna said. "Sarah wanted me to invite you to come stay with her for a couple of weeks this summer before you start college."

Elise suppressed a smile at her grandmother's subtlety. *Gavin knows all about Haighdlen, Nana. There's no secret.* Perhaps a trip would be exciting if she could convince her family to let Gavin and the other two join. While beautiful, Haighdlen was probably also a more enjoyable place now that it was not under a constant threat.

Elise lit up as a familiar figure emerged from the crowd and approached them. "He made it."

"Who?" asked Ruby.

"I can give you one guess," Joranna teased with a smile as she nodded over Ruby's shoulder.

Chewing her bottom lip, Elise watched her mother turn and come face to face with Charles.

"Hello, Princess."

Ruby stood frozen, staring at him as if he could not possibly be real. She opened and closed her mouth several times. "What are you doing? Who invited you?" she finally asked, glaring daggers at Joranna's and Elise's once she caught sight of their guilty grins. "Never mind. And it is just *Ruby* here."

"Forgive me," Charles said with an easy smile, taking in her full appearance before meeting her eyes. His own softened. "You look lovely as ever."

Time had also been generous to Charles, whose only sign of aging was the handful of silvery wisps of hair along his temples. Unlike Elise's family, he appeared to be made for the modern world's fashion, wearing a tailored dark gray suit that Ruby would have to be crazy not to notice. He turned to Elise. "I hear congratulations are in order."

"Thank you," said Elise.

Joranna patted Ruby's arm and nodded for her to introduce the two of them.

Rolling her eyes, Ruby stepped forward. "Elise, this is Lor—Charles. He is Richard's friend."

Liar. He's more than that.

Charles bowed his head. "Pleased to meet you, Elise. You may call me Charlie. At least, your mother used to."

A tense silence followed until a car horn honked nearby and Gavin's name was called.

Charles rested a hand in his pocket. "Please excuse me. I must go speak with your aunts and uncles."

"Let that be our sign to leave as well," said Joranna. "Ruby, you are good to drive Charles to the party, are you not?" Without waiting for her daughter's stunned reply, Joranna ushered the other grandchildren toward her van.

"Can you believe she did this?" Ruby snapped to Elise. "She knows better than to—"

"Nana didn't invite him," Elise confessed, biting her lip. "I did."

Ruby opened her mouth but no words came out. "Elise, how do you—"

"It's a long story, but I know you two are meant for each other," Elise said. "Don't be mad at Nana, either."

Ruby huffed.

"He's still crazy about you, Mom." Elise nodded to where Richard, Gwen, Sarah, and Liam were laughing at something Charles said. He tossed a smoldering smile over his shoulder at Ruby that would make any woman weak in the knees.

Ruby released a slow breath before shaking her head. "Elise, this is more than you realize. It would never work."

"Says who?" Elise challenged. She grabbed Ruby's hands with her own. "Mom, you have always had to put other people's needs first. I'm proud of your hard work and accomplishments, but it's time to put your needs first for a change. You had to stay away from Haighdlen for my protection and probably got settled here. Your degrees are not wasted, no matter what you choose, but I'm not a kid anymore. I have plans for my life. We can talk about them later, but it's your turn to live. . .wherever, and with whoever, that may be." Elise failed to suppress a devilish smile. "Not to mention. . .your legs look incredible in that dress. You're killing him."

Ruby laughed and tucked a loose strand of hair behind Elise's ear. "When did you grow up to be so wise?" She smiled as if seeing Elise as a woman for the first time. She cleared her throat and attempted a no-nonsense tone. "I won't make any promises, you know. He could turn out to be a complete cad now."

Elise chuckled. "I'm willing to place that bet."

Ruby kissed her cheek and nodded towards Joranna's van. "See you at home."

Gavin walked Elise to it before opening the passenger-side door for her. She thanked him with a kiss that was interrupted by the twins knocking and making kissing faces against the windows. Fortunately, the older three had enough sense to give them some privacy. Elise pounded the glass playfully and turned back to Gavin as his parents honked again.

"Will your mom be okay?" he asked.

"She's tough. I think so." A wry smile crept across her lips. "Plus, he's not wearing a ring. Fingers crossed."

Gavin chuckled. "Darcie will be proud of you."

"I think she will," Elise agreed. "I'll see you soon then?"

"Yeah, I can't wait. I love you."

"I love you, too." By this point, Elise could take a hint, as now *all* her cousins were fake retching despite Joranna's fussing. "I better go."

He waited for her to get settled before shutting the door with a wave and walked to his own ride.

Buckling her seatbelt, Elise stared at Charles and her mother through the window. "Do you think she'll be mad at me?"

Joranna lowered her head to peer out of the same window as Ruby softened her resolve and laughed at something Charles was saying. "I say she will thank you. . .just maybe not right away."

Elise chuckled.

"Richard gave him his blessing, I hear," Joranna said, pulling out of the school parking lot. "Goodness knows it is long overdue. Those two were made for each other."

I agree. Elise stared back at the passing school, realizing just how many changes were headed her way.

"I am proud of you, you know," Joranna called over the loud talking coming from the backseat.

Elise looked up from her bouquet and smiled. "Thanks, Nana." Her smile slightly faltered as a hint of mischief gleamed in Joranna's eyes. "What?"

Joranna offered an innocent wink and sweet smile in return. "Did you enjoy yourself?"

Elise glanced warily in response to her grandmother's loaded question. "Today?" *She can't mean what it sounds like, right?* After all, Horanis promised everyone would forget them. It had been one of the hardest things to get used to since being back home. Yet, there was a definite shift in Joranna's knowing stare. *There's no way she remembers.* "Sure."

Joranna drove in silence for several moments until her eyes lit up. "Oh! I almost forgot. I got you something." Opening the center console, she pulled out a gift-wrapped box.

"Nana, inviting Charles was your gift."

"Well, I wanted to give you another one." Joranna nodded for her to open it in the car. "I hope you like it."

Tearing the corner of the wrapping, Elise peeked at her grandmother for a hint. Encouraged to continue, she fully unwrapped and opened the box with a gasp. With trembling fingers, she lifted out a new diary and leafed through the blank pages, thankful it was not accompanied with a portal.

"Thank you," she said, leaning over to hug Joranna. "I love it." Lifting the front cover, Elise saw a small note written by her grandmother on the first page.

June 6, 2007

Dear Elise,

Your turn.

> *Love,*
> *Nana*

"Was it everything you wanted it to be?" asked Joranna.

This time, Elise did not question her grandmother's meaning. She closed the diary and placed it back into the box. Nodding, she imagined many more questions would follow when they were alone.

"It was," Elise replied with a wistful sigh. When Joranna slowed enough to make a turn, Elise thought she saw twinkling lights zipping in and out of the passing trees. She smiled. "It really was."

The End

Acknowledgments

I am incredibly thankful to God for giving me the gift of writing. His love, patience, and grace taught me that anything is possible with faith.

In 2007, Elise's journey began as an idea in a notebook. . .a passion project of a young girl scribbling away in class. Being able to share these characters with the world is a dream come true.

I wish to thank my editor, beta reader, family, friends, designers, and teachers. Additionally, I want to say thanks to my readers for supporting me. You are all an important part of my creative team. Words cannot express my gratitude.

More From Mary S. Catlin

    The Laurille Legacy is the first installment of *The Haighdlen Chronicles* series. After learning of her royal lineage in an overthrown kingdom, Elise Laurille is sent back in time along with her friends (and crush) to find the spy responsible.

    Restoring the Throne is the second installment of *The Haighdlen Chronicles* series. Haighdlen is once again cloaked in scandal after the spy escapes and Gavin goes missing. Can Elise and Gavin navigate through the mounting dangers and temptations to find one another again? Only time, and magic, will tell.

    For more information, visit www.maryscatlinauthor.com. Be sure to sign up for Mary's monthly newsletter, *Haighdlen Press*, for updates on her other projects! Thank you.